Return of the Sleeping Warriors

When Magic Awakes – Book 1

Petra M Costa

First published by Busybird Publishing 2017

ISBN
Print 978-1-925585-97-1
Ebook 978-1-925585-80-3

This is a work of fiction. Any similarities between places and characters are a coincidence.

Cover image: Petra Costa
Cover design: Kev Howlett, Busybird Publishing
Layout and typesetting: Busybird Publishing
Editor: Scott Vandervalk

Busybird Publishing
2/118 Para Road
Montmorency, Victoria
Australia 3094
www.busybird.com.au

This book is dedicated to my family.

Without their inspiration, this story would never have set seed in my mind.

Without their love, it would never have been given the nourishment it needed to grow.

Love you guys.

Contents

Prologue I
Legend of the Sleeping Warriors

It was written that there was a time when magic was so powerful it could shake the very earth.

There were those, the humans from the first realm and the dwellers of the second, who tapped into the source and drank deeply of its power.

Awash in unimagined magic they spared little thought for the delicate balance that was and always will be required to maintain life as they knew it.

Evil influences and seekers of power tipped the balance towards anarchy and chaos.

In desperation, the source, working through those with the skill to wield the power created a band of fourteen warriors and placed them on magical steeds.

From the blood of the magic wielders, mixed with the earth that they were forever sworn to protect, the bonded warriors were born.

To fight and defend, to awake and obey, whenever the land had need, and when the balance had been restored, the bonded would return to sleep, forever listening for the call that heralded the return to arms.

Through time they fought, for whenever evil was vanquished and they were allowed a period of rest, too soon another summons would come.

Over time the power of those calling dimmed and the fight to restore balance took more of a toll.

Until the last in a string of battles was fought and one of the shining warriors was slain and for a time the earth did shake not because of the power wielded but for the son that had been lost.

The legend states that the band sleeps, waiting for the day they will be called upon again. Thirteen warriors and their bonded steeds and one horse weeping the loss of her rider, half of what she once had been.

Prologue II
Hidden Idols

There was nothing Patricia enjoyed more than a stroll along the beach in early winter when the southerly had yet to grow its teeth and the waves were no longer quite as tame as during the summer months. She liked nature to be wild but just not so much so that it posed any real danger to herself. When she was younger, Patricia would have stood on the jetty with the wind blowing through her hair, salt spray stinging her face, hoping the clouds would bring the storm they boldly promised.

But she was older and wiser and she had arthritis to contend with as well as a six-year-old grandson who refused to slow down so his nanna could keep up. He had already found at least twenty seashells that were each so individually spectacular that not one could be left behind. Nanna Pat dutifully took out a tissue and placed the shells carefully in the centre. She admired the colour and shape of each before placing the bundle into her bumbag alongside the four-leaf clover that was really just a torn three-leaf clover, a rock that looked like a spaceship, and two dead beetles that apparently might be a new species.

By the time she had zipped everything up, little Master Tom had already moved on to a jellyfish that was probably wishing it had taken a left at the last wave.

'Nanna, come look. I bet this is not really a jellyfish but an alien scout come onto the sand so it can report back to base.'

Patricia was ready with a funny line about how all jellyfish came from Atlantis but Tommy had already stopped and stepped back. His stick had never quite made contact with the translucent mass and he looked earnestly at his grandma. 'Milkshake time?'

While she was still trying to work out how a jellyfish had made him think of milkshakes, Tommy's little hand had slipped into hers and they skipped off down the beach.

There were a lot of things that she didn't enjoy about getting old but grandchildren were definitely one of the perks.

Over their chocolate milkshakes they spoke about aliens, African safaris and the various flavours of ice-cream that you just could not live without. Before she had time to move aside the beetles so she could pay the waitress, Tommy was off and out the door.

He ran down the street dodging in-between the few people around them and veered down a side street, dutifully waiting until he saw his grandmother before turning another corner. Patricia followed him a ways, unconcerned as they were travelling in the general direction of the house they were staying at for the holidays. Tommy had found himself an old bric-a-brac store and ran inside before she had time to brush the hair off his forehead. She was almost out of puff. This little run through the side streets was more exercise than she was used to. She took the opportunity to stop and catch her breath.

While waiting for his little head to pop out of the store her heart skipped its first beat. It was only a twinge and may well have been the ice-cream sitting heavy causing her concern. Without knowing why she called out for Tommy as she stepped towards the store. She had only taken a couple of steps into the store when she experienced claustrophobia for the first time in her life, an overwhelming sense that there wasn't enough air. Her breath rasped through her lips in short shallow sips. The shelves seemed too high, seemingly poised ready to topple down on her, and the boxes were all crammed too close.

She turned in a slow circle and felt her heart skip another beat as fresh sweat beaded her forehead and upper lip. The smell of dust and furniture polish reminded her of all the things she hated about being old. She called to Tommy again as she rounded a corner and saw him reaching inside a dusty old box.

Tommy looked up at her with a puzzled expression on his face as if he understood she was in some kind of trouble and then turned back towards the box. He wrapped his little fingers around something she couldn't quite see. Patricia's chest was burning and she heard the whistle as each breath struggled to make its way into her constricted chest. When she staggered backwards, towards fresh air and the safety of the street, her breathing seemed to ease and her heart regained a steady although accelerated rhythm. This only made her panic worse and with a certainty that only half a decade of existence on this earth could give she turned back into the store knowing that Tommy needed her.

Patricia stumbled towards Tommy, knocking merchandise off shelves as she moved. Staggering like a drunkard she reached for Tommy with hands that no longer obeyed her commands.

With her vision fading, Patricia reached Tommy and knocked the doll he was holding from his hands and wrapped her fingers around his. Pain cramped her chest and as her consciousness slipped away Patricia held her beloved grandson's hands knowing she dare not let Tommy go.

Home Life

The moving van pulled up, followed closely by the sleek black BMW. Michael watched on with mild interest – it wasn't every day that you got new neighbours, especially ones moving in next door. His sister Dana was more curious in nature and had been hovering around the front yard all morning in expectation of the arrival.

'Do you think they have kids, Dana?' Michael asked, curious himself as to whether there would be any children and somewhat more importantly what they would look like if they did. As the car pulled silently into the driveway, he caught a glimpse of someone sitting in the back seat of the car, which the neatly stacked boxes and pillows had previously hidden from view.

Trying to appear casual, they kicked around a soccer ball and endeavoured to look anything but interested. They took in every detail as a tall man stepped out of the car. He had a stiff erect manner, which reminded Michael of someone with a military background. The man headed straight for the moving van, issuing sharp, clipped instructions.

The sound of a car door slamming shut brought Michael's eyes back around. It was hard to slam the door of a Beemer at any time, and he was surprised when he suddenly saw a woman standing next to the car. Her hand rested on the door as if ensuring it would stay shut as she quietly took in her surroundings. She had dark hair, a slight build and smiled coolly as if yet to commit to the suitability of this new residence.

'Not your standard typical door slammer there,' Michael mused.

'More like a Stepford wife, if you ask me,' Dana said.

Michael, not being as well-read as Dana, looked as her quizzically. 'Pod person?'

'Got it!'

Michael nodded and looked back toward the action. He expected the woman to reach for the back door of the car, to help the person who sat in amongst the boxes but this woman dropped her hand and moved towards the front of the house, as if the back seat and its contents held no interest to her whatsoever.

'Charming,' Dana whispered.

There was movement at the back seat of the car that caught Michael's attention. Boxes were being carefully shifted aside and a boy that Michael estimated to be Dana's age came into view.

He easily managed to step out of the car without scattering his belongings all over the driveway and moved with a conversation of energy, a deliberate manner that suggested everything this boy did was planned well in advance – strange in a person only a little older than Michael himself. This boy's movements were so very different to Michael's casually athletic style that by its very contrast became a point to note.

The car door was quietly closed and with obvious deliberation their new neighbour turned towards them both.

Even before their eyes met, Michael knew he didn't like this boy, that he didn't like this family.

Dana and Michael had been brought up to trust their instincts – first impressions and gut feel – those things you didn't second guess. Michael's gut was recommending that he stay well clear of this particular kid. His bearing was distinctly un-childlike and Michael on some level perceived him as a threat.

The dad's military aspect and the mum's cool smile all seemed off. Wrong. Unapproachable. The whole family had brought with them a vibe of unease that reverberated deep within him.

It had taken them less than two point five seconds to come up with their verdict and there was never going to be a chance of a retrial. These people were never going to be *their* kind of people.

'God, Dana, can it get any worse?' Michael asked in an effort to lighten the heavy mood that had settled over them both, nudging his sister to indicate the white cat that the boy carried carelessly under his arm.

They were a family of dog lovers, where cats and their owners were openly mocked. But even this small attempt at levity had failed miserably.

'Buddy, I truly don't believe it can!'

Once Michael realised eye contact had been made, he went for the old faithful 'nod your head' option in way of response and he was fairly certain Dana had done so also.

The new kid looked straight back at them both, no smile, no acknowledgement, nada. He locked eyes with Michael nevertheless, long enough to make him feel like nothing more than an insect being examined, ready for pinning to a board. Michael wanted to break eye contact, feeling that in some way even looking at this person would be deemed as a confrontation, though he felt slightly childish, Michael refused to even blink.

With a sneer the boy turned away, as if the two of them were somehow beneath him, not worthy of his time.

'Simply charming!' Dana echoed her previous comment.

Michael gauged this new neighbour to be about the same age as Dana, which made him around sixteen, not even two years up on him. Not old enough to warrant this kind of dismissal. The new kid was opposite to Michael in every way: black hair where Michael was blond, fair where Michael was olive, coldly detached where Michael felt himself to be in sync with the world around him. For reasons that he could not quite identify, Michael was left feeling tense and guarded.

Dana seemed to feel the same. 'I have a bad feeling about this. I really don't think it can get much worse!'

* * *

And it didn't take long for the animosity to grow.

Things started out small and petty, as such things so often did. Balls kicked over fences disappeared, or if they did get returned were found to be flat and 'inadvertently' punctured somehow. If Michael and Dana had friends over for a swim, their new neighbour would find that a burn-off was required and smoke soon billowed over the fence in noxious waves. If they were outside having a kick and listening to some music, power tools were revved up and the music drowned out by the steady thrum of screaming engines. Marcus was usually the one behind the disruptive behaviour and any request for a reprieve was ignored or refused. Some people just enjoyed making an arse of themselves and Michael had to give him credit, this new kid had a real knack for it.

In a cruel twist of fate, Michael found himself being introduced to his neighbour by his home group teacher at school. Fate wasn't so harsh as to have placed them in classes together but it forced them into an environment where the petty harassment could be expanded to the school day. It felt like Marcus had been tormenting him for years, when really, it had only been for a little over six months. It hadn't taken long for Marcus to collect a posse of overzealous bullies ready to ruin Michael's day at the first opportunity.

Michael, though, had a tight group of his own. And it didn't take much to avoid a bunch of kids who didn't even know their school had a soccer pitch.

But even then there were still run-ins: Michael had his phone knocked from his desk, the screen smashed. He had a locker door closed on his fingers. When a leg was stretched out on the stairs to trip him as he ran for class, Michael wasn't exactly ready for it, but he was used to jumping legs and he'd been blessed with fast reflexes and a finely-tuned sixth sense that kept him out of all kinds of trouble. So mostly, he found Marcus little more than a minor irritation.

But unfortunately things did not stay small and inconsequential.

* * *

Michael lay back in bed wondering how a day that had started so well ended so badly. How he had not seen it coming.

Michael had been in his element. Playing soccer was what he did best. It was a big game. It might just be summer comp but the skill levels of all the teams involved were high. And there was talk that there were going to be scouts at the finals, so they had to put in a solid performance. No-one could have disputed that Michael had worked hard. Two assists, one of them a long ball that allowed Jeff to run onto it and put it away with so much force the goalkeeper's hands would have been stinging if they had come anywhere near it. The second assist, a floating cross that allowed Justin to volley the ball straight over the goalkeepers head.

With only a few minutes left in the game the scores were level.

Michael had the ball and was looking for Jeff when he saw an opening in front of goal. A quick shot of adrenaline flooded his system but he kept his head.

'Hard and low, aim for the corner.' Just like Toby had drilled him. The ball spun into the corner, the goalkeeper dropped his head having barely moved in the ball's direction. The opposition tried to rally but their defence kept their composure and locked the game down for the last few remaining minutes.

The ref blew the full time whistle and it was all over.

He was focused only on his coach and teammates.

He was jubilant, and barely registered the faces of the other team as he shook their hands at the end of the game. The adrenaline was still pumping through his muscles. His legs felt tight and his heart continued to race. And it was then, as his back was being slapped and his hair was being tousled with calls of 'Michael!' ringing around him, that he felt the brief moment of apprehension. Had the hairs just lifted on the back of his neck? Before he even had a chance to react, there was a searing pain in his left knee and it buckled beneath him, dropping him unceremoniously to the ground.

Shouts rang out around him. 'Michael, are you alright?'

'Micky, what's wrong?'

'Mick?'

Having been on the receiving end of more than one kick to the knee during his last nine years of soccer, he knew exactly what had happened. But he just couldn't figure out *how* it had just happened. The pain in his knee blew all thoughts out of his mind and he reluctantly lowered his eyes, drawn by the pain, needing to see just how bad the damage was. His eyes had shifted focus and he caught sight of an all too familiar person walking nonchalantly off the pitch.

Marcus.

Even i his own mind, the word sounded like a curse. 'Hate' might have been a strong word but Michael felt it in that moment. Marcus had had *no right* to even be out on the pitch! He wasn't a player and he definitely was not an official. The prick did *not* belong there. The pitch was where Michael felt the most secure and this arsehole had intruded on that with his very presence.

If Marcus was there it had been for one reason and one reason only – to take his best shot. Unfortunately, it appeared that that shot had been a pretty damn good one.

Michael figured his chances to play in the finals were probably ruined.

In the confusion that followed, Michael was stretchered back to the club rooms surrounded by his teammates. He registered even the tiniest bump as a tearing pain that ripped through his leg. Through all of this, he grit his teeth and steadfastly refused to cry out. If this had been an ordinary injury he was sure he would have been more vocal but he simply would not allow Marcus to hear his pain. He knew without any doubt that Marcus would be in the background somewhere enjoying the fruits of his labours. He was never one to miss the opportunity to revel in the moment.

His teammates, in their state of outrage, wanted someone's head on a platter, the general assumption being that the opposing team had taken Michael out in retaliation for the winning goal. Michael, oblivious to all of this, was in no state to clarify the point.

Even through the ever-escalating demands for some kind of retribution, the racket seemed suddenly to quieten. Michael breathed a sigh of relief as the pain he was experiencing eased. He knew that these two things happening simultaneously meant only one thing: his mother was close.

Nicola materialised with cold pack in hand, quietly cutting a path through the people gathered around Michael. The chaos calmed in the sphere of his mother's influence and she was able to walk towards him without saying a word.

She didn't push through the throng like a normal frantic mother trying to get to her injured son's side; she didn't ask for people to move aside as she stepped forward to administer first aid. She only had basic first aid training but typically chose to work outside the circle of traditional medicine. Despite this, whenever someone was injured on Michael's team, she turned up and everybody knew to move aside and that was exactly what they did.

When she reached him Michael's mother smiled down and gently placed the cold pack against his knee. Michael could not contain the gasp when she flexed the joint to check the extent of his injury. Her dark blue eyes closed and her trademark frown line appeared between her eyes, which meant she was completely focused. Michael squeezed his own eyes shut and involuntarily sucked in a breath through clenched teeth, when he felt and heard the crack. The pain in his knee briefly became his whole world but still he heard his mother clearly as she whispered into his ear, 'Work with me now on this, baby.'

She still insisted on calling him 'baby'. He had given up protesting years ago, but in that moment he didn't really care. He felt only his mother's hands and listened to her whispered words. The cold was replaced with radiating warmth that penetrated deep into his knee and throbbed outwards. All sound in the room, although already uncommonly subdued, seemed to back even further away and Michael wondered if he were about to pass out as the baking heat flowed up his leg, almost too much to endure. But Michael had known what to expect; she had done this to him before and he knew he was only dealing with a small fraction of the discomfort. She stood quietly for almost three minutes. No-one else in the room seemed to notice the strange scene in front of them, hadn't registered the fact that the cold pack had been thrown absently to the side. When she finally took her hands away, the sounds returned and he no longer felt faint.

'He's fine. Nothing's broken,' his mother reassured everybody and the tension lifted.

Quiet conversations were replaced with a normal level of noise as his teammates finally celebrated their win.

There was no more talk of retribution or retaliation. People asked him how his knee felt, but no-one really spoke about what his mother had done. Funnily, no matter what knocks his team took, they always seemed less serious after his mother had administered her brand of first aid and nobody ever thought anything more of it. It was just taken as a given; they were all young and bounced back quickly. Was Michael tough or just plain lucky? A little of both. Michael knew that some of this was true, but it wasn't the whole truth, not even close to it.

He lay back in bed with his left knee slightly bent unable or too afraid to stretch out entirely. With his tousled dark blond hair he looked like the soccer player he so wanted to be. His hair was damp with sweat and there was a strained look around his eyes but these were the only signs that something was on his mind.

Michael tried to relax but the projector in his mind kept replaying the day in never-ending high definition. He was used to injuries; he played the game hard, but fair – bruises, sprains, the occasional cut to the head were all part of the game. You either walked it off or got out of the way and let your teammates get on with the job. But to be injured outside of play … Michael closed his eyes, steadied his breathing, feeling the pounding of his heart ease somewhat. Breathe, relax … as the projector in Michaels's head slowly faded and finally turned itself off he felt his tension and anger slowly drain away. He didn't believe in dwelling on things and what was important at this moment was how lucky he was. His mum had already 'worked' on his knee again that night and that was why the swelling had gone down. Thanks to her he could already bend his knee and by next week Michael was sure he would be able to play again. His mother would see to that. Which left him the task of resolving the problem of Marcus.

But what was he going to do? *That prick from next door had just gone too far*, he thought. He had been a right royal pain in the arse from the day that he had moved in. It wasn't the first injury he'd sustained because of Marcus but it had been the first open attack. And now it appeared that Marcus had finally found a way to get to Michael both physically as well as mentally. He'd found something that Michael really cared about – his ability to play soccer. He had seen some on the best players in the world knocked out of the sport due to something as simple as coming down onto an ankle wrong. A full kick to the side of a knee could take you out of the sport for life.

His mother might have been able to fix a lot of things but he didn't really want to test just how far her healing abilities stretched. And there was the obvious cost to her that needed to be considered. Michael had noticed how her hands shook when she left the changing room, how she'd swayed as she walked out of his room earlier today.

Michael continued to think, not to refuel his anger, but simply to look for an answer. He needed to find a solution and he needed to find it fast. If he knew his mother, she would be in again shortly under the pretence of checking on him, and she would have sensed by now that he was troubled. In their house, whether you wanted to or not, troubles were shared. This was all good in theory, but in reality that meant he would have to talk this problem through with her and that talk would no doubt limit his options greatly.

Cold logic or not, simply decking Marcus seemed like a pretty good option.

* * *

Michael wasn't aware that his mother had been watching him from his doorway for over five minutes, quietly leaning against the doorframe, wondering exactly what he was thinking. She couldn't help but smile. He always lay the same way in bed – head resting on one or both hands, looking like he didn't have a worry in the world. His features never appeared troubled, even when deep in thought.

The dark blond hair, always unruly. When he was young he wouldn't allow it to be cut because that was not how his favourite soccer players wore their hair. Now it had just become his style – untouchable … untameable.

But today he had been touched.

She hadn't seen him go down, but she had felt the pain, followed by the momentary flash of anger when he realised what had happened. In her mind the details were blurry, but two images had come across quite strongly. One was intense anger and the other was of Marcus.

Lost in thought, she jumped, as a hand dropped upon her shoulder.

'Shit, Dana,' she whispered. 'You scared the crap out of me!'

Carefully steering Dana away from Michael's room, Nicola glanced back quickly to ensure Michael was resting. Lost in his thoughts, he hadn't been disturbed by the interruption.

Michael's sister was not going to be easy to deal with. Dana was protective of her younger brother and fiery just like her father and she was obviously in no mood to be herded anywhere so they settled on hovering just outside of Michael's bedroom door.

* * *

Michael lay with one hand resting behind his head, no change in his outward appearance but his ears were now tuned into the conversation going on outside of his bedroom.

'Is his knee going to be okay?' Dana asked in a clipped tone.

'Sure, he'll be fine. You know how fast Michael bounces back.'

'Don't treat me like a child. I saw it! I saw his knee! I heard him scream.'

Michael flinched slightly as he overheard this comment, partially because screaming didn't sound overly heroic but mostly because it made his knee throb in remembered pain.

'Oh it hurt him, no doubt about that, but everything is back in place now and his knee just needs a little help repairing itself.'

'And next time, are you just going to up and heal him again?'

Even from his room, Michael could hear the hostility hovering just below the surface of his sister's words.

'Why would you think there was going to be a next time and why are you so angry?' The unspoken subtext of 'why are you so angry at me?' was heard by all.

Dana gave a loud impatient sigh. 'I'm angry because I saw the whole thing! I saw Marcus walking around in the crowd during the game. I wondered at the time why that bastard was there. I thought he was probably hoping to see Michael miss a goal or make a mistake. But I got so wrapped up in the game I forgot all about him.'

Michael couldn't see Dana from his room but he knew she would be showing signs of her annoyance in her restless pacing and her fists would be clenched against her legs. His own heart rate was beginning to rise and he could feel his fingernails digging into the palms of his hands. He forced himself to take a breath, not wanting to miss any of the conversation. He was now sitting up in bed listening intently.

Before his mother had a chance to answer, Dana continued, 'I was trying to make my way over to Michael, to congratulate him, to congratulate them all, when I saw Marcus again. He came across the ground from the other side, so he wouldn't get caught up in the crowd. I was close enough to see his face but not close enough to do anything. I called out to Michael, to warn him, but everyone was calling out to Michael, so he couldn't hear me.'

Michael would have interrupted her there and said that he had heard her on some deeper level, because something had made him look up. He had seen Marcus' face just before the pain hit.

Dana continued on, her words faster and filled with more anger as each word was uttered. 'If you could have seen his face, Mum! There was no doubt he was going to hurt Michael. No doubt! But what could I do?'

'Let me get this straight, you're saying that Marcus did this on purpose. That you saw him approach Michael? And that Michael's knee was no accident?'

'No accident?' Dana voice turned hard and sarcastic. 'The bastard jumped so he could put even more force behind the kick.'

Michael phased out on the next few moments of conversation because the image of the creep from next door jumping up and landing his best shot kept replaying itself in his mind. He might not have seen it happen but his overactive imagination was happy to turn the projector back on and supply a playback nevertheless. With each replay the throb of his pulse in his temples intensified, his shoulders tightened, his anger built.

This shit is going to have to stop, Michael thought to himself. His musings were interrupted, when as predicted, his mother walked into his room. Dana obviously had said all she intended to say on the subject.

'Micky, how are you feeling?' his mother asked, as she sat casually next to him on his bed.

He had automatically moved over slightly to allow her room because she never stayed for 'just a moment'. 'Muz, I'm fine. It's just … well I don't know how much more of this guy I can take. I heard Dana fill you in on what happened. But what are we supposed to do? If we approach them, they'll swear blind they were nowhere near the ground. Geez, I wouldn't put it past them to have a bunch of people lined up ready to swear they were all at church this morning.'

'To be honest, I'm not sure what to do. Direct confrontation with them does always seem to end up the same way. You could ask around and see if any of your friends saw anything?'

'Come on, think about it. If they had, he would be the one recovering right now!'

'Fair call. So what do we do?' The question was asked quietly, without doubt, without judgement.

'Maybe nothing just yet. I want to get through these finals. Mum, the scouts will be there. You know how much that means to me!' Michael heard how his own statement turned into a plea.

'Yeah, I do,' his mother replied.

'We've got our holiday coming up, so until then I'll just have to steer clear of him. When the season is over … well, then we'll see.'

'Sounds like a plan.'

'Mum, will my knee be okay?'

'I'm working on it as we speak!'

Only then did Michael feel the heat from her other hand resting casually against his left knee. Once noticed, he embraced the warmth as it spread through him and he knew sleep would overtake him shortly. As he drifted off he heard her whisper in his ear. 'Twenty-eight and always baby, twenty-eight and always!'

In the dreamy twilight state, halfway between worlds Michael couldn't remember how this particular phrase had come into being. His mother had been sending him off to sleep with these words for as long as he could remember, but he knew what they meant. 'Love you without limit, always and forever.'

'Back at you Muz!' he managed to murmur as sleep finally took him.

* * *

She had spoken with her children about Marcus before. Ever since that family had moved in next door they had been nothing but trouble. Damaged property, hate mail, the works. She knew that if it were not for Sheba, their black Doberman, dutifully protecting their home, more damage would have been done but today it had moved outside the circles of home and school.

Today lines had been crossed.

Today one child had deliberately hurt another. *What was wrong with these people?*

She wasn't sure she would be able to keep a lid on this particular situation much longer and truth be told she wasn't sure she truly wanted to.

Today you went way too far! Michael's mother thought to herself.

Holiday Life

His mother had delivered on her promise and his knee was as good as new. It was lightly strapped but more as a precaution than a requirement. Dana, who had now become Michael's personal bodyguard, kept a constant lookout for Marcus. This time Michael bet that if Marcus tried something, Dana would make sure he came off second best. He smiled to himself at just how seriously she had taken the whole thing. Michael had a tendency to focus on the moment. He had a game to play and at that particular moment it was his only concern.

Dana on the other hand, couldn't get the sound of her brother's scream out of her head. It made no difference in her mind that their mother had 'fixed things'. That wasn't really the point. Marcus had hurt him, really hurt him this time and she did not intend to let it happen again. It was because of her diligent scanning of the crowd that she was the first to notice the scout arrive. He was easy to spot – he went straight over to the coaches and Dana watched as several members of both teams were pointed out. Quite a bit of time was spent discussing two players in particular. One was the goalkeeper from the opposition. She had no idea of his name but she had seen him play and he was fantastic – he had reflexes that had to be seen to be believed. The other was her little brother. Dana watched as the scout nodded and then moved back into the crowd.

Michael already had his game face on, already too busy to notice. Michael was the kind of person that Dana would almost class as having some kind of attention deficit disorder if she didn't know him so well. He took nothing seriously. He was one of those easygoing types that infuriated her. Nothing really made him angry. He was always calm, happy to just live in the moment.

Except when he played soccer. Then he became a whole different person.

Committed.

Focused.

Driven.

He was that person now, even during warm-ups. He joked with his teammates, seemed relaxed and laidback, but she could see that he took in everything. This was the soccer final and Michael would be absorbing every detail. By the time he stepped out onto the field, he would know which players were stiff, which were troubled by nerves, and which players would be the ones to watch out for. Dana followed his gaze and knew that Michael had decided that the opposing goalkeeper was the one he would have to beat.

* * *

Michael had known it was going to be a hard game. The defenders were nervous. They weren't talking to each other, so he was able to use this to get through the back line a few times but even with the added pressure, the opposition's goalkeeper was on fire. A couple of quick crosses soon loosened Jeff, their striker, up and he made himself dangerous in front of goal. Michael had set up a couple of tries but Josh, the Royals' goalie, had the knack of knowing which way to jump. He either delicately tapped them up over goal and out of play or he took them clean. He hadn't made a single mistake.

The defence had inadvertently tripped Michael in front of the goal giving away a penalty. With a quick glance at his coach Michael stepped up to the penalty mark to take the kick.

He felt the usual tension as he got into position. He reached down, casually touched his left boot, where his lucky signature lay. His nerves calmed. His mind cleared. He walked back from the ball and took a deep breath.

He could feel every sinew, every muscle in his body. Autopilot kicked in and he ran forward, struck the ball, making it look like he was going low and to the right, but he knew this goalie would be ready for that move.

Michael relied on instinct and took the riskier move of going for the top left corner, harder under pressure, but it felt right. The goalie dived right, his first and last mistake for the day.

Michael didn't see the ball spinning in the back of the net – he was already jogging away. He never watched once the ball left his boot; he just *knew* whether he had scored or not. A smile broke across his face and the roar from the crowd confirmed that the goal had hit the mark.

His teammates jumped onto his back, celebrating the first goal for the day. Michael calmly high-fived them all and ran back into position. He wasn't the captain – in fact he was the youngest player on the team – but the confidence he exuded rubbed off on those around him.

In the dying minutes of the first half the Royals scored a goal to even the score.

Although Michael was able to get past the Royals' defence, sending a beautiful curling corner kick into the goal square, they just could not convert.

The scores stayed even until thirty minutes into the second half. And then a quick pass resulted in a goal. The Royals were ahead 2-1. Their defence finally found their rhythm and parked the bus. Michael managed to get through a couple of times but Josh was having one of those games and nothing was going to get past him.

Michael felt proud of how his team had performed. His team had kept pressuring until full time. But they lost, and that never tasted sweet.

* * *

The mood was sombre in the car on the way home. Michael didn't want to hear about how well he'd played, didn't want to know that they had played a great game. He wasn't a sore loser, he just liked to win and felt bad for himself as well as his teammates. He wasn't the arrogant individual people sometimes assumed him to be, he just felt at home when he was out on the pitch and it showed. He had always been pretty handy with a ball and had a knack for making the ball do what he wanted it to do. He'd tried many sports, enjoyed them all in their own way, but he was made to play soccer. He wasn't big enough for Aussie rules, wasn't patient enough for cricket and didn't like the solo nature of tennis. He had the fast, lightly muscled build of an attacking midfielder and was able to read the play and his teammates well enough to get into position to finish off if required. And that was what he really loved most about soccer, the teamwork.

When he played, whether a simple practice session or a final, it felt good. He was just as ecstatic when Brian saved a goal as when Jeff scored from a corner.

He didn't like to lose but he still loved the game.

When they got home he went straight upstairs to change and finish packing for their upcoming holidays. Dana followed him upstairs.

'Micky, you do know it was an absolute cracker of a penalty?' Dana walked into his room and bent to help him fold some clothes.

'Yeah, Dee, but did you see Brian's face when the second goal got through? He was devastated.'

'Nobody could have stopped that shot. When it comes down to one-on-one like that the striker should beat the goalkeeper. And he's had a brilliant year. But geez Michael, how that damned goalie kept out some of your tries, I'll never know. Man, he was on fire.'

'Thanks!' Michael curtly replied, shoving some more clothes haphazardly into his backpack.

'You know what I mean.'

'Yeah, I know. Did you see that corner that he managed to knock away? In any other game that would have been a goal!' Michael continued pushing more clothing into the bottom of his bag. When he turned away to rifle through his drawers, Dana silently removed the screwed up mess of clothing, refolding and repacking what was appropriate before she placed the rest into a pile to put away later.

'You know what, I saw the scouts talking about you before the game and I watched them and I swear they spent as much time talking about you as they did about that goalie.' Dana's face broke into a beaming smile. 'It was such a great game to watch! You may not have won but you killed them out there. They had two people marking you, you're lucky you even scored. I gotta admit, I was proud of you. And Mum, she can hardly speak she was screaming so much and Dad well I think he may have blown a woofer valve!'

'I heard Mum. I think the whole ground heard her.' Michael's smile had finally returned. 'Well there's always next year.'

Dana walked out of his room to finish her own packing, happy now that Michael was smiling again.

* * *

The smile didn't last long. Michael was outside grabbing some bathers hanging over the back of a chair when Marcus called out from over the fence.

They lived in the suburbs of Melbourne, with parkland out the back and neighbours on both sides. They had a pool surrounded by sandstone paving, a manicured green lawn perfect for goal practice and despite the drought, bushy conifers along the fence line. Unfortunately there was an area just above the barbecue that was clear of any foliage. And that was where Marcus chose to raise his sneering face.

'Heard you lost your team the game, Michaela. Heard you had two chances to cross but decided to go for glory and it didn't quite pay off. Did you freeze Michaela, when the pressure was on or couldn't you stand sharing some of the glory?' Marcus' face hovered just above the fence line.

'Always knew you weren't a team player. It has always been all about you. And today everybody saw that!'

Michael bit his tongue and tried to ignore the remarks.

'I must admit, after all of your screaming last week, I was surprised that you could even walk. Didn't you have some trouble with your knee?'

Michael threw his bathers to the ground and moved towards the fence. He had never dealt with Marcus over the knee incident and now his soccer season was over so he had nothing to distract him. He had every intention of just grabbing Marcus by the hair and pulling him over the fence. And as he walked forward with that sole thought in his mind, Sheba intervened.

The boys were too wrapped up in their hatred of each other to notice the black shape running silently down the garden path. When Sheba jumped onto the barbecue and stood snarling, level with Marcus' face – the moment was broken.

All thoughts of violence were replaced with laughter. Marcus' ridiculously high-pitched scream coupled with the fact that Marcus had dog slobber all over his face was too hilarious. Dana was by the back door holding out a dog treat for Sheba, obviously having organised the whole viscous dog charade. Sheba furiously wagged her stumpy tail as she trotted over and looked adoringly up at Dana with her grinning doggy face. It all became too much.

Dana kept it together for a few moments longer than Michael, enough time to praise Sheba then she too burst out laughing.

She threw her arm around her little brother's neck. She had to stand on tiptoes to do this but she was still the oldest and in these little ways she liked to remind him of that fact. All their lives people had asked them whether they were twins. Although her hair was long and perfectly groomed it was virtually the same shade of blonde as Michael. She stood a head shorter than him, but they shared the same golden skin tone and delicate features. Her eyes were a shade darker than his, closer to chocolate in colour but they both possessed the composed, comfortable air that made them seem older than they were. Michael was strong and athletic. Dana was graceful and fluid in her movements. Their resemblance was striking.

'Micky, what do you think, next time, I let Sheba have him for breakfast?'

'Nah, he isn't worth the trouble and she'd get indigestion.' Michael lent down and whispered to Dana, 'But if you can get her to make him scream like a girl again, well that I'd pay money for.'

They walked back inside together to finish packing. They were leaving the next day for Noosa and were supposed to have had their bags packed days ago.

* * *

Michael needed the break more than he cared to admit. Things with Marcus had been getting out of hand, and he knew the situation had to be addressed. He just wasn't sure how to go about it. If Dana and Sheba hadn't intervened the other day with Marcus he wasn't sure what would have happened. Marcus managed to get under his skin in a way few others could. Michael had taken an instant dislike to Marcus for a number of reasons. It would almost be nice to have had his instincts proven wrong for once.

A family holiday, with his cousin Ashley, aunt and uncle was just what he needed. Getting up each morning to the sound of the waves, taking a run before breakfast, eating whatever he liked, then spending his days, surfing, swimming and sightseeing. Dropping into bed each night and waking up the next morning to do it all over again. The simple nature of a beach holiday was relaxing in more ways than one. No arguments about what to eat because everything tasted great – seafood, sushi, steak. On holidays he worked up such an appetite during the day, so Michael would eat whatever was put in front of him.

His mother and Uncle Brent were also enjoying the opportunity for cook-offs. They'd come up with amazing breakfasts and elaborate barbeques. His uncle's garlic prawns were just ahead of his mother's seared scallops and that night they would be going out for a fancy dinner to celebrate the last day of holidays. But there was still one more day to just kick back and enjoy the surf, ride the waves, one more day to forget about everything for a while.

So how could it be, only minutes away from the beach that his feet were still dry? Michael had gone for his morning run, eaten and thrown some stuff into his backpack ready to spend the day surfing.

When the dads were left in charge of the last minute packing, Michael opted to hang with the girls. Happy to have been able to get out of helping with that particular task, he had bundled into the back of the car ready for the quick drive to the beach. They were almost at the car park when his mother had spotted something. 'Sars, take a left down there. We haven't seen this strip of shops before. I wouldn't mind having a quick look.'

Aunty Sarah easily cut in front of the car on her left and had them parked before Michael even had time to protest.

Michael was once again about to enter another in what seemed like a never-ending stream of knick knack, retro clothing and general junk stores that his mother and aunt always insisted on having a quick look at.

'Quick' doesn't even exist in their shopping vocabulary, Michael thought to himself. He could actually smell the beach, they were so close. Surely they wouldn't be much longer. If he were wearing a watch, he would have looked at it, just as a means of quantifying his dismay.

Michael leant up against a post outside of the store his mother and aunt had entered. Ten minutes in and the tapping of his foot was supposed to be an overt hint that it was time to move on. But no-one noticed: they were too wrapped up in their shopping.

It looked like he had no choice. He was going to have to give in and look around the thrift-shop-come-museum.

'What the hell fascinates you about these places anyway?' Michael cursed as he stepped towards the store. It was a complete mystery to him, but couldn't his mother find them! You'd be right in the middle of the trendiest surfy strip in town and his mother would somehow turn a corner and find these stores that look like they belonged in a different century.

Michael was used to his mother. He'd been on the receiving end of her special gifts all his life so most of her peculiarities to him seemed somehow normal. It was only when he started school that he even realised that not everyone's mum fixed bumps and bruises with just their hands rather than cold packs and band aids. He thought that all mums could feel or even smell when their children were getting sick or could look at their aura and ask what was wrong.

The healing hands he had too often benefitted from to complain about. The special insights were tolerable if sometimes annoying and intrusive and the crystals, Wicca and spiritual healing books were admittedly quite cool. Her unspecific, all encompassing 'feelings' simply drove him crazy.

So it was no surprise that it was one of those 'feelings' that brought them to this place.

'I just need to have a quick look!' Michael did an unflattering impersonation of his mother. 'Yeah, great, that was half an hour ago, Mum,' Michael mumbled to himself moodily, as he took the first step into the store. He would find Dana and Ashley and see if a three prong counterattack could move their mothers.

Before his first footstep had even landed he felt uneasy. Three steps into the store and the combined smell of dust, mothballs, old furniture polish and an undefined aroma that smelt suspiciously like mouldy oranges made him almost rethink the whole thing

Maybe he could just wait a couple of minutes more, outside. But his lack of patience won out.

The surf was waiting …

* * *

He found Dana pretty quickly. There was no surprise when she glanced up at him, and looked as bored as he felt. She'd been working her way through what looked like an old army locker, next to which hung a soldier's uniform with some book that had been put behind glass, nailed to the nearest post, making it a piss-poor kind of display in Michael's opinion. Giving the book a brief glance he was able to work out that it was some kind of journal, written by a man who had come over on the First Fleet.

The small yellowing photo wedged into the left-hand corner of the case showed a young fair haired man with eyes so startlingly pale they must have been blue, standing proudly in full uniform. What appeared to be the same uniform was haphazardly hanging behind the glass.

Michael almost felt pity for the guy. He'd obviously been proud to be in uniform, proud of his accomplishments and now they both appeared to have meant nothing to anyone save himself. How else would his story and belongings have found themselves gathering dust in a place such as this? Surely someone would have cared enough to have kept his things in an attic at least.

This feeling remained until he noticed the eyes of the man in the picture, the pride that shone from them. There was also some cruelty there and Michael suspected it was due more to the power of the uniform, and not the duty it was supposed to represent. He shuddered to think how this person had used his power and for a moment the pity he felt transferred to the unknown 'others' that had most likely suffered under his authority. Dana looked up at Michael questioningly, sensing the shift in his mood, obviously seeing how his eyes had turned steely.

Michael laughed at himself. 'The apple sure doesn't fall far from the tree, I swear, I'm getting as kooky as Mum.' Here he was, feeling what so very closely resembled hate for a person he'd never known, based purely on a single glance at an ancient photograph.

He laughed harder than ever with the realisation that his mother would find that a perfectly reasonable method of assessment, at least Michael wasn't so far gone that he didn't recognise how crazy that particular concept sounded.

Dana joined him then, not because she got the joke, just because he did and with them that was sometimes all it took.

This lightening of their mood went as quickly as it had come and the resigned look they shared was all the information required to confirm his earlier assessment, she was dead bored too.

'Come on, Michael. Let's get out of here. This place reeks and looking through dead people's stuff just seems wrong, it makes my skin crawl.' Michael couldn't have put it better himself. The place had been bugging him from the start and he was just about to join her when something near the bottom of the locker caught his eye.

It was a small carving that could almost have been described as a doll, half buried under folded blankets, clothes, old shaving kits and other ancient travelling paraphernalia.

It was the doll that had stopped him mid-turn.

Before he had time to think, he had the doll in his grasp, carefully examining the strange curiosity. It just didn't make sense. Why would the soldier have wanted to bring such an ugly little thing all the way over from England? Surely it must have been dropped into the locker by accident.

Michael decided that this was one mystery he was happy to leave unsolved. He carefully placed the doll back under the blankets. Actually, quite a good deal further under the blankets if anyone was keeping track of such things. Dana grasped his shoulders and turned him — not altogether gently – away from the locker, and they were about to start the search for Ashley when he heard a strange sound, almost like words but somehow muffled, which stopped him once again.

He uncovered the doll.

He'd not seen anything that could have caused it to speak. Surely they didn't have that kind of technology back in the 1700s. He tentatively prodded the surrounding blankets causing the doll to roll over. As it touched his skin he quickly withdrew his hand. For the life of him he couldn't see a ring-pull or any kind of clockwork mechanism that might explain how it could have spoken.

So what had he heard?

It had sounded so much like words, maybe not English, but words nonetheless. Having had the thing touch him for a second time, Michael felt the unaccustomed need to wash his hands. Michael was no germaphobe, like the girls in his family, but at that moment he empathised with them completely. He stepped back, hoping for a casual air, and reluctantly settled on wiping the palms of his hands down the legs of his jeans in a vain attempt to ease the building need to scrub his hands clean. Although Michael was intrigued, certain the thing had said something, he felt an unease, the kind of disquiet that was supposed to be the sole province of sci-fi movies. The strength of that feeling would not allow him to even contemplate picking it up and giving it a thorough examination.

'Michael what's up?' Dana asked looking somewhat concerned.

'Would you believe, I think I just had one of Mum's feelings?' This quip was supposed to lighten the mood but the statement sounded all too real to both their ears.

Michael reminded himself of his own inability to swallow the idea put forward by most Hollywood filmmakers: that some primordial relic, ancient tomb, alien spacecraft – whatever – actually had the ability to raise the hairs on the hero's neck just by its presence. It was ludicrous, but here he was wiping his hands down the front of his jeans for a second time, endeavouring to get rid of the itchy, burning sensation he felt in his palms.

'How disgusting.' Ashley rounded the corner, curling her lip to add weight to her opinion. 'Put that thing down!' To Michael's dismay the thing had somehow found its way back into his hands. There was no argument, this thing was just plain wrong on so many levels.

It stood about twenty centimetres tall and was a dull, dirty, faded black. It had stringy, oily hair that looked to have fallen out in clumps over the years and long movable arms and legs that although skinny had overly large joints harbouring a definite swollen appearance.

With hands and feet that were way out of proportion to the rest of its body, this thing would be winning no beauty pageants. The stomach was the thing that tipped the scales on the ugly-meter. It was distended as well, not the healthy, rotund belly sported by Buddha or Santa Claus, this had the stretched, emaciated look you saw on the news when there was a story about children overseas who were suffering from malnutrition. And if all that weren't enough, the doll was smiling a cocky 'I know something you don't know' smile.

'Hey Michael, come on, you can't really be thinking of buying that thing?' Dana's question brought him quickly back to the present, which was a relief because if he were to tell the truth, he'd lost all concept of how long he had been standing there holding the damn thing.

It was at that moment that his mother and Aunt Sarah rounded the corner, both weighed down by the piles of gypsy-esque style clothing, jewellery, candelabras, books and other general bric-a-brac they always seemed able to find. He quickly dropped the doll and wondered why he felt ashamed and was so desperately hoping his mum had not caught him touching, let alone holding, the thing.

Michael almost wished he had been caught looking through some of the 'inappropriate reading material' he had seen scattered around the place. At least then there would have been some reason for the guilt.

Luckily, Michael's mother never saw the doll, but her face showed that she was well aware that the three of them had been up to something and whatever that something was, she most certainly would not have approved.

Dana and Ashley dutifully exclaimed over their respective mothers' purposed acquisitions and thankfully the moment was broken.

Finally, clothing and funky jewellery bought, they were out of the store and heading for the beach, the smell of the surf and the warmth of the day almost enough to make Michael forget about the doll and the unease he had felt … almost.

Unbeknownst to him, the unease his mother felt took a little longer to fade.

* * *

Nicola hadn't been certain what had made her ask Sarah to turn down the street. She really had nothing she wanted to buy and had been looking forward to the beach as much as everybody else. But something about that street had caught her eye, and once she had a notion in her head it was hard to shift.

Her sister, Sarah, ever up for the shopping experience was happy to accommodate, so without much discussion their morning plans had changed.

It was to an old smelly store, nestled in amongst the more fashionable holiday shopping outlets that Nicola had been drawn.

She stepped over the dusty well-worn step and the first feeling of disquiet tickled at the edge of her mind. Regardless she still wanted to have a look around. She was certain there was something interesting there. As always she looked through the jewellery first. Not one for purchasing from deceased person's estates, regardless of the potential bargain to be had, she moved on to the case of jewellery made from local stones by local talent.

But her usual love of crystals and semiprecious stones was dampened by the ever-present nagging sensation that kept her roaming from one corner of the store to another.

After about twenty minutes, she was starting to suspect that she had misinterpreted things, gotten her psychic wires crossed somehow. Most likely she was just getting a migraine or coming down with something – God knows it had happened before.

Each time she rounded a corner or entered a new aisle she felt sure that whatever it was she had been searching for would be sitting there waiting and every time she felt an overwhelming disappointment when nothing interesting appeared before her. The gentle tug directing her would give an almost painful yank and within seconds, almost in response, her head would fill with a strange buzzing interference.

She had managed to collect some funky clothes and she continued to pick up more things in the same random fashion but she knew that none of these items were what she was searching for.

And just when she felt her patience snap, caught in the process of dropping all of the clothes in a heap, her mind was given a merciless yank that nearly knocked her from her feet. Less than a second later the buzzing intensified with nauseating strength.

Somehow the two forces seemed to be ripping her apart, tearing her in different directions. She turned, completely disorientated by this inner turmoil, all equilibrium lost. She struggled to control the conflicting signals swamping her mind. A final independent feeling punched through her chaotic thoughts, wiping out any desire to find some mysterious object. The feeling was dread, so closely bordering on fear that she stumbled around the next corner at a near run, nearly knocking Sarah over, who had materialised in front of her with a similar stack of clothing. A look of concern crossed Sarah's face when their gazes briefly locked.

Entering a new aisle, vision blurred and stomach reeling, knowing her sister was one step behind, Nicola found Michael standing before her flanked on one side by Dana and the other by Ashley.

But only Michael concerned her at the moment. Her fear was centred entirely on him and the guilty expression he threw her way wasn't making her feel any better.

Her eyes scanned the immediate area, looking for something dangerous but at that moment, the migraine she had feared blossomed. The buzzing flared briefly and she gave a warning glance back towards the children. She hoped they would drop everything and follow as she hurried towards the front desk, more to stop, get her balance and compose herself than any desire to buy the items she'd collected.

Nicola leant against the front desk and purchased the couple of items she still held. Her sister mouthed a quick 'Are you okay?' which she acknowledged with a nod, and admittedly she did feel somewhat better especially when she saw all three kids standing outside the store.

Her palpable relief at seeing them outside only lasted until she stepped down onto the sidewalk herself, when she realised the feeling of unease had not been left behind in the shop where she hoped it belonged. And as the trickle of sweat ran like a cold finger down her back, it felt all too much like her fear was what had chosen to come outside with her.

* * *

'Coffee!' Aunt Sarah suggested and no-one argued. Nicola's headache passed as quickly as it had come and the Coke she ordered was helping to settle her stomach, but she still felt restless. Michael, although obviously disappointed by the delay in getting to the beach, still managed to sit and enjoy his iced chocolate. She spotted his casual looks of concern and smiled back reassuringly. Both of her children had their own way of making sure she was okay.

'Who's up for the beach?' she asked pushing up from the table, taking deliberate care not to stumble in any way. If a soothing walk along the beach couldn't settle her frayed nerves she wasn't sure what would.

Michael immediately cheered and everyone jumped up ready to go.

* * *

It took them less than ten minutes to get to the beach. Her husband and brother-in-law hadn't arrived yet, so they looked around and found themselves a nice place to set up their towels and tent. The kids grabbed their boards and were off. With Sarah already engrossed in the book she was reading lying a few feet away in the sun, Nicola decided to grab her board to see if the waves would be kind to her.

It was only later as she sat in the tent after innumerable failed attempts at catching a decent wave that she realised she had left the bag of clothes and other junk she'd purchased under the table at the café. Knowing herself well enough she had to acknowledge that this probably had been no accident. She didn't possess the ability of self-deception. Although she was aware that she may have subconsciously left the bag behind, suspecting that it somehow contained the source of all her bad feelings, deep down she also knew that it was a feeble attempt, and that it had failed miserably.

* * *

Nicola would have been surprised to hear that just ten minutes after leaving the store, Joseph and Brent entered it. They had finished the packing in no time and headed off for the beach straight away. Joseph had been thinking of his wife and quite uncharacteristically wanted to buy her something. Not a present, of course … he couldn't get too carried away. More a memento of their holidays. She loved that kind of stuff. Joseph had tried a couple of stores, already way beyond his usual limit, when a picture hanging in the window caught his eye. And the style was right up her alley.

Usually he wouldn't consider buying her a picture. She liked to paint and would probably take it as some kind of artistic slap in the face if he did. It looked like the kind of artwork usually found on the covers of the fantasy novels he always saw her reading. Joseph thought that the picture might 'inspire' her – so that was the pitch he would throw her way if required.

He wasn't sure if it was a print or an original – he wouldn't be able to tell the difference between the two anyway. What he saw was a young man on horseback, who had a definite hero thing going, sword held high, some foggy villain in the distance. He was sure Nicola would love it. On quick consultation with Brent, he decided that he would take the punt and buy it.

When Joseph entered the store he wasn't bombarded by

the unease his wife had felt, didn't suffer the sudden onset of a migraine, not because he wasn't sensitive (he was, just not to her extent). He wouldn't have felt anything because the source of the disturbance had left about fifteen minutes earlier when his family did. Nor did he have a feeling, a need to find something, he just wanted to buy a present for his wife, the only real difference between the two, being that one had found what they had both been searching for.

* * *

Michael enjoyed the traditional end of holiday feast. Uncle Brent and Nicola had their last seafood cook-off but it was a hard call as to who made the best dish. Michael would have voted for his mum's calamari, though only if it were a secret ballot, because they both took it kind of seriously.

Then it was a double-check to make sure everything was packed, and early to bed so the family didn't miss their flight.

Michael usually slept like a baby even when he had to get up early. So even though they had a flight to catch the next morning, Michael was asleep as soon as his head hit the pillow. He woke knowing his sleep had been troubled by bad dreams but he couldn't remember what it had been about. It had probably been brought on by his reluctance about going home. He'd had a great holiday. Michael loved Noosa, enjoyed the freedom of the place. And he knew Dana had enjoyed her time off from guard duty, although she missed Sheba. Marcus must have been playing on his mind a bit, and maybe the soccer scout a little too, because he felt unusually tense.

Either way, they made it to the airport on time and once their bags were checked and he was seated on the plane, he fiddled with all of the buttons then settled himself for the two and a half hour flight. Determined to make up for his broken night's sleep he drifted off and experienced his last untroubled dreams for a very long time.

* * *

Michael woke abruptly to an elbow in his ribs from Dana. The flight attendant had apparently been trying to get his attention. It took him a couple of seconds to understand what he was being asked. His mind eventually cleared and with some prompting from Dana he replied, 'No, he was not using a laptop, mobile phone or any other electronic device.' Apparently the word of a half-asleep teenage boy wasn't good enough, because he was asked whether he was sure.

Yes, he was sure! Michael thought as he turned to Dana questioningly. Dana bent her head toward his and whispered, 'Just answer her, she's had a bit of a rough flight.'

Finally Michael convinced the flight attendant that he did not have any hand luggage and that he wasn't using anything electronic. Now that Michael was awake and taking in his surrounding he realised that the seatbelt sign was on and that the plane was bouncing around a bit. He smiled up at the attendant to apologise for his abrupt response but she had already moved to the next aisle. She asked the same question to the people sitting in front of them, while distractedly running her free hand over her head, obviously trying to smooth the now not so perfect hairdo. She held on with the other hand to the back of the seat, professionally riding out each bump.

'You could sleep through anything,' Dana accused

him, obviously amused by his ability to snooze through a noticeably rough flight. 'It's been like this since just after we took off. They keep reminding everyone to turn off everything electronic and they have just started working their way through the plane checking row by row. I told her you'd been asleep since take-off but she insisted I wake you.' Dana looked worried as the plane lurched through another pocket of air.

'Is there anything to worry about?' Michael asked.

'I don't think so. We've been circling over the airport for about thirty minutes but we're supposed to land soon. It's not the weather. Something electrical by the questions they keep asking. My bet, some idiot with a mobile phone just had to google something.'

The stewardess made her way to the front of the cabin and spoke with her colleagues. Moments later the captain announced that they would be landing.

'They obviously found the idiot,' Michael said to Dana as he checked his buckle.

* * *

The half an hour delay on landing had made a lot of the passengers irritable. So when it was announced that there would be a delay with their luggage, Michael found a wall to lean against where he could see the carousel without having to stand in amongst the crowd. So he was in the perfect position to hear all of his fellow passenger's remarks.

The common consensus was that the flight had experienced some electrical disturbance and the baggage handlers were being forced to put all checked luggage through extra security screenings. Most people felt that this was reasonable; others felt that security had missed something and now the passengers had to endure an unacceptable level of inconvenience. Michael didn't care much either way. Dana had brought him an iced tea so they stood together and waited for the first of their luggage to appear.

He grabbed everyone's bags off the carousel as they arrived, piling them together where Nicola and Sarah could organise distribution. They were walking towards the exit when Ashley, labouring her way behind Michael, called out. She must have run to catch up because she grabbed Michael's arm and asked, 'Michael, isn't that your backpack?'

Michael, annoyed, looked back towards the carousel which now only had a couple of items circling unclaimed. Ashley was right: one of them was his backpack. But the sight made him feel nervous. Would security be watching him as he collected the bag? He hadn't even realised he had left it behind but he felt real reluctance as he walked back and collected it. He grabbed one of the straps and looked left and right, expecting someone to tap him on the shoulder like they did on TV.

Michael hurried to catch up to his family and held his backpack, bumping against his leg as he walked. Obviously the mood of the other passengers had rubbed off. Even though the backpack was not over his shoulders he still felt a weight of tension descend.

* * *

Its sleep was restless again. It had been waking more often of late, only to find Itself still trapped in the stiff wooden body that had been Its prison for an eternity.

What had disturbed It this time? It detested the sleep but greatly preferred the ordeal to Its waking wooden torment. But this time It detected a difference. It smelled evil, caught the unmistakable whiff that might mean release, escape.

Its form had been picked up by a young male and It shrank away from the touch. This one was too pure, reeking of goodness. But there again, It detected the scent, it was on this boy, not coming from him but one he had been in contact with recently. How could It use this, use this disgusting creature to enable Its own release. Suddenly It perceived that someone close by was scrying. Old defences rose and It sent out a mental shield making certain to control Its power. It didn't need to overreach Itself like It had done with the old woman, forcing Itself into an unwanted period of inactivity. It carefully examined those that had blundered upon It. There were other presences apart from the juvenile male and close by now, another that harboured the delightful decadence. But these also were pure, revolting, before examining them further It stopped to check whether Its interference had worked and laughed when It realised It need not have wasted precious strength. An older female, protective of this young male, had already buckled under the little amount of power It had sent her way, The scrying, if it could even had been called such, already clumsy and erratic, faltered and died. No further risk lay in that quarter.

Its defences now relaxed, It contemplated returning to the sleep but decided to endure their stench a moment longer, hoping to grab another sniff of malice. It sensed that they often came in contact with the source of the evil and therefore It reasoned would in all likelihood come in contact with it again and that was something worth pursuing.

It shivered delightfully when It felt a wave of pure energy seep through the barrier, just when It needed it. The barrier had been leaking more of late and It took a brief moment to consider this strange fact but wasted little time contemplating Its good fortune. It inserted mental fingers, exerting pressure on the breach to try and release just a little more energy, just enough to disrupt the bindings long enough for It to stay awake and endeavour to attach itself to these two and hitch a ride that might just bring It to the source of the evil. And as a trickle of energy flowed through the breach and entered Its body, It pooled Its waning strength and struggled to accomplish what was needed. Its efforts were rewarded and It was able to move Its wooden form. So as the two sickly sweet creatures turned away to leave, It made the jump and was able to alight undetected on the strange pouch the male carried on his back. It burrowed down inside, through layers of reeking clutter, hiding itself, preparing to go along for a ride. If that ride might bring an opportunity for escape, It would endure this boy's stink. And with that accomplished It allowed itself to smile, dimmed Its presence to avoid detection and fell back, not into full slumber, but not truly awake either, waiting for any sign that might signify release.

It felt fear for a time when It checked Its surroundings and found Itself isolated. It had a strange sense of movement but could not at first detect the energy as It expected. Things were different. Panicked, It searched for and found the owner of the satchel It was riding in and a measure of sanity returned. After a number of attempts to examine Its surroundings, It found that the ground was somehow far below and they were somehow above. It knew that Its searching had for some reason created fear in those of authority and having this unexpected confirmation of Its power, It was able to return to Its dreams.

Dreaming again of destruction. Dreaming of anarchy. Dreaming such sweet, sweet dreams.

Life Gets Freaky

Due to his mother's strange notions of 'self-sufficiency', Michael found himself faced with the unpleasant task of unpacking his bags from their holiday. Nicola had conveniently left to stock up on what she called the essentials, which translated to 'we have no Coke in the house and while I'm out I'll grab some milk and bread as well', fully expecting all the dirty work to have been done by the time she returned. It was as he started this arduous job that he fully experienced a taste of the strange world that his mother lived in full time. He had experienced inklings, had hunches, but as he unpacked, he was hit full force by a 'feeling' so strong he had to stop what he was doing for a moment. This foreboding was accompanied by images that flashed through his mind in such close succession he was unable to fully grasp any of them clearly. Hazy grey images, black shadowed figures, even for just for a second, the unmistakable dark red of blood.

What was going on?

Why was he having these visions?

After standing motionless for more than a minute with no recurrent vision, he decided to store the information for later reflection and possible discussion with Dana. He still felt slightly shaken but without any obvious cause for his unease he decided to get the already unpleasant task of unpacking finished so he could move on to more important things like playing PS4.

Almost incomprehensible amounts of sand poured out of every pocket, shoe and sock he removed from his backpack. He kept feeling the urgent need to remove his hands from the backpack. He was getting jumpier by the second and had almost convinced himself there was some spider or other dangerous creature sitting at the bottom of his bag, waiting patiently to sting or bite his hand the next time he reached in.

'Don't be such a baby,' Michael muttered under his breath. Scolding himself he reached down to grab the remaining clothes before he lost his nerve.

Michael's world changed as he reached into his backpack to clear out the last of his stuff. The sensation he felt when his fingers brushed against something near the bottom made him jump backwards. He snatched his hand out so fast that he backhanded the corner of his bed in the process.

'What the hell?' Michael cursed as he sucked on his grazed knuckles.

He had put a good metre of distance between himself and the backpack. As he nursed his slightly bleeding knuckles, he swayed as another series of images flashed through his mind. Stronger than before: a strange shadowed figure appeared, exuding an agitation that he had not noticed the first time. There were flashes of blood that he assumed to be his own grazed knuckles, all accompanied by a measured pounding – almost like a heartbeat but with a more complex rhythm. The strange drumming drove away the images flooding through his mind and his own heart rate slowed into some kind of sympathetic harmony. Once his thumping heart had quietened the strange beat slowed and disappeared.

He sat on the edge of his bed as his vision cleared, trying to work out what had just happened. Maybe he was coming down with something. He hadn't eaten in a while and knew low blood sugar could make you feel faint, make your ears ring. Not an exact match to what he had just experienced but still he was no doctor. As Michael sat trying to explain away what deep down he knew to be beyond his comprehension he noticed the strange lump in his almost empty backpack.

He had a crazy notion as to what was causing the bulge. But it shouldn't be possible. He had shoved that stupid doll way back under the blanket of the soldier's chest back in the thrift shop. He most certainly had not picked it up again, and there was no way he had walked over and made an offer to buy it from the craggy old dude behind the counter.

'No way.' Michael tried to convince himself that he was just letting his overly active imagination get carried away. Surely the lump was just screwed up clothing. He could feel a kind of dreadful eagerness emanating from the backpack.

These ridiculous thoughts must be caused by fatigue or low blood sugar. 'That's it, I'm hypoglycaemic!'

His aunty was always feeing faint, disorientated and

downright grumpy just because more than an hour had passed since her last snack. After a couple of bites on a little more than a carrot she always perked straight up. He had always thought of her as a tad dramatic but she was obviously on to something.

'Problem solved.' He hadn't eaten in a while. It had been at least half an hour since his last decent feed. Hadn't he heard similar stories about people fainting, hallucinating, seeing and talking to people that weren't even there just because they needed to eat? He felt comfortable with this explanation. His heart rate may have slowed, but his fingers still tingled from the adrenaline rush, goose pimples still covered his body and the hairs on the back of his neck were still raised.

Humanity may have come a long way but the flight or fight instinct still linked them to their earlier, less evolved beginnings. Having decided to go downstairs and grab himself a muesli bar, Michael tentatively got up from the bed and slowly backed away until he was firmly pressed up against the wall. Not able to take his eyes off the backpack, reluctant to even turn his back for a moment, Michael stood, muscles tensed, poised, waiting.

'Either go get some food or open the damn bag. Make a bloody decision!' He reasoned that all he needed to do was lift up the flap on his backpack and take a look but he still couldn't move. 'Worst case, it's the stinking doll. So what, throw the stupid thing in the rubbish and be done with it? Better still, burn the bastard!'

While standing and mumbling curses to himself, Dana entered his room.

'Michael, what are you going on about? I can hear you from my room. What are you planning on burning? And who's the bastard?'

'You better not have anything to do with this?' he

yelled, trying to hide the fact that he had jumped when she entered. This random question was asked more to salvage some semblance of control rather than in any real belief that Dana might know what was going on.

'I suppose this is your idea of funny?' Michael asked gesturing wildly in the direction of his backpack.

'What are you talking about?' Dana's puzzled expression was to be expected, her look of disquiet wasn't. Dana wasn't laughing, her eyes glued to the backpack just as Michael's were. She obviously had no conscious idea of what was going on but it looked like some warning bell had already gone off in her head just the same. She stepped towards the backpack and Michael's paralysis was broken. He grabbed her and pulled her back so that they were both now standing with their backs against the wall.

'Michael what the …' Dana's temper always easy to provoke, showed itself in both the sound of her voice and the look on her face, but was dampened when she noticed Michael's grazed knuckles. 'What have you done to yourself?' Dana checked the damage.

Snatching his hand away, not wanting to be distracted by a silly graze, Michael stepped in front of Dana, placing himself between her and the bag.

'Don't go near that bag. Please!' Michael kept a strong grip on his sister's arm.

'You're starting to freak me out, Michael!'

Michael was somehow sure that he had felt that greasy headed little doll as he unpacked his stuff. He even thought that he had heard that muffled voice again, but with all the other images and sounds that had been flooding his mind he couldn't keep things straight. His priority now was not muesli bars, grazed hands or even understanding what the hell was going on, he just wanted to keep Dana away from the backpack.

'I can't explain right now. Stay here, next to me.' This wasn't the time for explanations of what he'd just experienced. He needed to keep her safe. Michael's mind raced through the options available. How do you remove a threat that doesn't make any sense?

Dana uncharacteristically made no move to push him away, searching his face, trying to understand what was going on.

'Micky, just take a breath … what's up?'

The whispered voice grew louder again as he tried to formulate his response. He shook his head and was able to block out the distraction.

'I think that doll is in my backpack!'

'Tell me you didn't buy that thing!'

'Of course I didn't buy it. Why the hell would I? I don't want you touching it. It's not safe.'

'Not safe? You're not making any sense.'

'Danes, I swear to you, I thought I felt that doll in my bag. I think I even heard it speak.' With the simple use of the name 'Danes' Michael had convinced Dana that there was a real problem. It was a childhood nickname that he only used when he was in trouble and it showed her instantly that he was trying to hold it together.

Dana didn't bother arguing any further. She didn't question what doll he was talking about. She remembered the horrible thing from the shop. It had freaked her out then and the thought that it was in the room with them now freaked her out even more.

'I swear, I thought I felt it in my bag, that's all.'

As the seconds ticked by, Michael was feeling less certain, more stupid. In the time he had taken to turn and explain things to Dana the backpack now looked less ominous.

Michael finally realised he had little choice. Keeping as much distance between himself and the bag the whole time, he edged his way over to his cupboard. His eyes darted back and forth between the bag and Dana. He grabbed a golf club from his cupboard and slowly closed the distance. Giving Dana one more look to say 'don't you dare move', Michael gave the bag a few good smacks with his five iron, then waited a couple of seconds before he hooked the arm straps with the head of the club. Holding his breath, Michael shook the bag.

Both of them jumped as a pair of balled-up socks fell to the floor. Dana turned, looked into his eyes and without a hint of ridicule or scorn, she gestured for him to hand her over a club of her own. Without a single comment made they began checking the room. They methodically looked under the bed, inside cupboards, and rummaged through the piles of dirty clothing he'd already unpacked. Dana even stripped his bed down and remade it just to be sure.

By unspoken consent they had decided to make sure that there was nothing out of place. That they were looking for the doll was never said. That the idea made no sense at all was never questioned. They had both felt something and wanted to be sure that if they found anything they could and would deal with it.

All they found was some sand under Michael's bed. After a trip to the beach, sand always seemed to find its way into everything. There seemed nothing more they could do. They'd searched his room thoroughly and found not a thing. But Michael couldn't shake the feeling that there was something more he should be doing. Dana obviously felt the same, if the way she was clenching and unclenching her fists around the handle of her golf club were any indication.

But without any divine inspiration as to what that thing was, they looked at each other and mutually agreed that the remainder of the unpacking could wait.

Being teenagers, they resorted to the tried and true remedy for most maladies of the mind: they decided to watch some television, trying hard to convince themselves they weren't running away.

* * *

The journey was worth it. The disgusting juveniles had brought It to a place of power, a place where the energy flowed from the breach in powerful waves. It could feel that the evil was close by, also drawn to this weak point in the barrier. There would be no returning to full sleep. Its strength was coming back and the ancient bindings were unravelling. But these children could not provide the fuel It desperately needed to complete Its release, could not be coerced to aid It. But when the stupid boy injured himself the smell of his fresh blood almost drove It into a frenzy. His blood held the taint of those that had bound it eons ago. Here so close and unprotected stood the descendants of the Enemy. Not only was a debt owed but these two, with the power that flowed through them, coursing through their very veins, It would be able to break the bindings instantly.

It tried, desperate, whispering into the unbelievably defenceless mind of the young male and succeeded in nothing more than using up some of the strength It had managed to gather.

It needed to get away from these people – 'The Enemy'. It should have recognised them by the relief felt when the older female left Its vicinity. It had known that she sensed Its presence more acutely. But even with her higher level of perception, she was merely troubled, only using the power in the most rudimentary way, sending out useless searchings, ignorant of the fact that she had even attempted to use the power. That It had felt relief when such a feeble user of power left Its presence should have given It an inkling of their hidden lineage.

But what were the chances to awaken in the presence of the Enemy, to sense aid so close by, and all of this to occur in a time and place where the power flowed through the breach at its strongest?

It would ponder this when It was safely away from these.

It revelled in their stupidity, realising how far this bloodline had declined, knowing they posed little threat but still they diverted too much of the power It needed and thereby restricting Its freedom. These few would resist Its release, albeit unwittingly; it was in their blood. As long as It remained near these, It would not be able to complete Its release. The first binding was already failing but the others still held strong. It knew Its goal was close by and with the power left flowing around It the final vestiges of the first binding were shucked away.

With freer movement, in the moment the male was distracted, It scrambled under his sleeping place. The stench was almost intolerable but necessary. These two juveniles had armed themselves and in Its weakened state It was vulnerable. When the disgusting creatures almost blundered across Its hiding spot It converted their sweet sweet fear into the energy It desperately needed. It had scurried for cover again, enjoying the irony of using these two as a power supply.

It watched on disdainfully as they searched only with their eyes, brandishing their crude weapons, looking for what their minds still refused to accept and It laughed as they made the mistake the weak minded always do. They never thought to look above. They all believed that anything evil must hide in the shadows and It amused Itself with images of their destruction as It hung from the curtains, dangling silently above their very heads. It would wait, store Its energy and when It could, It would travel to the evil so close by and affect Its release. But in the meantime It would spare some energy to toy with these children, and play with their minds. There was a debt that needed to be paid – their ancestors had been the ones responsible for the binding. Now after all these eons of captivity, It found Itself in a position where It could slowly shred their minds and then, with luck and careful planning, consume what remained.

It was owed this pleasure.

Dreaming

Michael knew he was dreaming. He'd found himself there too often of late: a strange grey land, void of feature or depth, where the air itself felt thickened, claustrophobic. It was like a place waiting to be or what was left behind when creation had moved on. He moved through the suffocating nondescript void where deadened voices whispered in his ears, just beyond his ability to hear or understand. He felt drawn to the voices as if they held the answer to some question he had long puzzled over.

As in past dreams, he found himself walking deeper into this strange place, unable to track or discern distances travelled. If not for one foot constantly falling in front of the other, he would be unable to register any forward motion. As Michael plodded onwards, the voices (or was it just one voice?) became more insistent, hurrying him to some other place, urging him to run. He failed to take notice as the landscape began to change, to clarify. The landscape had begun to *be*. He barely noticed as the atmosphere thinned and became easier to breathe, more like true air.

For Michael, distances merely passed.

It was when a sharp pain cut across his left side, unable to draw breath that he slowed. Attempting to ease the building stitch that was making breathing difficult. Only then did he take the time to survey his surroundings.

It was still a grey place, but where once it had been devoid of feature, it was now populated with a multitude of withered trees that looked like they had long forgotten the feel of sunlight.

Those trees, a slightly darker shade of grey than the thick oppressive surroundings that harboured them, were smothered by a yellow growth that was more than likely responsible for their unhealthy appearance. This fungus was the only thing around that looked to be thriving.

As was sometimes the case in dreams, his body moved without conscious thought. Of its own volition he found his hand drawn towards this parasite.

Something within screamed for him to pull his hand away, but he was fascinated by the texture of the fungus. Would it be spongy or firm? Would it resist as he probed or would he find his hand welcomed by its soft embrace? At the last possible moment, the fungus moved toward his hand, bulging and increasing its mass somehow in an effort to make contact. Once his fingertips registered the wet warmth of the thing, Michael finally managed to draw back.

The shrill shriek of disappointment was so intense that he 'felt' rather than heard the resonance, stumbling, he hurried to move away before he found himself mesmerised once more.

Backing away he discovered that the ground was damp and covered in decaying debris. Michael hoped it was nothing more than leaves because, at that point, he also became aware that his feet were bare and splattered with mud and some other undefinable substance. His legs were torn and bleeding from a disturbing number of scratches and cuts. It was obvious that he had been running for a long time and through some less forgiving terrain than where he now found himself.

A strong feeling of disquiet entered his mind and was chased away as the voices raised themselves to a new level that made his ears ring. Michael clasped his hands to his head, stopped and tried to steady himself. He forced himself to calm and gradually his heart eased its erratic beat. He needed to focus, felt deeply that there was much more than dirty feet and impaired hearing at stake here.

Slowly, he was once again in charge of his own faculties and he reluctantly decided to continue on.

As his first footstep touched the ground, he fell to his knees and the voices that screamed in his mind reached a piercing crescendo. He clutched his head in near intolerable pain.

It was only when he turned back towards the dying forest that the pain eased. He watched, resigned yet wondering why the voices so desperately wanted him to remain in this forest. Frozen, fearful of movement of any kind. Desperate not to trigger the return of the pain.

The monotony of the scene before him was broken as a dark shadow appeared with a familiar person following one step behind.

'Little Michaela, What brings you to this place?' Marcus smiled, sweeping his arm around to take in the surrounding as if they were somehow of his making.

'Oh, that's right you have little choice. *We* decide where you dream now.' At the mention of the word 'we', Michael tried to make out the other figure who remained always in shadow. He squinted, leaning ever so slightly forward, needing to discover the identity of the hulking figure that wore shadow as a cloak and walked with the stalking, disjointed gait of a wind-up toy. And when for a moment it allowed its face to be seen, Michael recoiled in horror.

A silent 'No!' fell from Michael's lips as he turned in an attempt to run.

The creature's lips stretched and emitted the screeching voice that dropped Michael once again to his knees. A single droplet of blood trickled from his left ear as he forced himself to crawl away, realising the futility of that action, knowing full well that the doll had finally found him.

* * *

Michael didn't feel refreshed as he woke each morning. Truth be told, he felt drained, as if something were being taken from him every night. He didn't know how he was supposed to combat this. He couldn't sleep, and no matter what he thought of before he went to sleep, he always found himself in the same circumstance – the scenery would change slightly but the characters were always the same.

For over a week he had been enduring the recurring nightmare of that damned freaky doll. It had started only a couple of days after he experienced the strange vision when unpacking from his holidays.

He spent each day dreading what the next night would bring. He was reluctant to discuss the whole thing in too much detail with anyone, for fear of being mocked, for having childish fears. He'd always had nightmares as a kid, probably more than normal. His mother would always press him for details, and usually she'd be able to say just the right thing. She would sit with him, promise to be there if he needed her. 'Twenty-eight and always' was their motto.

'Can I come into your bed, Mum, if I get scared? Can I call you?'

'Always baby, that's what always means.'

He was too old to call her now. He should be able to take care of himself.

Over breakfast, Michael tried to keep a low profile, quietly pouring himself a bowl of cereal, walking to the kitchen table to eat, rather than the bench were everyone else was congregated.

He hunched over the bowl, trying to make himself as inconspicuous as possible.

His mother pulled up a chair and sat next to him.

'You've been very quiet lately. Are you feeling alright?'

'Didn't sleep well,' he mumbled back knowing this was not going to be the end of the conversation but giving it his best to close it down quickly.

'Bad dreams?'

'Yeah, I suppose.'

'Michael, they either were bad dreams or they weren't. If you don't want to talk about them just say so but don't give me half-arsed answers.'

He realised his mistake. Nicola was easy to annoy in this regard. Rarely did she care if he chose not to tell her something but she hated it when people didn't answer questions directly, even worse if they answered a question with a question.

'Fine! I've been having nightmares. Nightmares about Marcus.' Michael felt Dana's eyes turn in his direction at this point.

His mum just kept looking at him, eyebrows raised, knowing there was more.

Michael knew just by this small gesture that there was going to be no holding back so he told her all he could remember.

Dana had sat herself down at the table by this stage and Joseph had left the kitchen at the very start of the conversation with a quick, 'I'll leave you to it.'

All seemed to be going fine and then she asked about the fungus. This seemed to interest her as did the withered trees but when he mentioned the screeching noise he actually saw her go pale.

'Can you describe it, baby? What happened when you heard that noise?'

'I wanted to get away, Mum. But you don't understand, the noise stops you, it's just too painful!'

'You felt actual pain in your dream?'

'Do you think I would look like this if I only had Marcus calling me names each night?' Michael was getting annoyed himself now and was about to continue when Nicola interrupted him by grabbing his arm and looked him straight in his eyes.

'You call me baby, whenever this happens again, you call me okay!' She said this as an imperative and for the first time that he could remember her words didn't make it all better. She had made him more fearful of sleep because he had seen past the concern in her eyes where the fear lived.

* * *

Michael didn't know why he didn't tell her about the dreams of the horse. Maybe his mum would make him fear the horse too, and he didn't need any more fear right now.

He only now realised that he'd been having these dreams for as long as he could remember dreaming. When he was younger the dreams where the horse appeared would leave him feeling empty and disappointed. Always the sound of drumming in his ears. And he recalled little else of the details. He had always remembered being chased through lands of impossible imaginings but little more.

It was only now with his current nightmares that for some reason he was able to remember the other dreams in full detail as if something had been freed. The smoky grey mare would chase him and Michael, fearful of what it wanted, ran. He knew she needed something from him because he could feel her desperate longing, almost as an ache. When the mare finally caught up with him, and she always did, she would stand, head proudly held high. She would then lower her head so that her eyes were on a level with his. Her large dark grey eyes penetrated through his, hiding none of the intelligence behind them. She would stand patiently as if searching for some truth or awaiting some revelation. The desperate longing pounding from her like a heartbeat. When Michael stood mutely and did not respond, she raised her head and walked silently away.

It was almost as if the nightmare of the doll had unlocked these hidden memories. Michael could now remember them in clear detail although he wished he couldn't. He may have feared the dreams of the doll, but his action when he last dreamt of the horse shamed him.

Having already endured the now ritual Marcus/doll nightmare for the third time in one night, Michael fell unwillingly back into sleep, tensing, waiting for the first impulse to run. He felt shock as the silent longing washed over him. He knew the horse from some distant repressed memory was back.

He didn't know if the relief he felt was purely due to the fact that the doll was taking a break or because he was somehow grateful for the return of the horse. He was tired of running and so he stood and waited as the horse walked up to him lowered her head and asked her silent question.

Michael had never feared the horse herself. But he knew the horse needed *something* from him, and what that was, Michael did fear. He knew it was no little thing and when he didn't respond he knew she left him disappointed in some way. Having endured the physical as well as mental pain that had been inflicted on him this night, Michael had nothing left to give.

'So what do *you* want from me?' He spat the words at the horse.

'It's bad enough that they want me out of the way. But you, what piece of me do you want?' And as the words left his lips he wished he could take them back. The smoky grey mare lowered her head further and Michael saw a single iridescence tear fall from her white lashes.

She turned slowly, did not look back, kicked up from the ground and was galloping though the air, running for the first time away from Michael. And her ache had now become his.

Michael had woken knowing he had made a terrible mistake.

* * *

He thought he had managed to endure his mum's questioning without snapping too badly. He just couldn't stop replaying images of the doll walking by itself, whispering in his ears every time he closed his eyes. Michael detested the concept of Marcus somehow enjoying his misery, however ridiculous that seemed. And his greatest concern was that the doll was ever increasing in size, always bigger than it had been in the store. Each time he dreamed, he knew it became more powerful.

That one iridescent tear hung heavily on his conscience.

Dana quietly followed him upstairs when he'd managed to break away from his mother's probing.

'Micky, can I come in?'

'Well by the fact that you're sitting on the end of my bed I would say that you really don't care about my answer!'

'Fair call. But Micky, you need to know. You're not the only one dreaming. I'm having dreams too. Just not as freakish as yours.'

'What? You let me endure Mum's inquisition and didn't help me out. You just sat back and listened!' Michael was furious that he had been left looking a fool when Dana was in the same predicament as him.

Completely ignoring Michael's mood, Dana continued, 'Mine aren't quite the same. They start the same way but as soon as the voices start, as soon as the doll appears, well … they change.' Michael looked up at that moment, wondering why she had stopped, and found Dana blushing.

'Change, change how?' Michael demanded. His anger was still bubbling just below the surface. He didn't want to lash out at Dana but he had no other target available and if she kept being so obscure he would have little choice.

'Well you know that painting Dad bought Mum on holidays?' Again Dana hesitated.

'Oh for God's sake, Dana, just give.'

'That guy, you know, the one on horseback. He comes and the doll disappears, the voices stop and I wake up!'

Dana normally the more articulate of the two blundered through this explanation, obviously embarrassed by the whole thing.

Michael, having sat down next to Dana on the bed during the conversation, jumped up and blurted out, 'What horse? I mean what colour is the horse!'

'What difference does that make!'

'Dana. What colour was the horse?' Michael spoke each syllable distinctly barely able to contain an emotion he was unable to identify but would later realise was jealously.

'Black, the horse is black. Just like in the painting, aren't you listening!'

Michael breathed a sigh of relief, and then they continued to discuss their dreams. He still didn't mention anything about the grey mare. It was somehow too personal …

'Couldn't you have been a bit more imaginative?' Michael laughed to himself.

'The typical knight in shining armour type, riding a war horse, waving a flaming sword, saving damsels in distress.'

Normally he would have used this as ammunition for some hardcore teasing. But being so close to breaking point, fearful of even discussing the full extent of his escalating alarm he would have gladly swapped with her, called himself a sissy and taken the resultant teasing and still counted himself ahead in the game.

'Have you wondered why the doll is in your dreams and the …' struggling to find the right words Dana settled with, 'this guy is in mine; we came across them both in the same shop on the same holidays.'

'Yeah I have actually!' Not being able to help himself, Michael paused for dramatic effect. 'You just think the guy is hot, admit it. That's why he's in your dreams!' Michael was glad to have something to laugh about. Each time he mentioned the dude on horseback she blushed, which to Michael was just hilarious.

'Be serious! What are the chances?'

'I am being serious. Couldn't you have picked someone more imposing, maybe a hero with a bazooka rather than a flaming sword?' Michael punctuated this statement by waving his arm around in a less than heroic fashion.

'I'm sick of having the mental shit kicked out of me every night. If I had a bazooka I would happily blow the living crap out of the next entity to visit my dreams, be it wooden creepazoid or fluffy pooh bear. Why don't you send your boyfriend over and ask him to save my butt tonight?'

Although Michael was joking, Dana had brought up a valid point, why were they both dreaming of things found during the same holiday. If his mum had taught him anything about coincidence they were almost always more than what they appeared. Coincidence, meant providence trying to tell you something. The problem was in the interpretation. Fate spoke its own language and the deciphering was usually way beyond his ability or his motivation to interpret. But getting little more than twenty minutes decent sleep per night, his mind just wasn't up for the challenge of unravelling the mystery. Quite frankly it most likely would not have been after a week of solid slumber.

'Dana have you also wondered why Marcus ... why is he all of a sudden in our dreams?'

'What?' Dana had clearly not been listening to anything past the comment about her boyfriend.

'Dana! Earth to Dana! Marcus. Why him? Why now? It's not as if he moved in yesterday.'

'Michael I have to think some more, you might be on to something. I'll talk to you later.'

With that as a parting comment Dana left his room and left him alone for the remainder of the day. Michael hoped he hadn't offended her with the 'boyfriend' comment. Girls could be so touchy about that kind of thing.

* * *

Dana wasn't offended about anything. She just thought Michael may have hit on something. What he hadn't realised was that everyone in the house knew he was having nightmares. Everyone could hear him muttering at night, and with the foul moods he woke up in, it wasn't hard to put the pieces together. But to find their dreams were so similar … that changed things.

When Michael mentioned 'her boyfriend', although she knew he was joking, it gave her an idea.

That night Dana waited for the quiet muttering and occasional cursing to stop. She could hear Michael easily from her room and when the sound of his tossing and turning stopped she watched the clock for an extra ten minutes, just to be sure Michael was finally asleep and then snuck into his room.

When she saw his face Dana's first reaction was to wake him. The look on his face frightened her. Michael had always been prone to nightmares but they had never made him look scared. He would usually roll over and just go back to sleep. Worse case he would call Mum, and she would sit with him and talk and he would be off to sleep again shortly after. He stoically took whatever life dished out without missing a beat.

He wasn't fearless, but his usual level of self-control was quite remarkable. Soccer had seen him need stiches in his head once and a schoolyard accident had resulted in him splitting his knee open down to the bone. Neither time did he even break a sweat, the mere flick of his right eyebrow all the giveaway that he felt any pain or registered some anxiety. To see Michael look so lost now made Dana genuinely uncomfortable.

Dana contemplated calling her mum, but surely if there was something really wrong, Nicola's radar would have been the first one to go off. So Dana decided to put her plan into action and test her theory.

She pulled out the painting that she snuck into her own bedroom days ago and gently she slid the painting under Michael's mattress, just as she had been doing for herself each night.

She sat with him for a while and his rapid breathing eased and he looked to have fallen into a more comfortable slumber, so she crept back to her own bedroom hoping that the protection the painting had given her would now pass over to him.

* * *

Had she stayed longer and realised that only about five minutes passed before Michael was thrown once again into the same recurrent nightmare, Dana would have realised that her plan hadn't worked. Michael cried out in his dream and as the doll's piercing screech tore through him, a single drop of blood trickled from his left ear.

Blood could flow in both worlds.

* * *

Dana wasn't the only one watching over Michael's dreaming. Nicola had tricks up her own sleeves that her children had no idea about. They knew she was unique, had gypsy blood that went back generations. They knew she could sense what they were feeling, but they didn't know she could pick up parts of their dreams.

Nicola had battled her own dream demons during her childhood and because of this had developed the ability to block unwanted visitations. She had also learned a certain level of dream control. All ancient cultures spoke of shamans that could enter the spirit world. She had done a lot of reading in her youth about a number of different cultures specifically in relation to dreaming. Along the way she had picked up some useful tips.

Childhood illness had given her the time and the incentive to learn more about other planes of existence. *When fate decides to stop your heart on the operating table, you sometime see more that you may have been meant to.* In some case it leaves doors open that should have remained closed. Nicola had decided to not only put a mental foot in the door to hold it open but to learn as much as she could so she was able on occasion to sneak through this door and see what was on the other side.

She had never spoken to her children about this, not wanting them to be scared of every bump in the night, every creature to enter their dreams, but she always put them to sleep with the thought that they could call her if they needed her. Both children knew she meant 'call her into their dreams'. She wanted her children to know that dreams were not just a movie where the script had been written, a place where they had no control. She needed them to know they owned a certain amount of control and could call allies if needed. When one of their dogs Titan died when the children were young he became part of their night-time litany.

'Don't forget you can always call Titan if you need him. He'll bite any monster's bum clean off!' The kids had loved the concept and laughed whenever they imagined monsters' bums being bitten. Dana especially took to this notion and would wake most mornings telling stories of the adventures she'd had with Titan the night before.

Lately she wished Michael had taken to the concept as strongly as Dana had. When he spoke to her of his recent dreams, she became scared. She couldn't put it more plainly. Real pain in dreams was rare, but not unheard of. To have the pain inflicted on you by the same entity each night – through sounds that drove you to your knees – reminded her too closely of her own childhood nightmares to dismiss it.

She decided to try and drop in on one of Michael's dreams and see for herself to assess the danger. Joseph had gone to bed when Michael had and they had both entered the land of dreams at about the same time. Nicola waited and smiled proudly as Dana snuck into Michael's room and sat patiently ensuring his sleep was untroubled. When Dana had finally gone to her room to do some homework, Nicola decided she couldn't afford to wait much longer. Dana was a night owl and would be up for hours yet.

Michael would be dreaming in mere minutes. It didn't take long for the first stage of sleep to wrap Nicola in its embrace. With care born of many years of practice she was able to take control before she slipped off into her own dreams. Thinking of Michael, focusing on his cheeky smile, his tousled hair, his easy athleticism, her son was easy to find.

She almost woke herself when she experienced the first wave of fear and instinctively tried to remove herself from danger. Knowing it was coming from Michael she forced back this natural reaction and focused. This was what she was here for, but she hadn't prepared herself for the intensity of his emotions. They washed over her but she was unable to pick up many clear images. Nicola decided to embrace the fear, let it flow through her in an attempt to see what was causing such strong emotions.

A flash of rampant hatred forcefully ejected her from the dream. She woke gagging, struggling to keep the contents of her stomach down, acid burning the back of her throat. Nicola had little solid detail to go on but she'd proven to herself beyond any shadow of a doubt that Michael was in real danger.

'What could hate us so?'

There was a huge difference between dreaming something from your imagination to having something beyond imagining enter your dreams. Michael's dreams were being controlled, and she was even more frightened by the fact that what was entering his dreams had the power to not only detect her but eject her within seconds. She had been kidding herself that she could control this situation. She hadn't even been left a moment to influence things at all.

Nicola felt trapped by the bed sheets twisted around her legs and kicked them away as if they were the cause of her problems. Feeling a moment of panic when they briefly tangled with her feet, she struggled out of bed, quick shallow breaths and clammy skin physical evidence of her fear. Why hadn't she realised something powerful was at work earlier? She had been plagued recently by random visions when she was working on the most mundane things: the slicing of mushrooms that turned into pustulent fungus ready to swallow her fingers; trees in the park becoming dying remnants scratching against windows ready to drag her outside; a simple leaf blown onto clothing becoming a scurrying insect trying to burrow inside her clothing. She had laughed it all away as just being a product of a ludicrously overactive imagination.

Something had been beating against her own mental barriers while she slept and manipulating her thoughts during the day but she had not recognised the inherent threat at first. Hadn't even contemplated the fact that her children were also being targeted.

Michael's dreaming was impacting not only his own waking life but hers as well. Whatever they were up against, and there was no doubt this was a fight, blurring barriers, merging worlds. This was something that she'd not only never experienced before but had never even read about.

She kicked the persistent restraint of the sheet away and walked purposefully towards Michael's room. She sat beside him and brushed his hair back from his forehead, his skin as clammy as hers. His breathing was ragged and his body was tense. He looked like any teenage boy in the grip of a particularly nasty nightmare.

She paused for a moment, gathered her thoughts, then murmuring half-forgotten words, sent her energy towards him. Breathing a sigh of relief as the tension slowly left his body, she'd almost been paralysed by the fear that she wouldn't be able to reach him.

* * *

Joseph later found her asleep, curled up on the floor next to Michael's bed, her hand resting against his arm. His blankets were wrapped tightly around her. Either Michael had woken and covered her or she had unconsciously stolen the blankets from him as she so often did from Joseph. Of one thing there was no doubt – he was surrounded by idiots. Joseph walked away and left them to sleep, oblivious.

* * *

The days passed, Nicola had little choice but to continue to search her many books, some passed down from generation to generation through the hands of her ancestors. Gypsies were not one for sharing their secrets – they didn't have their own written language; the wealth of knowledge they possessed was passed down through word of mouth. Nicola strongly suspected that some of the knowledge passed through the bloodlines like some form of genetic imprinting. She had not needed to learn how to use her hands to heal, she just could. She read auras because she could see them and they made her feel a certain way. Dana sometimes saw people who had passed on and had a way with animals that was uncanny. Michael was so in tune with his own body, there was little that he asked of it that it was not able to provide, without effort.

But the gypsy book was like a double-edged sword – it had a way of answering questions without words. Insightful dreams often accompanied the perusal of a book touched by the gypsies, images and recollections not even your own and not all of them simply insightful. Gypsies worked on a transactional basis. What was given came at a price. And the cost was not always able to be mutually agreed upon before the transaction took place. There was no way to barter with a book. This was a risk that she would have to take. The information gained by the gypsies as they passed through other cultures was invaluable. From Russia and all the way through Europe the gypsies travelled, persecuted, but forever gathering knowledge. They had no hesitation in sharing and recording the knowledge of other cultures in the standard written form.

Unfortunately this book, like most in her collection had references to dreaming and research took time and she felt that this was one thing she had very little of.

In the meantime she sent Michael what energy she could and placed as many protections over him as she knew. Whispering each night 'twenty-eight and always', wishing she could do more.

* * *

To feed again felt so good. The journey between the neighbouring houses had dangerously depleted Its energy level but the wonderfully corrupt souls It now resided with were eager to help. The power flowed through Its body and broke the second layer of bindings, those locking It into the wooden doll. It found itself fully in the second realm and It had willing accomplices, helping It, feeding It as It worked to break down the barriers that kept the flow of power locked so enticingly away. So close it could taste it, yet unable to gorge.

The delightful evil of Its new disciples knew no bounds, they happily let It feed on the strength of their own offspring, offering their spawn and more for what they imagined as small sacrifice for the ultimate reward. Little did they know that this would suffice only in the short term, to return to the first realm and release the hordes – to rule again, to reave again – would require a much greater fuel supply and these creatures would only be the first to be consumed. Disciples It had found in Its long history were never in short supply and this new age that It found Itself waking into only seemed to crave salvation all the more. Little did they know that salvation came in many shapes and sizes and very rarely what was expected was delivered upon.

Its daydreams would be nothing but pure joy if not for the nagging sensation that something was resisting Its attempts to break the remaining bindings. It had not been able to exact revenge on its persecutors. It had been able to toy with the Enemy, but little more. But this resistance was not from those of the stinking bloodline, they had no knowledge of the power they could wield, contemptible fools that they were. Manipulated and ejected from the realm of dreams with ease.

This felt like something else, something ancient. It would continue to feed, grow strong and monitor this resistance. But it was hard to retain control when so much lay before It defenceless, so easily corrupted and consumed. Its rapture was barely diminished.

It was free, It was fed and It would not be stopped until it had had Its fun.

Knowledge is Power

Dana sat with her chemistry book lying open in front of her, keyboard pushed absently to the side as she massaged her forehead with her fingertips. Who really cared about double displacement reactions when her brother was relying on a painting of a knight in shining armour to save him? There must be something more she could do – she had to protect her little brother. Dana hissed in frustration, her mind circling around the problem, but nothing came to mind. She knew there was no point talking to her mother. She suspected something, of this Dana had no doubt. Her mother's ears had literally pricked when Michael mentioned the pain in his dreams but Dana saw no figurative light bulb going off. Dana was no mind-reader but she could read body language. And her mum's body language had been a little too like a mouse sensing a cat was near but not yet realising which way it should run. Dana would give her some time to work it out. Nicola would not stay a mouse for long, and being a mouse was not in her nature.

Deciding to log off her computer, she wasn't getting any homework done anyway. She would check on Michael again and then think some more. She systematically saved or closed each tab she had open and absently sat looking at the screen in front of her, headphones continuing to play a song she barely heard.

Her thoughts chased each other around as she absently typed 'I need a hero' into Google. She came back to the moment with Bonnie Tyler's 'I Need a Hero' playing in her ears. She had to smile – it was one of her mum's favourite *Singstar* tunes. She consistently butchered it, but she did so with an amount of gusto that always made Dana sing along. The fact that the song finished long before she had worked out why it was playing was a testament to how distracted she was. In the same unconscious manner Dana cleared her search and typed in 'knight in shining armour' and was surprised when the screen filled with a range of results. Selecting one result at random she found herself reading about the legend of King Arthur. She'd heard of King Arthur and the Knights of the Round Table and had even watched some of the TV series *Merlin*. What Dana wasn't expecting was the mass of information and debate about whether King Arthur had actually existed. Dana had just assumed he was a fictional character. She considered for a moment whether the painting she had could be a representation of King Arthur and turned towards Michael's room.

She was fairly certain King Arthur would not be riding into any dream to save her brother. The whole notion of

Michael needing saving was wrong to her. Dana pushed back into her chair and with mounting frustration she rubbed at her dry itchy eyes. Her vision blurred but the tears on the back of her hands remained unnoticed. Dana took a shaky breath and forced herself to exhale slowly.

This was so wrong!

Michael was the hero type. He was the one who defused situations, and calmed people when they were getting defensive, or worse still, aggressive.

Dana had watched him neutralise situations when bad soccer calls caused tension and looked to be about to turn into an all in brawl. Dana even remembered him talking down a parent who went berserk when their son had been benched. He soothed people, reassured them and placed himself as a physical barrier when they were in danger. He shouldn't be the one who needed saving.

Taking another deep breath to steady herself, she lifted her head and forced her shoulders back. Dana needed to find a solution. She relied on Michael's calm. He balanced her and she needed to fix things not just because he was her little brother but because she felt a kind of discord building inside her. She felt like an animal caught in a trap and it was only through slow steady breathing that she managed to unlock tense muscles. Desperation would leave her unable to think clearly, so she methodically stretched her fingers and started tapping on the keyboard, following one link to another, hoping that something would jump out at her.

Images of knights from as far back as the fifth century flicked past her unblinking eyes. Knights with shields, swords, and often on horseback – protectors of the innocent. One image after another, some inspiring, some frightening. Some rode with their flaming swords held high, obviously the possessors of great magic, fighting in worlds she couldn't fathom let alone recognise. Warriors who slept awaiting the call spread across so many cultures.

Dana stopped following the links. She felt hollow as she hit shutdown on her computer and turned away just as the picture of a knight on horseback vanished while her internet browser closed. The knight's chest-plate seemed to glow as the rest of the image faded and Dana stood lost for words, staring at the now blank screen.

She couldn't move.

Her mind was busily processing what she had just seen.

How could she not have recognised it earlier? The design worked into the centre of the knight's chest-plate matched the rune work on the knight's sword on the painting now resting under Michael's mattress. She knew this without doubt because she had seen the rune work before, had copied the exact pattern from an old family heirloom, a book passed down from generation to generation believed to contain the history and beliefs of the oldest of the gypsies.

Her mother's ancestors.

Her brother's ancestors.

Her ancestors.

She impatiently logged back on to the computer. Her questions more focused this time, she slowly refined her search.

* * *

Hours later Dana sat back, her head a blur of disconnected ideas. She had tried to follow the rune though cyberspace. She'd found many legends of warriors that guarded the realm, from Odin and his hounds to the Knights of Allaberg, some containing runes too similar to the one she knew to be coincidence. The rune also followed the gypsies through Europe but this avenue of investigation proved somehow more elusive. There seemed to be more information on mythical warriors than on an actual people that still existed today. 'Gypsy' she found was a generic term used to describe nomadic people. She was after the more romanticised story of the Romani. She found many interesting websites that gave her a horrific insight into the persecution of the Romani that continued to this day.

But what caught her interest and had her scurrying through the roof at five in the morning was a piece of information about English rule and the exile of gypsies to Australia on the First Fleet. She knew there was a box in the roof space that contained their great uncle's investigation into their ancestry. He had become interested in the family history when he was diagnosed with cancer and the box containing everything that he had uncovered had found its way into a box in their roof. Dana remembered table talk of great great grandfathers that could read palms and lay their healing hands upon you. Though she had always zoned out – it had always seemed fairly ho-hum. Her own mother could heal and she along with many of her family had visitations from family members that had passed away. None of it was really earth-shattering. But she now had a connection between the gypsies and some of the family that came over from England. A tangible connection.

A diary of sorts.

Dana held a battered leather-bound notebook in her hands. Some of the pages were stuck together where the book had been exposed to water but she was able to make out some entries that described the journey of a girl named Kitty.

This is London! I wish we had never come here. Everywhere I turn is another house, another body, another building. The smells of this place! I hope my new brother or sister comes soon and safely so we can quit this place and return to the road. I know my mother fears for the babe but I have overheard the elders and it is 'the burden' that plagues and forces babies from the womb, misshapen and blue, not the road. Only those families given the task of safekeeping suffer. If only father were not so strong in the power. But he is, so we must do our duty and suffer the burden placed upon us.

Dana skipped forward in the diary and found that a baby had been born to Kitty's family, her little brother, though there had been some unnamed 'problems'. They were about to return to the road when they had been rounded up and sentenced to exile.

So it is done. We are to be exiled to a new land. Sentenced as criminals with no trial. Why? Because we are Romani, gypsies, thieves, and worse. They throw their words like spears to pierce our souls but we know our true purpose. To suffer the burden.

Dana found no further details about this burden until a later entry.

The day started as most days do. The creaking of the boards and the swaying of the ship was a constant that could not be escaped. Father stood under the heavy wooden grate and held out our metal cups to catch what fresh water he could. We are treated like animals. Even on a ship of convicts we are still the lowest of the low. This has given us some form of protection. The others fear us and so we are able to maintain a certain distance. Though I am certain even some of our meagre possession have been seen. I see them looking at our little pile of clothes with longing, believing some treasure is hidden there. Father tells me not to worry but I have seen their covetous glances. They have no idea, with their stories of gypsies and our hidden stores of gold! If they only knew! There is no treasure. The wooden idol my father keeps hidden is no prize but a burden beyond their understanding or their power to control.

Dana nearly dropped the journal at the mention of the wooden idol. Was there any chance that she could be talking about something other than the doll plaguing Michael's dreams? Unfortunately the next couple of pages were stuck together and Dana was unable to separate them. The next legible entry brought threads of information together.

I had feared him from the very start. With his eyes as pale as ice, he had the look of a vessel with no soul. Of course it would be him that was tempted, that responded to its call. I woke to the sound of his boots marching towards us and knew we were already lost. As the first kick landed on my father's head, his muffled scream woke my brother. I sat immobilised, cradling his small body in my arms, my hand held across his mouth to stifle his cries. I thought only to keep him safe and squeezed back into the shadows, ashamed not to have reached forward to protect my father, but unable to do otherwise. My mother launched herself at the soldier but weakened by the recent birth, she was thrown into a corner. Mercifully, my view of what happened next was blocked by the crowd. So many people were eager to grasp what they could. When I was finally able to unlock my muscles, my brother had cried himself to sleep and my parent's bodies were gone, probably thrown over the side of the ship like the rubbish the English thought them to be.

The connection seemed obvious: the soldier with pale eyes must have been the same soldier whose uniform had hung in the store in Noosa. Michael had reacted to the photo instantly, and so had she. Was it possible that the doll had called to them? No, she couldn't believe that. They hadn't even wanted to touch the doll let alone pick it up and bring it home. There were only a few more entries in the book. Dana read through them, feeling Kitty's pain and her rage.

I have searched. The doll is gone. Good riddance! Let him have his 'treasure'. He will soon find that the doll is nothing to be coveted. I curse the man that brutalised my parents. My father would be shamed but I curse them all.

And finally: *The doll is gone but the burden is not. In my searching, I found the book of lore in my father's possessions. I do not know how it is possible that such a precious treasure found its way into my father's keep but it needs to be protected and kept safe. I have remembered what my duty is. As I hold the book I feel comforted by the many hands that have held the book before me. I hear their voices.*

Dana sat and puzzled over the last entry. Was Kitty still touched by grief and looking for some form of solace? Had she heard the book speaking to her? She had never felt anything other than fear when she had handled the book but that was probably because she knew how much trouble she would be in if her mother found her touching it. Dana had to find the gypsy book and see what was inside it.

Enough Is Enough

Michael had little to be excited about lately. Dana kept rabbiting on to him about a connection between gypsies, books of lore and some legend about sleeping warriors. She insisted that an old diary she'd found gave her some insight. He really didn't care – how the doll was connected to him, how Marcus had found a way into his dreams – it was all irrelevant. His nightmares were out of control and his waking life seemed to be following suit. He was struggling to focus on the basics, so unravelling a mythical legend was beyond him at the moment. He found himself dreading what might be around each corner. Food was eaten but not tasted, TV watched but nothing recalled. His days faded into each other. The dreams were the only thing that possessed any kind of clarity.

His mother, much like Dana, spent most of her time with her head in a book and he felt tense each time she entered the room, scared that she would want to talk to him about *things*. Just looking at her made him nervous. He'd seen her fear and didn't want to expose himself to more of it. She was the one who was supposed to make things better. She was the one who never panicked. He'd exposed her to some fairly extreme emergencies in his time and unfortunately he'd had to watch her undergo some intense medical treatments himself and through all of it, he had never seen her flinch.

'You're like your mother, hard as nails, just plain stubborn. It's like you both just refuse to let anybody or anything else win.' His dad usually said this just before walking out of the room, hands held above his head in defeat after Michael had stoically refused to back down over some trivial thing. But what Joseph had never realised was that most things were not trivial. Most things led to bigger things, so almost all things were important.

So now he found himself angry at his mother. She was supposed to be his rock. He felt that she had let him down. He knew this was wrong, unjustified; she was hardly sleeping either, continually looking for an answer. But still if this thing could beat her, then what chance did *he* stand?

He didn't know what he might say if she caught him at the wrong moment.

'Mum, why haven't you fixed this?

'Mum, I think I'm going mad!'

He was scared because he feared her response would be: 'I know, darling. Them's the breaks!'

So he lay in bed deliberately pretending to be asleep when the rest of the family left Friday morning to pick up fresh bread for a late breakfast. His school had a curriculum day and his dad had decided to have a day off to spend with the family. Normally, Michael would have relished the opportunity with his dad but he just didn't want to have to explain his appearance, apologise for his mood or hide his mounting sense of disillusionment. His mum had checked on him before leaving. She brushed his hair back before kissing him on his forehead and then tiptoed out of his room. He kept his eyes tightly closed and let out a long breath when he heard her feet running down the stairs.

* * *

Michael listened for the unmistakable rattle of the roller door as the garage closed and waited a couple of seconds before he heard his father accelerating down the street. He kicked the blanket off his legs and stumbled into the bathroom, threw some cold water on his face, slapped his cheeks a couple of times in a vain attempt to wake himself up and shuffled back to his room. He dragged on the first pair of tracksuit pants he could find and didn't even bother changing the t-shirt he'd worn to bed. Grabbing his runners and Sheba's lead, he went out the laundry door. Sheba ran around him enthusiastically, licked his hand, smelt his shoes and then bit the lead, eager for a run.

Michael jogged lightly for the first couple of minutes, giving Sheba some slack while she smelt posts and methodically recorded the movements of all the animals in what he was certain she believed to be her domain. He didn't have the patience that Dana had and was soon increasing his speed and reducing his indulgence. Sheba got the message and they fell into the rhythm of an easy run. He liked to run: it was the monotony that he found relaxing. The steady sound of his breathing, the measured beat as his feet pounded against the dirt track – all created a quiet place where he could just be. He was exhausted and he could feel the unaccustomed weight this added to his legs, but that was good. It gave him something to work against. Each step he felt the extra tension in his muscle and concentrated on keeping his stride open and relaxed. And with every step he left a little of the tension behind. He wasn't running away from his troubles altogether; he was just temporarily running them away.

* * *

When he walked back through the door he felt at ease until he spotted his mum sitting at the kitchen bench, obviously waiting for his return. He contemplated turning back around but that would be running away. A brief moment of anger flared. Couldn't he have been left alone for a couple of minutes, to keep the peaceful buzz for just a moment longer? He sighed and walked towards the bench.

'Baby, sit down. Your father and I have something to talk to you about!'

They *both* wanted to speak to him. His dad was not much of a talker, so when he was involved Michael knew it was not going to be a light-hearted discussion about what to have for dinner. 'Dana!' his dad yelled, 'Come down here, Michael's back!'

His anger left him but his melancholy returned. It looked like everyone was going to have a part in the conversation.

Resigned, he slid into the chair, and slouched low, waiting for the inevitable. It appeared like this was turning into an intervention. Surely they didn't think he looked that bad because he was doing drugs or something. He thought Nicola had understood. He had explained to her about the dreams. He had truly thought she'd believed him. He shook his head not understanding. How could they have misjudged him so?

Come on! Michael thought. *I'm only fourteen! I've just come back from a five kilometre run. Give me a break.* No matter how bad things got he still needed to keep in shape – his dreams, his real dreams, not his nightmares, depended on that. He had to focus on what he could control and thankfully his body was still one of them. If he wanted to be the best, he couldn't let a few bad dreams and a dirtbag from next door stand in his way. She should have understood that.

Dana came barrelling into the room and almost fell trying to get to the seat next to Michael at the kitchen bench. It was the first time in days that he'd seen her smiling but he was so wrapped up in his own resentment it didn't impact his mood in the slightest.

'Go, go – Mum play the message. Play the message!' Dana was jumping up and down in excitement.

Michael, annoyed by his sister's behaviour, finally turned and looked at her. She beamed back at him, nudging him good naturedly. She motioned impatiently for someone to play the message. Michael finally realised that the faces around him were *all* beaming.

'Buddy, there was a message on the answering machine when we got back from the shops,' Joseph announced.

His parents nearly pushed each other over in an effort to get to the machine first. His mother tried to slap his dad's hand away but there really was no contest and so Joseph was the one to finally push the button.

'Joe, Nicola, Dana, Michael, hope you all had a great holiday. Sorry to be bothering you so early but I just couldn't wait to ring at a reasonable time.' Michael knew the voice. It was his coach, Toby. 'Please call me when you get a moment!'

All eyes turned excitedly to Michael.

'Yeah,' was all Michael was able to manage in response.

'Michael, your dad called him back!'

'You are not going to believe it.'

'Buddy, you did it, you bloody did it!'

'The scouts were at the finals. They called Toby – they want you to participate in a special summer program. Michael, you'll be training this summer with the state team. They liked what they saw. You're in!' Michael had never seen his dad this excited. He had managed to say it all in one breath.

Dana and his mother were now hugging each other jumping up and down around the kitchen gesturing wildly for him to join them.

Michael sat dumbfounded.

'Buddy you're in!' His dad had now rounded the bench and grabbed him into a bear hug. 'You. Are. In.'

This was no intervention – this was a celebration. It had nothing to do with nightmares, just dreams. He was one step closer to his. All of a sudden he found himself jumping up and down in a circle with his mother and sister.

He couldn't believe it.

He was in.

* * *

Coach Toby had come around earlier in the afternoon to personally congratulate Michael and to tell him exactly what he was in for. In two weeks' time he would start training with the state team. For ten weeks, twice a week. Wednesdays and Fridays for two hours of skills and fitness work. Saturdays would be game day. He most likely wouldn't play much but the experience of training with the state boys was such a great opportunity. Even if he managed to get out on the field a couple of times the experience would be invaluable.

'There's a meet and greet on Monday so it seems you'll have a long weekend.' Michael had no complaint about that.

* * *

His mother had already been on the phone and a celebratory dinner had been organised. Coach Toby promised to pop in for a beer and after that the rest of the day flew by in a blur. Before Michael knew it he was sitting down at his favourite Japanese restaurant, eating and celebrating with his family. Aunty Sars, Uncle Brent and Ashley were there. His grandparents from both sides were jokingly arguing about which side of the family the soccer talent came from. With his mum's dad being German and his dad's parents being Italian, they both claimed that the gene ran in their family. His aunt just shook her head and quietly ate her food.

Michael regretted the thoughts he'd had earlier, but couldn't help but laugh as his Ope and Nonno argued.

Toby managed to pop in as promised and declared it had nothing to do with genetics.

'You're both wrong. We all know it is because of my training. Now whether you buy me a beer or a wine, please pass me a drink so we can celebrate!'

* * *

Michael was excited as he lay in bed that night. One hand rested behind his head, one knee slightly raised. After his parents had said good night, Dana snuck back into his room to congratulate him one more time.

'Buddy, you must be stoked!'

'I can't believe it! Dad's off to golf tomorrow morning. Do you mind coming out tomorrow and kicking the ball around a bit, so I can get in some practice?'

'Sure buddy, no worries. You're not going to make me get up too early are you?' Dana took one look at Michael's face and knew the answer. 'Man, what time?'

'Eight?'

'No way. You do your running thing and Mum can drive us to the ground when you come back'

'Sure, thanks, Dee Dee.'

Dana got up off of his bed and on a whim stopped in his doorway and whispered back over her shoulder, 'Twenty-eight and always, buddy.'

'Back at ya, sis!'

* * *

By the time Dana dragged herself out of bed the next morning, Michael had already taken Sheba for a run, had a quick shower, eaten breakfast and was busily getting Dana's things ready so she could come with him and get some practice in.

'Mum's ready to drive us to the ground as soon as you've had breakfast.'

'Good morning to you too, Michael,' Dana responded moodily. She was not suffering from the nightmares like her brother, she just always woke up in a less that an agreeable mood and had been up three nights running researching on the internet.

Michael just let her be and by the time she'd eaten her toasted sandwich she was back to her normal self.

'Hey Micky, how did you sleep last night?' Dana asked this casually as she put her plate into the dishwasher. 'You look pretty good this morning.' She could hear their mum in the laundry and knew she would be listening for the answer.

'Don't ask. I don't want to waste any more energy even talking about this again. I just want to focus on the good stuff right now. So can we make a deal? I'll let you know if things change and you promise to do the same. It's bad enough *they* can control my sleep but I will not let them control my days as well.'

Dana could hear the desperation in Michael's voice and she forced a smile onto her face. She had a lot to talk to him about but he needed this, to enjoy the moment so she decided that it all could wait, just for another day or so. 'Yeah that's fair!'

'Now hurry up and get changed,' Michael said. 'I'll meet you in the car!' Michael was so full of nervous energy he virtually chased Dana up the stairs.

'Mum, you ready to go?' Michael called out.

'Yep, did you grab the gloves? I don't really fancy breaking a nail stopping one of your shots!' Michael knew his mother had heard their conversation and was showing her agreement to let things go for a while.

'No offence, Mum, but gloves or no gloves you haven't been able to stop any of my shots for years.'

* * *

The car was already reversed out and waiting in the driveway. Dana came running, grabbed the water bottles sitting on the front table as she went and slammed the front door behind her.

Michael had gone through the garage to grab their soccer boots. He ran to the hook where they always hung, grabbed Dana's pair and looked around for his own. They weren't where they were supposed to be.

Perhaps Dana had already grabbed them, but why then would she grab hers and not his? As he puzzled over this, he checked around and doubled back past the front door to see if someone had already put them at the doorstep for him.

Michael suppressed a moment of annoyance. He ran to the car and threw Dana's boots through the open window to her, asking where she had put his.

'Aren't they on the hook?'

Michael felt his level of anxiety rise somewhat. Would he have asked if they were on the hook? He had a bad feeling – these were his lucky boots they were talking about. They had been signed by Tim Cahill. Dana had seen to that. When they both attended a soccer clinic last year, he had no chance of even getting close to any of the players but Dana being in the girl's squad was able to get closer. Waving Michael through the crowd she boldly asked Tim if he would sign Michael's boots. Since that day onwards he'd never worn a different pair. He was convinced that he played better when he wore those boots. And now they were gone.

'Mum, have you moved my boots?' Michael asked this leaning through the window.

'No, Michael. Check the boot.'

He searched around, knowing his boots were not in there anywhere. He'd packed the boot himself that morning.

No-one had moved them. So something had happened to them. Q. E. fuckin D. You didn't need to be some kind of genius to work that out.

'They're not here!' Michael knew he was yelling. He could feel his recently reclaimed control slip.

'Calm down. I'll call Dad and see if he knows where

they are. They'll probably be in his car.'

Michael checked the time, wondering if his father would have finished golf yet. He slammed the boot shut in a futile display of anger and leant back against the car waiting. He could feel the perspiration running down his neck.

'You look quite distressed little Michaela. Lost something?' The moment Michael heard Marcus' voice he knew he wasn't going to find his boots. Marcus was leaning casually against the wall of his own garage less than ten metres away. Checking his nails with a distracted air, not bothering to make eye contact with Michael.

'If you've touched my boots I swear I'll ...' Michael moved in Marcus' direction.

Uncrossing his legs, Marcus meticulously smoothed his shirt then ran his hand over his waxed back hair before turning to Michael with a contemptuous sneer.

'You swear you'll what? All I ever see you do lately is run. That or fall to your knees. Do you think the boots can make you run fast enough to get away next time?'

Michael jumped the fence before he had time to think. He managed to register the sound of a door slamming closed behind him but paid it little attention.

'Just give me my boots back.' Michael had stepped forward, with only inches separating the two boys.

The door slamming had obviously been Dana and she now stood at his back. 'Michael, what's the problem. Leave the creep alone!' Dana had placed her hand on Michael's arm trying to calm him.

'Dana, he's taken my boots!'

'Oh, how sweet. Big sister here to defend her little brother. Little brother getting ready to run again! You guys are such a cliché!'

'Just give back the boots you thieving little bastard!'

Dana's fiery side had started to show. Dana may have been small but she could handle herself. It was obvious she'd been itching for some payback.

Marcus smirked openly into Dana's face not bothering to deny the claim. He paused as if listening to an unheard voice and his smile grew wider. Marcus shifted his focus back to Michael, ensuring eye contact had been made between them, and then with an arrogantly lifted eyebrow, he played his next card.

Michael registered these small mannerisms and tensed in anticipation. Michael was not ready to defend, or even deflect, for the target was not what he expected it to be.

Marcus moved forward with unexpected speed and shoved Dana backwards.

Michael watched as she fell backwards. All the self-defence training in the world didn't help Dana when a small fence lay behind her legs. There was no way to stop her from falling, though he reached out in a futile effort to try. Michael watched in slow motion and saw her head hit the rock.

The blood stood out vividly against the pallor of Dana's face. The sound of her head hitting rock echoed in his ears. Then time jumped forward, the next few seconds a blur. Michael was now running on autopilot and his autopilot was majorly pissed.

Marcus was down before Michael had time to realise a punch had been thrown. His left fist had connected high on Marcus' right cheek, splitting the skin under his eye.

Adrenaline flooded through Michael's system. Ablaze with anger so intense it crowded out all other thought.

'You never touch her, you understand, not my sister. You have a problem, you take it up with *me!*' Michael barely recognised his own voice, it was so distorted by the rage flowing through him.

Michael reached down twisting his fist into Marcus' shirt and dragged him to his feet.

He resisted the instinct to allow his anger full reign. He glanced sideways. Needed to make sure Dana was okay. In that second he registered his mother, already beside Dana, holding something against her head, and whatever it was, it was red now with his sister's blood. Dana sat up, looking, searchingly, directly into his eyes.

Michael squeezed his eyes shut and turned his fist, tightening his grip, twisted Marcus' shirt so that in now restricted his breathing. Michael could hear Marcus' panicked panting turn into a wheeze.

'Michael,' Dana pleaded. 'He's not worth it. Let it go!'

He opened his eyes and looked down on Marcus through the patchwork of black and red that so predominated his vision. He shook his head. He didn't want to hear Dana and he didn't want to listen to the voice deep inside that told him to back off.

Now he could get even, get payback for all the nights of pain when Marcus just stood by laughing.

* * *

Time, playing its own game, seemed to stop for a moment. Michael realised the sound of drumming remained, drowning out the internal voice that screamed for vengeance. For reasons that he did not understand the rhythm soothed him and he uncurled his fist, letting Marcus drop back down to the ground. Michael walked over to his sister, reached down and helped her up.

Michael turned back to Marcus. 'You will never touch her again. You will give my boots back and you will keep your little friend away from me. I don't care how you do it, but you get it done.' His voice sounded a little more like his own but held a degree of authority that he'd not heard before.

Even as he walked away, images of turning back and exacting some revenge played across his mind. Dragging Marcus back to his feet, landing another punch. Simply walking back over and kicking him where he lay. Although sickened by the imagery, the anticipation of the thud as his foot connected still made his legs tense.

Dana felt the turmoil radiating out of Michael.

'Michael!' Apparently her voice could hold some authority when it needed to as well.

He squeezed her shoulders and they stepped over the fence together. Their mother was one step ahead, continually glancing back to make sure they were following.

As Michael's foot cleared the garden bed and landed on the driveway, Marcus voice followed him. 'Keep running, we know where to find you both!'

The loathing with which this threat was issued stopped Michael. The promise it held forced him to turn.

Blood was freely running down Marcus' face. He had made no effort to wipe it away. He stood, chin thrust forwards, as if the blood somehow vindicated him.

The cold smile returned.

Marcus had finally learned how to push Michael's buttons and threatening Dana was a very persuasive button.

What choice did Michael have?

And as he dropped his arm from around his sister's shoulder laughter rang out in Michael's head.

Laughter that luckily Michael realised was not his own.

And for once he thanked the dreams, for without them

he may not have recognised the voice for what is was. If the very sound of the doll's laughter had not replayed itself over in his dreams so many times, he might have confused it for his own inner voice.

Michael knew the doll was playing in his mind, implanting images, escalating emotions.

He refused to be manipulated further. He wrapped his arm once again around Dana's shoulders and ignored the ranting he was hearing in his own head.

* * *

Nicola hastily ended the call, not bothering to leave Joseph a voice message as she watched Michael jump the fence. When Dana followed, her apprehension grew and she jumped out of the car. Both kids could handle themselves but with the tension that had been growing of late she didn't want things to get out of hand.

When Dana was pushed backwards, Nicola's hands instinctively flew out to stop her fall even though she was over five metres away. She had halved the distance in the time it took Michael to knock Marcus to the ground. She saw him register the sight of blood and watched as the look in Michael's eyes changed.

She had seen something similar before but never this. Never in such a pure form. Michael's eyes held a mix of cold calculated logic driven by one emotion alone, anger. Michael had always been a champion of the underdog. She had many a story, going back as far as his pre-school days, all relating to his unflagging efforts to even the scales, to right the wrongs.

This aspect of his nature was something that she was both fiercely proud of and also secretly fearful of. What she saw in his eyes told her she could have been five centimetres away and still would have been incapable of making the slightest impact on the outcome.

Having seen Dana's blood herself, feeling her own emotions chill and harden, Nicola was quite certain her own expression held the same cold sharp quality.

Nicola had to focus on Dana. With her jacket already ripped off and balled up, Nicola quickly applied pressure where Dana's head had connected with the rock. Head wounds liked to bleed and this one was doing its level best to impress.

She dared another glance towards Michael who looked ready to land another blow on Marcus. But as she looked deep into her son's eyes she was shaken by what she saw.

The intensity in his eyes hadn't lessened. The required justice had obviously yet to be appeased, she was frightened by what might be needed to return the warmth into his eyes. But Michael, she reminded herself, was no thug. His own internal rule-book, the tenets that he had set himself from early childhood would not allow it. So she stood, knowing as a mother, she had to let this one play itself out.

The two boys glared at each other, with Michael daring Marcus to do something. When he didn't react, Michael loosened his hold and Marcus fell to the ground.

Nicola couldn't believe her own ears as Marcus deliberately baited Michael to return to the fight. As she felt Michael hesitate, she had a sense triumph – alien and vengeful – wash over her. She threw Michael a warning glance to ensure he wasn't going to allow himself to be manipulated. Wondering where this emotion was emanating from, her eyes roamed the general area, fearful of some other danger.

Catching movement, she saw the curtain on the front

window drop back into position. But not quickly enough for Nicola not to have seen the dark hair of Marcus' mother as she endeavoured to remain unseen.

What kind of woman watches on as her son bleeds? she asked herself, then quickly ushered her children inside to what felt like safety.

* * *

What had just happened? It had the situation under complete control. The sacrificial lamb was dutifully acting the puppet. Jumping to every string It pulled, every suggestion It whispered into his mind. Hurt the girl to get to the boy. Make her bleed. And she had! The energy that poured from the boy when he allowed his hatred for the lamb free reign was intoxicating, to feed from the Enemy, rapture. And with the hatred, the barriers dropped. It had access into this boy's mind. It sent the images of revenge, of payback and he received them, without much resistance. The boy had a hidden skill for violence. His body literally thrummed with the hidden rhythm of a natural born aggressor. If it could only be tapped … what an unexpected resource to feed upon. The mother, so focused on her bleeding child, barely noticed any disturbance.

But that hateful, cowardly creature didn't follow through. Its lamb was lying dutifully sacrificial. What little defiance born to him had already been drained for Its needs. And to have the boy turn and reject this opportunity to finish him, to think himself above further bloodshed was nothing less than insolent.

It forced the puppet although already beaten to one last goad, to force the boy's hand. Threaten the girl. The thrill that came from the lamb at this suggestion was an unexpected pleasure. Maybe there was more depth to this husk than It had first expected?

With the bait taken the boy turned to finish what he should have accomplished without prompting. Its laughter echoed through the unprotected minds surrounding It.

And then nothing. A barrier. A void. The energy supply simply stopped. How could this happen? It screamed Its outrage. Looking for the source of such power and found only a mother's natural defensive instinct. It had cried Its triumph too early and she had heard on some level and intuitively defended her young. How she had formed such a protective barrier, one that It was unable to penetrate. Surely she had no memory of her ancestral knowledge. If she did, her attempts would not be so clumsy, It would have to ponder this.

But she would pay for such an affront. Denying It Its due.

She would pay. She would pay through her children.

The time for playing was done.

Behind Closed Doors

As the door closed behind him, Michael expected the yelling to begin. But his mother was focused on Dana so for the moment he felt safe. With her trademark cool calm efficiency Nicola had Dana seated in the bathroom, first aid kit open, saline, antiseptic, gauze and steri-strips already laid out neatly with near surgical precision.

'Michael, put a cold pack on your hand. I'll have a look at it in a moment.' This was said without pause, her hands continued their work on Dana's cut.

Dana had her head lying on her crossed arms, leaning against the bathroom bench, so that the cut was easier to get to. The rock that she had hit when she fell had caught her on the bone behind her right ear, so that the blood had flowed freely down her neck.

Although the bleeding had stopped, as soon as his

mother began cleaning the cut it started again and the sink was soon full of gauze soaked in saline solution and blood.

Dana was not quite as controlled as Michael. She had a tendency to freak out when she saw blood, especially her own. Michael suspected that this was also the reason Dana was sitting the way she was. If she saw what was dripping onto the bench she would start to panic.

'Okay baby, almost done, I need to trim away a bit of hair so I can put on some gauze.'

The hair had already been trimmed away when Dana protested.

'Mum, don't cut my hair, what … shit … what the hell … *Mum*!' Dana jerked away as the antiseptic was wiped across the now cleaned cut.

'Sorry darling, should have warned you, the antiseptic stings a bit.' Dana's head had already been gently pushed back down so it lay again against her arms. 'Almost done.' His mother looked at Michael and they both shared a smile.

'Michael, can you clean that mess I've made up quickly while I finish bandaging Dana's head?'

'Sure, no problems.' He was as unhappy about seeing Dana's blood as his mother was but they both found her queasiness slightly amusing. If Dana looked up now and saw the mess around her she would lose it. If his dad got home early from golf he would probably pass out. The image of this made Michael chuckle to himself as he bagged up the rubbish in the sink. He grabbed some tissues, washed down the sink and wiped away all of the traces of blood he could find.

Michael nodded towards his mother and gestured for her to make sure she cleaned off Dana's neck before she let her get up.

His mother nodded back smiling. It seemed strange to

smile while his sister was patched up but his mum had everything under control and sometimes you had to laugh, even if you couldn't afford to do it out loud.

'Baby, can you go grab some of the ointment Uncle Brent gave me. It's in the cupboard above the fridge. Dana, I'll just put some of that on and you're done.'

'Thanks, Mum,' Dana replied, unconvinced.

Michael handed her the jar that looked like nothing more than Vaseline. She passed him the face washer she'd used to clean Dana's neck. Michael's smile left him as he detoured towards the laundry and threw the face washer into the sink, covered with Dana's blood it somehow appropriately landed on top of the jacket that his mother had used to staunch the bleeding in the first place. Michael felt the anger flare again at the sight of the jacket and he noticed his hand throbbing from where he had hit Marcus. He rubbed his knuckles that he now noticed were beginning to swell and suddenly wondered what was happening next door at that very moment. Before he had much time to think about it he was called back into the bathroom.

Dana was sitting up now with a patch on the back of her head and a light bandage to keep it in place. Her hair covered most of this and if not for the dark circles under her eyes and the greyish tone to skin she could pass as someone trying to pull off a strange new fashion statement.

'I'm fine you don't need to ...'

Michael's hand had already been placed into a bowl that his mother had at some time filled with warm water and a multitude of other ingredients. The water almost looked like tea and it stung slightly where his knuckles had been grazed. Leaving Michael's hand soaking in the bowl, Nicola left the room. She could be heard opening and closing cupboards, obviously packing her things away.

Dana was still sitting next to him on the edge of the bath. Her hand kept touching the back of her head but her eyes continually dropped to his hand soaking in the bowl on his lap. The room now smelt of a combination of antiseptic, tea tree oil, lemongrass and other fragrances that he was unable to identify. Some of these smells were wafting up from the bowl in his lap and Michael suspected that the bags lying at the bottom were probably another of his uncle's concoctions.

His uncle loved to cook and had begun dabbling with roasting his own coffee beans. This had led to mixing teas, which had in turn somehow turned into homeopathic hand creams, ointments and oils. His mother loved them and had taken to using them as part of her own healing routines.

'Thanks, Micky!' Dana tentatively broke the silence.

'For what? Standing by and letting some guy hurt you? Yeah you're welcome!' Michael's tone had turned bitter.

'For stopping some guy from hurting me further.'

'I shouldn't have let him touch you …'

'You couldn't have known that he would. Honestly what kind of person does that?'

'I should have known! I've seen what he's capable of!'

'In dreams, Michael. No-one could have thought that transferred over into reality. For goodness sake don't do this … Don't make this your fault.'

Dana was interrupted as Nicola walked back into the bathroom.

When she lifted his hand out of the bowl, she towelled it dry and rubbed some ointment into his knuckles. Whether it was the homeopathic remedies supplied by his uncle or his mother putting some of her healing energy into the mix, either way the swelling was already starting to go down, although his knuckles still throbbed.

'Sorry guys, this is no-one's fault but mine.' Nicola continued a conversation she'd not been a part of. 'I should have seen this coming. It's not as if there haven't been warning signs. But now we must take back some control.'

Both children sat forward eagerly.

'Now we're going to go next door to apologise.'

'You've got to be kidding! There's no way I am walking over there apologising for having this done to me!' Dana pointed at the bandage wrapped around her head as if Nicola needed some reminding.

Michael's understanding of how his mother thought was a little deeper. He dropped his head and stood up ready to go. There was no point arguing. Michael knew by the fact that she hadn't already exploded, that his mother backed him completely. She understood what he'd done and why. But another person had been hurt and unfortunately for them, in her book this warranted apology.

She might not be a typical mother in many regards, but in this she acted as the textbook would have dictated: 'You punch someone in the face, you apologise.' Michael was sure she would not have phrased it that way. She would have made it all about karma, about control, about only using force as an absolute last resort. Michael simply walked out of the bathroom and waited for them both to meet him at the front door.

* * *

Michael rapped on the door and they waited awkwardly for a while before the door was answered and then were allowed to step into the front entry. No suggestion to move further into the house was offered. Marcus' mother held the front door, indicating that this was to be a very short visit.

Marcus' father walked down the hallway in what seemed an orchestrated fashion and glared at them with hands held behind his back, as if to prevent further entry and impose himself physically upon the situation. Michael thought he had done rather a good job at both.

'What exactly is it that you want?' he asked in a clipped military manner, eyes boring into Michael.

'We have come over to apologise for what happened earlier between Michael and Marcus and to ...'

'Your thug of a son ...' Marcus' father interrupted. Endeavouring to impose as much control over the conversation as he had on the setting.

But Nicola was not so easily intimidated.

' ... and to try and understand exactly why Marcus pushed Dana. If you could please ask him to come downstairs, I think we can get this sorted out fairly quickly.'

'How dare you come into my home and start issuing orders! We'll do no explaining to the likes of you.' His hands had now dropped to his sides and were balled up into fists, his knuckles white with the strain. Michael noted this small change and stepped forward so he now stood beside his mother. He made sure Dana stayed behind him by gently pushing her back a step, she resisted but he was not taking any chances this time.

As if the anger and insult had not even been heard, his mother glanced up the stairs where Marcus now hovered and spoke directly to him. 'Marcus, thank you for joining us. I'm sure you heard us talking. Michael ...'

Michael mumbled an apology that was completely ignored by everyone. His mother had already turned to Marcus' mother. 'You know you should really attend to his eye. At the very least it needs an icepack!'

'Your son assaults my child, does that to his face and

then you come over here and have the audacity to give me lessons in parenting.' Her voice held a note of anger that to Michael sounded manufactured. The only time it sounded genuine was when she mentioned the lesson. But again as if ignoring the remarks thrown at her, Nicola continued, 'I would hardly call it an assault. Marcus, go grab yourself some ice and then come back. I would like to try and understand what happened today.'

Marcus started to walk towards the kitchen but his father made no move to shift aside. He forcefully turned Marcus around, placing an overly firm hand onto his shoulder. Michael couldn't help but notice Marcus wince as his father's fingers tightened. Instinctively, Michael took a step forward and this time it was his mother's turn to extend a restraining hand.

'Your son,' Marcus spat back, 'punched me in the face for no reason. He jumped over onto our property and assaulted me. If I hadn't been able to defend myself the attack would have continued.'

'He's right, I saw the whole thing from inside ...' Nicola had been completely focused on Marcus until the mother spoke then she turned, left eyebrow raised and interrupted her mid-sentence.

'Kids, go home. I'll see you in a few moments.' Nicola turned and gave them both a gentle push towards the front door.

'Mum, I don't think ...' Michael whispered, but the look he received made him pause midsentence, turn and leave. Together he and Dana walked back towards home.

As they stepped over the now infamous fence, Michael thought he heard a door shut.

Michael hesitated.

'We give her ten minutes and if she isn't home by then we go back with a cold pack, as a peace offering. Sheba can walk over with us.' Dana smiled.

'I like the way you think!' Michael said.

Less than two steps later: 'Can you believe I did that with just one punch? Man, his eye was completely swollen shut.' After a quick Rocky imitation and an episode of near hysterical laughter, Michael and Dana closed the front door behind them and sat down to wait, alternating between hysterics and concern.

* * *

They both jumped up when the front door slammed closed. Joseph had just gotten home from golf. They'd been waiting almost ten minutes.

Joseph took one look at Dana's head and overreacted.

'What the hell! Dana! Are you okay? He seemed to alternate between anger and concern and kept looking towards the kitchen expecting Nicola to walk through the door and explain what was going on. Without this direction and not knowing which emotion to settle on, he wrapped Dana in his arms. 'Baby, what happened to your head?'

'I'm fine. I just sort of fell over and hit my head …'

'Well, where's your mother?'

Michael and Dana looked at each other, not knowing how to answer an awkward silence stretched out between them.

'Is she alright?' Panic had started to creep into the edge of his voice and the kids knew they had no choice but to answer.

'She's next door, talking to Marcus' parents. Marcus actually pushed Dana and that's how she got hurt …'

'He what? He pushed her over. He ...' Joseph shot up furious, already storming towards the front door.

'And Michael decked him, Dad. You should have seen him!' Dana couldn't keep the excitement and pride from her voice.

'Michael decked him?' He'd stopped, hand poised ready to open the front door, a small smile played across his mouth.

'Dad, he had hurt Dana. I didn't plan it, it just happened!'

Joseph turned towards his son so that Michael could see his expression. 'Don't apologise Micky, you protected your sister, that's just fine in my books.' This time he wrapped both children in his arms. 'That kid has been asking for it for a long time!'

He ruffled Michael unruly hair, kissed Dana on top of her head and headed towards the front door.

'Let's go get your mum!'

* * *

Before they reached the door Nicola hurried through and pulled them all into an anxious embrace.

'Thank God you're all okay!'

Michael could feel her shaking as she clung to each of them, squeezing them uncomfortably together. When she finally pulled away Michael noticed the tears running down her cheeks.

His mum didn't cry. She was a rock. She hadn't missed a beat during this whole event and now she was crying.

She kept reaching towards each of them, including his dad and running her hand down their faces as if not believing that they were all okay.

'Could someone please grab me a Coke, I need to talk to you all.'

They looked at each other not knowing what to do. Dana walked around to the bar fridge and grabbed the drink. By the time Dana handed the can of Coke to their mother she had settled somewhat. She sipped straight from the can and Michael could see that although she held it with two hands they were still shaking. At least some colour had come back into her face – when she'd walked in she was as pale as a ghost.

They all sat waiting, fidgeting, not knowing what to do. Purely to break the prolonged silence, Michael asked, 'Mum, why were you worried about *us*?'

'Because, I couldn't sense any of you! You have got no idea how frightened I was. One minute you were there, like you always are and then suddenly you were all gone.'

'But Mum you told us to leave. I didn't want to go but you gave me the look.'

'Michael baby, you did good, great. No, I don't mean you left, I mean, I couldn't feel you. Always, always I know you are around me. I am just so used to it. And when you suddenly weren't there, I panicked. It felt like a piece of me had been ripped away, I just couldn't feel you,' she repeated, 'any of you. At all. The thoughts that went through my mind … my God, I thought I had lost you all. I thought I was … alone!' Her hands had started to shake again and Dana sat next to her on the couch and curled her body in against hers in an effort to ease some of the shock.

Still confused, Joseph said, 'I don't really understand. Why did you even go next door?'

Hating to see his mother so upset, Michael thought he would help and fill his dad in on some of the details.

'To apologise, Dad!' When Michael saw his father's face

harden he wished he had said nothing. His mother raised her hand to stop the tirade before it even began.

'No, Micky, that was part of it, but not all. I don't like violence, you know that. But truth be told, I wish I'd been the one to punch that kid after what he did to Dana. No, actually I wish I had hit that woman. Did you see that boy's eye? She hadn't even touched it, no cold pack, nothing.' She shook her head as if trying to keep herself focused. 'But that's not the point, I went over there to try and find out what the hell was going on. What they might know about everything that has been happening lately. I thought if I asked the right questions I would be able to read something. So that was the main reason we were over there. Right from the start it was clear that they were all lying. No special insight required there; they're just a bunch of born liars.'

Michael took a moment to look away from Nicola and exchanged a meaningful glance with his sister. They both knew how much their mother hated deceit. And her choice of phrasing only highlighted to both of them how distressed she truly was. Usually she would come out with something much more convoluted to describe a simple lie, typically using an analogy or metaphor to drive the message home. The fact that she referred to the people living next door simply as 'born liars' without taking the opportunity to impart a moral lesson spoke volumes.

'The only truth to come out of their mouths was that the mother stood by and watched it all.' Nicola didn't notice their silent exchange. 'But Marcus, although just as obviously lying, was easy to read. I could almost hear his inner voice boasting the truth. The whole thing was a set up from the start, an elaborate charade – the boots, everything. He had just been waiting for an opportunity to spring his trap. That boy actually has Michael's soccer boots hanging above his bed in his room, like some kind of trophy! What is wrong with these people?' The question was purely rhetorical and his mother continued with another aggravated shake of her head.

'But when Michael didn't bite, when he wouldn't start the fight, Marcus saw Dana purely as a means to an end.' His mother paused and reached again for her drink. To Michael it looked like she was trying to find the right words to continue, to buy herself a little thinking time. Dana obviously sensing the same thing, quietly asked, 'He has them hanging over his bed? That's kind of creepy, Mum.' Dana glanced around, gauging everyone else's reaction.

'Hang on, what boots?' His dad looked around still confused.

'Don't worry about the boots. They're just boots! Don't you understand? Marcus wanted a fight with Michael, tried to engineer the whole thing. Was happy to write Dana off as collateral damage in an effort to push Michael's buttons. I could read this in him. It was right at the front of his mind, not guarded in any way, almost like he wanted me to know. Then when I probed further … bam … a wall went up around me. It was like a physical thing. I could still feel their hatred, the same hatred that I felt when I saw her peeking through the front window as she watched the fight. But I couldn't read any of them anymore.' Pausing again to collect her thoughts, shaking her head in apparent disbelief, she continued. 'I have no idea why they hate us so much, but they do. I don't know how they put up that wall, cut my connection to you, but they did.' Her voice was starting to break.

'I don't ever want to feel that again. You are not to go anywhere near them again. You *don't understand*, they want to hurt you both.' She paused looking at them each in turn.

'Don't look at me like I am some sort of nut!' She sounded almost hysterical. 'I'm telling you to stay away from them, I don't want you anywhere near them. Do you hear me?' When she saw they were both listening, Nicola calmed slightly.

'Am I understood?' Her voice broke at the end but the force with which this demand was made gave them little option.

'Yes, Mum!' Dana and Michael answered in unison.

The family conference quickly disbanded and Michael followed Dana upstairs, both keeping unusually quiet.

The image of his lucky boots hanging over Marcus' bed was something Michael knew he would have trouble just walking away from.

* * *

As the kids walked upstairs neither of them heard Joseph as he spoke to Nicola.

'You end this Nicola. I don't care how, you just end this. I will not have my family in danger. I will get the police involved. I don't care how crazy that is going to make our family look. If you don't do something, I will.'

The Calm Before the Storm

Michael was resigned to the fact that there was not going to be any soccer practice that day. He couldn't expect Dana to play with a fresh head cut and he wasn't certain he could focus himself. The thought of his boots hanging over Marcus' bed was an irritating distraction that he couldn't seem to block from his mind. He continually found himself gritting his teeth, clenching his fist, internally seething at an image of Marcus kicking back with Michael's boots in his hands and laughing. Knowing that Michael knew he had them.

Based on the conversation he'd overheard Nicola having on the phone, he and Dana were going to be staying over at Ashley's house that night, so even if he knew what to do about his boots, any action to get them back would have to be delayed.

He was already half packed when his mum walked into the room and raised her eyebrows at the sports bag and pillows already piled neatly next to his bedroom door. Michael had thrown his old backpack out during the last hard garage day and no-one had protested. The backpack had just never felt right since their holiday to Noosa.

'Going somewhere, Michael?' His mother smiled again for the first time since her return from next door.

'You're not the only one who can read minds, *Mum!*' Michael watched as her eyebrow arched even higher.

'Okay, so I heard you on the phone to Aunty Sarah,' Michael admitted as his mother walked into the room and sat down on the edge of his bed. 'Thought I'd get myself ready.'

'You okay after today?'

'To be honest, I'm trying hard not to think about it. If I do, I get really pissed, and to be honest, confused. It just doesn't make sense. Why are they doing this? I just don't get it.'

'Nor do I, baby, but until we know more, we just have to stay well clear of them.'

'Yeah, I know Mum. I get it!' Michael stopped himself for a moment. He knew his anger at Marcus, his inability to act, was flowing over into this conversation and he didn't want his mother to pay for that. Frustrated, he paced the room. His mother waited patiently for him to continue.

'Mum, how long is that supposed to work for? I don't want to be critical but it isn't one of your more brilliant plans. It's not exactly a long-term strategy. They do live next door. We go to school together. We're going to cross paths.' Michael knew he was pushing it but she had to realise that just steering clear of them was not a solution.

'Can you give me a couple of days, Michael? If I don't know more by then ...' She shrugged uncertainly.

Not wanting to press the issue, Michael replied as casually as he could, 'Sure Mum. We'll talk in a couple of days.' Michael knew his mother would struggle with this approach as much as he did. He wished he could do something to help. Everyone wanted an answer and she wasn't used to being in the position of not being able to supply one. Without being able to think of anything that could actively help solve the problem, Michael stopped pacing and sat next to her on the bed and threw an arm around her shoulder.

'Can you do me one favour, Mum?'

'Sure, baby!'

'Kick the ball around with me a bit before we go.' Michael stood up and grabbed his soccer ball from where it lay on the floor.

'Is that all you think about?' Nicola smiled and tried to grab the ball from his hands. He held it above her head and then juggled the ball on his knees until she gave up and walked out the room.

Soccer wasn't all that he thought about but it was high up on his list. Family was up there too and he just wanted to stop her worrying about things for a while. He could tell she thought that this was somehow her problem to solve and if clowning around with the ball made her forget about it for a minute, then a clown he would be. The fact that he had little intention of just letting this go was almost irrelevant. Marcus and Michael had something personal that needed settling and although Michael did intend to try and avoid Marcus, he was self-aware enough to know that his boots would not remain in Marcus' possession for long. He had yet to figure out how this problem was going to be resolved but he knew he would be the one resolving it.

* * *

Dana couldn't hide what she'd found for any longer. She wanted Michael to see the research she'd put together. The whole concept of letting him enjoy his moment had been taken from her by Marcus and the stolen boots and spilt blood. Dana waited, listening to the sound of the conversation between Michael and their mum wind down and skipped into his room and closed the door behind her before her mother had even made it down the stairs.

'Michael, I need to show you some stuff.' Dana dropped the pile of paperwork on the end of his bed and began shuffling through things before he had time to speak.

Michael was balancing the ball on his knee as she looked at him. There was a brief flare of frustration and the ball was knocked to the floor. Dana could be crazy fast when she wanted to be.

'Stop dicking around! Come sit, look at all this. You know I read up on your knight in shining armour theory.' She glanced in his direction and shook her head with an all too familiar lack of patience.

'Don't start!' Her look forced all the 'boyfriend' comments he had lined up to remain unspoken.

'Well I found the same symbol that Mum has on that gypsy heirloom appearing with the images of knights. Not just on one image, but sketches, paintings, carving from points of history spanning centuries.' Dana then started working her way through history about knights that started at the turn of the century with the Ostrogoths, moving into the 5th century with stories of King Arthur and on through medieval times with the crusades and the Knights Templar.

Michael tried to focus on the information Dana was giving him, but found himself fascinated by the printout instead. There were photos of rock reliefs in Persia, tapestries from France, pictures from the *Codex Manesse* in Germany. Michael scanned them all. Looking at the horses, then finding himself drawn to the faces as if he would recognise something if he searched hard enough. Many of the pages he leafed through were of kings knighting squires but Michael was compelled to search for the scenes of battle. There was some horrific detail of knights riding into battle. Michael could imagine the weight of the armour, the smell of the horses, the pounding of the hooves. He was lost in the detail when his eyes found something familiar. He was pulled back to the moment, searching the page in his hand trying to work out what his subconscious had picked up on and his conscious mind was unable to grasp. What detail was he missing?

His eyes flew over the image, searching the faces, examining the details of the standards.

Dana shuffled closer to him, looking over his shoulder, sensing that he had found something. She was holding her own printed page and Michael glanced briefly down at what she was holding and immediately knew what had caught his eye. It was the sword. He looked back to his own printout and found a group of knights in the background, one slightly ahead of the men he was riding with. His sword had the same emblem on it as the page Dana held.

'It's the guy in the painting I have under my bed.'

'Your boyfriend?' Michael asked without mockery.

'Yep and these two images span over five hundred years.'

'That's not possible.'

'No it's not, but what's even less possible is this.'

Dana held up a picture of a brightly coloured wagon. An image completely unrelated to what they were currently talking about: a gypsy wagon being pulled by horses down a dirt track.

Michael looked at her confused. Then he looked back at the horses. They were large, heavy draft horses, their harnesses adorned with ribbons and amulets. Hanging in amongst the ribbons was the same emblem that their knight had on his sword.

A distinctive symbol, a circle made of branches, and in amongst the branches was a dragon. Poised above its head was a sword that was held suspended by its own tail.

It was a uniquely disquieting insignia: the dragon seemed powerful but somehow less so than the branches surrounding it.

'I don't get it, Dana. How can the same emblem be on the knight sword as on the gypsy's wagon?'

'Don't worry about that for now. Ask yourself how can the same symbol be on the book Mum has in her bedroom and how can this diary,' Dana threw the notebook on top of the pile of papers, 'talk about not only the book but the doll?'

* * *

They mounted a quick search of their parents' bedroom but had not been able to do a thorough job because Nicola kept yelling for them to get ready. They both sat back on Michael's bed, feeling defeated at not having found their mother's book.

'She must have moved it. Should we ask her about it?'

'I say we have another look for it tomorrow then and if we can't find it we have no choice but to suck it up and ask her about it. Maybe she has no idea of the connection. I don't know.' Michael paused rubbing his head. 'I'm so tired, I just need a night off from these dreams. I need a full night's sleep. I haven't had time to process any on this. Can we relax at Ash's house and work at what we're going to do tomorrow?'

Dana wasn't sure. The thought of turning her back on this, even for a night, made her nervous. But she hadn't been the one not sleeping, so it wasn't her call. She felt like things were spiralling out of control, so as a precaution, she packed up the papers and carefully placed them in her bag along with the painting and some other essentials. Michael may have wanted a break but she was not going to be unprepared in case the decision was taken out of his hands.

* * *

Ten minutes later Ashley poked her head into Michael's room and, before she even said 'hello', she criticised the music he was listening to. He threw a dirty t-shirt at her just for the fun of it. By the time she'd finished shouting at him and had failed miserably in her attempt to throw the t-shirt back in his face, Michael was already by her side with an arm over her shoulder. Ashley was younger than Dana but older than him and she had almost made it a religion to keep Michael aware of his place in the pecking order from what seemed the beginning of time. That had all changed years ago when Michael finally became taller than both girls. He had been taller than his sister since he was eight, but Dana had never played the 'I'm older' or 'I'm taller' card. Dana had always been the most self-assured of all of them so she had never bothered pointing out what she saw as insignificancies.

Ashley looked at things differently and as a result reminded him of any height and age deficiencies whenever she thought he needed taking down a peg or two, which in Ashley's defence had been quite often. From the moment he had been tall enough, which was around when he turned twelve, Michael had taken to throwing his arm over Ashley's shoulders and looking down at her with a mocking grin. The joke had become old but the gesture remained.

'Ha! Ha! Michael you're *so* hilarious. You really are. And here I was coming over to see if you needed any help carrying stuff over for tonight. Well now you can carry it yourself. I'll just go and see if Dana needs any help! And please don't bring the AC/DC! I think we can live without your Angus impersonation for one night!' Ashley tried to walk out of the room indifferently but not before Michael managed to wrap his other arm around her in an exaggerated bear hug.

'Love yuh too, Ash!' Michael mockingly kissed her check then spun her out of his arms towards Dana's room.

Ashley walked towards Dana's room laughing, trying to work out how Michael had managed to spin her out of his room carrying a soccer ball.

* * *

They wasted little time getting ready to go. Even with all the joking around the tension refused to lift.

They walked downstairs together, each carrying a bag of some kind. 'Mum, we're going over to Ash's now!' Dana yelled out.

'I'm in the garage, guys.' They heard her muffled call back.

Michael was first to find her, mucking around with some old paint in the garage.

'We're off to Ashley's as ordered. Need some help?' Michael reached up and grabbed down the brush Nicola had been trying to get down off the higher shelf. He felt some misgivings as he handed her the brush. He didn't understand why but he felt like he was deserting her.

'Thanks, baby. I've got it covered. You go and see if you can get a good night sleep for a change. Okay?' She reached up to his face and gave him a kiss on the cheek.

Dana obviously felt as uncomfortable as Michael and asked, 'You sure? We can stay and help with whatever painting you plan on doing.' Dana actually went so far as to put her bag down and picked up a brush.

'No guys, I'm fine. Just touching some things up. You go. You took quite a whack to the head.' She reached forward and plucked the brush out of Dana's hand, gave her an identical kiss on the cheek, and bustled them all out of the garage.

With a 'love you guys' and a hug for them all they found themselves walking down the street towards Ashley's without further debate. All feeling like they had been manipulated by a master.

Ashley came out of her daze still carrying Michael's ball. She threw it back at him and Michael nimbly tapped it from foot to foot while keeping pace with the girls.

'What do you think Mum's going to paint? I can't think of anything that needs touching up.' Michael continued to tap the ball, one foot then another with the occasional knee thrown in for good measure.

'Did you notice the paint she had out? It was the paint from our old swing set. I saw the colours: yellow, blue, purple. That set has been gone for years. I can't imagine what she could be planning on doing with it.'

'Your mum loves to paint,' Ashley said. 'She's probably using those colours on a new piece. What you both need to do is fill me in on the Marcus fight. I've been dying to ask. Don't spare any details. My mum just told me that there had been a little scuffle. But that's not the impression I'm getting. Dana, you're obviously still majorly pissed. Michael, you're too worried to remain mad and your mum, well, she was so focused on what she was doing that we managed to get away with only one hug each.' Ashley phrased this as question and statement alike.

Ashley was able to pick most of this from their body language. They were a close family and she knew each of their ways. Dana's shoulders were bunched up under her bag and her hand was clenched tightly on the shoulder strap. Michael had his soccer ball – no change there – but where was his usual flamboyance? He might have been kicking the ball around in a way that most people would struggle with standing still, but she could see that he was going through a rotation, as if his mind was focused on something else. And Aunty Nic, well she was almost the most obvious give-away that something was wrong – she never just gave you *one* hug. Ashley was concerned, but being a teenager, she was mostly intrigued.

'So guys, give. The suspense is killing me!'

Ashley's enthusiasm for gossip broke both Michael and Dana out of their own individual reflection and they started on the story of the insane neighbours next door. The mood seemed to lighten whether because of the retelling, steadily gaining its own momentum, or because of the distance they were slowly putting between themselves and Marcus' house.

* * *

It was only a little over a five minute walk to Ashley's house so it had always been their practice to spend a lot of time at each other's houses. They had walked the route many a time so that they were able to put their full attention to the task of discussing the possible reasons for this twisted behaviour of the people who lived next door.

Michael, now completely engrossed in his part of the tale-telling, had them both convinced that the neighbours were most probably psychopaths and anything from midnight sacrifices to strange cult worship seemed more than plausible.

'Anything that makes Mum scared has got to be something serious. Ashley, you didn't see her face when she came home. She was terrified that something had happened to us.' Michael looked towards Dana for back-up, expecting Ashley to question whether the great Aunty Nic could get scared. Ashley had a special bond with their mother. They understood each other, both being able to read people in their own ways.

'Terrified! Why?' Ashley wasn't questioning, she just seemed to be having trouble comprehending. Michael knew how she felt. If he hadn't seen it for himself he would have trouble understanding how a verbal fight could leave his mum so shaken.

Michael nodded towards Dana to take up the story. She would have more chance of making Ashley understand than he did. They were so completely wrapped up in the moment that none of them realised that they had stopped walking.

It would have taken quite a bit to distract them at that point in time. Funnily, 'quite a bit' chose that exact moment to hurtle itself down the road towards them in the form of Old Man Stevens' Rottweiler, Madison. Dana was almost knocked flying when the dog got away from him and came careening down the hill, completely out of control. Michael made an instinctive grab to his left and managed to clutch Madison's collar, quite a feat with the dog weighing in at over fifty kilograms and who had built up momentum in her downhill race.

Michael, still commending himself on his lightning quick reflexes, released the collar when Madison turned on him with a snarl. The foam from her mouth flicked in all directions as she snapped at anything within reach. If not for Dana's way with animals, Michael was sure he would have been going back home for more first aid.

Madison looked plain vicious, half-crazed, not at all herself. With Madison they were far more likely to be pronounced dead by drowning in excessive dog slobber than by her biting them.

Old Man Stevens stood with his hands on his knees trying to catch his breath.

'Sorry kids, don't know what's gotten into her. Thanks Michael.' Mr Stevens took another gulp of air. 'You sure saved me a nasty spill. I couldn't keep up with her! She didn't hurt you did she?' Another gulp of air. 'No, surely not, not my Maddy. She's fine now, I think. Thanks kids.'

Mr Stevens was an older man who had a tendency to hold all parts of a conversation himself. Today was no different, except that each sentence was punctuated with the need to take in a breath. He was also noticeably nervous and shakily removed a handkerchief from his pocket to mop his brow.

Michael shared his concern. Madison always walked quietly by Old Man Stevens' side. She never pulled on the lead, as if she knew her own power. She outweighed her owner and could easily hurt him if she were overexcited when on lead. Michael had never seen her do it before and he'd known Madison for years. He had walked her himself a couple of times with Dana when Mr Stevens was not well.

'She was fine until we came past your street. Don't know what spooked her. She seems fine now, doesn't she? You sure seemed to have calmed her down some.' This was directed at Dana who was still talking quietly to Madison, bent down in front of her so she could be at her level – at risk of the aforementioned death by drowning that was usually such a high possibility when you allowed your face anywhere near Madison's mouth – talking to her like she were a frightened baby.

' … but still, just to be safe, I think we'll go the long way home.' And with that, he turned Madison away from their street and after a few paces seemed to regain some level of control.

Michael returned the wave as Old Man Stevens offered a distracted farewell, continuing to glance nervously back over his shoulder until he rounded the corner.

'That was weird,' Michael said light-heartedly.

Dana didn't laugh. She was still crouched, with a puzzled look on her face, where she had soothed Madison. 'Madison was scared. She didn't want to bite you, she just desperately wanted to get away. I'm sure of it. There are too many weird things happening lately. And all of these weird things seem to involve them.' Dana turned and pointed in the direction they had come from, her hand pointing almost towards their house, but slightly to the right, towards the house next door.

'I know you want a break but we have to talk about this some more,' Dana said. 'And this time, no leaving things out just so you appear more macho. Okay, Michael?'

He hadn't thought he'd left anything out but as he

pondered Dana's remark he realised that maybe he had underplayed things. His blood encrusted nose that he noticed most mornings was maybe more than just a repetitive nose bleed. Hadn't he even found some blood in his ear one day? Was there more to it than him just thrashing around and nearly knocking himself out?

Now that he was running though things, cataloguing them all, he remembered so clearly the laughter he'd heard when he hit Marcus. He hadn't time to really think about the fight, since he'd been too concerned about Dana, then with their mum. If hearing a doll that tormented your dreams laughing inside your head whilst you were seriously contemplated beating the person in front of you senseless didn't rate, then what did? Was he trying to hide things? He didn't think so. Things had just spiralled out of his control before he had time to address them.

'Deal! Too much is happening and not just to me now.'

Michael repositioned the bag on his shoulder and continued walking down the street towards Ashley's house. When the girls had caught up, just to ensure Dana didn't get too carried away with herself Michael continued the conversation. 'But you know that means you're going to have to talk about your boyfriend too.' Michael skipped forward dodging a bag swung through the air where his head had been a moment earlier. He laughed at the colour in Dana's cheeks and wondered why Ashley would be blushing too.

* * *

When the three of them ran into Ashley's kitchen, Aunty Sarah already had three plates of warm walnut loaf ready and waiting.

'Dana, how's your head, sweetheart? Oh Michael, you look just awful. I can't believe you're not sleeping well either.'

Dana and Michael just looked at each other. It was obvious that the two sisters had been talking to one another. Nicola would have filled her sister in on the fight, maybe discussed Michael's dreams. She might even have spoken to her about the altercation between herself and Marcus' parents, but they had both picked up on the word 'either'. A word indicating that someone else wasn't sleeping.

'Ash, haven't you told them about your dreams yet?' And without waiting for a response: 'Well, when she does and I'm sure she will, can you please let me know what's upsetting her? We would all like to sleep a night through for a change.'

Aunty Sarah, although trying to appear blasé, was obviously quite concerned about all of their recent inability to sleep well. Her remark may have been phrased as a question but there was no confusion. She wanted details of what was going on. She was giving them a chance to discuss it themselves first but there was no doubt that she expected to be kept in the loop.

'Aunty Sar, can we eat these outside?' Michael was already walking towards the door. He needed to get outside, the tension he thought he had left behind them came crashing back down and he felt like he was about to explode with nervous energy and at the same time implode with this weight that he just couldn't shift.

'Yeah, sure kids, but watch the weather. I swear it feels like it will rain soon.'

They looked back over their shoulders as they left the kitchen, leaving Aunty Sarah to clean some microscopic piece of dust that only she could see. She mumbled all the time to herself about how she hated humid weather, hated the oppressive feeling that always preceded a storm.

But there wasn't a cloud in the sky and it wasn't really humid either. But Michael felt strongly that the storm they could all feel coming had nothing to do with the weather anyway.

* * *

It was convinced that some hidden memory remained. It tried to penetrate into the minds of the ancient enemy living so close by, so easy to access, but it had yet been able to find a way past the first tantalising layers. The protections they raised were not conscious so It was unable to unravel them easily. It would have to wait until Its strength grew. It was getting fed regularly and needed to test Its skills, hone Its technique. Maybe It had grown clumsy with Its eons of imprisonment. Luckily the others of this world had not the unconscious protections that the Enemy possessed.

The world It had been awoken to was ripe for Its release. It could play in people's minds, inserting thoughts, creating emotions and as these weak souls were so ignorant of their own motivations they had no inkling that the intention had been planted by another. Its sphere of influence was only a couple of dwellings around on all sides, but that gave It about eleven separate families to slowly destroy. And the energy they produced as they fought and schemed just fuelled It further. The animals still sensed Its presence, and had not lost their ability to detect Its meddling. They even tried warning their chosen companions but the ridiculous creatures refused to listen. They actually thought themselves above the animals – more advanced than them.

Pathetic beings, it served them right. They deserved to be fed upon. They were nothing more than cattle in their reduced state.

They had lost so much knowledge and were not even aware that they were something less than they had once been.

It would feed where It could. Eventually the Enemy would succumb. They were the only minds not freely open to manipulation. But what infuriated It the most was their unwitting diversion of energy towards the resistance It had detected. It knew some ancient being was drawing closer and that was the only thing in Its current state that gave It any reason for concern.

No matter. Being undetectable made It untouchable.

The Storm Breaks

Once they finally got themselves settled, camped out on trundle beds in Ashley's room, they turned to each other to finally have their chat. What little had remained of the afternoon had been taken up with dinner and then a movie that none of them paid any real attention to. Ash confided in them that she was having dreams too and that hers went along the same lines as Michael's.

Ashley looked at them both with desperation, hoping they would both understand. 'They were just a foggy memory until Michael made the boyfriend comment. That seemed to open a floodgate of images. I felt uneasy when you spoke about your dreams, Michael, but it was more like I was remembering part of a movie. I knew it ended badly but not the whole story and with no real specifics.'

Ashley continued on as if she didn't have the courage to pause for long. 'I had no idea Mum was even concerned.

Now I find out I've been keeping the whole house awake with dreams that I can barely remember.' Dana reached forward and placed her hand reassuringly on Ashley's arm. 'Sure she had asked me about them but when I honestly couldn't recall any details we were both happy to let it be.'

'But now it's a completely different story, our parents have worked out that we're all having basically the same dream.' Dana was in analyst mode, her mind busily trying to fit this new piece of information into the puzzle.

'I can't believe I just forgot them. The woods ... the screeching noise ... the repugnant fungus. It's true that my dreams aren't as *intense* as Michael's.' Ashley turned apologetically to Michael who just shrugged back with an 'it's not your fault' kind of acceptance.

Ashley said, 'My dreams just don't evoke the same level of emotion.'

'Your dreams haven't "evoked" the same fear that mine have. Don't apologise for that. I am glad you guys have been let off a little easier. I wouldn't wish this shit on anybody. Maybe it was because you both have that "hero" protecting you. Honestly the guy sounds like a bit of a lame-arse to me but if he's protecting you guys then he must be on our team.'

'Are we certain this guy is on our team?' Ashley asked somewhat desperately. She'd noticed the sky darkening outside her window and felt a tense apprehension at the loss of daylight.

'Positive!' Both Dana and Michael responded in unison. One with absolute conviction, the other wondering where his conviction came from.

Michael hadn't dreamed of the knight, but he had no doubt they were on the same team. And although he felt uncomfortable with the idea he knew his belief had something to do with the grey horse. Michael was mulling it through when his thoughts were interrupted by Dana's excited exclamation. Some of the pieces fit together better than others.

'It's the distance. Your dreams aren't as intense because you're further away from the source. Remember Madison was fine until she came past our house. That scared her to the point where she would bite whoever tried to prevent her from getting away. The fight happened outside Marcus' house. Mum was terrified when she left their house because she couldn't feel any of us. Their house is ground zero.'

'Ground zero. It's not a disease,' Michael said. 'Marcus and his parents are behind this. They're using the doll somehow to influence things.'

'I think they're helping but maybe that doll is the one controlling things. They may not know they're being used. I'm certain they're just puppets.'

Michael was shaking his head as he paced the room. 'Surely the doll is just a means to an end, an implement to focus what they are doing.'

Dana sitting cross legged looked introspective. Michael didn't think she had heard him.

'Remember, it was the puppets that broke your head open. Dana, don't let my ...' Michael struggled with the word, but now the time for honesty had come he didn't want to be the first to break, ' ... *fear*.' Clenching his fists, he forced himself to take a deep breath and then continued, 'Don't let my *fear* of this doll cloud things.'

'It isn't, Michael. The stuff on the internet – and the diary – have somehow opened things up for me. We cannot discount anything as being unrelated. We all hated that thing the minute you first picked it up at that store yet it managed to get itself here. That is not the action of a puppet. The doll and the book go together, the diary tells us that. Now we have to work out how and why and whether we can do anything to stop it.'

'Come on, Dana, I can believe the shared dreams. I have to. I can almost believe in knights that never die, but magic dolls that transport themselves into your house, well I can't get my head around that. This situation is freaky enough without us making it into a full blown horror show.' Ashley was struggling with the recollection of her dreams. Dana was asking a lot of them both to accept gypsy links and supernatural phenomena as part of normal life.

'Ash, you weren't there when Michael unpacked his bag. We hunted around his room with golf clubs and still felt exposed.'

'You think that doll is still in my room?' Michael asked having not put the pieces together in the same fashion as Dana.

'No, I think it made its way next door. The same way it made its way into your bag in the first place.' Dana had relived the anxiety she felt when searching Michael's room. Back then she'd been able to rationalise some of the fear away, now she realised that reason was only causing her more concern. Because what had been possible in her mind had just taken a quantum leap. Now she had to accept that her fears were well-founded. She understood the real danger Michael had been in and she had no idea how to protect him.

Ashley had been trying to dampen her growing distress. The logic didn't make a difference to her. Ashley read emotions. And there was real fear coming from Michael and Dana. This convinced her where nothing else could have.

'So what do we do?' Michael asked.

'Ashley and I have this.' Dana reached into her backpack and pulled out the painting that she'd removed from the frame that afternoon and rolled up into her bag. 'And you will only sleep when we're watching you. The first eye flicker, the first moan and we wake you. And hopefully the distance can protect you as it has Ashley.'

'Don't forget we have Mum working on this too now. She said to give her a couple of days. I've been putting up with these dreams for weeks, a couple nights more won't kill me. Tomorrow though, we have to talk to them. What Dana's found changes things. It just has to.' Michael stretched out in his bed it what he hoped was a relaxed manner, took a deep breath and relaxed his body as he always did. With his left hand casually resting behind his head, he crossed his feet and announced he would take first watch.

The phone rang unexpectedly and loudly. Dana let out a yelp and Ashley gave a startled shout. It was Michael who laughed the loudest when he heard Aunty Sarah call to say it was their mother ringing to say goodnight.

* * *

Sarah had not been surprised when her sister rang to say the kids were sleeping over. Ashley's recent nightmares had unsettled her and Sarah found herself also having trouble sleeping, always waiting for the cry that she knew would come. It had been intermittent at first, but when it progressed into a nightly event, Sarah felt herself tense as night approached. So much so that when she felt herself start to nod off, delicately balanced between the lands of wake and sleep, she would jerk suddenly, dropping back into the waking world with a physical start, certain that she had heard Ashley cry out.

Her relief at having the kids sleep over was soon replaced with concern. Nicola had explained about the fight. Sarah had been shocked to hear Dana had been hurt but not overly surprised that the fight had occurred. They all knew it had been brewing for some time.

Her concern grew when she heard the details of Michael's dreams and what Nicola had found, or more to the point, had been unable to find when she tried to enter his dreams. Sarah had watched her sister through years of illness, watched as things that had been special about Nicola become stronger.

When Nicola explained that she had no choice but to consult the book, Sarah asked her to wait. Surely they should consult the book together. They had no idea of how it worked exactly. You could flick through and read some passages but before too long your head would be spinning with voices that were not your own.

Nicola planned on doing more than flicking a few pages. But Sarah's protest made no impact. The argument was lost before it had even begun. Reluctantly, Sarah conceded the point – the kids needed to be protected and she could achieve that more easily if they were all together. Hopefully the distance would continue to provide a form of defence. Nicola would be fully occupied trying to wrest answers from the book of lore. Having the kids safely away would give her more focus. Sarah agreed on every point but still wished there was a better way.

Sarah's style might have been less flamboyant than her sister's but it was more suited to the job of protector. Sarah smiled to herself as she picked up her sewing and prepared for the night ahead.

* * *

Since the children were out of bed again, Uncle Brent offered them a hot chocolate. He melted chocolate drops, muttering to himself as he warmed the milk, mixing the two together before serving them up with marshmallows.

Michael greedily drank his down and was first to get a shot at what was left in the pot. Sarah gave them each a small bag of herbs that she'd sewn that afternoon in the hope that it would help them all sleep well. They were instructed to place the bag under their pillows. Dana grabbed a ribbon off Ashley's bedside table and tied hers around her neck.

Michael lifted his pillow to place the packet of herbs underneath; he stopped to smell it first and noticed his head swam slightly as he inhaled. He wasn't certain what to do – his plan had been not to sleep at all and he didn't want to drift off accidentally, so he settled on placing his bag to the left of his pillow just to be sure.

Dana had laid the painting between the three of them, next to a bottle of nail polish on top of a Hollywood gossip magazine. Michael wasn't certain what occult properties the girls seemed to think lay in the nail polish or movie gossip but he had no energy left for comment.

'I'll take the first watch and wake you when I get tired!' Michael announced before the girls got too involved in their current conversation. Michael grabbed a bottle of Coke and some chocolate that he had snuck into his bag. He reasoned that if the caffeine and sugar combined didn't keep him awake nothing would.

'Be sure to wake us. Sleep tight, buddy,' Dana whispered. The house was already starting to fall quite. Uncle Brent and Aunt Sarah had either turned the TV off or turned it down because Michael couldn't hear it any longer.

'Yeah, sure. Now go to sleep.'

Michael was conflicted; anything had to be better than just waiting. What he was waiting for, he wasn't sure. He didn't know why that night felt different but it did. The oppressive air they'd all felt building over the last couple of days had manifested itself into a real storm after all. Michael had no idea how the bureau had missed this one coming. Melbourne's weather was notorious for sudden changes but this was not going to be a light sprinkle.

The clouds had begun building in the early evening. Just before sunset they turned a bruised brown, which indicated they were in for some wild weather.

Michael had been brought up to love storms. Very rarely did they cause any damage in their area, but the pyrotechnic displays were always awe inspiring. His dad especially loved an impressive display of lightning. He usually turned off all the lights and just sat inside watching the clouds circle, waiting for the first strike. Michael closed his eyes and welcomed the first flash of lightning as it played across his eyelids knowing his dad would be sitting at home doing the same thing.

Although Michael was on first watch and dutifully waiting for the next crack of lightning, he found it hard with the girls incessantly gasbagging about things that Michael did not have the time or the patience for.

'If you two are going to talk about such shit,' Michael hissed under his breath, 'I'll go to sleep first. I just can't listen to any more of it.' He rolled over on to his side. There was no point in the three of them being awake. It already seemed like an eternity had passed since they went to bed and Michael just wanted to pull his head under the covers and have a normal night's sleep for a change, storm or not.

Exhaustion, mental fatigue and an overdose of sugar took hold and so against all his best laid plans, Michael fell heavily and unceremoniously into sleep all the while listening as the girls talked about some actor that had recently taken their fancy ... and without noticeable transition the land of dreams enveloped him.

* * *

He could hear waves crashing against the shore of a beach. And the sound soothed the tension from his shoulders so that he was able to take a deep breath. He could not see any water but there was sand as far as his eyes could see. It appeared to be just after dusk and a heavy fog was starting to roll in, rapidly reducing the area of clear sight.

There was no fungus and no forest this time so he was content.

There was no-one else around. No living thing of any kind. He strained, ears trying to pick up any sound other than surf. As he listened to the mesmerising roll of water on sand and his body began to sway with the rhythm, he became less certain.

Was it really surf he heard? It had taken on a different timbre – it still possessed the same rhythmic quality, but now it sounded more like breathing. He circled around, told himself it was just to survey the scene, take in the sights. But he soon started to turn faster, breathing more heavily now. He felt strongly that there was something to see, just beyond his field of vision. If the mist were to part, just for a second ...

Suddenly, he realised he didn't want it to part. He did not want to see what was beyond.

Michael knew what was waiting.

The repugnant doll.

The way it moved now, with more animation than

before only served to draw more attention to its corpse-like extremities. Michael could sense it was bigger than it had been in any dream previously; its power emanated through the mist, its hatred, a palpable force beating against Michael's self-composure. And as if all of those things weren't enough, Michael knew it now had allies and they were looking for him, searching in the mist not content any longer to wait.

'Wake me up, girls,' Michael mumbled to himself as he turned in tight circles.

The mist continued to surround him, thickening and then thinning as if trying to part.

'You can wake me up now!' Michael stopped circling and started jogging in one direction then stopped himself as he had no idea if he was running into danger or not.

He felt panic wrap its fingers around his chest. As his heart rate increased, he involuntarily picked up his pace again.

He twisted backwards as he ran, looking over his shoulder for what he knew would be following him.

Michael had dreams before when he ran and didn't get anywhere. This was not one of those times. He could feel great distances as they passed behind him. A part of him was aware of invisible barriers separating before him. They felt like spider webs breaking against his face. He scratched at them, desperate to remove any fibres that remained. But the land these barriers separated remained shrouded by the mist. Hidden. He feared what he couldn't see and pleaded repeatedly under his breath to be woken.

His panicked mind focused only on escape and his senses were heightened while trying to detect where the strike that he knew must fall would come from. He sensed more than saw a black shape pacing him. Felt somehow unthreatened by this shape and the first clear thought overrode some of his panic.

What was Sheba doing here in this dream?

A voice he knew and loved screamed out to him: 'Michael, they can't follow you, they can't break through, they need you. Go back!'

He slowed. He would have thought nothing could stop him, as his panic was so intense. But the rock in his life – his mother – had spoken, screamed, and she was able to get through where others could not. He knew who needed him and he cursed himself understanding that he had left them behind to fight alone.

He turned and ran. He would not leave them behind for anything in the world. He felt ashamed and retraced where he had left them.

'I should have known when I didn't wake that it was because they were here with me,' he told himself. 'Should have known they needed me.'

Nicola's voice allowed him to regain control. Panic had clouded his judgement and he vowed to never let that happen again. He ran and if possible, faster than before. Calling their names with his mind, screaming to them with all his heart.

They heard him. And his mother had been right. They needed him.

* * *

Dana laughed softly as she listened to Ashley criticising her favourite actor's current girlfriend. The term 'bimbo' had been mentioned, the woman's fashion sense ridiculed and her acting ability put into the shredder. Ashley had just finished dissecting the current photo shoot she had seen of the notorious couple strolling away on some beach, when Dana found herself gently curling her toes into the soft sand underneath her feet. She opened her eyes lazily to find Ashley beside her, standing in the middle of an endless sand dune continuing to talk, seemingly unperturbed by the change of scenery.

Dana could no longer focus on Ash's words. They were being drowned out by the steady hammering of waves in the background. The sound wasn't loud but she could hardly hear Ashley any more, although not overly loud the noise somehow beat painfully against her eardrums, driving out everything else. One hand pressed against her ear, Dana tried desperately to reach out to Ashley with the other. Her vision was obscured by the sand blowing in her face and she had the irrational feeling that this world was trying to keep her from Ashley.

Dana staggered forwards to where she hoped Ashley still stood. The world continued to dissolve around her. She had to get to Ashley soon because Michael was sure to be in worse trouble. Her knees buckled under the onslaught of the sand and she dropped to her hands and knees but continued to crawl forward. She knew Ashley was near.

The sand pooled around her thighs and she couldn't move any further forward. Dana, fearful of the danger Michael was facing, closed her eyes and with all other senses withheld from her, reached forward using instinct alone. As her fingers curled around Ashley's arm the world solidified, coming back into focus. Dana's eyes were drawn to the two figures just now behind Ashley's shoulder, plodding forward, eating up the distance separating them.

She turned, pulled violently on Ashley's arm and ran. Ashley continued to speak softly as if she were completely oblivious to her surroundings. Dana suspected she might not be aware of the danger because she wasn't fully asleep yet, not fully dreaming. And Dana was sure that wouldn't offer Ashley any protection.

It wouldn't stop what was coming.

She turned to urge Ashley to move faster, to run, half dragging Ashley behind her. And then Dana suddenly dropped to the ground, the wind knocked right out of her as she ran head first into some unseen obstacle.

* * *

They couldn't break through. Break through what? Michael had no idea ... some kind of wall or barrier? He could see them, could almost touch them, but there was a cold elastic nothingness that lay between them. The girl's desperate gaze broke away from Michael's to look back over their shoulders. As the mist finally parted Michael was able to make out the terrible figure that stood behind them. *But it couldn't have gotten so big, could it?*

That doll was now a larger than life monster, bigger than any bear he'd seen at the zoo. It bared its teeth now, apparent in ways his imagination had failed to fully capture before now. Stringy black hair hung plastered across its heavy brow. Deep set dark eyes looked up through the layers of bone and hair, burning with an unhealthy intensity. The mouth was crammed full of finely pointed overlapping layers of yellowed teeth. The thin lips were in constant motion, stretched to the point of tearing, sliding across teeth, ceaselessly murmuring its words of hate.

And Michael heard every whispered word.

Yet he was unable to hear the girls when they were so obviously screaming.

He needed to get to them soon. Why did this place let its whisperings travel to his ears, when the screams of his family had to be felt rather than heard? He still had no idea how he had gotten through any barriers in the first place.

Blinking away tears of frustration, Michael beat against the near invisible barrier. It was as insubstantial as a heat haze, and took each blow without showing any signs of weakening. Dana and Ashley pounded uselessly against the other side, their efforts creating a thickened light that rippled out like raindrops falling on oily water. And as the force was absorbed, the light slowly disappeared. They both seemed so small, so diminished by the monstrosity that was closing in behind them.

As the doll strode closer, it looked as if it were carved from charred wood, glistening in oily sweaty patches on the roped muscle wrapped around bone. One arm swung clumsily at its side, the other resting on the back of Marcus' neck. The swollen joints made the hand look more like a gnarled root yet the fingers easily dug into the hollows of Marcus' collar bone. Thick cracked claws curled almost delicately around the edges of bone, tapping occasionally as if emphasising a point.

Its pace was slow and measured, as if savouring the moment.

Where once it had been small and ugly, now it was large and powerful and its whisperings turned to peals of unholy laughter as it closed in slowly, relentlessly on what Michael knew it viewed as prey and what he thought of simply as family. He had to do something and as the girls shrank from the horror that loomed behind them, he called out for help to break through.

* * *

Dana felt herself carried forward. Ashley crashed into her back, knocking whatever breath she had left out of her protesting lungs. Her forward momentum stopped and she whipped backwards as if a bungie cord had been wrapped around her entire body and she had suddenly reached its limit. Desperately trying to suck in air that had been knocked from her she untangled herself from Ashley and shimmied backwards all at the same time.

Ashley's attention had finally been brought into the here and now and if Dana were to be quite frank it wasn't helping much. Ashley was screaming, seemingly not aware that it was Dana that she was beating against as she desperately tried to regain her feet. Dana raised one arm to protect herself and used the other to try and grab one of Ashley's frantic swinging arms. All the while she was trying to keep her eyes on the thing slowly and menacingly walking towards them.

How had Michael slept at all if this was what had been waiting for him each night?

The doll shuffled towards her, twice the size that she was. It lumbered on legs it seemed unable to fully control. It had a disjointed gait as if it were a puppet with a master still learning their trade. But the distance between them was being eaten by its stride nonetheless. With dangling greasy hair and black charred skin, it shambled forwards with Marcus strolling one pace behind. Both faces broke into what resembled a smile, one a dark stretched rictus, foreign and inhumane, the other cold and empty, drained of any humanity.

* * *

Michael wiped his eyes, hoping that if he could focus on the swirling haze in front of him he would be better able to find a way through. But almost as if a hand had fallen on his own shoulder, Michael was somehow fully connected to his family and it was their presence that clarified his vision. He'd known their touch all his life.

They had always been able to find him and feed him strength whenever he needed a boost. And he needed that now. Michael didn't have to turn; he let their strength flow through him and he added his own.

Michael threw himself against the obstruction separating him from Dana and Ashley. He clawed, bit, thrashed against the barrier. Furious that something so unsubstantial would dare to try and keep him from them, keep him from saving them. He felt a small bundle clenched in his left hand but had no time to look to see what he had picked up. Energy crackled from him as his hammering turned into something more like an animal frenzy, but still he retained one single, simple thought: *he would not leave them*. This may be a dream, but abandoning them wasn't an option.

It was then that he felt the wall give. Not break or shatter dramatically, but thin just enough for him to stretch through and circle their wrists with his hands. With one hand he grabbed Ashley and with the other Dana and he lost hold of the small bundle as it fell to the ground unnoticed.

His feet dug deep into the sand. Playing some horrific kind of tug o' war. As he strained to break the barrier's hold, Michael felt his parent's strength, and that of his aunt and uncle, wrap around him, lending him weight, helping him to pull the girls back through.

The elastic quality of the barrier gave somewhat and Michael tightened his grip. The bundle Michael had dropped simmered and exploded in an almost unseen puff of smoke and the barrier before him weakened further. Knowing he only had seconds, and with only one heave left in him, he summoned up every last scrap of his remaining strength and threw his body backwards.

And they all fell in a heap, safely back on the other side, just the three of them. His family's touch had vanished.

* * *

The girls were crying. Michael held them and cried a little himself.

Ashley broke the moment to scramble backward, pulling them along with her. Ashley, fully in the dream, was hideously aware now. She was the only one still facing the tear in the barrier and she could see what Dana and Michael could not.

Their friends were still coming and they were not going to give up easily. The creature seemed to be growing, as if it fed off the pain and terror that it caused. Something else had changed about it too. It still had that sick, gaunt look, but it now seemed stronger somehow. 'Vibrant' would be the wrong word … it was the exact opposite of vibrant. It had the strength of a fever, the potency a disease possesses as it eats away at its host.

And its host was right by its side.

Marcus.

Way back in the distance Michael could sense endless hordes waiting to join the battle, hollering and yammering for release. His legs had turned to jelly, there was just no run left in them. Maybe it was because he felt like he had already run a marathon and back. Or maybe it was just the way a rabbit feels when the headlight first landed on its back. All he could hear was his heart. How could he not, it had decided to relocate to his throat. But there was something else. Something more was beating away at the back of his mind.

'It's him, he's coming.' Dana's voice sounded wrong in this place. It seemed like an environment that should only support a whisper.

'Who are you talking about?' Ashley obviously shared Michael's view about shouting as he had to strain just to hear her.

'Something's wrong. He can't get to us. Michael please do something!' Dana voice had taken on a shrill quality that Michael didn't like one bit.

'What do you expect me to do?' Michael yelled back. He couldn't even take his eyes away from the barrier. The smoke released when the small packet had exploded ran up like thread and knitted the barrier together wherever it touched. As the last of the tiny packet was consumed, the billowing blue vapour turned into a harmless clear mist, leaving only a small smouldering pile of ash – all that remained of his aunt's sewing.

The creature having reached the barrier was clawing relentlessly in its effort to reach them. Marcus smirked as he watched the events unfolding in front of him.

Michael couldn't even move. Any hope that remained drifted away with the last wisp of blue, as it curled up and dissolved before his eyes.

'Michael you broke through. You're the only one who can help him!' Dana screamed. Ashley rushed towards the barrier as if everything had finally gotten too much for her and she dived towards the ground.

Everything seemed to happen in one heartbeat, in one drawn breath. Ashley held her hand up triumphantly and threw a small bundle towards the barrier slowly being shredded by the oversized doll.

Dana suddenly realising what Ashley was doing, ran forwards and pulled her own bundle from around her neck, just where she had tied it when Aunty Sarah gave it to her before going to sleep.

Dana yelled back, 'Michael help him!'

Two silent small explosions drifted up from where the girls had thrown their bundles and as the blue smoke billowed it ran up the edges of the tear and drew them together. But the bundles were too little and the doll was too large, too vicious and their gifts of protection soon started to smoulder and die. With this small opposition depleted the doll continued its relentless tearing. Finding the weakened spot it reached its clawed hand through.

At that moment the black shape Michael had seen running beside him, the one he had assumed was Sheba, jumped at the barrier, snarling as only a dog protecting its masters can. The doll shrank away from the snapping teeth, pushing Marcus into the position of shield.

But it wasn't Sheba; this dog was bigger, much more heavily muscled. And at that moment Michael realised what Dana had known all her life. Sheba wasn't here. It was Titan, their dog that had died years ago. He had no time to contemplate the fact that his mother had been telling him the truth all his life, that Sheba protected them in one world and that Titan protected them in dreams. His mother had been telling him strange things all of his life and if he started to believe even half of them, his life would change dramatically.

'Michael hurry, *help him through*. Titan can't hold them forever.' Michael finally relied on his instincts and ran forward, grabbing his sister with his left hand and Ashley with his right. Whether to reassure them or to comfort himself, he didn't really know, he just did. Pulling them back behind him, to what little safety he could provide and just as Dana had, he found physical contact made things more focused, stronger. The voices although coming from a long way off became clearer. One was louder that all the others.

'You must do it together and you must do it *now*,' Nicola screamed.

Michael didn't know what to do.

But Dana knew something Michael didn't. Dana's back straightened, she held her head high and held the enemies gaze as she called a name. She had been dreaming of a saviour and knew that he was on his way.

'Ashul! Awake, come, we need you!'

Michael's rational mind put the 'Back in Five Minutes' sign out … leaving only the irrational.

Michael used the last vestiges of strength to scream with all the force left to him. 'Ashul, whoever you are! Wake! *Wake up you lazy bastard*!'

The sky blazed with a sudden flash of light. The twilight they'd been trapped in fell away to reveal a land that *desolate* came nowhere near close to describing. In was in that moment, blinded by the sudden flash of light and near deafened by the crack of thunder, that the sound beating away in the background became clear.

It was the pounding of hooves – many sets of hooves galloping towards them. And as with all dreams, it was in this moment of revelation that Michael woke. Not gracefully, but thrown forcefully back into the real world.

Back to the crash of thunder. The storm had finally broken.

* * *

It turned and slashed out at the boy cowering beside It. How had they managed to bring him through? How had It not recognised what the resistance represented? They must have known more than their conscious minds acknowledged to have shielded their thoughts so completely. And that damn boy, he walked through the barriers that It had created to trap them as if they were nothing more than a feeble spider web. Saving those detestable girls, the Enemy, when it was about to feed fully for the first time since It had escaped from the bindings. It wanted them. It was owed them. It had almost tasted their souls, eaten of the Enemy and to have them snatched away at the last moment. Protected by a guardian in the second realm, a guardian It had not even detected. It may have just lost its best opportunity to thwart the loathsome children, the damned spawn of the Enemy.

And now they had been joined by one of the ancient warriors. One that walked the world many centuries before the eons of imprisonment had even began. The Sleeping Warrior had been woken, It had only a short time before he regained full consciousness and was joined by his brothers.

It had to act fast, before they understood their advantage, but It could not think with the rage of Its defeat tasting harsh and acidic on Its tongue.

So It turned looking for something to destroy, something to pay for what had just happened, slack the rage that so consumed It and It found only the boy. He would not survive any attack; his life force was too depleted, so with no other choice available It went out ranging, out into the lands of dreams to find some release on the many minds that fled before It.

The Gypsy Book

Nicola settled in for sleep. There were no more excuses. No more delays. She had spoken with the kids at Sarah's and they'd been fine. The phone still lay next to her since she found its presence conforming. She felt an almost superstitious need to keep the phone close – whilst it remained next to her she felt connected to her children. She knew that she would not put the phone back on the bedside table that night.

It was ridiculous, but tonight was a night when the mystic held sway. She found it was impossible to convince herself that she was being neurotic and illogical as she lay in bed with a book older than she could fathom laying against her chest. Her arms were crossed almost religiously around the book, fingers tracing the pattern of the silver symbol embedded in the cover, inhaling the scent of book

– a combination of leather and the oil and perspiration of the many hands that had held this book before her, the hands of her predecessors, her long distant relations. She had no real understanding of how the book worked. She had flicked through its pages over the years. There were sections that contained lists of spells for anything from the removal of warts to safe pregnancies. Charms, potions and philtres were written in so many different languages her mind boggled at the distances the book had travelled. Mostly the book of lore contained stories, warnings of where not to travel and who not to cross, what animal – if seen at certain times – could be an omen or an evil spirit to be avoided. The tales within held warnings for wary travellers, but it also gave charms and rituals that could be employed to ensure safe passage.

She had only ever looked through the book with curiosity, had never looked for anything specific, or more importantly, required its help. She had no doubt that if she asked, the book would answer.

Nicola just had no comprehension of how the process worked. Images of the book flying open, pages turning until they stopped on an illustration of the doll had crossed her mind. Old episodes of *Charmed* and *Supernatural* had coloured her imagination with a fanciful notion of the how the book might respond. On some deeper level she knew the path before her was not so simple. As she thought about what the path might be, voices whispered in her mind as if trying to support and reassure her. She felt an unexpected comfort as if she were being cradled by those long since passed away.

She breathed deeply and tried to clear her mind. She could hear her husband locking up downstairs, knowing he would be watching over her, ready to intervene if she gave any indication that things were going wrong. Pushing these thoughts into the background Nicola focused on the one thing that mattered: the gaining of information. She knew that if she found out why the family that lived next door were targeting her family she could work out a way to defend against them.

Why do they hate us so?

The voices echoed the call. Her breathing deepened. She felt her muscles relax. Her fierce hold on the book lessened slightly as she entered the early stages of sleep and her mind wandered through the layers of dream. For a brief moment she caught sight of Michael standing in sand with rolling fog surrounding him. His posture was relaxed and he looked content so she let herself be carried on, repeating her question to herself and whatever it was in the book that heard the call – *Why do they hate us so?*

The myriad of voices supporting her call intensified and suddenly the sound of pages ruffling as if blown by a strong wind wiped away all else. The part of her mind aware of her sleeping body knew the book was open and that the pages were indeed turning at an amazing pace. Her hands were now clenched tightly around the cover as if she were bonded to the book. And as the sound overwhelmed her, she felt like she was being pulled into the pages and knew that there would be no turning back.

The pace that she moved through the layers of dream increased as if she were somehow moving through the flying pages. The question she had asked now rang painfully through her head, magnified by the voices that echoed her own and the smell of dry parchment burnt her sinuses.

Why do they hate us?

She hovered over a scorched forest, as she had briefly hovered over her son. This time she saw a man wandering bewildered, dazed through the desolation. She had less than a moment to wonder what this might mean before her consciousness merged with his.

Why had this happened? Why was he here? Why was he alive?

He (she) had regained cognisance slowly, pulling himself out from behind the tortured stump that had once been a magnificent oak. The small wood nestled between two hills, purposefully selected for the binding due to its latent energy, was now a charred void. Surrounded by nothing that resembled the awe-inspiring trees that until recently had majestically dominated all that fell in their shadow. Trevlor.

Was she Trevlor now? This didn't feel quite right but all memory of her true identity was quickly fading, being overridden.

Whoever he was, he staggered to his feet.

Mercifully the screaming had finally stopped and the smoke began to settle. He heard the occasional crackle of smouldering debris but nothing more. His soul, trained to be in tune with its surrounding, registered the lack of any other sound. No chirping of birds, chatter of wildlife or hum of insects remained. The gentle rustle of leaves, moving against one another in their own delicate ballet, danced no longer. Just harsh, brittle noise replaced the symphony that had once been.

He wondered what he should do. Was he the only one to survive? Could that be possible? His instincts told him to run, to forget what he had witnessed and forever forget his dream of learning the powers. But something stopped him from fleeing. He rose slowly and got moving. Whether it was guilt or hope that controlled his urge to run, he was unable to determine. Still he felt compelled to sift through what remained, hoping to find someone who could take charge – no – take responsibility for what had just happened.

He stumbled from one scorched form to another, barely able to discern the difference between blackened stump and broken body. He searched on for authority, but soon even this small hope failed. Bile rose when recognition was forced upon him by the smallest of things. A portion of trim. All that remained of hard earned robes. An eye that peered mockingly from a skull. Small visual identifiers that gave definition to lives lost. Several times he stopped, body convulsing, tremors racking his exhausted frame, reflexes endeavouring to purge the stench, the taste that he was being forced to take in with every breath, but due to the fasting, he was unable to bring up any more than ribbons of bile. He sat with blackened hands dangling and draped lifelessly across his knees. Strings of saliva clung to his chin and his sunken eyes stared but for a time took in no more. The smell of charred flesh receded and a grey oblivion sheltered his tortured mind ...

The sound of the pages as they continued to turn returned and with it came a glimmer of the person Nicola was. She was not Trevlor, a young man driven to the edge of sanity. She knew she was a mother searching for answers and for some reason she found herself back above the scene of desolation being pulled by another force towards the dream of sand.

She saw a young athletic boy, running, driven by the terror of what pursued him. Bare feet pounding relentlessly as he ran through the grey landscape. His heaving chest desperately sucked in air. His rapid breathing and backwards glances fuelled the fear that gripped him. The boy cast another glance behind him and then pushed back the hair plastered to his forehead.

As she recognised this small gesture, one that she had seen so many times in *her life*, suddenly she was herself again. She was not just a mother, she was *his* mother. This was her son, Michael, running in terror. Nicola knew he was in danger and threw all her strength towards him as she likewise felt the book gathering its own resources to pull her back within its pages.

As the smell of burnt flesh once again assailed her nostrils Nicola was acutely aware that there were only moments to act. The grey sandy land that Michael was running through expanded. Saw the uncounted layers of magic and trickery that he had fought his way through and she saw her daughter and niece trapped behind those same layers. She held onto herself and yelled, 'Michael, they can't follow you. They can't break through, they need you. Go back!'

And as her energy level ebbed, the book not finished with her yet, wrapped her very being in the fold of its pages and forced her mind back into that of another, forcing her to receive the answer to the question she had asked.

He wept, for himself, for the lives lost. Mumbling to himself, he sat mostly motionless, lifeless, a body whose mind had taken brief refuge someplace else. Eventually he stumbled on, obligation alone able to re-join the two halves of himself, separated by horror and despair. The deep feeling that he owed it to the fourteen masters, those who had sacrificed themselves to bind the evil, compelled him. It wasn't supposed to have happened this way. His mind rebelled, shifted from memories in a heartbeat, flashed back to the confident men and women who had entered the clearing, expecting resistance and defiance. Expecting some losses maybe but that was all. Sure of their gifts and their ability to wield the power, in no doubt of the righteousness of their purpose, almost as if this alone ensured success. Trevlor wondered if failure had even been considered. It seemed shocking to him now, with the horrors lay bare before him. Could it actually be possible that at no time had any contingency plan been laid? Had it seemed so implausible to them that this evil would have its own allies, ready to defend?

Had they been so supremely confident, so arrogant?

He had never thought of them as such. He had looked at them with awe and what he saw as a child's simple trust, but now …

'Come along and learn,' was the message sent out to underlings and apprentices. 'Give your strength and we in return will provide knowledge.'

And strength, they had taken, in abundance. First one, then another apprentice, like a house of cards collapsing under immense unseen pressure. They dropped, drained

*of all life force by the unexpected rise in opposition. But
what choice did the masters have? Were there any other
options available to them? They could not allow the evil
free reign. It had already reaped enough havoc on the
poor defenceless souls that it fed upon. No, the master
had done what was required and the apprentices that
did not fall through exhaustion were silently slaughtered
by the unseen allies, ready to assist this evil to the very
end. With the night in turmoil, confusion and disbelief
at its peak, his beloved master broke the mental link
binding them and in so doing breached all protocols set
down in the doctrines and that alone was what had
saved him. Trevlor had fought him, had wanted to
give his all, his life, but an apprentice's strength was no
match for a master even when that master was taxed to
the limit.*

With this break in Trevlor's thoughts, Nicola's own true identity was able to break free and regain control. Flooded by adrenaline she fought the book for control. Like a drowning person struggling to the surface for another breath, she sent her mind searching outwards. Like blips on a radar, her family flickered before her. She grabbed clumsily for each thread of consciousness, her mother, father, grandmother, uncle, each pulled upon desperately to anchor herself. Her children were in danger and she had little time for action. The memories of a man named Trevlor demanded attention. She dragged on her family's strength and thrust all of this power towards her son, knowing her family would forgive her this harsh treatment.

The now dreaded sound of turning pages enveloped her and she was again enfolded in the book. Left with only a prayer that her son had heard her words …

He found himself seated again, propped up against the cooling remains of an undefinable molten object. Cradled in his lap was what he believed to be his master's head. Mesmerised by the steady tick and crack of cooling wood that had become so like a slowing heartbeat. He mourned equally for the lost masters as he did for the ancient trees. His flagging consciousness was suddenly and painfully dragged back into focus by a sharp sound. He struggled to get his feet under him as realisation stuck him, that this was the first noise to break the silence, one not produced by the dying trees or his own rebelling body. It wasn't hope or guilt that had him moving this time but the immediate clear realisation, the simple idea that maybe they had not succeeded, that maybe the binding had failed. The evidence, now that his adrenaline-filled mind began to function rationally, finally absorbed what he had been walking through. It had no look of a victory field about it but that of a massacre. The sound he heard was probably that of the victor come to collect the spoils.

It was the blackened remains of his master's hand that stopped him from running and which stilled the panic. The croak that had once been a commanding voice had dragged him back to this dismal place. With words spoken into his mind rather than the harsh growl his master was only now able to issue, he was told what needed to be done. And it was with his master's strength, along with all of his knowledge and power, gifted to him as he passed, that gave him the courage to take up the burden that had become his.

This time the shock of the numerous lifetimes of knowledge flooding her already overloaded circuitry forced her not only out of the dream but to full wakefulness. She remembered it all. Not only Trevlor's memories but those of the masters, the memories received as his master had passed. Nicola's mind was full to bursting and she had a very real fear the something might have been damaged with the extreme level of information being absorbed. She experienced a headache so intense she felt like she would pass out completely. Her eyes fluttered open and she reached across to make sure she was in her home and in her bed. Her husband lay sleeping beside her, caught in his own dream, arms tense, skin sticky with sweat. Nicola drew in another breath to ground herself. She was herself, she was home and now she needed to make sure her children were safe.

She managed to lift her head from the pillow and instantly regretted it. The pounding of what she hoped was only a migraine beat against her temples, radiated out to encompass her whole head. The pale light coming through the windows lanced into the back of her eye sockets and she squeezed her eyes shut in an effort to reduce some of the pain. Nicola watched as the light faded and was replaced with the red beat of her own heart. She needed to get up, wake her husband, and get to the kids.

She braced herself and tried to roll onto her side, but paused as the nausea swept through her. She struggled into a sitting position, not even realising the book lay open still on her lap. She sat for a moment elbows braced against knees riding the waves of pain and nausea, readying herself for the first step. Her head spun and eyesight faded. She fell back, unconscious. The gypsy book had not finished passing on its message.

With barely a split second's pause, her consciousness was thrown back into Trevlor's memory again. Aware of what was happening this time, she braced herself, trying to retain some small measure of herself, but nevertheless her memories, her personality, her pain were replaced by that of another, and the question that she had asked the book was the only thing of her that remained.

The question asked had yet to be answered. The book would not stop until the answer had been given, and whether it was understood was irrelevant. It had only to deliver what had been paid for … so Nicola became Trevlor one last time to receive the final part of the answer.

He cried again, consciously this time, when he found the black wooden form, the evil that had taken the combined powers of the great fourteen to bind. He wept as it twitched and burned in his hands. He ignored the doll's whispers as it spoke promises, first of supreme power, and when that lie was not believed, of vengeance that would be delivered swift and bloody. Its few surviving allies had scattered when the binding was complete and Trevlor knew at some point he would have to face them. But now was not that time. He wept not for himself, for he now had the strength and knowledge of a master. He cried for his children and his children's children, for they, his unborn ancestors, would be cursed with the responsibility of keeping this evil forever bound.

She woke and felt the tears running down her face. She and Trevlor had become one in their shared moment of grief. She now knew why *It* hated them so much, and she knew her family were the descendants of those who had imprisoned it so many centuries ago. The burden had now been passed on to the next generation. Her children were now *Its* warders and *It* would stop at nothing to destroy them. And the doll had once again found allies, equally willing now as ever to shed blood in its cause.

She reached across to wake her husband and that small movement proved too much to bear. She fell unconscious once more. Her mind needed time to repair itself from the strain of taking on a lifetime of memories. The enormous amount of information that had been thrust upon her tore away all sense of equilibrium. She had not been trained to absorb the power of the masters and so her mind shut down in at attempt at self-preservation.

Her children would have to fend for themselves.

Assessing the Damage

Michael lay there listening to the storm as it beat against the roof. His eyes were still dazzled by the light he hadn't really seen, his ears still ringing from the sound he hadn't really heard. It had all happened in his nightmare but to his body there was no longer any distinction. Being only a dream offered no solace and definitely no protection.

He could hear the girls breathing and he tried to let the sound soothe him, but the thought of their faces as they stood trapped behind a barrier was not easily pushed aside. He cursed his own stupidity. He should have known they needed him. Shouldn't have needed his own mother to tell him to turn back. Marcus was right, he did spend half his time running. But it wouldn't happen again, that he promised himself. Something had happened last night. Something had changed deep within him and he knew the next time he would stand.

He fists clenched as something locked into place, as if his thoughts had in some way sealed some kind of bargain.

Michael placed both hands on his forehead, rubbing at his brow, completely overwhelmed by all that was happening.

His fingers felt strangely gritty. Raising his hands for examination he found his left palm covered in a layer of fine blue powder. Wonder replaced frustration and Michael exhaled and gently blew away all that remained of his aunt's bundle of protection.

How had she known how to make such things and that they would need them?

How had his mother been able to find them and help them in the dream?

He knew his family was different, but it was becoming obvious that those differences were not as minor as he once believed. His parents had a lot of explaining to do. *They* would be the ones in the hot seat this time.

Dusting his hands off, Michael clapped them together, but the feeling of hot, tight skin made him wince. His hands were red, maybe even slightly burnt, and they were now both dusted with the dark blue residue. Shrugging, he sat up. *It is what it is*, he thought to himself, stealing one of his dad's favourite lines made him smile. Sometimes you just have to move on.

Both girls were already awake and had also discovered pile of ashes of their own. They had been silently processing all that had happened when Michael clapped his hands together and drew their attention.

'What are you smiling about Michael?' Ashley asked her voice shaking. 'Please share, because that was the most terrifying thing I have ever experienced and right now I'm seriously trying very hard not to burst into tears?'

Two things had brightened Michael's mood. One was the presence of the Doberman in the dream, Titan. He had always felt his mother was somewhat 'full of it' when she went on about Sheba protecting their home, and Titan protecting their dreams. Titan had died years ago and while Michael had been happy to believe in a doggy heaven, the very idea of him standing guard in dreamland just seemed too make believe. Dana had always bought into it though, had always believed that Titan would come when she called. He was blown away by his own stupidity as he remembered all the times he had made fun of Dana for this very concept.

Dana had recognised Titan instantly. He really did protect their dreams.

The other thought, simpler but somehow more profound was the knowledge that even in the land of dreams his family could reach him when he needed them.

Michael answered simply, 'I'm smiling because we got out of there intact. And more importantly, if my nose is still working, your dad is cooking scrambled eggs.' Michael above all things lived in the moment. Wars could be won or lost in your dreams but hunger would always be what you woke up to.

* * *

The smell of bacon and eggs wafting through the house threw all of their concerns into the background as they raced each other to the kitchen. Ashley who had jostled herself into the lead grabbed Michael into a fierce but brief bear hug, letting go to mess up his hair in a decidedly condescending fashion. Michael wondered to himself if he was ever going to become anything other than the baby of the family. Dana was twenty months older than Michael and Ashley a mere fourteen months. He'd been a head taller than both of them though since he had been twelve. But it seemed to make no difference. He knew the brief hug and ruffled hair was her way of saying *thank-you* and was way more than he felt he deserved.

Families looked out for each other. In Michael's view, it was in the job description and he didn't think he was in line for any promotions based on last night's performance. He knew he wouldn't allow it to happen again but he would still have to find a way to apologise to the girls. Once breakfast was done he would need to talk to them. He needed to ask them a big favour, to bend some rules. Michael thought that 'stretching the rules past breaking point' was probably more accurate but he had noticed something just before the crash of lightning had thrown them out of the dream and it was something that he needed to address.

* * *

Michael's stomach announced his presence as he entered the kitchen, and being the adolescent young teenager he was, food became his only immediate priority.

'Thought you guys might be hungry, hope scrambled eggs are okay?' Uncle Brent was one of a kind. He loved to cook and concocted all sorts of amazing dishes. If Michael had answered 'Actually I feel like eggs benedict' Uncle Brent's head would have ducked back into the fridge, face beaming and unerringly come out with all the necessary ingredients. No problem. But today scrambled sounded like just what the doctor ordered.

Michael happily took a double serve of bacon and noticed Dana going back for a second helping of hash browns. They all seemed to have worked up quite an appetite because Ashley, who normally struggled with a couple of pieces of toast, had loaded her plate as well.

Aunt Sarah was sipping on her first coffee of the morning when they sat down for breakfast, distractedly finishing up a telephone call. Michael judged that it wouldn't be long before she was starting on her second cup. She didn't just look tired, she looked ill. There were dark circles under her eyes; she was unusually pale and her normally bright hazel eyes were a dull brown. It took her a couple of moments, as if she were trying to compose her thoughts, before she got up and sat with them at the table.

'Kids, that was your dad on the phone, checking to see how you slept.' Sarah only then seemed to take in the plates piled with food. 'You all seemed to have worked up an appetite. Tell me you weren't up all night watching the storm?'

The three of them exchanged a glance, trying to work out how much to say. Up until that point Michael had felt sure his aunty would have somehow shared in the dreams, or at least parts of it. He was certain he had felt her presence.

Given that his mother hadn't rung, Michael guessed that neither Sarah nor Nicola had any clear recollection of what had gone on the previous night. This was a bonus that Michael hadn't expected. He knew that they had to talk to their parents, and he would, he just needed to get one thing sorted out first. An open and honest exchange with them would have to wait a few hours.

He would only get one chance.

Jumping in to forestall any possible complications caused by Dana's usual need to talk things through, Michael answered for them all.

'Busted, Aunt Sarah. I kept them both up half the night.

You know how easy it is to spook Ash when there's a thunderstorm.' Michael was ready to continue waffling on but his aunt just nodded, mumbling something about thinking she might lay down for a little bit if nobody minded as she was feeling decided off colour.

Sarah started to walk towards her bedroom, but Dana stopped her, at which Michael cursed.

'Are you okay Aunt Sarah?'

'Don't worry about me. I just didn't sleep well last night. I dreamt badly but I just can't remember what it was about. I can't focus on anything. I keep thinking it will come to me, that I almost have it but it … slips away.' This statement was accompanied by a butterfly like hand gesture. Michael thought his aunt was going to get distracted examining her own hands when she continued, 'When the three of you walked into the room this morning, I almost had it. It was so close but then it just, well goes … My mind fills with so many different images, I get completely sidetracked. I probably need to take a leaf out of your mother's book and go back to bed.' Dana threw Michael a superior 'I knew there was something up' glance.

Aunt Sarah was already moving in the direction of her room when Dana gently held her arm. 'Aunty Sars, What do you mean? Isn't Mum well either?'

'Oh no sweetie, no need to worry, when your dad called earlier …' Here she paused again as if thinking. 'I did tell you he called earlier didn't I? Anyway … Joe mentioned that your mum was sleeping soundly. Apparently he remembers her getting up at some point during the night but this morning she didn't even stir, so he's left her to sleep in a bit. So it looks like the storm must have kept us all awake.' The little eye contact that had been maintained during this conversation was broken and without further comment Aunty Sarah shuffled off to her bedroom and closed the door. Dana and Michael both looked towards Ashley to see if this seemed as off-kilter to her as it did to them and Ashley's face told the story. The tightening around her eyes and mouth spoke volumes.

Ashley asked her father, who was busily washing the dishes, 'Are you sure Mum is okay? Maybe you should take her to the doctor. She doesn't seem right.'

Michael had mentally added 'in the head' to the question. It wasn't polite but his aunty wasn't just acting 'not right' she was acting 'not right in the head' – there was a huge distinction. He had turned to follow his aunt's progress when Brent's response drew his eye back to the immediate conversation.

'Sorry Ash … I missed that … Did you want something for breakfast? I can make eggs.'

'It's fine, we've already eaten.' Ashley grabbed Dana by one hand and Michael by the other and dragged them towards her room. Michael winced at her grip but decided not to mention anything about his hands yet. She appeared stressed enough.

'What the hell is going on? They are acting like complete morons. They can't remember what they did five minutes ago let alone answer any questions. Should we get your mum over? I don't know … call an ambulance? Maybe they have had a stroke?'

'Ashley, both of them, I don't think so! Your dad was fine to cook eggs with all the trimmings without any problems. He just doesn't seem able to answer any direct questions. I think we need to go check my mum and dad first, so we can get some idea of what's going on, then work out what to do. It may be that after some sleep they'll be fine.' Dana had already thrown on clothes ready to walk home.

Michael nodded his agreement. He understood the impact of not getting a decent night's sleep. Anyway, he had no objections, he wanted to go home anyway. He was just planning a small detour along the way.

* * *

Michael rushed back to Ashley's room, eager to get moving, unsure how to tell the girls what he had planned. He was reaching for his shirt when Dana cried out, 'Look at your hands, what happened to them? They're burnt!'

Michael didn't want Dana to let his hands delay things. He needed her calm so he could start convincing her to break some rules. Dana, being the one most respecting of authority, would be the hardest to convince. Considering he was proposing breaking and entering he would have to tread gently.

'They're not really burnt Dana, they're just a bit stiff, sore. More like I've had them in hot water.'

'These are burns! You're lucky they haven't blistered!' Dana gently checked his fingers, then the palms on each hand. They were both equally scalded up to the wrist where the burn stopped almost in a straight line. 'Ash, go get some of your dad's cream. He must have made one up for burns.'

When Ashley had left the room, Dana softly asked, 'You got those saving us didn't you? When you reached through that damned invisible barrier, you got these burns?'

Michael didn't want to answer, the shame of having left them alone made his jaw clench. His whole body tensed and he moved to pull his hands away so he could continue dressing. Michael knew that was exactly where he had burnt his hands. He could remember the penetrating cold as he reached through and grabbed the girl's wrists. It had felt like blades of ice slicing into his hands.

The real concern now was how easily injuries received in a dream could translate back into the waking world. He now understood that they were all extremely lucky to have made it out of there with minor burns as the only visible reminder.

Dana had seen the look on Michael's face and her heart hurt with the pain she knew he was dealing with, however he may try to hide behind anger. Holding gently but firmly onto his hands she held his gaze and said, 'Micky, thank you! We were lost without you.'

'You almost were anyway!' Michael pulled his hands away.

'You're the hero in this. You saved the both of us.'

'I think you best save the "hero" for your knight in shining armour. I seem to be a better runner.' Resentment and anger vied for position in Michael's emotions. None of this could he hide from his sister.

'Buddy, you pulled us both through a barrier that we couldn't even budge. How did you do that?'

'I had help! Can we drop it?'

At that point Ashley came back into the room with a jar of cream which Michael massaged into his hands. It tingled at first and there was a strange crawling sensation as if the cream were working its way under the surface. But his skin soon felt less raw and the taut, tight feeling had gone. Michael flexed his hands, testing the movement. Maybe dream injuries healed differently because even his mum and her healing hands didn't work that fast.

* * *

While Ashley had been off hunting for hand cream she had taken a moment to check that her parents were okay. Having established that, unless she actually tried to have a conversation with them, they seemed perfectly fine. She was able to process all that had happened last night and had managed to work herself up into quite a state. She felt Dana's concern and Michael's misplaced anger when she walked back into the room but forced herself to hold onto her enthusiasm. She uncharacteristically waited while Michael flexed his fingers, noticing with relief that the movement was smooth and then burst out in an almost ecstatic fashion.

'We must have beat them!' Ashley exclaimed. 'Guys, can you believe it?'

Dana and Michael stared back at her not yet catching on.

'Can't you feel it? Things are back to normal. Sure, Mum and Dad are a bit goofy at the moment but I'm sure with a bit of rest that will all pass. That damned oppressive tension has eased.'

Michael stopped for a moment to take in what she had said. Ashley had a point: things did feel different, almost normal. He'd been labouring for days under the same tense dark cloud that he had not noticed until it had been lifted. But he wasn't convinced that they had won. A single battle, maybe, but Michael was certain that last night had only been round one. He suspected a lot of the shift in atmosphere had to do with the approach of the riders but it was not something easily explained.

He had no chance to try, since Dana had caught some of Ashley's enthusiasm. Her attention had finally shifted from his hands and for that Michael was thankful. He sat cross-legged on the floor a couple of paces away as Dana reached under her pillow to retrieve the painting. It had become her morning ritual to return the painting to its frame.

Dana gasped and she dropped both the painting and the frame.

By instinct, Michael checked the area, finding no obvious threat. And then his gaze finally settled on Dana. She was staring down at his hands. Her shock had been replaced with amazement. Following her lead, Michael looked to see what had so caught her attention.

He had caught the frame and the painting inches from the ground. When he'd heard her intake of breath he had been over a metre away, with pillows, blankets and other sleepover remains scattered all over the floor between them. There had been no clumsiness, his feet had known the right places to land and his hands had reached out without intervention to catch both the frame and the painting. He didn't think he'd even looked as he made the grasp for them.

He was fast, but not that fast. His mind flicked back to catching Madison's lead yesterday. That had been a moving target but he'd still made the catch. This was taking things up a notch. He shouldn't have been able to make the distance, not from a sitting position.

They exchanged a 'what the?' look. Michael realised that the oppression may have lifted but he wouldn't go so far as to describe things back to being any kind of normal he recognised. Yes the tension had eased, but that didn't quite weigh out the fact that Ashley's parents were walking and talking zombies, Michael had just made an impossible catch and he was sporting injuries that he'd received in a dream. Not to mention the fact that before Dana had been amazed by his catch she had been shocked by something she had seen in her picture.

Normal, he thought not.

Embarrassed by the attention on him, Michael chose diversion as his best tactic.

'Hey, I'm not lining up to become a member of the Prince Charming fan club but he doesn't deserve to be on the floor like a piece of rubbish. He saved our arses last night.' Dana looked at Michael and gave a tiny shake of her head.

Michael had done his fair share of saving arses but there would be no convincing him. He would either work it out for himself or he would continue to beat himself up about things. It was not something she had much control over. Dana knew she had to let him work it out on his own.

Michael noted Dana's disapproval. He had endured a life of suggestive and corrective body language from the females in his family. The head shake she threw his way, although not exactly subtle, was easily ignored. He had no intention of wasting time debating things with her when the result would be to agree to disagree anyway.

Time felt like it was slipping away from him. He glanced down to see what Dana had reacted so strongly to.

Previously the painting had a mounted warrior in shining armour, with flaming sword ready to strike, and a black stallion captured in the moment of rearing, challenging all who would dare come before them.

No longer did a single rider sit on a rearing horse: he was accompanied by a group of men, all of them now riding hard.

The lead rider was frozen, looking out towards whoever would be viewing the painting. His face looked tired and drawn. The horse he rode was covered in lather, with flecks of foam around its mouth, head hanging down, not held as proudly as it had originally been. The lead rider stared straight out of the picture with a burning determination that humbled Michael. The men that rode behind him all shared the same look of resolve. Only Michael noticed the grey horse that ran without a rider off to the left of Dana's hero.

The grey horse from his dreams was in the painting, he knew that for certain. Her eyes held a searching quality that the other horses lacked. It was this very aspect of the horse's gaze that forced Michael to hand the painting back to Dana. Michael was scared that if their eyes should meet, he would be dismissed. Just as he had dismissed the horse from his dreams these many years. He couldn't deal with that right now, not on top of everything else. He had plans for the rest of the day and he would need all the focus he could muster.

'Look at him! Just look at him! He looks half dead. What's happened?' Dana turned around, her eyes wide, and all the talk of things being normal quickly vanished.

'He's supposed to be our hero, right? So why does he look so wasted?' Ashley was now standing next to Dana, reaching for but not quite touching the painting.

Michael couldn't believe what she'd just said. The misplaced anger he had felt earlier became justified. Didn't she realise, he looked 'wasted' because he had ridden through worlds to save them. He looked 'wasted' because he had put his life on the line to rescue people he didn't even know and now he was getting criticised because he no longer look like the pin-up boy from one of her magazines.

'Are you serious? Ashley, we didn't win anything last night. We survived with our arses still attached because he got us out. He has a right to look "wasted" and just for the record he isn't ours, Ashley. I don't know why he's helping us but don't start claiming some kind of ownership.' Michael was breathing heavily now and he could feel the veins in his forehead throbbing. He had punctuated the word 'wasted' with condescending air quotation marks and he now had his finger pointed aggressively towards Ashley. He forced himself to lower his hand and turn away. He knew that he'd overreacted but he felt personally offended by her remark. *What exactly did they expect?*

'All I'm saying is a little gratitude wouldn't go astray.' Michael sat on the edge of Ashley's bed and dropped his head, elbows resting on his knees, all the anger drained from him. He had seen Ashley's face. She hadn't meant it the way it sounded but Michael had no intention of apologising. Knowing he'd overacted didn't mean that what he had said had been wrong.

Michael temporarily having the upper hand decided there was never going to be a better time to hit them with his plan. There was no way he was going to be able to make his request sound anything less than crazy but now that he was on the front foot he might as well give it a try.

He raised his eyes to ensure he had made eye contact, and deliberately interrupted Ashley as she began to explain herself. He hit them with the inevitability that had come into being when he had seen his boots hanging around Marcus' neck in the final moments of last night's dream.

'Guys, I'm going over to Marcus' to get my boots back.' Both girls jumped up in protest. He focused only on Dana because she would be the one that needed the most convincing, the one least likely to break the rules and in this case, the law.

'This isn't just some ego thing. Last night, in the dream just before I woke up, I was looking directly at Marcus. After all his smiling and gloating, when I heard the hooves and I had an idea of what was coming, I watched Marcus. I suppose I was savouring the moment for a change. Can you blame me after what he's put me through lately?' He looked at the girls, trying to see if they understood.

'It was the first time I had seen him uncertain, and actually scared. And when the sound of hooves became overwhelming he started stroking something hanging from around his neck, almost like you would a cross or a lucky rabbit's foot. It was my soccer boots. I think he's able to take strength from me. In the dream, and after last night maybe here too.' He looked at them both to make sure they were listening, to make sure they realised how important this was, how everything was becoming interconnected.

There was no doubt – their identical frowns confirmed they were both taking him seriously.

'They act as some kind of conduit. I think because those boots mean a lot to me. That's probably why he stole them in the first place, as a way to get to me.' He looked at Dana and her face had a hard look to it, knowing she had a lot to do with why the boots were so special.

'It freaks me out completely. I need to get my boots back today. Your parents are goofed out and we won't get a better opportunity.'

'We've been expressly forbidden from going anywhere near them. Mum believes they're dangerous, unless you've forgotten,' Dana reached up and touched the bandage, 'they've proven themselves to be exactly that.'

'She told us to keep away from the neighbours. Marcus and his family go out on Sunday mornings, every Sunday, and we know it isn't somewhere local because it takes them half the day. And their car comes back covered in mud. So we're not going near them. We are *not* breaking our promise.'

'Mum would never allow you to go over there.'

'No shit! But still I have to go. Look at your hero, Dana.

He needs help and I can't do that with Marcus hanging off me like a leech through those boots. And I think if he's sucking energy from me, he's sucking energy from all of us, parents included.' Michael pointed towards the lounge were Ashley's dad sat watching TV.

Dana wasn't going to make this easy for him. 'Nice try, Michael, but you seem to be doing a pretty damn good job to me, boots or no boots. You ran through barriers that flung us around like rag dolls. Tissue paper would have proved more of a deterrent to you. Catching things from over a metre away. These may be unusual circumstances but that doesn't mean we will sit back while you break and enter!'

'You're right,' Ashley said and Michael threw her a betrayed look. 'But my parents are sitting around like the village idiots and if there's any chance that there's some kind of energy drain, well I have no choice by to go with Michael. Are you coming with us or not?' Ashley turned to Dana with hope in her eyes. Michael just looked on, shocked that anybody was coming with him.

'I was getting there, Ashley. Give me some credit. I just wanted you both to take a moment to think it through. Now we've done that.' She faced her brother with a look of determination that would give the riders a run for their money. 'It has to be soon. We know Marcus and his family leave early and we want to be sure we're in and out before they return.'

'Let's go.' Michael was already striding towards the door, not wanting them to change their minds.

'Sheba's coming with us. I'm not going in there without her. Mum said there was something ... wrong over there, and we have more than enough reason to believe she's right. We get your boots and find out whatever we can while we're there. We won't get another chance.' Dana was obviously given up any reticence and was now fully committed.

* * *

It just could not believe Its luck. First It had been released after centuries of imprisonment. Just as those barriers that were created at the same time of Its captivity start to fail, unwitting souls, descendant of Its very captors, no less, bring It to a place of power, a place where evil already resided. Evil that is more than willing to help facilitate Its complete release. It is returned to the world in a time when minds roam the second realm unguarded, unaware that evil has once again joined them. And now after Its first miscalculation, Its first bitter taste of defeat, It sensed in the ether that those who brought about that very first failure, Its enemy, Its very oppressors were about to venture into Its seat of power. They had actually broadcasted their intention, allowing It time to prepare. The minds of the parents were easy to manipulate. They had been so severely drained by the battle, that with a little bit of interference, they were barely able to walk in a straight line. One still lay comatose. Weak fools.

But the offspring, thinking themselves so grown, so calculating, had deemed it safe to venture into Its domain because the family that resided there would not be home.

Just when It thought Its golden opportunity had been lost, another even greater one presented itself. Such arrogant imbeciles to come before It, close enough for It to drain them completely. A chance to destroy the Enemy's children in their more vulnerable form.

It was too delicious a thought. When It destroyed them It would have all the energy It needed to enter the first realm. It would have their life force which It knew was more than enough power to make the jump. And then without constraint It would drain every last descendant of the cursed enemy and then move on unopposed.

It had promised the parents they would pay through their children. In this It had not lied.

Reconnaissance

As the three of them walked back discussing strategies for the upcoming introduction to criminal activity they noticed that things were indeed far from being back to normal. The closer they got to home the more off-kilter things felt. Describing something beyond more than the standard five senses was no easy thing, so they didn't, or couldn't, speak of what they were feeling. Michael's apprehension mingled with more than a measure of fear unsettled him slightly. Whether it was the promise he had made himself to stop running or the change he had felt during the dream, he didn't know but he kept walking, determined to keep his resolve.

* * *

Dana was the one struggling the most. She didn't want to appear weak so she kept walking, and tried not to tremble. But she was being bombarded by strong emotions. Dana had always had an affinity with animals; she could read whether a dog was aggressive or just annoyed by the angle of its head. She had thought that she was just a good observer, attuned to the body language of animals. She knew zookeepers could read their charges, so was it so strange that she could read the animals she lived with. But what she experienced as she walked towards home was something completely different. She was being bombarded with the emotional signatures of the animals in the neighbourhood although she couldn't see any of them. She could somehow feel the panicked beating of a bird's fluttering heart, racing near to bursting, so terrified by strange impulses it could not comprehend that it would fly or die trying to escape. Dogs paced the fence of their homes looking for intruders, looking for weak points, stopping their pacing only to dig at the ground, trying to create a way to escape. Cats moved to the edges of their domain, finding a place where they could hide, sensing a predator was out there somewhere. These emanations were coming to Dana like stray radio signals on an old transistor radio, signals fading in and out. Strong one minute, disjointed the next, and from so many directions in so many different forms that she was struggling to keep track of her own emotions.

Could the doll be causing this too? Could its circle of influence cause this strange by-product? This idea didn't feel quite right. On some level her increased awareness was more akin to Michael's ability to move quickly when threatened. Something was changing them, enhancing them, and she believed it was the riders. They were closer now and maybe they'd brought these changes with them.

The three of them quickly rounded the corner and walked up the street. Michael strode confidently a pace or two ahead, Dana one step behind, head jerking as she tried to cover every direction at once. Ashley followed behind too, a hand rubbing against her temple as if trying to soothe a headache.

Dogs howled their distress and cats were perched in trees, tails bristling, defensively hissing down from the branches. Of the birds that usually flew so vocally overhead, there was no sign. Dana's senses couldn't pick up what was causing the animals distress but she felt a mounting tension building inside her regardless. Her pace had dropped as they entered their street, and she came to a standstill.

'My God, it's so oppressive. I'm finding it difficult to breathe. It just creeps up on you – then bam – you feel exhausted. Are you guys feeling this too?'

'It's the doll isn't it? I started to notice it when we turned the corner.'

'You've both been dragging your feet the last block,' Ashley said. Dana might be able to read animals but Ashley read people.

'Yeah, I think you're right. I want to test the theory. A couple of minutes won't hurt and Marcus is still home anyway.' Dana pointed up the street. You could see the house from where they were standing. A silver Lexus was parked in the driveway. 'They always leave the BMW and take the Lexus.'

Michael nodded his agreement. They routinely left early on a Sunday morning, and generally returned late in the evening. And the silver Lexus always returned looking to have done some hard driving. By Monday afternoon the car was freshly detailed, washed, with the rims polished, and the tyres blacked. Michael had always admired how the father looked after his car, somewhat obsessive but it was a nice vehicle so he respected that. Now it seemed ominous. What had he been trying to hide? Well perhaps when they finally got into their house they would find out.

* * *

Dana had noticed that the tension built as she got closer to home. She wanted to make sure it was not just her mind playing tricks on her. Her apprehension about breaking into Marcus' house was causing her heart rate to skyrocket. Only by retracing their steps would they be sure that the oppressive tension was related to home. They couldn't do anything until Marcus had left and this would serve both to test her theory and keep an eye out for the Lexus. By walking back to Ashley's and then a couple of blocks beyond, they were able to monitor both the animals as well as their own behaviour.

The weight and tension that had slowly built just as slowly eased. Birds flew overhead whistling to each other, cats sat on porches watching intently as strangers passed through their domain then returned to grooming or just basking in the sun. The level of influence seemed to be directly proportionate to the distance from home. Dana smiled. It explained a lot. It even explained Madison's strange behaviour yesterday. Satisfied, Dana gritted her teeth, readying herself for the animal's distress as she walked back towards home.

She didn't like what this particular experiment proved but knowledge was supposed to be power. They now knew how far the strange influence could reach. It extended to a couple of houses past Ashley's just short of the park and then quite abruptly stopped. It meant that Ashley's house was within the sphere of influence and therefore no safe haven.

* * *

Ashley was watching the faces of those they passed, trying to see if anybody else felt the tension. It soon became abundantly clear that this area was being avoided. The number of people out for a Sunday stroll was noticeably less when within the doll's radius. Those few out walking, hurried down the opposite side of the road, looking back over their shoulders as they quickly put as much distance between themselves and Michael's family's neighbourhood.

It would have been funny to watch if she had been oblivious to the source of the distress and were not feeling so suffocated by the tension herself. Couples strolling along happily would suddenly jerk into a funny kind of power walk, then lift into a stuttered jog, trying to look in all directions at once. It was as if they could not admit to themselves that they just wanted to run away. Ashley knew Michael would empathise with them completely. Logic was fighting a losing battle with the instinct to run and that loss of control was not a comfortable feeling. A middle-aged women in a t-shirt and jeans, jog-ran towards them, eyes darting in every direction. Ashley moved aside to allow the woman to run past them but she obviously felt the gap was insufficient, so she left the footpath and ran down the side of the road.

* * *

Dana was so overwhelmed by the vast amounts of turmoil emanating from the animals around her that she was taken by surprise when a dirty white cat flew out of the bushes in her direction. The cat showed none of the feline grace the species was known for, instead favouring its front paw as it ran. Its fur bristled where it wasn't matted and brown. Pausing, the cat shook its front paw as if trying to dislodge some annoyance. Dana managed to scoop the cat up into her arms and held it tightly, trying to soothe the animal's distress. She felt the tiny heart pounding within its chest.

As Dana stroked the cat she soon realised the brown stains covering its fur were not the oil from lying under a car as she had at first suspected but were actually dried blood. It was covered in a multitude of fine thin cuts, looking like it had dragged itself through barbed wire.

So wrapped up in the animal's pain Dana barely heard Michael when he said, 'Isn't that Marcus' cat?'

* * *

When they left Ashley's house it had seemed almost exhilarating. Michael felt like a character in a movie, travelling behind enemy lines, accessing strengths, exploiting weaknesses. *Mission Impossible* kind of stuff. But his hands were still greasy from hand cream used to heal the burn inflicted from reaching through magical barrier, and they were further slickened by the layer of nervous sweat that now covered his body. He purposefully rolled his shoulder back, took a deep breath, and forced his hands to flex. The skin on his hands, previously almost healed, grew painfully taut. When he recognised the cat in Dana's hands, Michael felt a moment of uncertainty. The animal was in a terrible state.

As Dana's fingers delicately combed through the matted fur, more and more abuse became evident. The skin was scored with a network of fine precise cuts, some scabbed over, almost healed, while others still wept a thin watery fluid.

Michael was no expert, but he knew a thin blade of some sort had been run repeatedly over the poor creature's back.

'Michael, can you help with her front paw.' Dana's voice betrayed the nausea she was trying to suppress.

Michael reached forward and wrapped his hands around the cat's left front paw. The cat flinched but whether it sensed he meant it no harm, or the residue of Brent's cream soothed it, the cat allowed its paw to be held. The skin had been chaffed raw by the thin rope tied around the front leg. The white skin was swollen and bruised where it had obviously tried to pull itself free.

Dana spoke gentle words and carefully removed the rope from around the cat's paw.

And then, suddenly bristling, the cat jumped out from Dana's hold and disappeared into the bushes, just as a four-wheel drive raced down the street towards them.

Michael's heart skipped a beat as the woman who'd run down the edge of the road was forced to jump back onto the nature strip. She was never in any real danger but the driver of the Lexus had deliberately made it closer than it needed to be. Marcus' family had been so focused on giving the jogger a scare that they didn't notice Michael, Dana and Ashley on the periphery of their vision.

The three of them stood looking at each other dumbfounded.

Dana held a piece of frayed rope in her hand. 'She chewed through the rope to get away.' Dana spoke in a quite measured way, defying the tears that beaded her lashes. Ashley wrapped her arms around her cousin.

'Dana?' Michael asked, finding it was hard to conceive the reality of the animal's abuse.

'You think we should reconsider?' Dana spat in anger. 'Are you joking? We get in, we get out. But we cannot let these *people,*' Dana spoke the word like a curse, 'have any hold over you.'

In some kind of strange confirmation the animals in the street started making more noise. Sheba and half the other dogs in their street could now be heard. They weren't barking madly as dogs sometimes did when a siren sounds in their vicinity, this instead was the barking usually reserved for the middle of the night – part whine, part howl. Dana could feel the warnings in the howls around her but she would not let them sway her. She could not let her brother's fate be left to such dangerous hands. Tears still hung from her lashes but she chose to draw strength from the animals' voices. Her posture changed, she squared her shoulders and took the lead walking up the street.

* * *

Michael took in another deep breath and this time clenched his fists in defiance of the taut skin. Sweat trickled down his back as he matched his pace with his sister and cousin.

He couldn't believe they were actually planning on sneaking into their neighbour's house. What were they thinking? These people tortured animals. Michael remembered how he had felt when he almost discovered the doll hiding in his backpack. He was certain that if it had dropped out onto the floor instead of just some socks he would have run out of his room with Dana alongside him. Michael reminded himself of the abject terror he felt when he'd been unable to get to the girls during the previous night's dream. He played back in his mind's eye the look on his mother's face when she tried to explain how she had felt when in Marcus' house. Alone and isolated. She had made them promise to stay away.

Doubts were starting to creep in. Maybe his mother had already found out what was going on. She had asked him to wait a couple of days, to give her that time to work things out. He knew Nicola was planning on doing something to gain insight into their situation. Her kooky side had always been a bit of a not so private joke. Michael had the thought that maybe they should check with her first before they took this decidedly huge step. She had called to him in the dream. She had reached out to him and fed him strength when he needed it. He was just about to mention all of this when Ashley spoke, echoing his own concerns.

'Michael, you're not having second thoughts are you?'

He said nothing. He'd feel like a git saying it out loud.

'We get Michael's boots, but anything weird and we're out of there, okay?' Dana's eyes burned with the anger she felt at what had been done to the cat. She was scared of what could happen to Michael.

Dana said, 'Surely Mum would have called and told us if she had found out something, wouldn't she?'

He glanced towards Dana, saw her push her hair behind her ears for the tenth time in about as many seconds and nodded in agreement. She looked determined, her eyes focused – and the hair twitch was the only sign of any nerves.

'We have to do this, buddy. Last night, Ashley and I experienced firsthand what you've been dealing with for weeks. Just now I held in my hands a defenceless animal, tortured for some sick purpose we have no ability to understand. I know we can't stop it by going next door. I'm not that naïve. But we can get your boots back and I think we *need* to get your boots back as soon as possible.' Dana wrapped her hand around Michael's arm. 'Micky, I just cannot leave you exposed to them any longer.'

Michael pushed his apprehension aside and embraced the relief of finally taking action towards something rather than running away from it.

* * *

Sheba quietened as soon as Dana's feet touched the path leading down the side of the house. Michael could hear Dana whispering softly to her even before they reached the gate. As soon as the latch lifted, Sheba nosed her way through and joined them in the front yard. Bumping against everyone, pushing her head up under Dana's hand for reassurance. She managed to lick Michael's hands at the same time but stopped when the taste of the Uncle Brent's cream kicked in.

They had decided that they needed a cover story just in case they were caught breaking in, one that included Sheba. And no-one denied the reassurance a huge black Doberman provided.

Michael threw one of his balls over the fence. If anybody asked, they were just going in to retrieve it. Seemed plausible enough to him. It had happened often enough before Marcus moved in. Michael had become a little more careful when balls were returned deflated. Taking Sheba would also give them additional cover if anybody found them in the house. Part two of their cover story, even more ridiculously flimsy, was that somehow Sheba had gotten into the house and the three of them were just getting her out before she did any damage. Michael was positive that no-one would buy the story. But would the truth be any easier to believe? Sometimes implausibility was on your side.

When you live in the suburbs, kids often jumped each other fences to retrieve balls. They lived in a street where the lawns were always mowed, the flowerbeds blended into each other with little distinction from one property line to the next. The trees soared only slightly higher than the oversized aerials on the roofs of second storey houses. People waved to each other as they walked past. No-one would look twice as three kids jumped a gate. It was all very suburban.

Michael decided to go first. It was a standard paling gate, there more to separate the front garden from the back than for any measure of security. And it wasn't going to be hard to get over. Michael had no problem with the initial jump. He grabbed the top of the gate to pull himself up, shifting his hand position for balance and jerked his hand back as a sharp pain tore into his palm. With a little more care Michael tried to get a hold that didn't hurt quite so badly. Michael hauled himself up, swearing profusely the whole time.

* * *

As he sat poised ready to jump down to the other side, Michael saw the small sharp pieces of wire that had been hammered into the top of the gate. His cursing intensified – what kind of sick twisted individuals would secure their house in such a way, this was no suburb ruled by gangs? Did he have spring traps in the flowerbeds to look forward to? Balancing between the fence and the gate, Michael had a better vantage point from which to inspect what had torn his hand open and he whistled, mentally thanking whoever must have guided the placement of his second grip. Safe handholds were few and far between up there. Glass shards had been embedded amongst the wire. He'd been very lucky.

Shaking his head, Michael wiped the blood dripping from his palm onto the front of his t-shirt and unlocked the gate without bothering to bitch and moan. He wouldn't get much pity from the girls; they were all too tightly wound. Sheba at least gave him a nudge as she pushed by. Dana and Ashley were so wrapped up in their impersonation of normal kids retrieving a ball that they walked past without noticing the blood that now streaked his top.

* * *

It was all really quite easy. The laundry door wasn't even locked. This saved one of them from having to squeeze through the cat flap. So without any further incident they found themselves inside the kitchen.

Michael had been in there before, but that was when the Adcocks had lived there. They'd been nice people. And like most kitchens he'd ever been in, theirs had been warm and welcoming. This kitchen was the same, nothing had been changed structurally but all personality had been removed. There were no tea towels hanging off the oven door, no school books on the bench and the fridge was no longer covered in family pictures. It felt like a place of study rather than the centre of a home where family gathered to talk about what had happened during the day. Michael could imagine things being tested and analysed here, maybe even dissected but not prepared and cooked.

As they walked through the house, everything continued to feel *wrong*.

They headed up the stairs, the sound of their footsteps dulled by the heavy carpeting underfoot. They went straight for where they thought Marcus' room would be. The place seemed dark and cold. Sunlight was streaming in through the windows but it didn't seem to warm the rooms.

Sheba walked right beside Dana. Not running ahead, not jumping all over the furniture, not acting as any normal happy-go-lucky dog should when faced with a new area to explore.

And somehow, most unsettling of all, it didn't smell right. All homes had their own distinctive smell; it's the signature of the family that lives there – a mottled combination of cooking smells, soap, aftershaves, perfumes, sometimes smoke from an open fire, scented candles, oils – all the smells of normal family life. And there's always that undefinable aspect, that elusive element that makes each house unique.

It took Michael a while to recognise what was wrong. Here there was no smell. Nothing.

It was the simple absence of this house's signature that screamed that while it was a house, it certainly was not a home. Small distinction maybe, but in this context it meant a lot. Michael couldn't pick up any scent at all and he only used his sense of smell to enhance his other senses. Sheba relied on hers as the primary method for analysing her environment. She tested the air and whined quietly, confirming she was equally unsettled.

Even though Michael could detect no discernible aroma there was something that made his nose tickle, almost burn, like when he'd been to the snow and his nose felt like it was about to bleed. It was so cold. Michael was finding it difficult to pinpoint the sensation because it also reminded him of walking into the chemistry room at school where the smell of ammonia and other unnamed substances left his nose wishing it was anywhere but attached to his face. He didn't know how to describe it, but Michael knew that Dana and Ashley were reacting to it as well, because more than once he saw them wipe at their faces and then inspect the backs of their hands afterwards as if they were expecting to see the tell-tale trace of blood that signified a nose bleed.

At this point, Michael again asked himself how much of a good idea this really was. It was only now on reflection that it occurred to him how easy their entry had been.

'Are we sure about this?' He paused to look closely as each girl making sure he had their attention. 'Are we even sure this is even *our* idea?' The girls just looked back and shook their heads. It had dawned on them too that maybe the force that was influencing the neighbourhood may have also been manipulating them.

'Too late now. We get your boots and we're out of here. I don't care if we find out anything else useful.' And with that, Dana reached forward and opened the door into Marcus' bedroom.

It was like walking into a vacuum.

The room looked as one would expect any young kid's room to look. All except for the fact that the room had no personal touches. It was the kind of room Michael had seen in department stores selling kids' furniture or a display home. No posters, no toys, no dirty socks or jocks thrown into the corner. It certainly didn't look like Michael's room that was for sure. There was one obvious exception to this rule, one personal touch. Michael's boots hung above the bed.

Ashley had moved to investigate a table in the corner covered by a cloth. *Black of course,* Michael thought, *what other colour would it be?* It was covering a variety of different things, undefinable purely by the shapes they created but noticeable as separate items all the same. Michael had a good idea of what one of the lumps would be.

Dana followed Ashley as she approached the table, huddled together, hesitant to get too close. Sheba was still walking next to Dana but a half pace behind. All of their apprehension levels grew as Sheba's perpetual whine deepened into a growl low in her throat. She sounded like a dog trapped in a corner, not aggressive but certainly unwilling to go down without a fight.

Michael retrieved his boots, slung them around his neck and walked over towards the girls, wanting to put himself between them and the table. He felt the cold, dark vacuum as he approached. Michael was struggling to breathe. The air was just too thin somehow. He saw Ashley reach up with one hand and brush it across her face again. This time her hand came away smeared with blood.

Something about the room had made them all unconsciously feel as though they were about to get a nose bleed, and now one of them finally had.

'Okay, Ashley, if you must see what's on that table, let's just get it done.' Dana reached over and pulled off the sheet.

The doll looked exactly the same, no bigger than it had in the shop. Nothing like how it had appeared in the dream. Next to the doll was a wooden bowl and behind that stood a mirror.

Michael's heart beat faster. The girls sucked in quick shallow breaths beside him. Sheba whined softly, her hackles raised and her body crouched as if anticipating an attack at any moment.

This was what they had all expected, since Marcus had first appeared in his dreams with the doll. Michael had known that it had somehow passed into his possession. There was nothing here to cause such slow mounting terror, no still beating heart lying on an altar, no dismembered head, no severed limbs. He could see a doll and a bowl. Cursing in frustration he hissed at the girls, 'Maybe we should have brought Dana's old Barbies and had a nice little dolly tea party.' But Michael knew there was a problem, he just couldn't pinpoint what that was.

'Michael, open your eyes, look at the mirror!'

As he did, there were three very frightened faces staring back at him. Ashley's nose bleed had gotten much heavier. She had been forced to hold her shirt sleeve against her face. But he was sure that was not what Dana had been referring too.

'I've got my boots – we're out of here. We have got to get Ashley home.'

Michael paused … finally understanding what his conscious mind had been trying to block out.

The image in the mirror was not an exact reflection of the room.

He could see the three of them clear as day but a second image shimmered there just below the surface. It was the landscape from the dream, the grey void they had barely escaped the previous night. It was clearly visible as if the reflection of the room they stood in was merely a window dressing and that the mirror held the true reality.

And as in his dreams, Michael watched on, impotent observer as his hand reached towards the shimmering image, reached with the hand that he had cut jumping the gate.

He could also see his enemy looking back at him. *Which should not be possible*, his mind screamed. The doll was facing them so the reflected image should have been the back of its head, not its face smiling broadly. And it was animated in this second reality in a way he never wished to see in his waking world. Adrenaline pumped into his bloodstream and Michael's already racing heart reached a new dangerous level. Through all this he looked on helplessly as he continued to reach forward and in silent parody the creature reached back towards him, mirroring his movements.

Its already wide smile extended as a drop of blood left Michael's hand, and instead of falling towards the tabletop, it flew straight towards the mirror, hitting right on the creature's image with a wet slap. Michael stood transfixed as his blood was slowly absorbed into the silvery surface. Before Michael could stop it, another drop left his hand to follow the other and more were sure to follow.

Michael realised his blood was being consumed by the creature and he forced down bile that rose in his throat.

As each drop of his blood was absorbed into the mirror, the reflected reality of the bedroom faded and the grey landscape became the clearer view. The other reality became closer. What would happen if more blood were to flow ... would the grey void take over? Something whispered in Michael's mind that that was not quite right, but it was pretty close. It was this realisation, this abject fear that allowed him to break the spell controlling his movements.

'Ashley, quick, get out of here!' Michael yelled. If his small wound could cause such a shift in the realities what would Ashley's pouring nose facilitate? Dana, having already come to the same conclusion, had positioned herself between the mirror and Ashley.

Some sort of balance had been disrupted. The two realities, now in conflict, caused an equilibrium shift and the basic laws of physics altered. Dana, being closest to the mirror was being drawn toward it. She reached out to stop her forward movement and her hand hit and then slid, not off the mirror, but through it. Her hand penetrated up to the wrist and the pain and fear the immersion caused was written all too clearly across her face.

Michael moved uncannily fast and wrapped his arms around her waist. A similarly intense scramble was being made by the doll to pull Dana through the mirror. Dana had braced herself against the edge of the table on which the mirror stood, but even with Michael holding her she continued to slip forward.

But Sheba had been pushed beyond any animal's endurance, her desperate whining giving voice to her terror. Fighting all of her instincts to run from this unnatural place, she thrust her head into the mirror and grabbed Dana's hand in her teeth. Her back legs scrabbled against the table as she struggled to find some purchase. With Michael's help they were able to break the mirror's hold. Sheba continued to drag Dana sideways, then took a guarding position until Michael was able to half carry, half drag Ashely and Dana out of the room.

Michael's backwards glance as he hauled the girls from the room was to see one final drop of his blood fly towards the mirror. This time instead of hitting and being slowly absorbed, the doll was able to break through the surface long enough to snatch the drop from the air.

Its cry of triumph followed them as they ran home.

* * *

Was it luck or planning that had made the Enemy bring their dog, litter mate to the guardian in the second realm? It had no doubt been warned. Well, no matter, It had not been able to gorge Itself as planned but the few drops of power that It had consumed left It light-headed and giddy. Their blood had flowed so deliciously freely and that little amount, so potent, had been enough to enable It to break, however briefly, through into the first realm. And there was no bolt of lightning, no hidden magic to sear Its true flesh. It was now certain that the barriers were almost down. That had been Its final concern. Could It survive in the first realm? Would Its true form survive? Now It had Its answer. No real magic remained. Time and energy were all that were required to complete Its release. And both seemed readily available. It may drain the family's offspring earlier than originally planned, for It no longer needed to preserve the child for use as a host. It had only to gather enough strength then It could simply walk through the mirror.

It screamed again in triumph, so that all with the power to hear would quake in terror, knowing Anarcus would soon be coming back into their world.

Comas and Crazy Neighbours

Michael struggled to get the girls out of the house. Their hasty retreat didn't go nearly as smoothly as their covert entry had done. Dana tripped on furniture. Ashley stumbled as she ran, hampered by her need to cover her face so she didn't leave a trail of blood throughout the house. Sheba circled them constantly, one minute in front of them, the next nipping at their heels, frantic for escape.

Michael hoped that the obstacles being placed in their path were purely a spiteful gesture and not through any reason for delay. The scream that still rang in his ears promised that they had escaped nothing and the trap had yet to be sprung, mocking his chances of getting the girls to safety. If he turned to look would he see that It had shucked off the remnants of the mirror? That It had clambered into their world and was just a couple of paces behind. Ready to grab the first who stumbled.

Fear clouded Michael's thinking and dulled his reflexes but he refused to turn and look over his shoulder. He knew if he succumbed to the voice in his head they would all be lost.

Michael saw the girls turn and he dragged them relentlessly forward. He had found something in his dream last night and he used it now to keep his eye fixed on his goal: outside, escape, home.

Michael stumbled out through the back door. He relied on instincts alone to guide his movements. All of his other senses couldn't be trusted. Furniture had moved to block his path. The floor had felt uneven under his running feet and the walls themselves seemed to warp around him. He ran with his hands clamped around the girls' upper arms, supporting their movements, guiding their steps.

Desperate to get the girls safely away, fearing the ground was about to open under his feet, Michael ran directly towards the back fence, the quickest way to get them out of there. Reluctantly releasing his bruising grip, he boosted the girls over the fence. As Dana dropped out of his line of sight he registered the bloody hand print that he had left on her upper arm and felt a moment of alarm. They must have left a blood trail through the house; the furniture had been strewn everywhere. There was no way they could pretend it never happened. But then again, the doll knew everything. Attempting to cover their visit to the house was pointless. The doll would tell Marcus' family they'd been there.

Certain that the girls were safe, Michael's focus shifted to Sheba. She ran whining along the fence, back and forwards, sniffing madly, torn between wanting to get to Dana and needing to protect Michael. Michael tried to direct her around towards the side gate where they had entered but he couldn't budge her. Before he had a chance to yell for assistance Dana called from her side of the fence. Only then did Sheba run towards their home, her stumpy tail pointed down, the closest she could get to having her tail between her legs.

Michael followed closely behind Sheba and gripped the boots hanging from around his neck. Michael locked the gate behind Sheba and doubled back to jump the fence. He wanted to follow Sheba; but he didn't feel like having to explain his appearance to any passers-by. The cover story of retrieving a ball wouldn't hold much water now that he was covered in blood and stunk from sweat that only outright terror could generate.

His feet had barely touched ground and he was already sprinting towards the open sliding door.

'Oh man, look at your hand!' Dana had already placed a cold pack on the bridge of Ashley's nose in an effort to stop the bleeding and now directed her concern towards Michael.

'Don't worry about my hand! Are you okay? Dana, you fell into the mirror!' Michael looked into her eyes and saw the pain she was trying to hide. Her hands were steady, but her voice was strained and her body posture showed everything. Her fear may have diminished but had yet to subside and the triage style approach she was taking to the situation was fooling no-one.

Dana mouthed the words 'Get Mum.'

Michael understood all too well the need to force control upon a situation that had spiralled so quickly away. He left the girls to run upstairs, where he hoped his mum would still be sleeping. He nearly crashed into Joseph as he came running down the stairs at the same time.

Michael searched for an explanation of his dad's sudden appearance but Joseph had already pushed past him rushing towards the kitchen. As Michael watched on dazed, Joseph picked up the phone with shaking hands. He fumbled for a dial tone and then slammed the phone down when he couldn't get one.

'Dad what's wrong … what's happened?' Michael felt an emotion he didn't want to acknowledge enter his voice. 'Dad, where's Mum?'

'Michael, what? Get my mobile … it's on the front table … call triple zero. Tell them to send an ambulance.' Joseph's olive complexion was pale and his eyes darted about with a *this can't be happening* kind of distraction. Tell them I can't wake your mother.'

Michael raced down to the front table, numbly grabbing his dad's mobile as instructed. He dialled twice before he saw the 'no service' message on the screen. Dana, having heard some of the commotion, was running up the stairs. Michael followed, his hand in the air hoping to get a signal.

What were the chances of both the landline and the mobile being out at the same time?

Michael knew the chances were slim. He intended to find reception from his parent's bedroom window anyway. The coverage was always best from the front of the house and if that didn't work, well then … well then … he would just have to run and get help.

In his parents' bedroom, as Michael saw his mother's face, for the first time in some time his footwork failed him. She lay on her bed, face deathly pale, one eye slightly open with a little bit of the white showing. Her feet were hanging over the edge of the bed, one more so than the other, as if she had fallen backwards when trying to get up.

It seemed staged, as if she were only pretending to be unconscious.

Michael registered Dana having followed him up the stairs. She had already run back from the bathroom with a wet face washer.

'Did you get through? Is the ambulance on its way?' His dad looked up at him from his kneeling position beside the bed. His voice held a note of pleading Michael couldn't remember ever hearing before.

Michael turned the phone towards Joseph as if in explanation. 'No service. I can't get any service.'

'Keep trying.' And then his dad lifted Nicola from the bed and started to carry her down the stairs.

He was on the first step when Michael saw her raise her arm. Joseph was halfway down the stairs with her when Michael heard her say, 'Always'. It was barely above a whisper but he knew she had said 'always'. He was at the bottom of the stairs before his father had even realised she was now conscious.

Dana burst into tears when Nicola said, 'Ashley baby, give me that cold pack, I've got a splitting headache.'

* * *

It took a lot of convincing, but Nicola was nothing if not persuasive. They left her to rest on the couch without getting an ambulance.

The telephone service returned shortly after that decision had been made, with their first call being to check on Aunt Sarah.

They were all been directed to clean themselves up before Aunty Sarah got there. She was notoriously squeamish. So with the gore washed away and clothing changed they just looked like shell-shocked survivors.

Michael had listened while his mother explained why an ambulance wouldn't be necessary. The conversation had been stilted, the pain in her head obviously still troubling her. And no-one wanted to push the issue too much while she was plainly having trouble focusing her thoughts.

Nicola would explain more fully when everyone was together.

Michael couldn't believe how things had spiralled out of control in less than a day.

Hell, a little over a week ago, soccer finals and some frightening dreams were all he had to be worried about. He had been sure that if he spoke about his dreams in too much detail he would come across as a complete nutbag. Do not pass *Go*, go straight to the loony bin, where backward buckled jackets were all the rage.

Now his mother had somehow been rendered unconscious asking an ancient book for the answer to a problem, a problem that had recently only held sway in his dreams but had now made the jump into the real world.

Michael wished that it had been as simple as insanity.

* * *

Michael decided to walk out the front to wait for his aunt and uncle. All of his unasked questions felt like a palpable accusation and he couldn't stand being cooped up with them any longer.

Fresh air couldn't hurt.

'Micky, we all decided to go next door.' Dana had followed him and sat beside him on the doorstep. 'You didn't force us. I'm the oldest. If anything I should have been the one to put a stop to the whole stupid thing. But what's done is done.'

While Michael heard the truth in Dana's words, he also heard the tremor in her voice.

But how could he explain to her that he should have stopped them, that he should have protected them, that it was somehow his duty to do so? Dana would take it as chauvinistic bullshit. But deep inside Michael knew better. Nicola had only risked the book at his request. Splitting her awareness between the book, and sending Michael all of her energy, may have been what almost broke her. He had asked for her help and she had put herself in a coma in an effort to provide it. He was doubly to blame.

'Remember this morning, when you were trying to tell me how much of a hero I was and I said I had help. Well, Mum was that help. I did this to her.' With this admission another wave of self-recrimination hit Michael. Twice now he had let them down and he resigned himself to the coming reproach. Michael wasn't quite prepared for Dana's anger.

'You're such an idiot.' Dana raised her voice. 'Did you somehow forget that you were not alone last night? Did you honestly think you were the only one she gave strength to? And for the record, Mum wasn't the only one helping, I felt Dad last night too and Aunt Sars and Uncle Brent all pouring their energy our way. You seem to be walking around under this misconception that this is all about you!' Dana was on a roll and was not about to let up.

'Sure, I give you the fact that up until today you have been hit the hardest. No doubt about that. But Michael, you ran through barriers that Ashley and I couldn't budge. Whether you realise this or not, you saved us last night and again today. You got me out of that ...' Michael was sure she was going to say 'mirror' but again he was wrong, ' ... room and you virtually carried Ash out of that house.'

* * *

Dana felt the effect of the last twenty-four hours take hold. She raised a shaking hand to brush the hair out of her face and sat for a moment to compose her thoughts. Mum always said Michael had a knight in shining armour complex. No-one could be as all sacrificing as he expected himself to be. Chivalry was certainly not dead in Michael but she wished it didn't come packaged in continual self-recrimination and pig-headed stubbornness.

Dana knew that given time and space he would ease up on himself and put the matter aside, not to rest, never that, but at least aside. She sat frustrated by Michael's stubborn attitude. Needing a distraction before Dana smacked him upside the back of his head, she decided to analyse the implications of what had happened today. Dana had started breaking things down into unemotive easy to handle chunks when all of her thoughts were pushed aside as Marcus' parents' car pulled up.

If Dana believed that her capacity to be shocked for the day had been reached, the assumption was blown away when she saw Marcus get out of the car. Deep down, she was ashamed to admit it: a part of her was pleased by what she saw. Marcus deserved some payback for his kick to Michael's knee. Everyone else might have forgotten but she still heard Michael's pain echoing in her head. Somehow what she saw didn't feel like justice. She wanted it to, but it felt so hollow.

Marcus' hands were bandaged past the wrists and his eyes had dark circles beneath them making his already pale complexion even more ashen. His parents also looked washed out. In normal circumstances she doubted she would have noticed anything further. She might have questioned their fashion sense. It was warm day yet the shirts they wore were heavy and loose fitting.

As they roughly pulled Marcus from the car, the mother's sleeves lifted slightly to reveal bandages just past her mid forearm.

'Oh God, Michael, I realise what that bowl is for.' Dana looked at her neighbours disbelievingly, talking in a whisper. 'They're bleeding themselves, Michael, to feed the doll. They're bleeding their own son.' Dana promptly turned and vomited into the bushes.

As soon as Marcus was out of the car, his parents' withdrew inside, and so Marcus hobbled towards the front door unaided. This was the boy who had stood by watching as an evil entity tortured him in his dreams night after night. He was, not to put an over dramatic spin on things, the enemy.

So why was Michael having to restrain himself from jumping the fence, pushing past the mother and smashing the father in the face for good measure? Why did he feel so damned gut-wrenchingly sad to see Marcus' pain? Michael's muscles thrummed with the energy that begged to be released. He had actually taken a step in Marcus' direction when Dana placed a restraining hand on his shoulder.

'You saw what happened when just a splattering of blood hit that mirror. Well what do you think will happen if three people let a lot more than a few drops find their way across to the other side?' Dana asked, her voice barely audible.

'His parents are happy to literally feed him, and themselves, to it, drop by drop. God, their cat! That explains the cat.' Dana face paled even further but this time she swallowed the bile down and pulled Michael away, back towards the step. She regretted her moment of pleasure when she saw Marcus' injuries. She wished her uncle and aunt would hurry up. How long did it take to drive a couple of blocks anyway?

* * *

As they sat waiting for Ashley's parents, still overwhelmed by their recent discovery, they watched as another scene unfolded in front of them. It appeared that the day was about to pull something else out of its never-ending bag of tricks.

Mr Jeffries, from a couple of houses up, came walking casually up the street, looking this way and that, like he was checking who was out and about today. It was still fairly early Sunday morning and things were quiet.

Mr Jeffries appeared to have had some troubles getting himself dressed that morning. Aunt Sarah would have said Mr Jeffries looked like he had gotten dressed in the dark. He had thrown a navy blue suit jacket over the top of his red and white flannel pyjamas. He was shuffling along in what were obviously his wife's fluffy pink slippers. If all this wasn't absurd enough, he must have put his toupee on backwards because it was perched on the top of his head as if it were about to sprout legs and bound down the street.

'Dana, please tell me you're seeing what I'm seeing?' With all that had happened today, topped with what he had just seen next door, he was once again not overly certain about his own perception of reality, let alone his own sanity.

'What the hell ... he's not about to do what I think he is, is he?' Dana looked back with a ghost of a smile hovering at the corners of her mouth.

Neither of them answered the other's question. They just sat and watched as Mr Jeffries walked up the Sanderson's neat patterned concrete driveway. Michael noticed the small paper bag Mr Jeffries was carrying. He had missed that small detail at first sight as he had been so transfixed by the renegade hairpiece. Mr Jeffries shuffled up the couple of steps to the Sanderson's porch and Michael watched as Mr Jeffries bent down, carefully placing the bag on the front mat, suspecting what was going to happen next.

'You have got to be kidding me ...' Michael managed to whisper. Mr Jefferies rummaged around in his suit jacket pocket and pulled out a lighter, lit the bag, rang the doorbell and shuffled away leaving one pink slipper on the porch step behind him.

Every kid knew the prank about lighting a bag of dog crap and waiting for the unsuspecting householder to come and stamp out the flames, even if most of them have never performed it themselves. They had heard kids brag about it, had seen it in the movies. But to see an adult execute this exact same stunt seemed almost unreal. Dana and Michael sat still for a moment, looked at each other and burst out laughing.

All of the pent up anxiety and fear chose this moment to come pouring out in a torrent of hilarity, leaning against each other laughing, waiting, trying desperately to stifle their amusement long enough to witness the front door open and see the prank reach its expected conclusion.

And then the simple joy of laughter was stopped dead in its tracks.

Mr Jeffries wasn't giggling merrily as Michael had expected. No-one was home and the door stayed shut. Mr Jeffries walked away with a face that showed barely contained fury and then detoured into the carport past Mrs

Sanderson's parked blue Falcon. As he walked past her freshly washed car, Mr Jeffries removed a set of car keys from his other pocket and purposefully scratched them down the side of the brand new car.

Mr Jefferies finally smiled but with an expression that reminded Michael a little too much of their friend from the mirror.

And what really got Michael's feet moving his arm wrapped protectively around Dana, was the question: what would have happened if someone had been home?

Making Plans

A lifetime ago that just happened to be yesterday, Nicola had watched her children walk down their normal suburban tree-lined street toward her sister's house for a sleepover. She had hoped they were walking towards some form of safety. The plan had been simple – get her children far enough away so they would be safe and that she could prepare in private. She had promised Michael she would find answers and she had no intention of breaking that promise.

First she had placed some basic protections around the house – some special symbols painted in discreet places, or crystals buried at certain points of the compass, then she was on to her shopping. She didn't have much time. The jeweller, having already worked with her before, knew she only did things when the moment was right. She had called him months ago to request that settings be made, to her specific design. He was happy to accommodate when she rung requesting the jewellery be collected that day. Nicola had only to pick the crystals and wait for them to be set. Everything had gone perfectly to plan.

When she finally arrived home she rang the kids at Sarah's and they had seemed safe and relaxed, so she readied herself for the gypsy book.

The aftermath of that encounter was that she spent what felt like an eternity in a coma-like state, locked in her own mind, struggling to find herself. In the final seconds inside the book, she had shared Trevlor's memory, the moment when he had been 'gifted' with the generations of his master's memories. Each memory, each personality, became entwined and entangled, vying for ownership of her body. She had no training with which to suppress or even stem the sudden flood of information.

The rest was, as you say, history! But so many histories. Her head swam with the lifetimes of memories that passed through his mind.

How had Trevlor survived? She knew he must have – that was what the book had needed to tell her. The onslaught of the masters' memories had just been an unfortunate timing issue. To the book, it meant nothing. She had needed to experience the binding, needed to know about the burden of guardianship. Most importantly she needed to know why the doll hated her family.

Nicola had gotten her answers. She knew her family were the direct descendants of the very masters who had bound the doll. She had no idea how she was going to explain it to everyone. Since she had woken she had trouble stringing any thoughts together let alone coherent sentences.

At first her thoughts had remained clear. She had easily

convinced Joseph not to get an ambulance. Her need was immediate and the objective singular. Her overtaxed mind could still handle that. But when she tried to move past the immediate and process what she had learned in the book, she literally felt parts of her mind shutting down.

She was certain she had blacked out again a couple of times but Joseph was busy with the kids so she kept this small detail to herself.

* * *

Now that everyone was gathered, they were all looking at Nicola for answers. Sarah was fluttering around fluffing pillows, checking Nicola's temperature. Joseph was thankful that someone had taken over and had gotten himself and Brent a beer.

The kids sat perched around Nicola expectantly.

There was just so much to say.

She took a deep breath ready to try and explain, looking at the faces of her children first. Joseph had cleaned them up pretty well. There was really no sign of any blood remaining …

My God how had she not registered the fact that the kids had been covered in blood? Ashley's t-shirt had been soaked through from what she now realised had been a very bad nose bleed.

Jumping bolt upright, Nicola grabbed at them, running her hands up and down their arms, looking, feeling for injuries.

This couldn't have happened last night. What had she missed? What had happening while she was fighting to find herself again?

Her mind flooded with images.

Dana's arm being swallowed by some mercury-like substance.

Michael reaching forward, his own hand dripping.

Sheba, teeth bared, hackles raised.

Ashley holding her hand to her face, her top lip smeared with blood.

Dana falling … God no … towards the doll.

Her overtaxed mind struggled with so many different images and finally put the pieces into place. She could not believe what they suggested. Suggested! Who was she kidding? Confirmed.

Headache or no headache, she did what any parent would do. She exploded: 'You went next door! When I expressly forbid it, you went next door? After I warned you! Told you they wanted to harm you! What the hell were you thinking?'

Dana tried to speak but she had no chance. 'Do you know the danger you put yourselves in? Don't you dare try to answer me and explain this away. Don't you dare! You have no idea what we're up against. My God, Michael, you barely got them out of there.' Her voice had lost all of its power by the end. Her vision was dimming around the edges and she knew that if she did not calm herself down she would likely pass out again.

Nicola sat back and waited for the room to stop spinning. She couldn't afford to black out now.

'He did get us out, Mum!' Dana answered defiantly. 'But how can you know that?'

'Know Dana, what don't I know? I can barely remember my own name but I know that after you escaped that damned doll in the second realm you go after it in the first?'

'Realms?' Brent asked. 'Nicola, what are you talking about?'

As everyone tried to absorb Nicola's words, Joseph moved protectively towards her. Her hand was pushing at the side of her head like she did when a very bad migraine was taking hold. What disturbed Joseph more was her slightly slurred speech.

Sarah jumped in with the answer: 'This is the first realm, the waking world. The second realm is that of dreams. The void is a small part of the second realm.' Sarah said this almost robotically, the information recited by rote. She wasn't thinking about what she was saying, trying to understand what the hell was going on herself. Sarah felt disconnected and disorientated. She continued to speak to give herself time to think and her sister time to recover.

'Nicola attempted to get some answers from the book. Anything that could help with the dreams. I made the kids some charms to protect them while they slept.' Sarah ticked things off on her fingers, 'But that was last night …' her momentum slowed and Sarah turned to look at Brent confused, 'then Joe called us about twenty minutes ago.' Sarah glanced at Brent again. 'I can't remember anything in-between. I've lost half a day.' Her voice cracked showing the signs of the fear that had crept slowly into the room.

We haven't got time for this, Nicola thought wearily to herself. By the time Sarah and Brent were able to shift the fog from in their minds, precious hours would be lost. *There's too much we have to do.* Knowing the danger the children were in, she racked her aching brain for answers. Wanting to scream her frustration she forced herself to calm down. She closed her eyes and tried to concentrate, feeling her heart beat erratically. Voices in her head spoke incessantly, clambering to be heard. Overlaying it all was the dense white noise that signified her grip on consciousness quickly slipping away.

Realising Nicola was close to fainting, both Sarah and Joseph reached forward simultaneously, each grabbing a hand, hoping in some way to keep her conscious.

In that moment of flesh on flesh contact the part of Nicola's overstressed mind that held Trevlor's memories gave her the answer. She now had the knowledge, and some of the power, of the masters. Without the luxury of time for preparation she hit them all gathered there with as little information as she could, but enough to make them understand.

Graphic images of a wooded glade flashed into Sarah and Joseph's minds. They both jerked backwards as the vision was forced upon them. They were unable to move. Nicola kept firm hold on their hands having no choice but to share a little of what she knew.

An animated monstrosity held in the centre of this wood, thrashing against its restraints. Robed figures circling, chanting, energy cracking from their fingertips. In a fraction of a second, the vision changed. The chanting remained but it was now accompanied by screams as the robed men were slaughtered where they stood. Creatures beyond imagining fought with teeth and claws, ripping at the robes, tearing through the flesh beneath.

Sarah eyes bulged with the horror at what she was seeing.

Another abrupt change, an image of a young man standing alone, surrounded by scorched and smoking trees, holding a small black doll. The despair that emanated from this young man was palpable. A single tear ran down Sarah's cheek as she began to understand.

One final image: a mirror, a doll and three frightened children.

Each image came with insight and understanding. These were not merely visions but moments in time transferred onto another. Nicola tried to hold some of this back, not through a need to keep the knowledge to herself but in an effort to try and protect them from the weight it would place upon their hearts.

The doll that had been bound by the ancients wanted to be free. The descendants of these ancients, their own children, were the guardians of the doll.

The doll would destroy them all to get to their children. And if it destroyed them, the bindings would fail.

Sarah and Joseph slumped backwards, physically drained by the enormity of what had just been passed onto them. Nicola waved them away and Brent reluctantly stepped forward, knowing what was required. He had been able to glimpse some small fragments of the exchange, and steeled himself not to recoil when Nicola clasped his hand. But he failed.

Nicola's ears roared and swirling black spots swam across her vision. She endeavoured to slow the flow of information for the children but she needn't have bothered, their minds were more elastic and absorbed everything without question.

Proud of their resilience, Nicola smiled up at them. And then her eyelids fluttered closed and she passed out.

This time they all understood why. They knew she had shared only a miniscule fragment of the information that the book had forced upon her. And that small fragment had given them all varying degrees of headache and nausea. They had no choice but to let her rest for a while.

* * *

Though his own head felt ready to explode, Joseph felt a sardonic smile touch the corners of his mouth, before his wife had passed out she had the audacity to send him a 'to do' list.

* * *

Normally when given a list, Joseph would have dutifully nodded and then gone off to watch some soccer, cricket, anything. There was always some sport on TV. But today the list had been sent directly into his brain. It reverberated there painfully and he didn't think he had any choice but to accede to Nicola's wishes. The request had been sent with a level of stress that he doubted she had intended. He was certain that if he tried to do anything other than instructed, something might actually rupture in his head.

Not that he needed to be forced. Yesterday, he had gone to bed, believing his wife was half-mad and suspecting she had already driven him to madness also. He had awakened from a dream that frightened him so completely that any attempt at self-delusion seemed dangerous. His ability to discount all of the strange things that happened in his life as mere anomalies had been totally and utterly blown away. Yesterday his kids had been in real danger in a dream. Today his wife had somehow sent images directly into his head. She had mentally compelled him to undertake a list of instructions.

Last week, if asked, Joseph would have been forced to acknowledge that he believed in some of what went on around his house. Mostly he would have tried to argue coincidence and the power of suggestion as being the most likely explanation.

The truth was that he wanted it to be coincidence and merely mind over matter. He wanted to believe his life and more importantly his wife were perfectly normal. Then he could live in a happy cocoon of self-delusion where his wife did not have to deal with disease, pain and insights into the more unpleasant parts of life. It was his coping mechanism. But there comes a point where this kind of ignorance would endanger the very people around him. His wife's paranormal ways may have been the only things that prevented his children from coming to harm.

Suddenly, the rules had changed. He'd watched on last night, dreaming, yet knowing his children were in danger. Joseph was grateful that through his wife's intervention he had been able, even just a little, to help his kids. But to now find that this ancient evil wanted his children dead, that they were mortal enemies by virtue of ancestry … well he had to accept that. He'd always known his family was unique, and he just had to deal with the consequences. If his wife had told him he needed to go get some goat's blood and eye of newt he would have gone shopping and brought them back.

Luckily, Nicola had already done most of the work. All he had to do was check to see that some paint was dry, bury a couple of packet of seeds in the garden and get some jewellery out of her car. He had only just ticked off the last thing on his *mental* list when Michael called out that Nicola was awake again.

* * *

Michael hadn't left her side the whole time. Even when she was unconscious he could still tell that she was in pain. It was etched into her face.

Her eyes opened and she smiled and stroked his face, but Michael had noticed her wince when the light first hit her eyes. She was always trying to protect him and he wished that she didn't always feel the need to pretend that she was fine. Michael would have preferred it if she sometimes just chose to not 'suck it up'. He didn't think she realised just how much pressure it put on everybody else to maintain a similar level of control.

Her hand ran down his arm and stopped at his hands. They still felt burnt and the cuts on his left hand had only just stopped bleeding.

He felt the warmth from her hand intensify and so he snatched his own away.

'Mum, enough, save your energy. You need it yourself right now.' Michael got up and walked to the window hoping she hadn't noticed how frustrated he was.

With his back to the room he could still tell that all of the family had returned. A second later he felt his mother's hand on his shoulder. She had gotten up as if nothing had happened and cursed when she realised the sun had already set. She spun, grabbed the bench to steady herself, and reached over to pluck the bag hanging forgotten in Joseph's grip.

All business, Nicola handed each of them a small wrapped package. 'Put these on and don't let me see you taking them off. They're for your protection. I haven't given them to you earlier because with them comes a certain amount of danger.'

Michael held his package in his hand, testing its weight, watching his mother for further signs of fatigue. When she walked over and grabbed a Coke from the fridge he finally relaxed.

'Come on, open them up and put them on.' Nicola was doing her irresistible force impersonation. And after today she had a lot more force than she'd had previously.

Dana unwrapped a silver chain from which dangled a crystal pendant. The crystal was hanging in the centre of the same Celtic symbol that decorated the cover of the now notorious gypsy book. Ashley's pendant was identical but where hers had a purple stone Ashley's was pale blue. Both Aunty Sarah and Nicola had pendants of their own that they never took off.

Michael found that his was of a similar style design except his symbol and crystal were worked into the middle of a leather wristband.

'Mum, what's this all about?' Michael had noticed *the* glint in her eyes. As bloodshot as they were, Michael knew that look. It meant she intended butting heads with something, be it a maths problem she couldn't unravel, a dizzy spell she couldn't shake or some unacceptable opinion. Whatever the opponent, the force of her will or maybe just her plain bull-headed stubbornness ensured that in most cases Nicola prevailed.

Michael often found this infuriating. It was he who was always inevitably having some obvious truth banged into his skull. But now, knowing that this level of bull-terrier-like tenacity was on his side, made him laugh, just a little.

Nicola looked straight at him and for a moment the tension left her face as a crooked smile turned up the corners of her mouth. She obviously had no love for the situation they found themselves in. But the challenge was somehow separate – it brought out the best and worst in her. So when she answered his question with a casual 'Oh nothing much, darling, I just know a little more than I did yesterday. Tonight we're going to play some hardball!'

Michael couldn't help it, he felt excited. A bit of hardball felt just about right.

* * *

'We have a lot to do tonight and we don't need that damned doll getting in the way. So Sarah, you'll need to bind it. Use what you did yesterday with the protection pouches, but this time strengthen the bindings. The kids can help, and so can I.' Sarah nodded that she would try.

Michael was past questioning. When Nicola started to draw a picture of the doll, he dutiful corrected some minor flaws here and there but he let Dana have the most input. She had the same artistic streak as Nicola and more accurately pointed out the bits that were not quite right. Within a couple of minutes the sketch looked frighteningly close to the real thing.

'Okay, so now we bind it. We won't be able to hold it for long, but hopefully long enough so that tonight we can pull Ashul through the final layer.'

'Isn't he already through?' Michael asked, confused.

'I don't know how but you somehow managed to pull him into the second realm. Tonight we have to get him here, into the first. We create a link, a connection to him. You kids will need to form this link because you're the ones most attuned to him.'

Michael couldn't help himself. He had to give Dana a discreet elbow to the ribs and he laughed as the expected blush instantly crept up her checks.

Joseph picked up on this because he looked at Dana suspiciously.

'All of this needs to be done while we're sleeping. Once we have a lock on him, we create a conduit, a kind of bridge to connect us and then we put an end to their slumber and pull their sleepy arses through.'

'And who exactly are we talking about?' Brent asked looking from face to face, trying to pick up whether he had missed something.

'They are the sleeping warriors of legend. Protectors when the land has need.' Dana was happy there was finally some detail she could provide.

Nicola looked towards her daughter. 'And how do you know that?'

'It's called the internet, Mum.'

'Of course, why didn't I think of that?'

Michael had the distinct impression that his mother was somehow enjoying herself.

The sketch, now completed, was passed onto Sarah. As she reached into her handbag, Michael held his breath not knowing what he expected but it was certainly wasn't her travel sewing kit. She took a piece of cloth that Nicola had supplied and started to sew the sketch into a pouch.

The sketch had been folded intricately, similar to origami and as a result it was now much smaller. Sarah used an elaborate method of stitching that was far beyond anything Michael had seen before. She seemed to follow some design that appeared to have more to do with the binding than with actually holding the corners of the cloth together.

When Sarah finished, her face was covered in a fine sheen of sweat.

Michael wasn't sure what he expected but a spot of art and craft was not on his list. It seemed so mundane, so normal, so downright boring.

'Now to lock him down.' Nicola took the pouch into her hands and mumbled under her breath, 'You won't be expecting this will you, you little ...' Her voice trailed off but Michael thought he had caught the last word and it wasn't a word she used regularly.

Michael arms broke out in goose pimples as a cool wind blew lightly past his face. Nicola's hair moved in a delicate breeze although no windows were open. Her eye opened, and the right was more bloodshot than before. She had the frown line that she so often got between her eyes, the one that meant she was either getting very mad or very focused. Michael suspected that this time it was a little bit of both.

The tension in the room increased, but apart from the quiet breeze and the look of concentration on her face, nothing had changed, except now Nicola looked well and truly pissed-off on top of being exhausted.

'Damn it, I thought I would be able to do this. Thanks to last night, I know I have the knowledge up here ...' Nicola angrily tapped at her temple. 'But I just can't quite get to it. And we don't have the time for me to stuff around playing at Glenda the Good Witch of the West.' Anger and apology warred for dominance on her face.

Sarah stretched her hand out to calm Nicola, and her eyes softened.

His mother's stare shifted first to Michael's burnt hand then to Dana's, equally red and slightly swollen – a matching pair. When her gaze lifted, the blue had darkened with an anger held barely in check.

Dana gasped as a cold and strong wind gusted through the kitchen. Sarah's hand had dropped away.

Michael followed his mother's eyes – it would have been difficult to look away.

Not because support was no longer required, but because distance had come between them.

Anger had created the distance, not from family but from the floor. Hovering, feet slightly pointed, Nicola was suspended above the ground.

'Got you now!' she whispered and dropped back to the floor.

* * *

It was still relishing Its moment of triumph when It sensed something alter, something change. It recognised the feeling as magic being focused, but what a strange sensation. It was like nothing It could remember coming into contact with before. Strong magic, but wielded very primitively. What was going on? It circled around looking for the source of the disturbance and saw the air thicken and coalesce into what resembled strips of fabric. The flimsy strips flew aimlessly around, with more and more appearing, circling around Its head.

And It had to laugh – was this the best they could do? Was It supposed to return to sleep because a few strips of mindless cloth decided to appear? In a show of contempt It slashed out where the fabric flew closest to Its head and was annoyed to find the strips stuck to its skin! It reached to pluck the fabric away and found Its other arm similarly covered.

As It writhed around It found itself more and more tightly bound.

This could not be happening. These worthless souls were attempting a binding. How had they gained this knowledge? It had no time to try and work out how this had transpired. With each second that passed It was less and less able to move.

More and more tightly bound. It cried in frustration and lost all sense of time and place as It allowed itself to dissolve into a mindless, all-consuming rage.

Forging the Link

Michael had never been able to master the knack of going to sleep on demand. He found himself nodding off for what seemed like hours to wake with only minutes having passed. Frustration finally won and he threw back the covers and went to the toilet. Michael turned on every light, closed every door forcefully and a constant cursing followed him through the house. Dana yelled at him twice to 'Just go to bed and go to sleep.' Michael was at a loss as to exactly what it was she thought he'd been trying to do. He could hardly keep his eyes open but that didn't make getting to sleep any easier.

His mum must have had enough too, because she was waiting for him in his room when he stumbled back to bed. 'Problem?'

'I just can't turn my mind off. I can't get to sleep!'

'I'm having trouble myself. If I have to look at your father sleeping peacefully for another second, I may just …' Nicola kicked her leg at the air with a slightly wicked expression. 'How about we watch a couple of minutes of TV together, what do you say?'

'Sure, but Mum with all the hovering and sewing, I forgot to ask, why are the symbols dangerous?'

'Because they open doors.'

'So why make us wear them?'

'To keep other doors closed.'

'And you know this how?'

'I received a data dump last night like you wouldn't believe. Funnily, a lot of the information I received I'd already read in books. Some of the books I've read appear now to be complete rubbish, but others based on ancient legends were pretty spot on.'

'So you know all about magic now.'

'I have thousands of memories swimming around in my head. If I concentrate too hard on any one, I pass out, so no I wouldn't be calling myself a master magician just yet. Let's watch TV, I need to wind down a bit too.' Nicola lay beside him stroking his head like he had a fever. The last thing he heard before sleep overtook him was his mum whispering, 'Twenty-eight and always, baby. See you in just a minute.'

* * *

Nicola smiled as she whispered their family's secret adage. It had been shortened over time, but had originated when she'd asked Michael once how much he loved her. Being only three at the time, he'd answered with a string of random numbers: ten, three, two-hundred and seven. And then … 'Twenty-eight', said as if it were the biggest number in the world. From then on twenty-eight had been their personal number for infinity. When he had started having childhood nightmares, Michael would look up at her asking if he could call her during the night, and she had answered 'always'. She turned the questioning around, asking the same question with the addition of how long he would love her for, he answered, 'Always'. Over the years their family told each other how much they cared for one another by saying, 'Twenty-eight and always'. It never failed to make her smile – *twenty-eight and always* was what made her sun come up in the morning. She now knew that *twenty-eight and always* meant a hell of a lot more. It had been shortened, alright, but over centuries not years. This knowledge unsettled her a little but it was not something she could control, so she took the same simple comfort from the words that she always had.

* * *

Michael found himself alone in the grey void. It didn't feel like a beach this time. It just felt empty. He was expecting everybody to be there waiting for him.

Had something gone wrong? He couldn't build a bridge by himself. That was Uncle Brent's thing. He was the handyman in their family, not Michael. The uncertainty quickly started to grow into fear.

Michael started to get the unpleasant sensation he'd experienced too often in his dreams of late, that something unwelcome was hidden just out of sight, waiting for him to relax, to let down his guard and choose that exact moment to attack.

Scaring himself was not going to help, he knew that. But instinctively he had no choice but to start circling around. Just to make sure nothing was trying to creep up on him.

All he found was the fog's steady determination to close him in on all sides.

He wrapped his hand around the wristband on his right wrist and traced the symbol. The silver felt warm and the tiger's eye stone in the centre tingled under his fingers. The repetition made him relax and he used the pattern to force away the images of the previous night when Marcus and the doll had nearly gotten to Dana and Ashley.

He wondered if waking himself up was possible. The one thing he knew this time was that he would not run. That was somehow hard-coded in him now.

He jumped when he felt something push up against his hand.

Any dog owner knows the feeling of a pushy mutt begging to be scratched. It's a reassuring feeling – such a simple gesture that can't be measured or explained and was better to simply accept and appreciate. He noticed the positioning of his hand wasn't quite right. While that good feeling never left him, curiosity did make him look down.

It was Titan. He was much bigger than his sister and was much more pushy. Dropping down to his knees, Michael hugged him.

He was still hugging the huge mutt when Titan pulled his head back and gave a happy whine and Nicola walked over, looking very calm, and very at ease, as the fog of the void parted before her.

Joy lit up Nicola's features when Titan ran to her and nearly knocked her over in his eagerness to jump up and lick her face. He had a paw on each shoulder and he was taller than her when he stood up on his back legs.

Titan dropped down onto all four paws and allowed his mother to breathe. Tears stood out on her lashes but laughter rang out as a faint breeze blew her hair back from her face.

'Oh it's good to see you T-man. I've missed you so!'

Then Nicola looked in the direction the wind had blown from and said, 'I do believe your aunty has just arrived.'

Michael had always thought his mum looked beautiful but his aunty was something else, something more. Her hair blew theatrically about her face, splashing highlights he wasn't certain her hair usually possessed this way and that. She glided along about a foot off the ground. With brown hair and hazel eyes that looked one moment green, one moment gold, it was like a tree fairy had walked off the pages of a fairytale.

'Not all of us can fly around at home, so I thought I might just give some levitating a go while I'm here. It's funny, once you know it's possible, it becomes ...possible!' Sarah laughed as she looked over at Nicola, shrugging her shoulders, appreciating the moment of indulgence.

'Where's Ashley and Dana? Couldn't they get through by themselves?' Aunt Sarah scratched absently behind Titan's ear.

Before Nicola could reply, Michael saw Dana's face and then Ashley's appear before them. Then a heartbeat later they just as suddenly disappeared. Before Michael could register concern, they returned with bodies attached but this time stretched all out of proportion. They looked to have been made out of rubber and their limbs were skewed as if they were literally being pulled in different directions. One moment an arm would appear normally then it would undulate and elongate or expand in ever more erratic combinations. It looked frightening and hilarious at the same time.

Michael ran forward, not knowing what to do. Should he pull, push, what? He looked over towards Nicola and realised his concern was not shared, because to the witch sisters it seemed funny enough. Nicola was leaning against Aunt Sarah, both relying on each other to remain standing since their amusement was set to drop them both to the ground.

'Oh, Mum, come on and help us,' Dana pleaded. 'This isn't funny.'

'I'm sorry but if you could just see yourselves, your faces look all ...' Nicola couldn't finish. Still chuckling, she grabbed Dana's hand and Aunty Sarah grabbed Ashley's and they both just pulled, flicking their wrists as they did so and with a small popping sound the girls were through.

'Aunty Nicola. You really shouldn't make fun of us that way. It felt really peculiar. We could have been stuck like that forever.' Ashley was cross at both of them but more so with her aunt because she still couldn't quite maintain any level of composure.

'I'm sorry, no, you're right, but if you had seen how ...' Nicola twisted her face and wobbled her arms around and because everyone could see she was about to lose it again she stopped herself. 'Oh never mind. But no, you wouldn't have gotten stuck that way. You probably just would have been bounced back into a normal dream. Anyways let's get to work.' She then wiped the last of her tears away. The time for humour had gone; she was all business now.

'Sarah, can you help the boys through? I'll get these guys started with the summoning.'

'Why can't Dad and Uncle Brent get through?' Michael was confused again, which seemed like a permanent condition for him lately.

'Oh, I'm sure they can. They've had no reason to really try in the past though. It seems to come more naturally to our side of the family. Whether you like it or not, you'll sometimes find yourself here. Thanks to all of the memories I now have floating around up here.' She stopped to punctuate with a tap to her temple – a gesture that was fast becoming one of her personal mannerisms. 'I now know that the rumour of our family being descendant from gypsies was a lot more than just a story. It goes a lot deeper than that. The gypsies were our ancestors and the keepers of the knowledge of the first true magicians. That book, *their* book, seems to work as a kind of conduit for energy and having it in our possession gives us *all* a power boost.' She considered to herself that it also painted targets onto their backs but that might be something she should keep to herself.

'Anyway … although our enemy may still be bound, it most definitely will be listening.' As if to prove her words true, the quiet of the void was split with the same screeching howl that had followed Michael home yesterday.

'My binding won't last much longer. We need to get this done quickly. I'm sorry kids but the questions must wait for the morning. Now go with Nicola and start the call.' Aunty Sarah removed two dolls from the sleeves of her flowing gown resembling both Joseph and Brent.

Michael had to admit, his aunt was dressed the way one might expect a witch to dress: long, flowing, golden gown with lots of layers – all very ethereal.

His mum on the other hand wore the same old flannel pyjamas with teddy bears all over them that she always went to bed in. But that was his mum. She probably hadn't even considered wearing anything else.

Aunt Sarah wrapped ribbons around her wrists and then around the dolls. Michael's attention quickly snapped back to Nicola when she gave him a clip to the back of the head.

'Pay attention and focus on the job at hand.' Nicola's tone deserved a snappy response but Michael bit his tongue. Was it his fault that what Sarah was working on looked cool? He wanted to point out that his attention had been focused … just not on her.

The look on his mother's face suggested that she wasn't in the mood for his mouth.

He wondered when he was going to be old enough to for her to stop treating him like a child. He guessed never.

'Okay, guys you're up.' Nicola gestured for them all to gather around. 'We have to pull your friend through into this dimension. Since you're his link, we need you to make the connection. I need you to focus on him. Use whatever it takes, the sound of his horse, the way he looks. The stronger the image, the better. Once you have this locked in your mind, focus on it, strengthen it. I will find him using the connection you establish.' Directing them to all hold hands she closed her eyes and waited while they all concentrated.

Alright, focus … Michael could do that. He loosened his neck muscles and shook his head briefly from side to side, just as he would before taking a goal. He tried to think of the sound of Ashul's horse's hooves.

Imagining the flaming sword, he built up the details in his mind to give him more to focus on.

Michael had the image clearly in front of his eyes. It was the sword that had caused the blinding flash the night before. Michael hadn't been able to pull Ashul through – he wasn't really sure if he'd even tried though. But the three of them must have had gotten him pretty close because it was Ashul's flaming sword that had driven the doll back. Michael didn't know how the girls were faring but with his eyes closed he attempted to clarify the image.

He mentally layered detail, and as the imagery clarified, Michael began to sense movement. This unnerved him for a moment but a reassuring thought from his mother made him realise that this was the intention. He focused on the details in his mind: blinding white light, pounding hooves, horse rearing. The more focused the image, the greater the impression of distances flying past him.

He was tempted to open his eyes. Were they passing through nothing more than a grey void? He could still feel the girls' hands in his, so he knew they must be moving together. Focus was what seemed important now so he resisted temptation and kept his eyes firmly shut.

Michael could now hear the sound of the horse's hooves as they pounded, not in memory but somewhere in front of him, growing closer, racing towards them.

It was working. *They* were doing it. Michael could sense some of what was going through the girls' minds. Not reading their thoughts, more like being able to pick up on the pictures, recollections, sounds, anything they threw into the mix of the summons. These images and thoughts were becoming a tangible thing and Nicola was in some way using this to home in on Ashul.

Dana, ever the romantic, had a very Prince Charming kind of spin on Ashul. This heroic impression made Michael smile and he wondered what their mother would make of it.

Ashley focused on Ashul's appearance in the painting, particularly the modified version they saw that morning where Ashul looked exhausted yet determined. Every line of his body showed the strain he'd endured when summoned through realities. Ashley focused on the look of resolve that had shone from his eyes. This was her addition to the link.

Once he'd heard it, Michael couldn't get past the thunder of hooves approaching – it resonated within him. It became something more than memory and the thought circled around his mind vividly. It was that drumming he was best able to remember and focus upon.

He felt Nicola take this sound and use it to add an extra layer to the construct she had built. Dana's crystalline imagery and Ashley's ideas of resolve and determination all combined to create a multidimensional representation that gave her something tangible to lock down on.

As Michael felt distances fly past him he continued to focus on the drumming of horses approaching, knowing that this was his piece of the puzzle to reveal. And as the sound intensified his own breathing once again matched the tempo of the horse's hooves.

His mind briefly flew to that of the grey mare and he felt the slight shift in direction this change of focus caused. It was barely discernible but at the speed they seemed to be travelling, he registered the tug against his hands as his grip slipped ever so slightly.

'Focus, Michael,' Nicola corrected him. And he forced his mind back onto Ashul's horse, imagined the foam at its nostril and its breath as it fogged the cold air, racing ever onwards.

The sound of the horse's breathing. The snort of the other horses working hard. Strong and steady. How different to the inhale and exhale of breath that had always been the first warning that the doll was about to close in. And it was as this thought passed through his mind that all hell broke loose.

Michael's hands were ripped out of the girls' grip as he abruptly changed direction.

Nicola cried out, 'Michael, think only of ...' but Michael didn't catch what it was she was about to say; only an idiot would have needed to be told, ' ... think only of Ashul.'

Kind of obvious when you thought about it.

He was alone now, hurtling unguided towards ... towards what, he didn't know, but the breathing coming from all directions was getting louder.

A set of teeth clamped down hard on his left wrist and at that moment he lost the ability to track his own movement.

I have a very bad feeling I'm not going to like where I end up.

He certainly held no illusion that he was going to wake nice and snugly warm in his bed.

* * *

'Oh my God, Sarah, I've lost him.' Nicola let go of both of the girls and Dana and Ashley fell to the ground.

'What do you mean?' Sarah asked. 'What's happened?'

'No time. He's gone to *It*. He's gone to the doll.'

'No! How?'

Nicola had been so self-assured, so goddamned sure of her own powers. She had been playing various mind games most of her life and she had failed to realise how easily a mind could become distracted.

Michael had been the only one so directly exposed to both sides in the magical equation and only an overconfident idiot would not have thought to put some protection in place for this very eventuality.

She took in a deep breath to stop the scream she felt building. She tried to keep herself focused. 'Think, goddamn it! Think! But she was a mother and her son was lost and she needed to find him. Absolute terror tried to consume her, but she refused to leave her son with the doll. Not again. She needed to get to him.

Nicola drew in huge amounts of power. Sarah fell to the ground as she offered all she had to give.

Her skin rippled with the energy she'd taken in, but even then Nicola callously drew more. She sent out mental hooks towards Joseph and Brent and absorbed their power also, passing through the barriers to get to their energy.

Nicola lifted off the ground, as her dream-skin shed, layer by layer and once again as anger and desperation tore through her mind. And soon enough she wasn't just a forty-something woman in teddy bear pyjamas, she now flew through the churning sky in the shape of a huge silver dragon, roaring her desperation and fear as she soared towards a son that should have thought before he thought.

* * *

Michael came back to consciousness slowly. The first thing he became aware of was a tearing sound, as if material were being ripped, accompanied by vicious growling.

The next sensation was his shoulder hurting, the same way anybody who has spent the day unsuccessfully trying to get up on water skis experienced. His arms felt like they had nearly been ripped from their sockets. The left arm was hot and burning from where he thought he'd received a fairly decent bite from a very large Doberman trying to save his life … for the second time.

The last sense to return was sight and this was the last only because he was too scared to open his eyes. But the sounds that came to him, made his imagination conjure up images that wouldn't allow him to sit there with his eyes closed any longer.

Now if he had been in bed, he probably would have pulled the blankets up over his head and held his breath until the next morning.

But there were no blankets. And maybe no morning, so he opened his eyes and resisted the urge to close them again.

The doll struggled desperately to claw and tear its way through shrouds of white fabric. The pouch that Aunty Sarah had sewn the doll's image onto not a couple of hours previously had become strips of material that tightly wrapped themselves around the doll's body, making its form clearly identifiable. The delicate sewing, now thick ropes, intricately intertwined, hampered the doll's attempts to tear its way free. The fabric was being shredded by the doll's sharp nails, and glimpses of black could be seen through the gashes the clawing had created.

But Aunt Sarah knew how to sew and she must have thrown a large dose of magic into the stiches, because for each layer torn away another seemed to appear. The ropes reconfigured to restrict movement and the bindings wound themselves back up around the doll's body.

The creature struggled as each piece of fabric cut into its flesh. It screamed in frustration and, Michael hoped, pain.

A hand tore its way free and Titan lunged forward, clamping his jaws shut on the doll's forearm. He used his heavily muscled body to restrict its movements while the torn fabric knit itself back together, sliding back into place.

This should have been a relatively reassuring sight. The creature was bound. Titan was doing a fine job and Michael just needed to find a way back to his family.

But the magic was slowing down. Each strip that hit the ground took a little bit longer to start back up the monster's body. It wound a little looser, cut a little less deeply and allowed the creature to rip a good portion more material away every time it got a hand free.

Titan was also slowing in his attacks and not only was the thing able to get its arms free more often, but it was having increased success in controlling each attack.

It slashed at Titan each time it freed a hand and Michael had the impression that the pain inflicted on the dog gave it strength.

He couldn't just watch Titan being clawed to pieces for his own lack of self-control. He had to do something but the best he could come up with was to try and re-use the now still material for rewrapping and rebinding the doll.

His logic was simple: there may have still been some magic left in the material even if it was unable to renew its attack without aid. And considering no other weapons dutifully appeared in his hand, he grabbed a piece of cloth and set to it.

He successfully dodged a swipe of the creature's left arm and managed to wrap a piece of material tightly, binding the freed arm firmly against its body.

Titan's jaws snapped forward with quick fast bites, diverting the doll's attack so Michael could move in with another piece of cloth. Michael was pleased to note that the material seemed to gain strength from his touch.

They continued to fight as a team. Canine teeth snapping forward, followed by Michael with the cloth. But they couldn't keep it up much longer; they were both slowing.

Michael barely ducked a swipe that missed his face by mere centimetres. Titan was able to deflect the attempt but he hadn't gotten away unscathed. The doll had left another cut across his muzzle.

Taking in huge gulps of air, Michael stood back for a second, trying to regain some strength, when a new sound invaded his already overloaded senses. It was a cry, resonating through him, making his chest vibrate and his teeth hum with its strange multileveled pitch.

Whatever had made the torturous shriek, Michael suspected must have been carrying a mortal wound because the sound held such pain. It wasn't long before the creator of the sound soared into view.

A silver dragon.

Agony reverberated through its cries and darkened the very air it soared through. Michael turned away unable to look at such anguish and for the brief second before their gazes parted he thought he saw the pain fade ever so slightly.

It flew low over the doll in its attempts to shrug away the last of its bindings. It was when the dragon flew over for the second time that it opened its mouth and this time the pitch of its cry was different. Michael's head swam with images of light, and shadows flew from the sound, for it was one of pure emotion, the antipathy of the dark.

He expected agony, fury, even hopelessness. The dragon seemed to have held all of these emotions in its gaze when it first came into view. But what issued forth opposed every one of these emotions. It was the sound of joy, love, pride, of triumph.

He didn't know how it was possible to vocalise such emotions. Maybe only a dragon could. They resonated within him and lifted his spirits. Titan barked suddenly reenergised.

The doll recoiled as if the sound ate into its very soul.

Its struggles became frenzied, but the dragon's song had somehow given strength to his aunt's magic and each spent cloth writhed with renewed energy. The creature was soon bound tight once again.

The dragon circled and dropped its head and Michael was buffeted by the wind made by the dragon's landing.

Titan had no fear as the dragon settled at his feet. Bounding up to it, Titan jumped up to lick its face and the dragon welcomed the gesture, lowering its face expectantly.

It was this reaction that made the penny finally drop.

His mother had come to save him. He should have felt stupid and he knew that later he would but relief and gratitude were flooded his system so he just hugged her and following Titan's lead, jumped up on her back.

They flew back though nothing more than a complete absence of landscape. The grey continued without change. There was no up or down, no cold pockets or misty clouds. The wind against his face was the only way to judge that they actually flew.

Eventually they landed and Michael saw Dana sprinting towards him.

* * *

It lost all conscious thought. It had surrendered completely to the rage all consuming. It continued to fight Its bonds and occasionally injured the foul beast that protected the boy. Sensing all that was going on around It, the red haze of pure fury was in its own way enjoyable, impossible to resist and so It surrendered to it and welcomed the oblivion. And then too soon, the bliss of abandon was ruined as It heard the shrill, soul-rending cry that reverberated with love, pride and relief.

It had no recollection of what happened next. It was lost as It ripped and tore, dreaming, imagining that it was flesh not cloth that was being destroyed. It reluctantly began to come back to Itself. The realisation of these dreams, tearing flesh, sundering souls, could not be achieved if It did not gain back some control and begin to plan.

These few had to be destroyed. It had underestimated them, being held captive by nothing more than a child's trick wielded with unexpected power. It had given them strength with this little success. It had to control the rage. Put it aside to be enjoyed later when It could make them pay in a way that no other before them had ever paid.

It had survived centuries in bondage. A few moments more could be endured and the things It had imagined over the years of imprisonment would be visited upon those that had thwarted It once again.

Dreams could be made to last an eternity.

Building a Bridge

Sarah had successfully pulled Brent and Joseph through into the second realm and set them to the task of starting on the connection to pull the sleeping warriors through.

Her mind was on the verge of panic, but instinct told her that having everybody in the second realm strengthened them, so she got to work on that. Without having any way to get to Nicola, Sarah's next task was to reinforce her binding of the doll. With a deft flick of her fingers she'd made the pouch and its contents appear in her hands. She then set about the process of maintenance. Left weak by Nicola's transformation into the dragon, Sarah monitored the binding's deterioration more than anything else.

It was as if she were conducting a choir: small movements of her fingers caused thin strips of fabric to detach from her flowing gown. The strips ran down her arms, across the backs of her hands and with a quick twist wound themselves tightly around the pouch. The folded sketch had undergone a change when it transferred into the second realm. No longer was it an intricately folded piece of paper. The material was wrapped around a small simulacrum of the doll that now writhed at Sarah's feet. So tightly bound was the doll, the shape of the face and the hands were clearly visible beneath the layers of shifting cloth.

Sarah retained the same ethereal quality that she had possessed in such abundance earlier but it was now put in stark relief against the dark circles under her eyes and the erratic way her hands shook with each small movement, indicating that the process couldn't go on for much longer. She constantly stretched and flexed her fingers to get circulation back in to them, needing to keep them nimble. But the stiffness in her joints was becoming a problem, as each flex caused her more discomfort.

'I can't keep the doll bound for much longer, my joints are seizing. Any sign of them?' Sarah kept her eyes fixed on the squirming shape, fearful of looking away.

* * *

Nicola started to lose the shape of the dragon even before her feet touched the ground. Her body had started to tremble during their last few seconds of flight and Michael felt the scales rippling under his hands erratically.

Titan, being more in tune with what was happening, jumped to the ground as soon as he was able. Michael fell rather than jumped and turned back in time to see the small erratic undulations increase in intensity, until it appeared like he was viewing the dragon's scales through a shimmering heat haze.

Michael shielded his eyes as the heat and light intensified until, in a burst of energy, the dragon exploded outwards into a thousand tiny luminescent balls. Each came within touching distance from Michael before they stopped and spun suspended for a millisecond. Michael had time to recognise his own face reflected back at him from a myriad of surfaces, before the image changed to that of Nicola and the balls retreated. They were pulled backward by a great vacuum force, spinning spheres reforming, and then his mother stood where the dragon had been.

Uncertain and awed by what had just happened, Michael reached a tentative hand towards her. Nicola retained a silvery pale appearance and shook as if the transformation was not yet complete. Looking like a stiff breeze would scatter her to the winds, Michael hesitantly asked, 'Mum, are you okay?'

* * *

Dana had been watching as the silver dragon beat into view, and sensed the lack of rhythm in the down thrust of the wings. She was already running as the dragon, and Michael along with it, fell to the ground. She wrapped her arms around Michael as he jumped from the dragon's back and she was at Nicola's side a heartbeat later. Nicola retained a silvery shimmer, but she was also deathly pale, almost translucent. Her veins could be traced in a network under her skin. Dana could see her mother's blood as it pulsed, giving her a liquid quality that reminded her all too much of jellyfish washed up on the beach. She looked not only ready to collapse but also near to dissolving.

'I'll be fine, darling,' Nicola whispered as she managed to get to her feet with Dana supporting one side and Michael the other.

'I just need to see how Joe and Brent are travelling. You know, make sure they're working in the right direction. After all, I left before I could correctly align the link.' Nicola's voice held a slight tremor as she spoke. Without pause, she walked towards her husband with her children wrapped protectively in her arms. She had heard the shrieks of the doll as she flew away, and knew it was tearing through the bindings as each second passed. It was hard to keep the urgency from her voice.

'Here she comes, Brent,' Joseph said. 'While she's been off gallivanting and saving errant children we've been here working our butts off.' He rolled his eyes. 'Now she wants to check in to make sure we're working to specification.' Joseph walked over to Nicola, pushed a stray lock of hair behind her ear and gave her a quick hug, one that that encircled both children and may have lasted a bit longer than usual. He kissed Nicola on the cheek and indicated for Dana to get Nicola to sit down then dutifully updated her on their progress.

'Truthfully Monkee, we've been playing around at different ways of bridging the gap between him and us.' Joseph looked around with scorn for the nothingness that surrounded him. *Monkee* was a nickname for Nicola that only Joseph and her father used, coming out in moments of concerns, usually for her wellbeing. 'But this place is making the creation of a link difficult. No matter how much we try and force this place to our will, it resists our efforts. So your *bridge*, we do not have.' Joseph held up his hand to stop his wife from interrupting. 'But Brent may have found another way around that particular issue.'

'Nicola, shit you look awful!' This comment received a *move it along* look from Nicola. Sarah, who was now sitting cross-legged in front of an ever diminishing pile of rags, obviously concurred: 'Guys, there's no time for this.'

'Okay. Right.' Brent turned around and stepped away, and in two steps he could barely be seen. The fog seemed to solidify around him and within a few more paces it had almost obscured him completely. 'This place is tricky. It appears thin and insubstantial.' His voice appeared to be coming from nowhere. 'But it isn't. It has weight. The more you focus on the connection to the sleeping warriors the more this stuff solidifies around you and conceals the way.' Brent's fist suddenly punched through the grey fog and his face appeared in the hole he'd created. His head appeared disconnected, like a face seen through a portal, until his body forced its way back through the thickened mist. Swirls of grey clung to his legs like a cloak. 'And this is our trick.'

Joseph and Brent stepped further away until they came to a particularly dark place, a section of the fog that swirled thickly making them have to work hard to move forward. Eventually they had their shoulders pushed against nothing but the shapeless black of their surroundings and they were unable to move any further. They both turned and casually leant their backs against the resistance. It could barely be perceived by the eye, although where their bodies applied pressure the darkness churned and thickened as if fighting against their touch. 'As so, my love, we have not bridged the gap, but we have found a way to tunnel through it.' Joseph could not help but smile as Nicola stared wide-eyed at what they had created.

* * *

Sarah's once-deft movements were becoming more stiff and arthritic with each sweep of her hands. Michael hesitantly placed his hand upon her shoulder, fearful to break her concentration 'Thanks, Aunty Sars, your sewing saved me back there. Is there anything I can do to help?' She reached up and patted the back of his hand. 'Michael, I've got this covered, now go, hurry them up. I could really go a chardonnay right about now and there isn't any around here.'

So unable to help and reluctant to just stand around, Michael stepped into the thickened ether that was the opening of the connection to the sleeping warriors. He immediately felt a low level drumming. And with each step, it became more recognisable as the sound of hooves.

'While you were off seeing the sights,' Joseph informed his son, 'Sarah was able to get us started. We still need your mother to lock down the connection but if all of this commotion is anything to go by we're making headway. If you think you can keep your mind on the job, we could use your help.' As if to confirm how little time they had, a shriek of rage swept around them. The grey mist seemed to be trying to absorb their efforts to penetrate it.

Michael, ever the type to keep moving forward, heard his father's subtle reprimand but also picked up of the relief underpinning his words. The doll's cry, he ignored. It had been screaming in his head for weeks and was losing the ability to terrorise him. He endeavoured to get some kind of idea of what was going on before him. With each step the air seemed to thicken even further, where even breathing became difficult. His body perceived a resistance that his eyes were unable to discern, a darkening similar to the fog that somehow pulled the eye out of focus. It was the kind of thing that needed to be looked at sideways since his mind was unable to take in the whole. Logic did not rule in this place and Michael had to accept that.

Mimicking his uncle, Michael punched his fist into the

darkest point in front of him. The swirling grey miasma recoiled, streaming away from his hand. It was like punching into very soft plasticine that suddenly gave under the impact. He could now detect a dilution of colour around his arm, the thinning unlike the grey fog of the second realm. What was in front of him could only be described as an absence. It was more what wasn't in front of him. No colour, no texture, no density. Where there had once been something now there was nothing. It was into this emptiness they would send their call.

'Brent, quickly over here.' Joseph's voice held a note of wonder.

Michael had created a hole through the boundaries of the second realm and it resented such an assault. Just as air rushes in to fill a vacuum, so to the substance of the second realm was endeavouring to repair the breach. Michael was finally starting to understand what his mother had been telling him: the second realm was a place of pure mind and spirit. Anything physical was just a fabrication. A manipulation that could kill you, but a manipulation nonetheless. His fist had created a hole through the unseen borders and the absence left behind created a kind of gravity that pulled at Michael's mind as much as it did his body.

He suppressed his anxiety when his father and uncle plunged their hands into the absence of the tear. Fearful that they would be sucked through, Michael jumped forward ready to grab them both. The grey mist thickened, liquefying around their hands. A soft sucking sound accompanied the rapid movement as the grey of the second realm turned into a slurry that swallowed their hands completely.

Without thinking, Michael plunged his hand into the small area of the breach that remained. He was ready for the sudden pull forward, his balance obtained through years of mid-fielding. He braced his feet and resisted as the void tried to upset his equilibrium. The balancing act was as much mental as it was physical and Michael experienced a brief but strong moment of vertigo.

Joseph's hands appeared in the middle of the swirling grey, clawing back at the edge of the sludge. Brent pulled in the opposite direction, dragging the edges of the hole apart. It was like trying to dig a hole in wet sand.

'Great work, Michael! Can you keep doing that? You've broken through *and* you're somehow repelling it. We just have to make the gap larger, more stable.'

Michael thrust his hands deeper into the hole and this time felt the sludge recoil. His head swum with the same strange vertiginous pull of the *absence* before him and he had to resist the urge to step forward into it. It was like the type of sensation of standing on the edge of a very high cliff: some people recoiled, others felt an enticing pull.

It seemed no longer a liquid now. The more the second realm resisted the more malleable it became. The churning mist was now a sticky dark putty. Hands left impressions but were no longer engulfed. Brent was able to gain some purchase and pulled the edges apart. Joseph moved forward and ran his hands over these treacle-like dark edges, each touch accompanied by a soft crackle. Joseph's hands were emitting a kind of low-level electrical charge. His hair stood on end with the current that passed through his body. Where he hands touched the sludge, it had turned into a substance that was beginning to look and feel like blackened glass.

Michael felt the sharp sting of static electricity as Joseph worked methodically to turn the sludge to glass. Before him the absence yawned with a gravity that only Michael seemed to feel. He ignoring this pull, and so they worked together until the opening was large enough for a person to walk through. With this method of constantly moving forward, they had creating a tunnel of blacked glass. The pounding of hooves echoed harshly amidst the non-absorbent walls and the grey sludge seeped and oozed around the edges, trying to regain territory. Like any tunnel it had become colder as it deepened but the air was somehow thick and moist, making breathing difficult.

The breach called to Michael, to either step through or stop this intrusion altogether. Michael shook the thoughts away.

The tunnel had taken on an unpleasant smell that reminded him of homemade playdough that was long past its use-by date. Michael had learned in science that to smell anything you need to have breathed in thousands of tiny microscopic particles and Michael stomach flipped with revulsion knowing this grey ooze was in his body. The faintly off and dank odour was subtle yet pervasive.

'I think we're nearly ready to complete the link. Brent, can you get the girls.' Catching his breath, he casually leaned against the wall. 'Michael, this stuff really doesn't like you.' Joseph had to raise his voice to be heard over the pounding of hooves. 'I can feel it recoiling. Keep focused. This place will play with your mind given half a chance.' He offered this comment almost as an afterthought.

Joseph wiped sweat from his head, and a sizzle of sparks flew from his fingers to which he seemed oblivious.

The drumming reverberated through Michael's chest and felt like his own heartbeat. In contrast the cracking of the glass, when his father leant against it, made him jumpy and agitated. He was standing in front of what was basically a newly-formed black hole; he was certain that no light or sound would be able to escape the irresistible pull.

The weight of the air had increased, and a wind had developed as the air rushed towards the darkness, blowing Michael's hair across his face.

Michael's chest was aching with each breath. He could hear Joseph's laboured breathing next to him.

The glass created an almost perfect mirror. Michael didn't know what was worse looking into his own wide-eyed stare in the glass's dark reflection or when he chanced a glance directly into the black hole in front of him. The void whispered to him, daring him to jump though into the beyond. He did as his father told him and tried to ignore it. But he couldn't look away from the glass.

Small fissures had appeared now, sharp cracks echoing like gunshot off the walls.

* * *

'Come on, Micky, keep it together. Don't let it get to you.' Joseph must have seen how his eyes ran from crack to crack. If his dad thought this little pep talk had reassured Michael, well, he was halfway right.

Michael was not altogether as comfortable with the concept that this thing they were working against seemed to have a mind of its own, and was actively trying to scare the living crap out of him. And, Michael thought, doing an amazingly good job of it.

'Come on girls, you're up,' Brent called down the tunnel. His voice reverberated off the walls, creating a kind of sharp and painful feedback.

The tunnel was deeper than Michael had realised. *Or was this more mind games?* It stretched almost ten metres, slowly sloping down towards the gaping maw of the hole they'd created. The walls seemed to close in on the girls as they walked away from the light of the opening. The chill in the air caused the girls' breath to form clouds in front of their mouths as soon as they entered the tunnel.

Their breath-fog didn't dissipate like it should have, despite the wind. The thickening of the air had increased to such a level that it now had weight. The fog hung around their faces slowly expanding with each exhalation, and the dank, mouldy aroma registered on their faces.

Nicola walked down the tunnel towards them, barely creating any fog, since her breathing was so shallow. Aunt Sarah was one step behind, her gown flowing smoothly against the now slick black floor. This world seemed poised, waiting for the next intrusion.

'Now this is the hard part. We're at the point where Ashul has to come to us. We can then work together to bridge the distance between us. But we cannot go any further without his help. The void will actively fight us. It can fight in many ways but will usually try and turn your own fear against you. Michael can give you an idea of how that feels. Just focus on our goal, creating a doorway between this plane and his.' Nicola moved directly in front of the darkness – her hair snapping in every direction.

'We'll keep these walls stable, you call Ashul, let's get him through.' Joseph braced his feet apart and leant into the wall. Placing his hand flat against the smooth surface he moved as close to the breach as he was able. Brent took up the same position on the opposite side. Their stance suggested they were expecting some resistance.

'Okay, call him, babies,' Nicola said. 'Call him with your voices, but most importantly, call with your minds.'

And with that they all joined hands and called.

Michael fighting an unexpected moment of claustrophobia, wasted no time being polite. He screamed as loudly as he could, and if sheer volume counted for anything he would soon have this guy sitting at their kitchen table sipping on a cold drink in no time. The cracking of the glass reminded Michael of ice ready to shatter. The wind had picked up to a low howl and his hair stung as it lashed his face.

The girls' voices had joined his own calls and he was certain he could hear hooves drawing closer.

Michael's heartbeat raced with the rhythm of the pounding hooves. He felt the force of the walls pushing down against him. A shriek tore through the air and Michael was unsure whether it was the doll screaming its release or the wall finally giving way.

Moments later Michael felt the first razor sharp fragment tear at his cheek. He realised the walls were not just pushing down against them, they were breaking and fracturing under the strain.

* * *

Dana was a little overwhelmed as she walked down the tunnel towards her family. Michael's eyes kept flicking around as if he felt threatened and wasn't sure where the danger originated. As soon as she reached the bottom she felt herself struggling to breathe. She had never been claustrophobic before but she was fairly certain that this was exactly what she now experienced. The air felt thicker and the tunnel appeared tighter than it had moments before.

Dana struggled to listen as Nicola told them to resume the call. Not knowing that everyone around her had done the same thing, she closed her eyes and imagined the talisman-like figure of Ashul riding his ebony black horse.

She felt her mind slide along a tangible link, like an electrical current down a cable. She felt her mother's presence around her and wondered at her mother's ability to create such a thing. Dana became somewhat distracted and suspected her lack of focus had been a manipulation.

Refocusing, she clarified the imagery: sweat beading on Ashul's brow, his hair plastered to his head with the effort already expended in getting as far as they had. Dana reached out towards him and found her hand repelled by a barrier she couldn't see. She realised it was a barrier she had experienced before. Reflex forced Dana to pull her hand away. She had seen Michael's burns from passing through this barrier in a previous dream and she didn't want to endure the same.

Nicola's voice whispered to her from a great distance, promising to protect her if she only tried a little harder. And as if her mind had picked up on random transmissions, she heard her father swear as he staggered backwards. The wall started to shatter, and she glimpsed an image of Michael cursing as blood flowed down his face.

She pushed her hand forward again and saw Ashul reaching back towards her. The intense cold made her fingers ache as they broached the barrier.

There was a sound of shattering glass as the walls imploded.

The pain in her hand grew and she felt the skin split as the burning cold became too much. Reflexes tried to take over but this time she overruled them and clasped Ashul's hand as he bent down towards her. Dana found her hand locked in a vice-like grip. She suppressed a cry as the pain became almost unbearable.

She had thought breaching the barrier would relieve the agony not intensify it. Her hand felt like it was being crushed. When she looked up she saw Ashul's face but she barely recognised him.

Sweat ran into the creases of a smile that twisted his face into a mocking expression.

It was then that she heard her brother yell into her mind: *they had all been deceived.*

* * *

The pounding of hooves grew louder, and Michael mentally begged Ashul to approach more quietly. Didn't he realise they had a crisis on their hands? The last thing they needed was uninvited visitors when they were all so preoccupied with the job at hand. He could hear the curses of his dad and uncle as they struggled, desperate to hold the wall.

Shards flew in all directions. Joseph and Brent cried out, caught as the wall splintered. Michael too terrified to open his eyes sensed all this through their link, knowing the girls did the same.

Michael flinched as a sharp fragment tore down his cheek. He tasted the salty trickle of blood as it found its way into his mouth. His whole face was on fire and he feared at the thought of the amount of the damage being inflicted on the girls standing so closely beside him.

His throat was too hoarse to call any more, and his mouth had gone bone dry with the coppery taste that threatened to make him gag. So he called with his heart. It was all that he had left.

The sound of hooves was now deafening. The noise was frightening, rather than reassuring. It came to him in that moment, that he knew nothing of Ashul. He was nothing more than a picture in a sketch. A couple of internet searches couldn't prove a thing. And, he had only appeared when the doll had.

What if his purpose was to help the doll, rather than fight it?

They might have made a deadly mistake. It was probably too late to stop the summoning but surely he must let the other know of his fears.

He heard the tortured sound of the wall imploding inwards. More cries. Then nothing. He sensed the girls pulling back. Of their collective parents he could now sense nothing.

What had happened to his dad?

He sensed only the girls, and they were as scared as he was.

Could it be that they had been tricked into this summoning?
He heard the doll's cry and this time it sounded triumphant.
Could Ashul be just another enemy?
What the hell had happened to his parents?

He felt shame welling within, with the near certainty that he'd been duped and that the cost had been his parents' lives.

A sole voice cut through his thoughts, confirming his fears, a voice that demanded entrance, a voice that refused to be denied as it echoed around what remained of the bridge they had built.

Mocking laughter, insisting it was too late to turn back, too late to stop what had been started.

Hearing only the beating of hooves and the sound of laughter, Michael pooled his waning strength, determined to stop this impostor from making the crossing.

He was desperate to find some trace of his family, needing to know that they were safe. Searching for his father, looking for his uncle and finding them gone, not killed, not mortally injured by the falling wall. Something far worse had happened; he'd been abandoned.

Left alone as what remained of the wall came crashing down around his ears.

And as that thought flew through his mind, he called out to the girls. He wrenched all the energy that was available and rather than directing that power to stop the impostor's entrance, he used it to call for a person that he hoped, believed was their friend to finally come through.

Michael called out to Ashul *to come through now*. And with his mind, he punched through the barrier that was all that remained between them.

The void's carefully constructed delusion had been broken – it had miscalculated terribly.

Michael was ashamed to admit he had believed, albeit briefly, that Ashul was their enemy, not their friend.

But that his father had turned and ran when the wall they had built together fragmented, abandoning him, Dana, everyone! Well that was something Michael could never be made to believe.

The void had obviously never met his family. With this thought at the front of his mind what he desperately hoped was a 'friend' on a lathered horse burst through.

* * *

Dana's terror left her as she felt the change in her brother's sending. She realised that her hand had not breached any barrier, since it had been wrapped in a protective sheath the whole time. Her mother's protection very literally surrounded her.

Her face had been cut but her hand was not burnt. The void had tried its best to fool them all but her brother had seen through the lies almost as easily as he had punched through the last layers of resistance.

As Ashul broke through, he clasped Dana's hand and she was hauled up and onto the back of a horse. Her head banged against an armoured shoulder before she blacked out and returned to a safer sleep.

* * *

It had broken through the fibrous binding in which It had been bound and shook Itself as It sensed that they had succeeded in bringing the sleeping warrior through. It had fought the warrior before and so it seemed they would fight again. It smiled as Its body was flooded with the energy that was released as the foolish boy broke through the barrier between the planes. These very barriers had retarded the flow of power for so long. With every breach the power now flowed more freely. It was impressed; this was no easy feat. The boy would be a feast to savour, if he harboured even a shred of the strength that he had somehow managed to wield today. He had such raw strength, more than It could ever remember encountering before. And his youthful naivety was like the icing on the cake.

It sat and glutted Itself on the power, releasing the double-edged sword this flow of energy symbolised. Power was universal. If It received this amount of energy so did his enemies, but the difference was It had no concept of restraint, no notion of taboo. They were hamstrung by these values. So It relished the flood and wondered, which of Its comrades It would call through to join It first? After all, a feast had to be shared, just a little.

It had huge amounts of power to play with.

So It sat and smiled and released an old ally from bondage.

The Morning After

Michael woke to sunlight streaming through his bedroom window. As late in the morning as it was now, he didn't feel refreshed in any way. He had not expected to bounce out of bed, not after the night he'd just endured but this bone deep lethargy was something else altogether.

Time ran differently in dreams: hours in a dream could translate to only minutes. He knew this because he'd been mocked by the bedside table clock many times over the course of the last few weeks. The whole notion of the near endlessness of time in dreams had compounded his fear greatly. Infinity was not a concept easy accepted. Add pain and suffering and that created a place that sounded a little too much like hell.

But this time they'd been able to use time's elastic nature to their advantage. They had been able to spend what seemed like days building their bridge, fighting the grey sludge of the void and only one night had passed. No wonder his head pounded like he was coming down with a bad case of the flu. Stretching his arms up above his head Michael winced as a sharp pain lanced through his shoulders.

He wasn't surprised they ached; he'd come close to wrenching them from the sockets when he broke away from the group.

He sunk even deeper into his pillows remembering his own stupidity. His head protested the sudden movement and a wave of dizziness washed over him. *You're such a hero Michael,* he quietly rebuked himself, doing his best impersonation of Dana's voice.

Not being one to let anything as simple as pain and humiliation get the better of him, Michael swung his legs around and was forced to stop and sit a moment when the room and his head seemed suddenly to come out of sync. He grabbed the bed for support, and when that didn't help, Michael tried steadying his head.

He fingers traced over a series of cuts crisscrossing his face. They must have occurred when the dream wall splintered in front of him. He ran a finger along a scratch too close to his left eye for comfort, and suddenly felt the need to check on the rest of the family.

After a couple of failed attempts to get up out of bed, Michael stumbled towards his sister's room. Using the wall as a guide he made slow progress towards Dana's room and found her still fast asleep. She lay curled tightly in a ball, facing towards her window and away from the doorway. Relieved at finding her sleeping soundly, Michael hesitated only a moment before he lent forward and tapped her shoulder. His reticence was due in part to what he might find but mostly he hesitated because Dana didn't wake well at the best of times. And she liked being woken even less. If Dana felt even half as bad as he did she would be inclined to lash out first and ask questions later.

Dana sat bolt upright and turned towards him ready to explode. Her mouth opened and Michael tensed, explanation ready, but Dana only groaned. One hand reached up to push her hair aggressively back from her face almost tearing off the bandage wrapped around her head in the process. The other hand rested on her temple as if trying to stop her brains from leaking out through her ears.

As the last strands of her hair were raked away the full extent of Dana's injuries became clear. They winced almost simultaneously and mirrored one another as they both raised their hands to the other's face to more fully understand what they each saw. A network of fine razor thin cuts covered them both from brow to jaw line. Dana's hands also bore similar injuries.

'Oh my God, Michael, your face.'

'Dana …' they both started to talk but couldn't bring themselves to finish. Dana drew in a deep breath to control her accelerated breathing.

'Your arm is bleeding, the rest … well … it will just have to wait. Let's get that under control first.' Dana didn't want to think about her own injuries. Michael's reaction had given her enough indication of how shocking she looked. Right now she needed to focus on the practical not the emotional. If she thought for too long about the possibility of scarring she would break down and she had no time for that. For all she knew Michael was not the only one that needed help this morning.

Dana scooped up a t-shirt from her bedroom floor and wrapped it around Michael's arm. He had opened the wound when he'd reached towards her face. During her quick inspection she found a deeper set of cuts that ran from his elbow to his wrist. Being far better at handling the sight of someone else's blood rather than her own, Dana detoured past the bathroom to check on the rest of the family.

Michael was sure their wounds would heal, but the potential scarring concerned him. He didn't really pay much attention to his own sister but his mates assured him she was a knockout. He was certain half of his soccer friends chose to come to his place to hang out just so they could check out his sister.

Dana was keeping it together, he had to give her credit. The same thoughts must have been passing through her own mind but she focused only on finding their parents.

During the dream summoning, his dad had been closest to the wall and had been trying to hold back the shattering pieces when things dissolved into mayhem. Was it possible that his injuries were so bad that he was now in desperate need of medical attention?

Their tentative crossing of the lounge room turned into a fast paced run towards their parents' bedroom when their dad silently came up the stairs and intercepted them by putting a finger to his lips. He indicated they should continue downstairs to the kitchen.

Dana pushed Michael towards the kitchen bench and once seated unwound the t-shirt from Michael's arm. Finally Joseph seemed to notice their injuries.

'What the hell caused that?' Joseph started rummaging around the kitchen, trying to find something to put on Michael's arm, picking up first one thing and then another, not being able to settle on anything suitable. Michael was sure his father must have been asleep during first aid courses at school. He was still looking amongst the drawers when Dana passed him a clean towel from the cupboard. She had already put the kettle on to boil and was pouring some salt into a bowl, before Joseph even realised that he even had something in his hands.

'Titan did it, Dad. He grabbed me when, you know … He was just trying to save me.' Michael looked away before the disappointment he felt in himself showed.

'Has Mum woken yet? How's she feeling?' Dana asked.

'She woke up earlier, told me to check on you, and not to be too worried by what I might find and fell straight back to sleep. If she can issue orders she's fine. But there would be hell to pay if I didn't let you both know how great you were last night. I hope you both know I would never leave you.'

'*Daaad*. We both know that, but Michael was the one who saw through the deception. He seems to be making a habit of saving the day.' Dana placed the bowl in front of Michael and started to clean his arm. 'Maybe he isn't such an idiot after all?'

Michael winced when Dana's smile pulled at the cuts that crossed her face and looked away when a couple of the cuts started to bleed slightly.

Dana was nearly finished when Nicola walked into the kitchen. She looked worse than terrible. The circles under her eyes were as dark as bruises. Her lips were dry and cracked. Navigating the room methodically. Nicola steadied herself, first on a chair, then against a wall, traversing the kitchen floor like it was a ship's deck on a choppy sea.

Her legs shook with each step she took but she made it to the fridge, grabbed a can of Coke and dropped into the nearest chair before anyone had a chance to get to her and help.

'Come here, my angels!' She reached towards Dana and Michael and they both knelt dutifully before her so she could wrap them in a bear hug. She still had the strength to make them both struggle to breathe. 'You guys were fantastic. Has your dad told you how proud we are?'

'Yes, Mum.' Dana and Michael both rolled their eyes.

'Good, so let's get this mess cleaned up. Look at you both.' Nicola's head dropped, overcome with emotion.

Michael gave Dana a pointed look urging her to say something reassuring.

Nicola's shoulder shook as she sat with her hand covering her face. It took Michael a moment to realise she was moved by humour rather than distress.

Relieved and somewhat baffled, Michael shrugged and Dana shook her head indicating she had no idea what was going on.

'What?' Michael asked.

'You guys will believe just about anything! Just look at you both.'

Michael said, 'What? Mum, I don't get you. Dad said we did good to see though the lies.'

'He's right, you did. The void tried to trick you into running. Trick you into losing faith in the ones you trust. You did great to see through that but ...' She stopped to cover her mouth while she laughed again. 'Haven't you both asked yourself why these injuries don't hurt? Why we're not covered in the same type of wounds? I hate to point it out to you but both those wounds are nothing but an example of your overly active imaginations.'

* * *

Nicola rang Sarah to check on how their side of the family had faired. When she chuckled again, Michael took that to mean Ashley had an overactive imagination as well. Michael still wasn't certain exactly what that meant but he wasn't about to amuse her any more by asking. After discussing oils and herbs with Brent, she made some recommendations about channelling energy into the blend and then finished the call by saying she would leave things in Brent's capable hands. While Michael knew she meant it at the time, he also knew she would be double-checking everything again in five minutes. Classic obsessive compulsive behaviour.

Ash and her parents arrived a little later. Michael noticed that it was only he and Dana that bore any sign of injury. Everyone else looked tired and sore but that was all.

Uncle Brent was carrying an earthenware bowl covered in a tea towel and he placed it on the kitchen bench. 'Dana, come over so I can have a look at your face.'

He examined her for a moment or two, nodded his head twice then whipped off the tea towel and started scoping out great globs of thick green cream with his hands.

'Nic, you're going to want to see this. I did as you suggested, mixed the oils and cream together, but I think the little extra kick you mentioned has amped things up even more than *you* could have expected. Here take a look!'

Michael was about to ask about Ashley's face and her lack of any visible signs of injury but stopped himself as all words died on his tongue. Uncle Brent's cream had begun to work. He could do nothing more than stand there open mouthed. As his uncle smoothed the cream over Dana face, it bubbled and fizzed and if Dana hadn't been giggling, he would have been worried that it was burning her skin. The mixture spat and sizzled and the acrid yellow green smoke released as it effervesced further fuelled the impression that cream was somehow acidic. But Dana continued to chuckle and when it dissolved away so had all signs of injury. There wasn't even any redness. Her face was as smooth and clear as usual. The only remaining indicator that anything had happened was the residual fog suspended over Dana's head and even that was dissipating.

'Okay Michael, your turn.' Uncle Brent went through the same procedure with Michael, applying a generous amount of cream to his face. He could understand why Dana had laughed. It felt like having Wizz Fizz smeared on him. When the smoke cleared Michael's face only retained the scars that had been present since childhood. When Michael offered up his arm his uncle shook his head.

'Sorry, Michael. That will have to heal on its own. That's a real injury. I can help speed up the process, but your body will have to mend itself.'

'What do you mean a real injury, If anything, this,' Michael stopped to lift his arm, 'is less of a worry than my face. That was really hurting last night.'

'Yeah I know, but it didn't hurt this morning did it?' Brent said. 'I bet you didn't know it was hurt until you looked into a mirror.' Michael had actually noticed things were wrong when he touched his face and seeing Dana confirmed his exact injuries, not a mirror, but Michael nodded that he was essentially right.

'The wall shattering was part of the void's attempt to scare you off. Of course, it never shattered. It held strong for the entire connection. When your father and I build something, it stays built. But the void wanted you to think it had failed, needing you to so stop tampering with it. Breaking through the barrier is not even close to imposing a concept on the void, which is basically what Joe and I had done. The void is a place for dreams and it readily accepts them, but it will also endeavour to clean up after the event, and create a clean slate so the next dreamers have no residual images or emotions to cloud their experience. So it will naturally resist when a conscious thought is imposed upon it. When Michael, broke through one of the boundaries, you all experienced the void's response. It was all fabrication, but you,' Brent swept his hands around, indicating the three children, 'did not know that. Your mind cannot distinguish between what was suggested and the reality, so it created wounds to match those it believes were inflicted upon you. My potion just tells your skin to forget about it, sort of like deliberate amnesia. Understand?'

Well sure, who wouldn't? Michael thought, but decided to ask another question rather than make any more of a fool out of himself. 'But why can't you fix my arm? That didn't really happen either. That was just a dream too.'

Michael swivelled in his seat when his mum jumped in with the answer. 'Not at all! We weren't in a dream. Our conscious minds were in control, so we experienced the void to a deeper degree. Dreamlike, but most certainly real. Something conscious, something real inflicted those injuries. In your case, Titan, and previously, the doll. All real. Anything that happens there will affect your reality here, affect your body and your mind. If you were to get lost in the void, your body here would never wake. And God forbid if anything else were to happen, you can only imagine ...'

Die there. Die in the real world. *Nice.*

Michael wanted to move the unpleasant conversation along and asked the first thing that came to him. 'Well, what did you mean about speeding up the process for my arm? Show us what you've got Uncle Brent.' He raised his arm in anticipation of a miracle.

'My dad mixes magic potions. That's his special talent. I watched him this morning; it was really fantastic.' Ashy beamed, obviously very proud of her dad's skills.

'Thanks, Ashley. But up until today, I've only been playing around. But now … there's energy everywhere. I can only see it when I'm mixing, but Nicola told me to look for it and she was right.

'The barrier was only leaking energy before. But each time we tap it or touch one of its constructs we release more. I did some serious damage when I accessed the knowledge of the book. Last night Michael punched a hole straight into another dimension. And now I'm not certain the game will ever be the same again.'

'Mum, is that how you became a dragon?' Dana asked.

'I have absolutely no idea how I did that. It wasn't from a repressed memory. I was just so scared. I couldn't believe I had let Michael down so badly. I just needed to get to him quickly and the image of a dragon popped into my mind. It was the first thing to come to me. Lucky I have been reading *A Game of Thrones* because if it had been *Moby Dick* you may have had a ten tonne whale flopping about.' They all took a moment to smile, the ludicrous image of his mum as a whale just too absurd.

'Now we have more important things to discuss, like what are we going to do about contacting Ashul? I'm confident that we succeeded. With the way you guys were screaming at him and Michael punching clear through the breach we definitely brought him through, but what next?' Nicola looked around for suggestions.

They all jumped as they heard the front doorbell ring.

Aunty Sarah rose to answer the door and soon enough they all knew Ope had arrived. They could hear him telling Aunty Sarah she was too skinny, she needed to eat more,

'Where's Monkee? Is that lazy bum still in bed?' and 'Are all the little monsters here?'

Ope had lived in Australia since he was twenty but still managed to have a strong German accent. Skin weathered from a lifetime in the garden, landscaper by trade, he looked like a gnome come to life.

'What's going on here? Michael, why aren't you ready?'

'Ready for what?' Michael asked.

'Soccer. Or have you forgotten that you're meeting the other players today. Monday, remember, meet and greet? Stop looking at me like some idiot and get yourself ready!'

Michael was up in his room grabbing his gear, swearing profusely the whole time. But he stopped dead at his Ope's next words, heard faintly from downstairs: 'Can someone tell me why you have a horse ruining the back garden I slaved myself to death landscaping for you?'

Michael walked woodenly over to his window and gazed down upon the huge horse in full battle armour happily chewing on their grass.

Downstairs, Dana had also moved towards a window. She immediately saw a very tired, very familiar looking young man sleeping quietly under their sun umbrella, Sheba curled contently at his side.

Meeting Our Friend, Knowing Our Enemy

I t was a race to see who could get out the back door first. Sheba ran around them all, seemingly quite proud of her discovery and then settled at Dana's side, ready to receive a scratch as a reward.

'Well that puts it beyond any doubt now, doesn't it?' Michael whispered to Dana as he pulled his soccer shirt over his head. Michael felt some last remaining doubt lift from the group. In their house if Sheba liked someone, it was as if they passed some kind of unspoken test. Tradesmen had been turned away based purely on Sheba's opinion of them.

Michael glanced around: there was definitely only the one horse. The back garden was large, but almost every square inch had been landscaped. In-ground pool, sandstone surrounds, paved alfresco areas. It looked more like a tropical resort that a standard everyday suburban yard. And with the sun shining brightly down from overhead, the only shadows were under the umbrellas – nowhere for a grey horse to remain concealed. Michael wasn't sure whether he felt relief or disappointment. Probably a mixture of both.

Ope was systematically stamping grass back into the holes made by the horse hooves, seemingly oblivious to the irrationality of the situation.

Dana was looking puzzled at the horse when a quiet voice spoke from behind her. She jumped around, and sucked in a breath as she did so.

'We are bonded; he is my better, more noble, half. You cannot read him as you would another animal. But he is honoured to know you. You have provided much needed light during our journey here.'

Dana turned to Ashul standing less than an arm's length behind her. Ashul dipped his head towards Dana. His hair was matted and dark with sweat. Only when he raised his head and his tired gaze met hers did she realise he was just a teenager, only a little older than herself. His eyes although exhausted were a clear crystal blue. She felt the warmth of a blush creep up her cheeks and quickly turned away towards the horse.

These were the first words any of them had heard him speak and Michael for one was disappointed. Ashul was supposed to be the hero in this story: a warrior. Michael expected him to come in and take charge, not bow politely to his sister and talk about lights and better halves.

'I must apologise for my manners. You honour me with your call. All I can offer in return is my name, as custom dictates.' And he stood and bowed to all of them in turn.

'My name is Ashul. I am bound by blood and by honour to vanquish the evil that has been unleashed. I am sworn to protect those of the blood from the force that has once again re-entered the first plane. I will offer my life and knowledge to those who summoned me, as only those of the blood can.' He bowed again and stood as if waiting for instructions.

No-one knew how to respond and everyone was looking at each other expectantly when Ope, who had already created a temporary corral out of trellis and star pickets, jumped in. 'Well all that is just going to have to wait. It's not every day a man gets to watch his grandson play soccer with the state team. So tell your horse not to shit on my grass and let's get going.'

* * *

And soon enough Michael found himself bundled into the backseat of their car with a mythical warrior that they'd somehow pulled into their reality, wearing Michael's own clothes, on their way to soccer training.

Michael couldn't get past how young he was. The top was a little tight but in general Michael's clothes fitted Ashul. Surely this guy couldn't be expected to fight the demon doll from next door?

An overpowering silence had settled over them all during the short drive. Obviously in some effort to ease the tension, Nicola decided to make some polite conversation. 'Ashul, I'm curious. You mentioned that you're bound. I'm racking my memories but don't seem to be able to get a hit. If you don't mind me asking, how are you bound and by whom?'

'Well, mam, I was born to a different time, a time when magic resided fully in this, the first plane. It was a time of wonder and of peril. There were those who were strong in the ability to use and manipulate the forces of magic. Some chose to use this power to help, to better their lives and those around them. Some thought that those strong in power should rule and sought to gain control. And there were others who chose to just be, to use the magic as it felt natural, to let it flow through them if and when it desired. Over time the ability to tell the difference between the first two groups became harder and harder. Creatures of magic were formed: dragons, unicorns, gryphons, gargoyles. All were created to give the other group power and dominance. It became a time of war.'

Michael, while resolutely looking through the front widescreen, was nevertheless listening to every word.

The soft spoken warrior continued to tell his story, the soft hum of the tyres the only other sound in the car. 'Some of these creatures became a force of their own and they broke the bonds that had been created to bind them. They sought power for themselves. And through the war that followed the source of power was nearly drained dry. Much like a well servicing too many people, eventually the well turned toxic and became useless to all, worse still, poisoning those surrounding it. This was the unwitting result of the thirst for power.'

'Why not stand back and let them annihilate each other? A war of attrition. Those who remained given a poisoned power source. Eventually they would die too wouldn't they?' Michael asked. He didn't like the idea; it felt wrong but strategically it made sense. Having spent half his life playing video games where worlds were won and lost, sometimes the only winning strategy was to let the other guys duke it out and them come in and clean up afterwards.

'Michael, many a wise man argued the same point. But the land suffered. Magic is just another facet of the power that creates and binds the world around us. The power that gives every tree life and every child breath. If it fails, all fails. The risk was too great. So the third group decided it was time to step in. They did not fight in the war, for that was not their way. They decided that the wilder facets of magic should be locked away to protect all life, hoping that a time would come when harmony with the powers could be achieved. It was a huge undertaking and many generations did it take for them to succeed and many losses did they incur. All of the abusers of magic fought them, banding together as tenuous allies, turning the creatures that remained in their control against these few.'

Ashul fell silent for a moment. He had closed his eyes as if in some form of communion. Nicola turned awkwardly around in the front seat to look over the head rest and Joseph repositioned the mirror so he could glance back when possible. The cracking pace Joseph usually set when driving reduced as his foot unconsciously eased off the accelerator.

When Ashul opened his eyes he was looking straight at Michael.

'The power itself, although not exactly what you would call sentient, sensed that its survival was in jeopardy. Working through those strong in magic and true to the source, a race of warriors was born. Created of the blood of the chosen and of the land they needed to protect they were bound together by magic; their only purpose, only instinct was to protect the power and those who defended it. I am of that race – I was the first to be born.'

Michael, completely absorbed, hadn't even noticed the warrior looking at him so intently. Michael's jaw opened as he took in the words. This guy was talking like he had been there!

But he was only a teenager. It didn't add up.

'Wait, hold on a minute. Don't you mean you're one of their descendants?'

'No, master Michael, I am the first. I have fought all the battles through all the generations. More battles than I care to remember and I have been called to do battle once more. One of the creatures has broken the ancient bonds, and as its first shackle dropped away, so I first stirred in my slumber. And with each step it made towards this realm, I grew closer to awakening. For me to have come all the way through to this plane and not to have fought the battle in the void bodes badly for us all. Our enemy must have its own allies, ones that have taken a hand in its release. Ones that have already successfully managed to bring it into this plane.'

'So it was actually you in the pictures, the sketches, even the wall carvings? All of that stuff on the internet it was not just a knight with the same sword? It was actually you?' Dana asked but she had already known the answer and nodded; it made a strange kind of sense. 'The symbol on your sword, on the book, on the gypsy wagon – one for the warriors, one for the third group, the magic welders that remained.'

Before Nicola could ask where she had gotten all of the information from, Dana asked another question, 'Have you fought it before? The doll?

'Unfortunately, yes, fair Dana, I have. I witnessed its binding. It calls itself Anarcus. It is one of the Gezahnt, one of the evil races of magical creature brought into existence during the first wars. It lives only to control the magic that created it, but its first goal will to be to find and destroy those of the blood.'

Michael stared blankly out the front window seemingly not to have taken in this piece of information. He only snapped out of his daze when he registered that the car had stopped, parked outside of the state soccer stadium.

'And that would be us,' Michael murmured, grabbing at his water bottle, turning ready to follow Dana out of the back seat.

* * *

Michael had no time for nerves. He was too shell-shocked anyway. He was introduced to his training partners and thrown straight into warm-ups and drills. His body thankfully fell into its own rhythm. Dribble, pass, tackle, roll back; all came naturally. His mind struggled not to look to the sidelines where, standing with his family, was a straight-backed young man with an overly intent gaze.

As the intensity of training increased, Michael became oblivious to it all.

He was sitting on the bench, staring at the signature on his boots, breathing hard after a brutal period of one-on-one competitions when he heard his name called out for match practice.

He hadn't expected to have any game time, even during practice, let alone at the meet and greet. It was an honour to train with the state team. To be included in a game was extraordinary.

Ashul lent down and asked Dana quietly, 'Has he been selected to compete?'

'Yes,' Dana said. 'He'll be stoked. He's only supposed to train.' Dana's awkwardness had disappeared. She was nervous for Michael to do well – her heart was set racing.

The game started and Michael had been placed in an attacking midfield position. Dana could see that only two other trainees had been selected to play. She recognised Josh, the goalie from Michael's grand final. He was keeping for Michael's team. The other boy, Dana did not know, but he was playing on Michael and had already set himself up as someone to watch. He obviously wanted to get noticed and he played defence hard. Slide tackles seemed to be his specialty. Dana, who played up forward herself, had been on the receiving end of defenders that used their bodies well. She understood that the position needed to be played aggressively, especially when on someone as quick as Michael but she personally thought this guy played the game old school, where defending came close to thuggery.

Michael took a pass, ran down the left wing, a quick roller-coaster past their defender and he was in position for a cross. A tackle from behind clipped Michael's heels and he tumbled forward. The whistle blew playing the foul. Michael had managed to get the ball away and still had the free kick awarded to him and so the ball was returned.

Ashul leant forward, looking to jump the fence. Dana lay her hand on his arm to restrain him, a gesture that had become habit. She'd performed it so many times with Michael.

Michael looked over in her direction when he placed the ball at his feet, touching his boot as he did so. He scanned the sidelines without really seeing anything. He was focused only on the next few seconds.

Dana's hand dropped away and she glanced at Ashul. The look in their eyes was so similar. The determination. The focus. Dana held her breath as Michael stepped back to take the kick.

It was a good ball but their defence managed to clear the ball for a corner.

The game continued. And Michael continued to be marked and had to jump a couple of wide tackles. All the while Ashul stood watching every exchange, his hands wrapped around the fence.

* * *

Half time came and went. There was no score. Michael had been lucky enough to play the rest of the game. The thug-like defender had been taken off for a five minutes discussion with his coach but was back on the pitch, positioned against Michael again. The ball was moving forward. A high ball in the box, Michael was up, tilting his head towards goal.

Dana could see what was about to happen. Everybody could. Their heads collided. Injury time-out was called while both players were checked by officials.

'He is surrounded in power,' Ashul said. 'Why did he allow that to happen?'

'It's part of the game. That was a fair contest. Not a nice contest, but fair,' Dana responded not really understanding the question.

'Yes, I understand. But he could have stopped that. He could have used the power. He is bathed in it. Why did he not?'

Dana could feel her mother listening. Dana looked towards Michael and for a moment saw a shimmering light surrounding him. He appeared to be standing in the middle of a rainbow. Dana rubbed her eyes. Looking again, the heat haze had disappeared.

'Michael could have used power *here*?' Dana asked.

'The power surrounds him. He senses it. He reacts to it. But he does not draw on it.'

'Ashul, it's a game,' Dana tried to explain.

'A game of combat. And he does not draw the power.'

Dana rolled her eyes skyward. She had thought it was difficult reasoning with Michael. Ashul looked like he was going to prove even more of a challenge.

Distracted by the clouds overhead, Dana watched them form into a group that looked like horses running across the sky. The two in the lead darker than the others: one a black thunder cloud, the other a lighter shade of grey. Dana heard but didn't look away from the sky as her mother answered for her.

'It's a game and it wouldn't be right to use the power. It just … wouldn't be fair.'

'It would not be.' Ashul nodded his agreement, Dana only registering this movement from the corner of her eye. She was still focused on the clouds overhead. The black cloud continued its swift progress across the sky. The grey cloud shifted, reforming the horse with its head lowered as if in silent agreement and then broke apart.

'It would not be honourable,' Ashul affirmed.

Great, Dana thought to herself, as all traces of clouds were shredded by the wind. *As if Michael's knight in shining armour complex needed any more encouragement.*

Dana brought her gaze around and responded defiantly, 'If *I* had the power I would have smashed the guy.'

* * *

While It sensed their absence, It worked tirelessly, struggling to bring through the ally. It called on Its hosts and they bled themselves again to give it the extra power required to reach though and find another. There were so many creatures begging, willing to fight beside It. It chose to bring across a lesser power, one that would not fight it for dominance, one that would simply obey.

It also had to choose a power that could creep past the protections these novices had erected. Their juvenile use of the power indicated how little they knew – crystals, amulets, sacred seeds – all had their uses but they would only stop entities possessing of a body.

So it sought one that did not.

Those next door would be surprised by the amount of creatures It had to choose from, surprised by the sheer volume of those willing to take a hand in their destruction.

Tonight they would meet one of them.

The First Battle

After getting home from soccer, the phone had been ringing off the hook. Nicola tried to get them to all to sit down around the dinner table and have a bite to eat as if everything were perfectly normal. If Michael ignored the ancient warrior sitting beside them eating pasta for the first time in his very long life, then yes, it would have been. Although Michael did appreciate the food, he was starving and he thought any attempt at making this place feel normal was being a tad optimistic.

Dana sat playing with her food, unusually quiet, pondering some deep mystery, but Michael was just too excited to care. The phone just wouldn't stop. Michael had to keep excusing himself as soccer mates called to see how he had gone that afternoon in training.

While Michael had been walking around in a daze,

sullenly dreading each dream, his teammates had been counting down the days until Michael trained with the state team. The news of how well he had done had already spread. Each call was more enthusiastic than the last.

Giving up all hope of a relaxed dinner, Nicola sent Michael upstairs to prepare a place for Ashul to sleep. For a moment, Michael had almost forgotten that they had a house guest, being so wrapped up in the never-ending phone conversations and Facebook commentary.

Night was already upon them, he noted. In the last few weeks, he found his unease steadily building as the light level dropped, but this time he'd almost missed the shift from day to night, reaffirming just how much things had actually changed.

Michael joined Ashul when he went outside to check on his horse. Dana was sitting silently on the sunlounge with Sheba curled up by her side when they stepped through the back door. With the sun down and no cloud cover the stars shone brightly in the night sky. The moon bathed the backyard in a silvery glow. The sound of insects hummed loudly as Michael searched around for the horse.

'The horse isn't here, Michael. Can't you smell that?' Dana pointed out, lifting her arm so Sheba could jump up and investigate Ashul further.

'Well my sense of smell has never been as good as yours, Dana.' Michael felt like she was testing him somehow but he didn't know how this proved anything. Of course, now that she had pointed it out Michael realised the faint aroma of chlorine was the only scent that rivalled the green fragrance of grass.

Ashul patted Sheba's head and walked towards the lawn. 'My horse is here. He's just keeping his presence dim. All is in order. He is watching and guarding the second realm. You can go inside to sleep now.'

Ashul stood in the middle of the grass communicating with a horse no-one could see.

Dana watched for a moment, head tilted listening. It was obvious she had expected something. When nothing appeared she walked towards Michael and gave him a quick hug, her way of apologising for being short with him.

'Ashul, you know you're sleeping inside too,' Dana said from the back door, finally herself again. 'Mum won't let you sleep out here.' The absurdity of the situation obviously amused her.

'My place is to guard and protect. I will sleep here,' Ashul answered.

'Yeah right!' Dana laughed. 'Maybe you could have gotten away with *that* two thousand years ago.' She didn't bother saying goodnight. She knew she would be seeing them both shortly inside.

* * *

Michael lay back in bed, hoping to have a decent night's sleep for a change, not caring whether he dreamt or not this time around. He felt confident that protections had been put in place, and with a real-life hero lying in the trundle bed next to him, he felt relaxed for the first time in ages.

His mind had turned off before his head had hit the pillow. If Ashul had said goodnight or had any strange night-time rituals, Michael was unaware of it. He was exhausted and his body had finally thrown in the towel. He needed sleep and he had every intention of getting it.

When he found himself once again in 'the second plane' Michael felt a moment of annoyance. *Hadn't he done his bit for now? Ashul was here to help fight the battle.* Michael wanted a reprieve, just for a night.

His irritation was short lived. The difference in the atmosphere was obvious. For once the place he found himself in really did feel like a beach. A gentle breeze was blowing against his face and brought with it the subtle tang of salt. Water lapped gentle against a shore somewhere nearby. This place did not hold the same expectant quality as it had before.

It felt nice, peaceful, comfortable.

Michael hoped that Titan would come and visit. His old friend had saved him last night and Michael would have liked the chance to thank him, maybe to throw a dream frisbee or two. He hadn't recognised Titan when he'd first appeared, hadn't been looking for him the way Dana always did and he wanted to make up for that.

Having Titan around would make things … perfect.

Certain that Titan would bound forward any minute, Michael became mildly annoyed when what felt like minutes passed and Titan failed to show.

Having no knowledge of what ghost dogs did when they weren't protecting family, Michael felt sure he could spare a couple of minutes.

Wasn't this his dream?

Shouldn't he be able to just make Titan pop into existence with a mere thought?

Apparently not.

With little more than a salty breeze blowing in his face to distract him, Michael soon became bored by the monotony.

Great! Good dreaming, Michael. Put in a mental request for a soothing dream. Your subconscious dutifully delivers and here you are getting ready to complain to management. He was convinced that he must have been one of those people who were just never happy. And as a classic line from the movie, *Goldmember,* came to mind, Michael mumbled to himself in a bad Dutch accent, 'There is no pleeeasing you'. He then answered himself in a much better English accent, 'That's not right!'

Michael thought that he might just be the first person to sleep talk whilst in a dream. He wasn't certain if you could nod off in the second plane but he thought that he may just have managed the feat.

It was with this kind of ridiculous mental conversation taking place, oblivious to his surroundings, that Michael's internal dialogue was broken when he thought he heard Dana call.

The breeze had died down for a moment and Michael's ears rang with the silence that surrounded him. He strained for confirmation, listening for Dana's voice but heard only the wind swirling around him.

The rhythmic pounding of surf increased and the breeze although still gentle must have changed direction because the sound reverberated painfully against his eardrums. Michael strained to pick up any echo of Dana's voice but nothing more than the buffeting of air reached him.

With a heavy aching sensation in his chest, Michael realised he must have unconsciously been holding his breath.

It wasn't excruciating. He just struggled to take in any air. A heavy weight seemed to have settled across his ribs. Not that he needed to take deep breaths. He was in a dream, what was he worried about? He wasn't at training. He didn't need to run.

Everything was alright. Now that he thought about it, maybe aching was too strong a word. Maybe 'tight' was more accurate.

Deciding to walk it off, Michael attempted a couple of shallow breaths to ease the increasing pressure across his chest and found it too was difficult. Maybe if he could find the surf he could relax again and then everything would be all right.

But his internal dialogue started up again. Michael surprised himself by just how chatty he was this evening. He quickly pointed out that if he wanted to chill he would.

'Just shut up. It isn't going to happen!' Michael gasped out to anyone who could hear him. 'And just for the record my chest bloody well hurts.' Michael wanted to check on Dana. He was certain that she had called him and even if she hadn't, he still wanted to make sure she was okay just the same.

But couldn't Ashul fight some battles for a change. After all, wasn't that his job?

Hadn't that been exactly what he thought before he went to bed?

No! It hadn't been!

He had only thought that a normal dream would be nice. He had no intention of letting Ashul fight this war solo. He may have been some great ancient hero but he still needed all the help he could get.

Words of comfort entered Michael's mind. If he were to just calm down his breathing would ease. The lights that now speckled his vision would fade. The dream would grow calm and he could relax.

If he would just stop fighting himself ...

'Enough is enough!' he yelled using his last remaining breath, the gust of wind stealing his words as they left his mouth.

The annoying other voice in his mind could stick it where the sun didn't shine.

During this last string of dialogue a slow realisation dawned on Michael. This didn't feel much like talking to himself at all. It felt like arguing ... with someone else.

All too slowly he realised that something was manipulating him. *Again.*

He was pondering how to go about waking himself up when Dana's cry cut across his thoughts.

Desperation seized him. He was completely out of control in his own dream. The pain in his chest had become excruciating. Michael yelled with only a trace of irony – *wake up Michael, you lazy bastard.* And he managed to oblige.

* * *

Michael woke to find his chest a white-hot mass of pain. He was unable to draw breath. His room was dark but his eyes burned white from lack of oxygen. Michael's face felt like it was covered in a thick plastic bag. He reached up to claw at his mouth only to find a cold elastic substance where his face should have been.

He recoiled and the oily substance shifted to encircle his wrist. He shook his hand free but the price was a tightening around his neck. Cold tendrils raced down over his shoulders towards his arms, crisscrossing their way around his elbows, linking to a network already wrapped around his chest. Soon he would be completely bound.

With burning lungs and obscured vision, Michael kicked out hoping to wake Ashul. He needed Ashul to realise the danger before Michael's strength failed him completely.

Michael rolled to the edge of the bed, intending to use his last ounce of energy to fall on Ashul but he stopped mid roll. Looking through the striated black membrane, he realised Ashul would be rescuing no-one. He was far too busy trying to save himself. With hands and feet tightly bound the slime had coalesced into a semblance of an eel ringing his hands in a tight grip. Ashul threw himself repeatedly against his bonds but made little progress.

Michael's struggles slowed completely.

First one then another of the eels dissolved back into its liquid form with Michael unable to do anything except watch the black parasite's purposeful progress. In seconds it had moved from Ashul's limbs and now succeeded in pinning down his entire torso.

The seething black mass moved towards Ashul's face and thin tendrils, like black veins, raced up his neck. Some shot straight into his ears, others diverted and crept up his nose. Michael watched on, unable to make a sound. Ashul clamped his mouth shut but the parasite was able to force his jaw open, enough to slip in at the corners. It was like an awful parody of him eating pasta earlier in the day.

And, finally, Ashul ceased to resist. His eyes found Michael's, his gaze remained unnaturally calm.

In some kind of sick sympathetic harmony, Michael felt the mass encasing him shiver in pleasure at the domination of the warrior.

The oily slick raced up Ashul's body towards his mouth, endeavouring to pour more and more of itself inside him. Michael could see the cords on his neck stretched taut with strain but that battle had already been lost.

The liquid parasite continued to push itself into his mouth and Michael was horrified to see the black torrents streaming out of the warrior's nose to join back with itself and complete the mask that now covered his entire head.

The blue eyes remained fixed on Michael's. Viewing each other through a double layer of rippling film, Michael was sure his eyes held terror and fear. Ashul's still held that frightening resolve.

Michael tried to take courage from the gaze but he was paralysed by the shroud holding him bound.

Ashul went limp. His eyes blinked once, then remained closed.

Michael felt his own body give up the fight.

They had both been without oxygen for far too long.

Michael had nothing but peripheral vision left but it was enough to pick up some small movement. A very slow purposeful creep, as Ashul's hand moved across the floor.

In the slime's eagerness to enter Ashul's mouth it had slid up along his body pooling on his face, keen for entry. In doing so it had moved away from his extremities. Ashul must have anticipated this and allowed the slime's entry with that exact purpose in mind. Calmly accepting invasion so his limbs would be released.

With deliberate movement, this freed hand inched slowly toward something under the bed.

The control required to not tear desperately at the suffocating mantle must have been immense.

What seemed like an eternity later, Ashul's freed hand reappeared, gripped firmly around his sword.

Michael felt like cheering for him.

Get them, Ashul, make them pay, Michael mentally cried. But all celebration stopped and stood mute witness. In silent awe of what was happening.

The sword was not being wielded to free its bearer, but to free Michael.

The blade flared once as it touched Michael's face.

Whatever the slime was, a sound of agony ripped through Michael's mind.

The thick liquid pulled itself out of Michael leaving his mouth with a wet kiss.

Michael felt like passing out with the pain as air returned to his lungs. His body struggled, fighting the intrusion. Michael had to force himself to take each burning breath.

His chest lurched spasmodically, remembering how to breathe normally. His limbs tingled as the oxygen returned to his bloodstream and muscles.

With his body protesting every movement Michael rolled off the bed and found Ashul still covered in the black convulsing membrane but the warrior was otherwise completely still.

Unsure what else to do Michael grabbed the sword and begged it to work in his hand. He gently placed it against Ashul's face.

Nothing happened.

'No, no!' Michael screamed. 'That's not fair.' Michael hit at Ashul with the flat of the blade hoping for something to work. Watching Ashul's skin through the shroud start to change colour and fade.

Why had Ashul not saved himself first?

That was what they told you on every airline, on every flight Michael had ever taken.

Save yourself first so you could help others.

Save yourself first! Goddammit!

Ashul's fingernails were now almost blue.

His hand was almost the colour of his sword.

Michael realised what needed to be done; Ashul needed to wield the sword. It was his after all, he must power it somehow.

He hoped Ashul had some power left. Michael reached for his hand, only to find the slime had anticipated his move and was rapidly trying to cover his flesh, making itself a barrier between flesh and weapon.

But in this, Michael was faster and as the sword touched Ashul's skin, the slime screamed. A clear crystal sound rang out as if a bell had been struck. Placing the blade against Ashul's face, Michael was relieved to see the sword flare once again, fainter this time but still enough to do the job.

Michael slumped backward, sitting down with his head held in his hands, trying to keep it together. Ashul stirred and struggled to his feet. He leant on Michael for support and said the only two words that could have gotten him moving at that moment: 'Fair Dana.'

Well just plain 'Dana' would have done the trick but the thought sounded a little too much like hysteria so Michael pushed it aside. Lending each other strength, they raced to Dana's room only to find her covered in the black slime just as they had been.

Michael had seen the blade flare up for him, but now it blazed in Ashul's hand. Rather than having Ashul touch Dana with the blade, a bolt of white lightning flew towards her and the slime simply ceased to be. No time for it to scream its goodbyes.

Michael threw himself towards Dana and heard Ashul drop to the ground beside them. With Dana gasping for breath against Michael's shoulder, he looked to Ashul to thank him, and for the first time Michael saw something in his eyes other than resolve.

Pain etched across his features and Michael knew it had nothing to do with the pain of oxygen returning to his muscles.

* * *

Again It had been defeated, but It had time in abundance. The slime had returned and reported many useful facts. Ashul must have lost some of his foresight if he had not sensed this attack coming. The boy again surprised It when he was able to return in time to free his body. He wasn't stupid that one, naive yes, but naturally intuitive, able to sense thoughts that were not his own.

Useful to know.

It had scored one victory though. All four of the parents had been kept completely in the dark about what was going on, giving It some indication of how much energy they had expended. Also giving It an equally clear indication that they had no source available to them to recharge their powers. They didn't know how to draw fully on the power at will. They were mainly relying on their own life force, which was finite. Their scruples would not allow them to suck other beings dry like it was currently doing.

It had just to keep challenging them, keep sending them adversaries and they would inevitably destroy themselves. And if It threatened their children, well, they would destroy themselves all the sooner. The stupid mother had almost done that when she transformed herself into a dragon, almost drained her own sister dry in the process.

Yes, this might be quite easy after all. It had many, many more allies that It could expend in this war.

And when they were drained near death ... then the fun would begin.

Riding the Fleet

Nicola was troubled. She had wanted to get to bed early to catch up on some much needed rest, but shortly after ordering Ashul up to Michael's room and seeing everyone tucking in and ready for sleep she found herself staring at the ceiling. Sleep eluded her. Nicola was fully aware of the ridiculousness of the situation. For an outsider looking in, everything would have appeared normal: two teenage boys having a sleepover. Only closer inspection would reveal that one boy had a tired, strained look to his face and the other would have left you guessing. His eyes had a quality that only came from seeing and experiencing too much, but they held not an ounce of bitterness. To have endured so much and to still have such a clear unwavering gaze amazed her.

Succumbing to her nervousness, Nicola threw back the

covers and checked the wardings for another time. She had walked around the house with an oil pastel in her pocket, stopping occasionally to strengthen a line, smooth a curve or retrace a symbol. She doubted these last minute touch-ups were necessary, since she'd already double and triple checked everything. With nothing left to do Nicola went upstairs to give the kids another kiss and try to get some sleep herself.

When she walked into Dana's room Nicola found her daughter still awake reading. Nicola was sure that she had probably been rereading the same page for the last half an hour if the distracted way she placed it on the floor was any indication. Dana was fastidious about certain things and marking her place in a book was one of them. It was amazing what tiny things added up to create a full picture of a person. That so much could be read into the smallest gesture.

Dana shuffled over in bed to allow Nicola room to sit down.

'Are the boys asleep?' Dana asked quietly.

'Yes, I think so and surprise, surprise, your dad is too.'

'Ashul went to sleep okay? You should have seen his face when I told him you would make him sleep inside.' Dana chuckled for a second then her face clouded over again as if the image of Ashul awakened another memory.

'Mum, have you noticed his eyes?'

'How could I not have? They're almost frightening in their intensity.' Dana sat up in bed leaning forward, unsatisfied with the response.

'That's it. Nothing else?'

'Should I have?'

Slightly disappointed, Dana gestured for her to go take another look.

Nicola planted a quick kiss on her forehead and walked back past Michael's room to poke her head in one more time. Both boys appeared to be sleeping. Not wanting to disturb them Nicola whispered, 'twenty-eight and always' from the doorway as she turned towards her room.

Michael's muffled response of 'Back at yah, Muz!' was to be expected.

The quiet voice responding, 'And so we are sworn' was not.

She should not have been surprised. She had known he was one of the twenty-eight, one of the warriors sworn to protect the land. The book had given her that knowledge. But he was so young! He looked like he needed her protection not the other way around. He was so much like her own son.

Nicola realised that must have been what Dana had already noticed.

Their eyes were so similar. Michael's eyes were always smiling, always full of laughter. Unless someone did the wrong thing, crossed some line, unless he was truly focused on something.

And then his eyes held the same unerring quality as Ashul's.

Only moments before she had been congratulating herself on how much could be read into a simple gesture, how a page being left unmarked could indicate distraction yet she had needed Dana to point out how similar Michael was to Ashul. Michael was just a throwback to another time. He had a strong sense of right and wrong, but so did they all. Did he have a choice living in this family? It didn't need to mean any more than that. It couldn't mean any more than that, could it? With all of the knowledge flooding though her mind, a couple of similar characteristics left her more uncertain than anything else she had experienced in the last couple of days. And with these thoughts of brown eyes and blue she went and fell into a troubled sleep …

* * *

Nicola dreamt of running through the pages of a book. The ruffling of dry paper loud in her mind's eye. She was searching for knowledge and enlightenment. She had thought they were the same thing, but she had been mistaken. The words raced beneath her feet as the urgency building inside her drove her through page after page of indecipherable symbols. She glanced behind her and saw the paper curling as if placed too close to a flame and she knew time was against her. If she could stop for a second the meaning would become clear to her and she would have her answer. But there was no time. She could feel the heat building behind her, singeing the back of her hair.

The crystal-clear ringing sound cut through the dreams and caused the pages to shred and flutter away in a non-existent wind.

The words upon them remained and coalesced into a writhing mass of black.

And then Dana's scream pierced her ears.

* * *

Nicola woke at Dana's cry. It had not followed her back from her dream – it had originated here in their home and echoed throughout her nightmare.

She swung her legs out of the bed and ran towards her daughter's bedroom. She could feel Joseph only paces behind, the intensity baking from him mimicked her dream. She would not have been surprised to feel the carpet smouldering under her feet.

She staggered to a stop at the bedroom door. Her dream seemed to have followed her after all. For a brief moment she saw veins of inky black pooled around the edges of the window frame; within seconds it had leached out through the cracks and was gone.

A flash of white light followed its trail and Nicola turned thinking somehow the light had come from her husband. But it wasn't.

Ashul lowered his sword and the light faded.

Dana clutched at her brother, both struggled to breathe.

* * *

'It seems that the attack was focused directly on Fair Dana,' Ashul said, 'and Master Michael. I think that … I was just in the way. The rest of you were sent into an enchanted sleep, clouded by forced dreaming to prevent you from providing aid.' Ashul's eyes systematically worked their way through the room. His jaw clenched slightly when they fell on Dana but his gaze did not drop. When Dana spoke, Ashul flinched and a brief flicker of pain resurfaced in his eyes.

'But why us?' Dana asked huddled on the couch curled up against Nicola. Their lounge room had become the unlikely place for their war council.

'You are the guardians. You have been in close proximity to Anarcus. It has tasted Master Michael's blood. It would have used this as scent for its allies. You could have been anywhere and they would have found you.' Ashul said all of this as if ticking points of on a list. If Michael had not been witness to the warrior's actions and more importantly his reactions that night, he would have found the routine manner in which he ticked off these points disturbing. He would have hated this guy.

At the moment he just wished he did, because if it was Michael's blood they had used to track them down, then he was responsible.

'How did it get through our protections, past the wardings?' Nicola's hands visibly trembled. Whenever she tried to find the answer herself, thousands of memories would scream over the top of one another, clamouring for dominance until the pain forced all coherent thought from her mind.

'Because you're unschooled and unprepared. Because the knowledge you possess is overwhelming you. Because it has had thousands of years to prepare and you have not.' The words were not meant as weapons but they struck their target regardless.

Michael watched his mother's face as the words found their mark. He had decided that he would hate Ashul after all. Joseph had obviously come to the same decision because he now stood in front of Ashul.

'Because …' Ashul continued, without seeming to notice the anger directed towards him. 'I … failed.'

Michael had once again read things wrongly. The words had been meant to wound, but they were directed inwards. Ashul didn't need to be hated; he was doing a good enough job of that himself.

'We have our own allies. If I speak on your behalf they may consider training you. Come the morn we have a lot of travel ahead of us. So please everyone, bed and rest. Lightning and I will guard your sleep.'

'Your sword?' Michael asked.

And for the first time since they had met him Ashul laughed. For a brief second he looked young.

'Master Michael, your jest is appreciated. No, not my sword. My horse.' And with that he left the house, the smile fading completely by the time he made it out the back door.

* * *

The morning was cool and dew still rested on the lawn as Michael and his family huddled together outside waiting for Ashul to arrive.

Dana was the first to hear the sound of beating hooves. Following her lead they all gazed in the same direction and saw the air above the swimming pool shimmer as Ashul materialised. He rode straight through the pool fence as if it had no substance and then stopped. His horse reared up on the middle of the lawn. It was a very impressive entrance and with annoyingly changing emotions, Michael beamed at his approach.

'Forgive the delay, but the night has been long. Many a foe was summoned and sent back into the ether. Anarcus is still dependant on those next door for its fuel. They will not have the resources to launch any attacks for quite some time. I think we will have some peace over the next few nights. Let us hope he stays dependant for a little while longer.'

And with that, Ashul bowed first to Nicola and Joseph and then to Dana. Michael was beginning to feel a little left out when he strode over and clasped his forearm, nodding. 'I thank you, Master Michael. You saved me from great peril last night. I have brought Lightning and would be honoured to introduce you.'

The black horse moved forward. Michael took a tentative step to close the gap, not knowing what was expected of him. He didn't want to reach up and touch the horse, the gesture too intimate. So he settled on standing in front of the horse, awkwardly waiting for something to happen. Michael looked into the jet black eyes, intimidated, but he refused to submit to the horse.

Lightning's neck muscles relaxed and the proud head lowered slightly. What he thought might be gratitude seemed to soften the gaze. Releasing a breath he hadn't realised he'd been holding, Michael smiled.

The head instantly snapped up and Lightning shook his mane, not aggressively but not quite playful either. The horse took one step forward and Michael resisted the near overwhelming urge to step back. He knew he was being tested and that any sign of weakness would forever lower his standing. Michael felt like almost everything rested on this one exchange. He forced himself to step forward, reducing the distance between them to mere centimetres. Seconds passed and Michael stood eyes locked with that of the horse. The standoff was finally broken when Lighting snorted into Michael's face and stepped away.

Watching the whole exchange as if worlds depended on the outcome, Ashul paused in what appeared to be some form of silent communication. He finally nodded and turned to the group as if nothing had happened.

'I have sensed in my short time with you that many of the old bonds have been lost. I can feel that the connection to the power still flows strongly in your blood, but it is unfocused, confused. I have not the wisdom to teach you the ways, but I know of some that do. So if you could all please cloak yourselves I shall summon the others and we will ride. We go to our allies.'

* * *

It all sounded so heroic, so *Lord of the Rings*. Michael didn't want to be the goose that pointed out the he was not exactly magic. He had no idea of how to cloak himself. Luckily his dad stepped in.

'Not wanting to be the one to burst your bubble, but I think I speak for all of us when I say that we haven't the faintest idea of what you're talking about.'

'But I have seen you all do it. Can it be that you do not realise your use of the magic? Sir, mam, last night you checked on your children. Is this not so?'

'I always check on them,' Nicola said. 'I just don't want to make a fuss about it. I know they're getting too old for me to baby them. So I sneak around a little.' Nicola was almost apologetic. Joseph just bent down to pick out a weed hoping attention would soon be focused elsewhere.

'Well, I was only able to see you because I was watching from the second plane. You were both cloaked.'

'And Fair Dana, did you not enter the kitchen and remove some food from the cooling box?'

Dana also nodded somewhat sheepishly.

Michael was willing to place a healthy sized bet on what his chocoholic sister had been getting from the fridge.

Ashul continued, 'You are all able to cloak, quite well I might add. Just think yourselves invisible, think yourselves quiet, just as you all did last night.'

Michael quietly thanked Ashul for not mentioning that he had also checked on Dana. He was hoping he still had some reputation left to maintain.

'I am sure you are all excellent players in the game, hide and go seeking,' Ashul remarked, 'if you can all cloak without conscious thought.'

And now that Ashul had so blatantly pointed it out, Michael realised that they were. He remembered a time when his mouth had gotten him into trouble with a guy two years older than himself at school. Michael had not wanted the showdown the other guy had so desperately been seeking and had consequently been chased down past the shelter sheds during lunchtime in an effort to avoid confrontation. Michael compounded his error by getting himself cornered standing in the dark in the back of the shed. Hoping that he would not be found, thinking that if the dark were just a bit darker he would be okay. If he could just stay still and blend in like those chameleon lizards the bully would walk right past him.

Michael remembered it all so vividly. Holding his breath. Slowing his racing heart. Trying to just sink back into the shadows.

And sure enough he hadn't been found.

At the time it had seemed like blind luck, but now he realised it was magic.

Dana was smiling too. She was probably remembering some other chocolate pinching expedition where she had *almost* gotten busted.

All this time and they had been doing a *Star Trek*, activating their own cloaking devices and they hadn't even known.

So after a few failed attempts at cloaking, everyone managed to make themselves dim. The process was quite easy once someone explained that it was possible. Michael was starting to believe that a great many things were possible.

Watching his family shimmer before his eyes and then slowly fade was slightly nauseating. Looking in the direction that he knew them to be in caused a spiking pain behind each eye, as if his eyes detected something in front of him but they were unable to focus properly. Luckily everyone didn't stay dim for long and only moments later they all shimmered back into sight and the pain disappeared.

'Maybe we aren't as good at disappearing as you think,' Dana said.

'We could try hiding chocolate in the garden. I bet Dana could cloak herself in a heartbeat then. Now I know how she always came away with most of the Easter eggs.'

Dana refused to even dignify the comment with a response and gave Michael a look only older sisters were able to produce.

'We are all cloaked. You have done well. You are able to see each other only because you know the others surround you. Remember you are not truly invisible. This is a trick, a deception. You are forcing others' eyes away from you, making their vision simply slide off you. If someone has the knowledge that you are present, the glamour will fade and you will become visible.' Ashul explained and then indicated towards the side path where he had heard people approaching before anyone else had.

Brent, Sarah and Ashley appeared, talking amongst themselves as they came through the side gate all looking confused.

'I'm sure I heard them all. The cars are still here, so where could they have gone?' Sarah started to walk back towards the front yard.

Michael briefly considered sneaking up on Ashley and grabbing her from behind but decided against it when he saw both Dana and his mum looking at him disapprovingly.

Sheba, seemingly oblivious to any cloaking, ran expectantly from one person to the next and finally settled on sitting in front of the side gate. Obviously the horses had disappeared as well because Ashley's family seemed to have no concept that they had company of any kind. Which was probably for the best because even though they lived in the outer suburbs, huge war horses in full battle gear strolling casually around the garden could draw unwanted attention.

Ashul waved his hand in front of the group and Ashley's simultaneous squeal and jump in the air indicated that they had all become visible. Being a person of few words, Ashul hastily updated the new arrivals and explained the method for cloaking.

Ashul gave a short sharp whistle and the bonded were summoned.

They materialised, galloping over the pool as Ashul had. Their forms translucent until the hooves touched the ground. The backyard was crammed with horses stamping their hooves and snorting as they tried to find a clear space. Everyone was soon mounted up behind one of Ashul's band with Dana behind Ashul himself. Only then did Michael realise that no rider remained for him to mount up behind.

Looking up at Ashul questioningly, Michael felt movement at his side as a huge grey horse wearing silver tack stood beside him, shaking out her mane.

It was the horse that had been appearing in Michael's dreams since childhood.

This horse had always wanted something from him, desperate for Michael to acknowledge its unspoken request. He had been avoiding this moment for years and now he steeled himself to stand.

His strength almost wavered, the need to turn and walk away becoming almost overwhelming. Michael knew he had a choice to make: to move forward and accept what the horse offered, thereby accepting all of the craziness around him, or he could simply turn away, let Ashul and his band fight this war and forever deny the horse.

Michael could feel everybody's eyes boring into his back: family, warrior, horse alike, but the only ones at that moment that meant anything were those of the grey mare. Her eyes were proud but also restrained as if anticipating another rejection. Michael wasn't sure what he was committing to but he longed to reach out and repair some of the pain he had caused this magnificent creature.

His own mother's words reverberated through his mind. She had always brought him up to believe anything and anyone can let you down, and that was okay. But what was not okay was letting yourself down.

She believed this, and so did he. He only had true control over one thing, and that was himself. Letting himself down was the worst possible crime. And he had done this recently and had no intention of doing so again. It may have been a load of parental bullshit but right now it felt right.

This magnificent animal might forgive Michael but then again she may not. He had to accept the fact that his regret may not be enough. He only had control over the attempt to try and make amends.

Still uncertain of what was being asked of him, Michael lifted a tentative hand, hesitant to offend the proud horse that stood before him. He knew his decision would be irreversible, but knowing this, he stepped forward to reduce the distant. Something had changed inside him recently and he knew this change had only been one step towards where he now found himself. His path was linked to this horse, linked to the riders watching on so intently.

Michael waited. The final step was not his to make. He whispered the words 'I'm sorry' so quietly under his breath, no-one but the horse could have heard them. The grey eyes that had been clouded behind a layer of smoke cleared and the horse stepped forward.

Michael heard his mother call out to him.

But the grey mare had been waiting for this moment for centuries. She lifted her neck up to his hand and as the two touched so the connection was made.

The pealing of a loud bell echoed through Michael, drowning out Nicola's words of concern. His thoughts were flooded by smells, sounds and feelings that were not his own but somehow felt like part of him. His consciousness had been bombarded from an external source too many times in the past few weeks, and each time his mind rebelled, fought, and endeavoured to repel the intrusion.

This was different, this time the thoughts complemented his own; mirrored them, shadowed them and brightened them all at once.

Amongst the images and thoughts that raced through his mind a clear voice overrode the confusion. *'I am Smoke! You have made me whole again!'*

Emotions that he couldn't understand enveloped him: joy for the half of herself that had been found mixed with an unfathomable sorrow for a rider that had been lost long ago. Michael accepted all of the horse's emotions, for they were now somehow his own.

The bonded closed in around him – horses and riders – and he felt a part of them all. When the bell had sounded, when his flesh touched that of the horse, an instant connection to them had been created. It was like the feeling of walking out onto the pitch and knowing his teammates were there with him, and that they had his back. This was the same connection but intensified a hundred fold.

Ashul's face was an image of pure joy, for the first time since he'd met him, the look of intense awareness that so characterised his being had lifted.

'We are whole. After centuries we number twenty-eight again, as we were always destined to be.'

'No you damn well are not.' Nicola half slid, half dropped off from her mount, stumbling towards Ashul. 'He's my son. He is no sleeping warrior; he was not created from dirt and magic. I made him. We made him. She gestured frantically to Joseph who looked on not understanding the importance of what had just happened. 'You cannot have him!'

'The bond has been made. The connection was not forced. The acceptance, the bond, is mutual.'

'He is my son.' Nicola half cried, all strength gone from her voice. She could see the look on Michael's face. His hand had not moved. He had not flinched. She could see that he knew and accepted the bond.

'He is true,' Ashul countered.

'He is a child.'

'He has the soul of a warrior.'

'He is not meant to fight evil!'

'He has been for weeks.'

'*Please?*' Nicola begged.

'Smoke has been soulless since we lost one of our brothers,' Ashul explained. 'I know not how this connection has been made but I feel the truth of it. They're bonded to each other. They now feel and think as one. When we ride, we ride as one. No-one except one of the sleeping warriors has even ridden one of the fleet. But the times have changed. The barriers binding the wild magic are breaking. I know not whether this is due to the intervention of our enemies or because the source chose it to be so. But it *is* so.'

Michael heard none of this debate. He stroked Smoke's heavily muscled neck and without hesitation or conscious thought threw himself up in the saddle. Smoke adjusted for his weight, and her footing shifted slightly. Michael's body swayed in anticipation of the movement he had known was coming. Through the strange link they shared he felt every movement of her muscles as if they were his own. His heart rate slowed to that of the great horse and his breathing deepened.

They were in tune with each other.

Dimly he heard the muttered thoughts of the men of the band, joyful as well as confused. Michael could feel that they sensed a difference between them but they also recognised the bond. He had not been created of magic from a bygone era but somehow here he sat at home on horseback, ready to ride.

Sensing his thoughts, sharing his eagerness to explore, Smoke stamped her feet and with a tensing of her powerfully muscled hind quarters she kicked off from the ground. With a whoop from the men of the band their horses followed suit.

They were in flight, galloping through the air as if flying over ground, skimming over the top of the highest pines that lined the park behind their house. Within moments they were riding through clouds with the cold air beating against their faces. It was intoxicating.

'Ride at my left, brother. Smoke has long awaited the return to her rightful position.'

Smoke and Lightning surged ahead of the others.

Dana glanced over at Michael, who exuded unadulterated delight, emotions radiating out from Ashul in equal quantities. They were like mirrors to one another. It seemed strange to her that she had been the only one to see this coming. Perhaps her mum had been in denial. Always one to find Michael's enjoyment infectious she whooped along with the others. The joy of flight was something that she could easily become addicted to.

At first, they rode for the joy and the pure freedom of it. But soon, with unspoken counsel, Ashul imposed purpose on the group. Riding behind Ashul with her arms encircling his waist, Dana felt the change in his bearing.

They now rode on to find the hidden realm of their allies.

Finding Our Allies

Dana rode comfortably on the back of Lightning.

Ashul insisted she continue to keep a firm grasp of his waist. She didn't complain about this but felt amazingly comfortable flying and the precaution was unnecessary.

They rode through space, through layers of existence, through curtains that served to separate the supernatural from everyday life. All were ridden through with ease. Colours, texture, smells – never before experienced flashed past them in a kaleidoscope of sensation.

After a disappointingly short period of time, they returned to the ground in the deepest part of the bushland that surrounded their neighbourhood. Dana knew these woods like the back of her hand, having travelled hidden paths with Sheba and Michael regularly. She slid off Lightning's back with Ashul holding her arm for support.

The horses were huge and her feet dangled in the air for a few second before they crunched down into the leaf litter covering the path Ashul had brought them to.

It seemed to Dana that they had travelled distances that could not be counted in kilometres alone. The place they landed in looked like the bushland she knew so well; it retained the unique feel of native Australian bush but she couldn't place exactly where they were. The dry medicinal aroma of eucalyptus, coupled with the astringent smell of the introduced pine burnt at her nostrils. The undeniably unique scent spoke of home but she was sure their current whereabouts would not appear on any map. Even the most advanced GPS mapping system would fail to pinpoint where they had landed.

The tones of the animals in the area were muted also, not fearful or agitated, but subdued in a way that would suggest they tread lightly. There was no reaction to the sudden arrival of seven large horses and the riders. The birds rustled their feather but did not fly away, the smaller marsupials shifted positions in their sleeping hollows but did not run, and the insects continued to buzz about their business.

The current warm dry conditions had left the ground covered in deadfall, with each step punctuated by the crack of resistance. The forest appeared never to have experienced the touch of human feet. Pathways through the trees were low and close – old trails made by animals.

Dana chose to walk a little further away from the group. Uncle Brent and Aunt Sarah were content to wander around looking at some unique flowers they had discovered, Joseph was discussing things with Ashul and Nicola appeared lost in her own thoughts, distractedly kicking at the scrub.

Dana, not ready to discuss Michael's bond to Smoke, distanced herself further from the group. She was concerned about the implication of him becoming a bonded warrior. He had gotten himself into enough trouble before and now it was apparently his duty to do so. She hoped there was some kind of loophole that prevented him from becoming a full-time hero. She also had to admit she envied the connection he had not only with Smoke but the other horses in the group. Dana prided herself on her way with animals but with these horses she kept coming up blank. Deciding to keep her frustrations to herself, Dana walked through the dappled sunlight as it cut through the upper canopy. The light level dropped the further she moved away from the clearing. She looked up and the sun was still high in the sky but the trees were positioned in such a way that they greatly reduced the light around her. Having spent time in the bush before, she knew every forest has its own personality, sometimes welcoming, other times oppressive, and on rare occasions resentful of intrusion. Any bushwalker would understand. The bush had its own character and some areas were often not in the mood for visitors. Dana soon realised this forest wanted her out.

The others had caught up with her but all were cursing and annoyed. They were getting repeatedly tangled on any and every branch, twig and thorn. The native flora seemed to be deliberately placing itself in their way.

Aunt Sarah's hair had become so entangled in a thorn bush that she needed assistance because if she moved any further she would most likely be walking away with a bald patch.

Dana, being the most agile in this environment, was getting away pretty unscathed, so she went to Sarah's side to extricate her from the thorn bush's clutches.

Unnerved by the whole situation, Ashley jumped at every shadow, cursed every scratch and soon had everyone feeling equally uneasy. Moving deeper into the bush started to feel like a very bad idea.

Making headway was getting more and more difficulty so Ashul had no other choice but to send the horses away.

'Don't worry, they'll come when I call. Michael since you're now bonded, Smoke will return whenever you have need.' Michael had noticed that Ashul had finally dropped the master bit. He wasn't sure what it meant but it made him feel doubly accepted, like one of the gang.

'So why are we here exactly?' Nicola, never one to hold a grudge *much*, didn't bother wasting time being polite.

'We must go a little deeper to be sure. I'm hoping the faerie still reside here. I can feel that they once did but as to whether they still do, I have yet to uncover. Something is obviously resisting our intrusion. You have done well to control your fear.'

Sarah wiped sweat from her brow with a shaking hand and her other clasped Ashley's so tightly she had all but restricting circulation in her daughter's fingers.

'This could simply be an old deflection spell. Similar to a warding but its purpose is to create fear and thereby force trespassers away. I will need your assistance to enter further as we are not truly still in the woods. We are partway between two levels of existence, where I suspect many magical creatures still dwell. We must join together, broadcast our intent, but be wary, there may be other creatures still here, ones that do not wish to aid us.'

The last couple of metres were the hardest for Dana. With each step she took forward she noticed the reduction in bird song until no animal sounds remained. *What could have driven all animal life away?* She felt small and exposed and without the unconscious reassurance on the animal's presence her fear increased.

They stopped and joined in a circle to broadcast their intent. To Dana it felt more like a plea yet she felt some of the oppression lift.

'Something has changed,' Dana said. 'Somebody heard us. But there's still no animals here. I would have expected the birds to come back.'

Michael wasn't sure why Dana even cared about birds. Smoke whispered into his mind to stop and think. 'No bird song, no insects of any kind – it speaks volumes. Birds are the gossips of the animal world; if something were to happen they would want to be here so they could send out the news. For them to be absent means their fear has outweighed their curiosity.' The last word was said with an unmistakable note of superiority.

Michael hoped that these faeries would realise they were the good guys. If they had the power of the forest at their command who knew what else they were capable of.

Still the resistance continued to ease, but on the downside Michael had noticed that the trees seemed to be moving. He watched on in disbelief as the trunks of trees expanded, the canopy already ridiculously high now soared above them all, almost outside of his ability to focus on clearly.

Uncomfortable with the ever expanding distance between himself and the treetops, Michael looked down towards the ground. It was only then that he realised that it was not the trees that were growing but that *they* were shrinking. And the sensation was less than pleasant. Watching the world expand around him gave Michael a feeling of insignificance as well as mild vertigo. Michael worried how this must be affecting his mother, whether her dizziness had been brought on. He took a moment to turn and check and the pallor in her face said it all. She smiled back reassuringly, but didn't she always. Michael had no time to berate her. Something told him if trouble came it would be from the front so he turned expectantly.

In less than a heartbeat they were smaller than the tallest twig. Down on this level the bush took on a new and even more sinister aspect. From his now reduced perspective the trees were larger than most skyscrapers. A knot of tangled tree roots appeared as a large hill, higher than their heads.

Everyone looked around nervously. Most of Michael's new-found heroism had diminished with size. He was starting to gain a new respect for those fluffy little white dogs that always seemed ready to take on all contenders, even if that contender happened to be a huge dog at least ten times their size. Maybe they were just sick of being intimidated.

Michael was contemplating whether to attempt scaling a fallen stick to get some sort of visual bearings, when his thoughts were interrupted by the words, '*Prepare they come.*'

A steady pounding irregular but similar to the sound of hooves surrounded them.

'I think it best if we find a more defensible position, please all of you move in under the roots over there. Michael, sirs, please find something with which to arm yourselves.' Ashul had taken charge and had soon cleared a small area and herded all the girls together. Dana and Nicola took particular offence at the assumption that they needed protection. Both being quite accomplished in martial arts, they could handle themselves fairly well.

Nicola walked over to a thorn bush and carefully snapped off two wickedly sharp barbs that at their now reduced size resembled primitive swords. She carefully wrapped one end of each with a blade of grass to serve as protection for her hands. Michael followed suit thinking they looked more dangerous than the stick he'd haphazardly picked up and belatedly realised just how sharp they really were. Without the makeshift handle it would be all too easy to slice open his hand. Luckily, Michael followed his mother's lead early enough to get away with only a nick to the inside of his thumb.

The pounding was growing steadily louder and was soon accompanied by the snap of breaking sticks. Whatever was making all the noise was certainly coming in their direction.

Ashul had drawn his sword and positioned himself in the lead to take on the brunt of whatever attack was coming. Michael moved to his left and found himself trying to mimic the cold certainty Ashul projected. Joseph and Brent had each taken flank positions and were brandishing dangerous looking clubs. The girls had picked up something from the ground to defend themselves. None of them were going to go down without a fight.

So there they stood together waiting for whatever was to come. Michael thought to himself that he was well and truly over this being attacked business. He also felt perversely like he was going to burst out laughing at any second.

Michael was renowned for getting an attack of the giggles at the wrong moment, but he couldn't remember a time quite as inappropriate as this. He glanced over to Ashul. He was still looking ahead, still ready for whatever was coming, nothing in his expression humorous. If anything his face was a deadly mask of cold certainty.

But isn't that in itself somehow funny? Well to Michael at that moment it certainly was. He then made his next mistake. He looked at each member of his family in turn.

Some of what he was thinking must have been written across his face, because Michael saw Dana's lips twitch before she turned away from him. He had completely forgotten about being scared, or maybe his brain had just said, *Sorry, none left. We're clean out of stock of fear right now, please call again later.*

Smoke, sensing the shift, spoke sternly into his mind. Michael had battled grey sludge just the night before. He was now bonded to a magic horse and to top it all off he had been shrunk down to a size where the mythical Tom Thumb would seem a giant.

It was all just too much, too absurd and his mind/body responded in the only way it thought acceptable: it just refused to take the situation seriously. The last rational part of Michael's mind looked over to each of his parents' desperate for help, expecting the steely look that they both had down pat, but found that they too were purposefully not looking at each other. Just as he could not risk locking eyes with Dana, they too were deliberately avoiding eye contact with one another. Then Michael's eyes met his dad's gaze.

Joseph mouthed for Michael to '*stop it*' managing for just a second a half convincing look of reproach and, when Michael's expression didn't change, Joseph was the first to crack and everybody else just followed suit.

The last to go was Aunty Sars; she had managed to keep it together for a full second or two past everybody else.

Ashul looked on in disbelief. Just when one of them would get it together, another would burst out laughing. They tried yelling at each other, looking away, covering their mouths – all of the things you try when in this kind of situation and nothing worked. In the end they either fell or sat down and just let it happen. They let the laughter roll over them.

And so it was, as they were wiping the tears from their eyes, that Dana first realised the pounding had ceased and they were now surrounded on three sides by what looked like an army. Ashul, the only one still in a defensive position, kicked Michael's foot to get his attention and Michael looked up to see row upon row of the scariest looking creatures he had yet to come across.

These creatures were built to destroy; they looked completely alien but also oddly familiar. Their bodies were covered in hard armour plating, with six multi-jointed legs that looked capable of ripping arms clean off bodies. To top it all off they had a set of sharp deadly pincers on the front of their heads in place of mouths.

'They're huge bull ants,' Dana whispered, being the first to recognise the creatures. From Michael's angle they looked like something out of *Doctor Who*.

'You called and we have come.'

For a second Michael thought it was one of the ants that had spoken but soon realised the voice had come from the delicate creature riding upon its back.

At this, Ashul bowed. 'Lady, we had come to ask your aid. We seek your knowledge and forbearance as the veil had once again been breached.'

'We have sensed this and regret deeply that your sleep has once again been disturbed. We wish for a time when you may finally find peace. As always we will aid you, Ashul. Are these truly the ones you bring?' The beautiful faerie looked over them contemptuously with a wry smile curling the corner of her mouth. The smile didn't reach her eyes.

She was the same size as they were, which meant she couldn't have been larger than a centimetre tall. She looked exactly like the faeries from books and movies: graceful body, pointed ears, delicate wings. She even had on a dress that seemed to float about her body emitting a steady subdued glow.

'Come join us, *you* have *much* to learn and we have much to teach.' And from up on top of her giant ant she led them down into the ground not down a rabbit hole thankfully, that would have been just too much, but down into an ant hill.

* * *

It had lost track of them. Lost their scent. Surely if one of its brethren had succeeded in destroying them, it would know. It was currently too weak to call to its allies and make the inquiry. It also had no strength for scrying. Through the night it had called too many and found them all repulsed or expelled. Ashul had returned to the second realm and his power there gave it a moment of fear. He knew how to use the power, being born of it and he was also awash in a new kind of energy. One Ashul had not possessed before. It was not able to discern the nature of this power but It knew It came from those next door. It sensed two parts to this new energy and each had the signature of the boy and the girl. It made Anarcus' skin crawl. Ashul was covered in their stink.

In such a short time Ashul had somehow become one with these creatures. Many a battle had they fought and Ashul had protected many of the blood but something here was different.

It sensed that this could be Ashul's weakness. It had been waiting an eternity to find one and now It may just have fallen into Its grasp. If It could just unravel the mystery, find out what had changed.

It would watch and wait. Things were different this time. Ashul was different, the guardians were different.

And while they were elsewhere, It would escalate Its little games with those within Its influence. This host family were currently no more than husks, they recovered so very slowly, so It needed fresh fuel.

When blood was not available, anger, fear, jealousy all worked almost as well.

Fuel after all was fuel.

Cool Welcome

So they followed the faerie down the ant hole.

Michael was thankful that he had gotten all of his laughter out of his system because the initial friendliness, if it could even be called that, seemed to have dissolved into an all business mentality.

They were led through a labyrinth of tunnels and an equally amazing network of curling bridges that joined one section of their land to another. Michael doubted that even half of this structure had been created by the ants – he'd studied their ingenuity in school. The architecture was in tune with the complexity of an ant's domain but the extraordinary delicacy of the structure ensured that this was pure faerie work.

The bridges could never be described as bulky, utilitarian or even just plain functional. They all had distinct differences as if each were a separate work of art. Every panel was etched with elaborate carvings that seemed to whisper to him, calling him to follow their delicate swirls. The colours belonged only to the faerie realm: silvery purples and shimmering blues blended and mixed as if they were not truly static, and more in a constant state of flow. The tunnels too were not merely a method of travel between one place and another; they held an artistry that has to be seen to be understood. Each separate work complemented the one next to it and begged to be viewed and admired, in singularity and as a whole.

Nicola silently hoped she would have the time later to just absorb the wonder of it all. It felt like a place where batteries could be recharged, faith could be renewed and imaginations could soar free. All of which she felt in desperate need of. The burden the book had placed upon her was taking its toll. Her thoughts were fragmented and her soul was too. Her body seemed to be trying to house countless minds, each wanting their say and vying for ownership of the whole.

Their trek finally ended when they reached a large room with an intricately vaulted ceiling, softly illuminated by both the people that resided within and by the walls themselves. Each gave off their own glow. It was all very beautiful, but even more intimidating.

The one that Michael had named the faerie queen addressed Ashul. 'We have too little time for the task before us. We must start immediately. Ashul what have you observed of them, what form does their talent take?' She didn't seem to bother talking to any of them directly. Michael was already preparing to tune out, thinking how rude these little people were, when he was abruptly brought back to the moment.

With a simple movement of the faerie's finger, Michael was lifted off the ground and held suspended far above everybody's heads. She then flew gracefully but somehow menacingly towards him and Michael noticed that nobody in the room was moving, including the other faeries that crowded around the edges close to the walls.

He was in the perfect position to view all this being suspended several body lengths above everybody else's head. She stopped within touching distance of Michael and seemed to remove whatever spell she had placed upon the room and Ashul fell forward, suddenly able to move.

'You think me rude, young Michael, simply because I have not introduced myself, have not offered *you* the correct courtesies? You think we have the time to waste on redundant civility. As we waste time debating the political requirements of this exchange, the bonds are dissolving. For our enemies do not waste time with such pleasantries. They at least understand that time is running out. Would you prefer we sat around eating honey cakes and sipping some golden nectar like in one of your stories?' And as she said this, she reached forward and placed her index finger underneath his chin, her sharp fingernail not quite digging in but getting ready to do so if the situation changed. Using the sharp point of her nail she tilted Michael's head back to make him look her directly in the eyes.

Michael thought, *Yeah honey cakes sounded pretty good and even though she was the faerie queen and had crazy emerald green eyes that sort of hypnotised you, she was acting like a spoilt brat and ought to just chill out a bit.*

He was about to say exactly that when her nail dug in a little deeper as if reading his intentions if not his actual thoughts. Michael had decided that she was going a little bit too far when his mum suddenly materialised in-between them, pushing them both backwards, not with her body but with the air that she displaced just prior to appearing. Both Michael and the overzealous faerie were buffeted by the force as the air repositioned itself.

There was no doubt in Michael's mind that his mum had no idea how she had accomplished the amazing feat. If she had planned to intervene she wouldn't have been looking straight up as she had been when on ground level. But she regrouped beautifully and simply hissed 'Back off' in an undeniably threatening tone.

'Oh, so you are strong in the wild magic are you? Do you truly think that you can compete with my strength?' The Faerie Queen seemed to be issuing a challenge.

'No, but threaten my son again and you will give me little choice.' With the words said Michael could hear the anger leaving his mother voice. She just didn't have the energy to continue. She had been placed under so much strain and the fact that she couldn't maintain her righteous anger spoke volumes to those who knew her.

'We have come here asking your help but we will not be treated like this. We do not wish to compete, only to learn. If that isn't on offer, well then, we best be going.' Nicola then looked pleadingly towards Ashul for help. She was already slowly dropping back down to ground level. Michael doubted this was on purpose. Her strength had given out, but to her credit she made it look like a strategic retreat.

A commanding voice cut through the tension that hung heavily in the room and all eyes turned towards the source. 'That will be quite enough, Malcarielle. You best remember your manners or you will become little better than those we wish to defeat. My apologies, my friends. We've started off badly. I agree with the young man hovering above us:

honey cakes and golden nectar do seem to be in order. Please see to it will you, Malcarielle?' There was a stern dismissal in the voice.

An old man, also winged, but with a heavily lined face and wispy silver hair approached their group, his gnarled hands clasping an unassuming cane that was little more than a twisted stick. He seemed like the kind of person expected to be found mopping floors at school, all except for the wings.

Everyone was frozen, not by magic this time, but by his presence, by his ability to command everyone's attention. They seemed to be in awe of this ancient faerie.

'Ashul, my friend, I am glad to see you once again, regardless of the cause. It still makes this old faerie heart glad to see you. My apologies to your brother and his family. Malcarielle believes too much of the old tales. The walking folk have not entered our halls for many a generation and I think you caught her a bit off guard, and you know how she prides herself on knowing everything.'

'Azuradien, I am equally glad to see you again.' And for once, Ashul seemed to drop his cool façade and shifted to one knee in a bow of respect. When this gesture was waved impatiently away Ashul rose and clasped the still chuckling old man in a fierce bear hug.

'You have aged not a day, old one, and I swear on the one power that you are wearing the same robe you had on when last we parted. Malcarielle's temper seems to have improved somewhat, no?'

'Ah, she may be my daughter but she is not yet queen, yet she already has the temperament of one. But alas we must reminisce later. Please join me, we can eat and talk at the same time I think.' Azuradien then gestured towards a doorway that had not been there moments before. He smiled warmly at Michael and with a small flick of his twisted hand Michael was back on the floor, not lowered, just one minute in the air, the next, not.

It seemed to Michael that things were taking a turn for the better once again.

* * *

They sat around on what the faeries used for chairs, which were more like soft lumps protruding out of the floor that contoured perfectly to body shape. They were seated at a table that was in reality a large flat piece of condensed air that had risen out of the ground and hovered, supported by nothing that Michael could see. None on these things had been there when they entered the room. They had all just appeared at Azuradien's command.

The door silently opened and Malcarielle entered the room carrying a large shimmering silver tray in front of her, covered in various types of cakes, fruits, sweets and drinks that were fittingly enough served out of small flowers shaped like tulips.

'My apologies,' Malcarielle said as she offered them the tray. 'My father is correct, I've forgotten my place. I fear that my own dread of what is to come has caused me to act harshly. I handled this situation not at all well.' With that she turned to leave.

'Please, I'm sorry I don't know your customs here,' Sarah looked around to make sure she hadn't offended anyone, 'but we don't hold grudges. If we did my sister and I would have stopped talking years ago. Stay and help us work out what we need to do.' Somehow managing to make her chair extend so there was room for Malcarielle to sit down. Brent and Ashley shuffled along to the left wanting to allow her plenty of room to sit.

Michael didn't think it was the right time to mention that Aunty Sars had only been half right. She didn't hold grudges, but his mum sure did. Maybe 'grudge' wasn't the right word, but it was close enough.

Dana, Joseph and Michael smiled to each other as they had all noticed that Nicola hadn't said a word. They were all sure that at some point she would say something and none of them would want to be in Malcarielle's silky green slippers when she did.

All things considered, the meal went surprisingly well. The food was a little too sweet for Michael's taste and he left feeling like he'd eaten nothing at all. He was so engrossed in the conversation he barely noticed the renewed energy that was flooding through his system. This faerie nectar was like Red Bull on steroids.

'Ashul, I think Malcarielle asks a good question. You have observed your friends, so where do you think their powers lie?' Azuradien asked.

'Ah, that has been hard to ascertain. I have not much insight to give you. Up until today I had no idea that the wild magic was present in any of them. If not for Lady Nicola being angered, I do not think any of us would have known. Yes, she has managed great feats in the second realm, but the wild magic has not been seen for generations. Master Michael has successfully bonded to Smoke. I know not how this is possible but it has happened.' At this both of the faeries looked at Michael and then to each other.

'What does this mean, Father, a wielder of the wild magic and a mortal bonded? Does this bode well or ill?' Malcarielle seemed nothing like the self-possessed woman whom they had first encountered.

'I think it is both. In life there is always balance. For such powerful magic to be released now, the bonds most surely have been tampered with, if not partially broken. I fear what must have been released to keep the scales in check. You tell us that Anarcus is working to enter the first plane, but what else is brewing? This we must find out. But not before you are prepared. This is the role that has fallen to us.'

Azuradien seemed to ponder how to proceed when Michael felt the need to ask the obvious. 'Why don't you just fight them? You have the magic. You are already trained. What do you need to waste time with us for?'

'It is not our place. We are the teachers, the keepers of the lore. We are forbidden to enter into the battle directly.' Malcarielle seemed disappointed with this answer. Michael empathised with her earlier reaction a little bit more now. He had experienced himself how very difficult it was to watch and not be able to act.

'Sorry about labouring on this point, but we're at war here.' Joseph was getting riled up. 'My family has been endangered. Break the rules for God's sake, just get the job done. We're talking about evil, not somebody jay walking.' He couldn't abide rules just for the sake of them.

Azuradien calmly placed his hand on Joseph's shoulder to show no offence had been taken.

'Believe me when I say we've tried to break the rules. Many of our number will never ride the wind again as they perished in the attempts. Ashul can tell you stories of our young heroes, who believed that they would be able to overcome the covenant, only to have their magic fail them when wielding it to destroy. I myself would have been counted among this number, if my friend here hadn't managed to snatch me away when my magic protection failed me, I would no longer be among you today but I still carry the scars.' And with this Azuradien lifted the sleeve of his robe to show a mass of knotted scar tissue running up his forearm. Under the surface of the skin a liquid black current run up and down, swirling, seeking, writhing. The skin was moving and bulging in places as if whatever was under the surface sought release.

Michael's hands shook as a blunted head passed just under the surface of Azuradien's skin. His hands flew to his ears, trying to block out the liquid voices calling to him. He recognised this black current. He had had the same substance in his own lungs just the day before.

The voices begged Michael to free them, to just pick up the knife lying in front of him and release them. They would aid him. They were not the enemy. Couldn't Michael see they were the ones being held captive? Everything spun, Michael's vision blurred and he fell gratefully into unconsciousness. His last terrifying vision: his own hand wrapping itself around the pearl handle of the knife in front of him.

* * *

He returned to consciousness slowly, with Azuradien lying on the ground next to him. His left arm was covered in blood from the elbow down to the wrist. Michael's hand still held the knife as bloody evidence. And he thought to himself, *Oh God what have I done?*

Surrounded by faerie folk looking like each one of them might risk breaking the covenant to kill him, Michael lifted his hands in a simple gesture of supplication and was as surprised as everybody else to find five black eel-like creatures writhing in his right fist. They morphed and shifted trying for release, one moment insubstantial, pouring over his fist but unable to escape his grasp.

Repulsed, Michael was about to drop them when Azuradien sat up, commanding, 'Don't. In fear of all our lives do not release them.'

'Ashul help me … I can't hold them … I just can't … they're in my head.' At that moment Michael felt sure he would either vomit or faint. As he weakened, began to fail he suddenly felt the rhythm of his heart slow, the blood flowing through his body increased and his grip grew stronger. 'I am with you. Take my strength for it is yours.' Smoke had been unable to enter the faerie realm but the bond with Michael was still intact. With her aid Michael was able to ignore the pleas of the writhing darkness.

Fighting his own inner battle, Michael had not noticed when Dana fell to the ground. Malcarielle bent over her. Dana was deathly pale and equally still. Her lips the only things to move – in constant motion as if she were chanting. Malcarielle had her pointed ear above Dana's lips. Desperate to catch each word, her delicate hands soothed Dana's brow.

'Michael, she speaks to you. She says release them. She will hold them. Somehow she understands their real speech. She knows their purpose. They want to escape and possess us and if they cannot do that they will burn us all. But Dana is sure she can hold them.' Malcarielle was listening to Dana, reciting her words. But her voice did not contain any commitment, she was above her head in this and her searching eyes begged someone to take control.

'Guys I need some help.' Michael struggled to hold the slimy, seething mass.

Ashul looked like his worst nightmare had become a reality. He had drawn his sword and it was blazing, with heat and light rippling out, searching for something to strike. But there was no easy target.

Michael was about to plead again for help when a bolt of electricity shot through his arm. Luckily the current made his grip contract. Not through any amount of bravery, simply the human body's natural reflex to any amount of electrical charge.

Michael, listen they're about to kill you. You must let go. Dana's thoughts overcame the other voices in Michael's head. He turned and found that Dana had managed to sit up and Ashley was now holding her hand on her other side. Although Michael wanted to listen to Dana, wanted to believe that she had the situation in hand, he just couldn't let go.

It was like trying to jump into icy water, saying, 'Okay, jump *now*. Come on, on three, go on do it', and the three count has come and gone and still standing saying, 'What are you kidding?' Well, Michael was having an 'Are you kidding?' moment and he couldn't see how he was going to convince his hand to let the squirming mass of morphing black eels go.

Michael knew panic was starting to set in. He would have welcomed the oblivion if so much had not been at stake. *Panic* seemed like a comfortable place where his mind could close the door behind itself and only take down the bars it had placed across the door when and if it wanted to. But Smoke's calm influence remained and her strength forced the panic down, not out of his mind but behind a door of her making.

Looking around in desperation, Michael found his mum and refused to look away. She nodded in his direction, confident in Dana's decision.

Both knew Dana would never endanger Michael.

'Michael, *now!*' The urgency of her words were amplified somehow, holding a force close to imperative.

Michael released his grip, and a split second later another shot of electricity sizzled from the heads of the black eels. A bolt that would have left Michael's hand a charred ruin and his brain a boiled useless wreck.

If the situation seemed desperate before it should have been out of control now. Five oil-black eels snaked across the floor. The faerie king was still dripping blood and nobody seemed to know what to expect.

But mayhem did not rule. The strange calm radiating out of Dana remained, if anything it felt like it was being reinforced, boosted somehow. The eels tried to fracture into their true nebulous forms but Dana imposed her will. Her mumbling increased and the eels slid across the floor obeying her command.

Michael heard the soft hum that he recognised as the eels generated another charge. The hairs on his arms stood up painfully with the amount of static electricity in the room. Michael knew what was about to happen. Dana was about to get fried. Not a little charge like he had experienced. No, this was going to be a bolt to annihilate all in its path.

Ashul was trying to push his way through the group, moving around the edge so that he could place himself between Dana and the eels.

But Dana continued to encourage the eels. With soft whispered words Dana turned their own tricks against them, urging them to hold nothing back. They must destroy the girl in front of them or they would be trapped again, captured never to be released.

Ashley, Michael realised, was amplifying this message as well as broadcasting the general sense of calm that had taken over the group. The air itself was crackled with the electricity building in these eels.

Those closest to the source, Dana, Ashley and Malcarielle, all had sparks flying back and forward between them, with their hair standing on end.

In the moment that the hum rose to the pitch that signified imminent release, Dana turned to Joseph and whispered, 'A little help here, Dad.'

All eyes shifted in Joseph's direction, expecting to see his cool confidence. Dana obviously knew something they did not. The abject terror written plainly across Joseph's face suggested otherwise. Every aspect of his demeanour spoke of the fear only a parent seeing their child in mortal danger could experience, a parent knowing they would not be able to stop whatever was about to hurt their child.

The calm instantly dissolved. Surely Dana had not called the eels to her on a hunch. She would not bet everything on a sneaking suspicion, would see? For it was now blatantly obvious that whatever she thought she knew, she was the only one that shared the belief.

Dana had played her hand, wagering all.

Ashul had no clear target because too many people were in the way.

Michael could hear the turmoil of Ashul's thoughts. Desperate to save Dana, he pushed forward ready to throw himself the remaining distance.

Michael finally mobilised ran to close the gap.

Joseph's face broadcast the fact that he did not know what Dana expected. He didn't know what she had thought he could do. So he did the only thing he could think of – he jumped to put himself between the eels and his daughter.

Michael knew he wasn't going to get there in time.

Blue fire shot from Ashul's sword with a loud *crack*.

Too late.

At precisely the same moment, the eels now close enough to their target, released their charge.

Michael instinctively turned away to save his sight from the searing flash, the last thing he saw was his dad reaching out towards Dana with a gesture very much like his own earlier.

The image was burnt onto the back of Michael eyes and even with his lids tightly closed the horror of the penultimate moment remained.

The smell of fried flesh and ozone made Michael gag. He tried to blink away the afterimage and restore his sight even though he did not want to see what must now be before him.

When Michael opened his eyes, he first saw Joseph standing, shock written plainly across his face.

Nicola, however, was laughing, jumping up and down clapping, hugging Joseph, kissing him, just plain out of control. Brent and Sarah weren't far behind in joining them.

Michael was slowly able to piece together what he was actually seeing.

Dana and Ashley were sitting hugging each other, neither of them burnt. They hadn't been fried.

But it seemed that the eels had.

Malcarielle and Azuradien's expressions showed they had just witnessed a miracle they could not understand. Joseph just stood there smoking. And this was not to say that he looked cool, his hair, clothes, everything were actually smoking, electricity was running up and down his body, playing across his arms and legs, not burning him, just dancing across his skin.

Ashul, looked at Michael, both haunted and relieved. Joseph pointed towards the ground were the sooty outline of the eels remained and released a small bolt of lightning.

He casually blew the tip of his finger as if he had pretended to shoot a gun.

Becoming some kind of human lightning rod, Joseph had managed to intercept the charge shot towards Dana. And now he was able to disperse the charge running up and down his body at will.

He looked pretty proud of himself too, which made them all laugh, even Ashul.

Of the eels, there remained only an oily black powder where once they had writhed across the floor toward Dana and Michael thought with a laugh 'Too bad, so sad' which was his Uncle Brent's all-time favourite saying.

How had Dana known what their dad was capable of? Simple, the eels had inadvertently told her. They had been scared of him, scared of his power.

Grateful Thanks

To say the faerie folk were taken aback by what had just transpired was a huge understatement. Malcarielle had moved to Azuradien's side and looked at his arm as if she realised something needed to be done but was uncertain what that something was. Azuradien was more poised but still in a great deal of pain, staring at the walking folk with a mixture of astonishment and a healthy dose of fear that had not been present previously.

Some of the faeries hovered uncertainly off the ground. The more timid flew way above in the apex of the vaulted ceiling, creating a confusing flickering of light as they constantly shifted positions. The rest had moved back around the edges, dulling their glow as if trying to avoid notice, huddling, watching, waiting for direction from their leaders.

The scene before Michael was still chaotic so Michael could understand the faerie's concerns. The air still smelled of ozone and burnt eel and the floor was covered in their king's blood.

Nicola was the only one mobilised at that point as her first aid mode kicked in. She was already issuing instructions to get something to clean Azuradien's wound. The faeries responded like they'd been ordered by Azuradien himself. He empathised completely – Michael didn't blame them, his mother was quite insistent. Dana already knew what was required and had cleared the area surrounding Azuradien so she could work unimpeded.

All in all, the simple humans were handling this whole situation a hell of a lot better that the faerie folk. They were clearly shell-shocked. The facade of the faerie's emotional indifference had been shattered. Violence, even though wielded in their defence had been released amongst them and they were at a loss of how to respond. They stood apart as if scared that the tendencies may somehow be catching.

Michael felt like shaking them and screaming into their faces.

Didn't they realise this is what they had been dealing with for weeks? Ashul walked over and placed a restraining arm on his shoulder. 'Brother, you know not what has transpired here. You broke through a faerie's charms. You should not have been able to touch Azuradien with a blade, let alone slash his forearm from elbow to wrist. He is the strongest amongst them and you breached his natural defences.'

'I couldn't let them stay under his skin. I needed to get them out of him. I remembered how it felt to have them inside me.' Michael offered this more of an apology than an explanation.

'Your motives are not in question. If they were, you would now be bound beyond hope of release. It is just that what you did should not be possible. But then nor should that.' And Ashul indicated towards Joseph. Small amounts of electricity still sizzled across his skin like water, with static occasionally sparking off his hair.

Having cleared the makeshift triage area, Dana walked over and hesitated, obviously wanting to hug her dad but a little afraid of the electricity running over his skin.

'Dad, thank you. For trusting me. For saving me. Did it hurt you?' She reached a finger tentatively to touch him. 'Doesn't that burn?'

'Dee Dee, I'm just glad you are safe.' And Joseph wrapped his arms around her. The veil of electricity expanded to cover Dana and she laughed in surprise. When she stepped aside and the contact between them broke, she felt a slight zap but nothing that could be considered painful.

Dana couldn't help but remember the time he had whipper-snippered through a power cord. Mum had gone absolutely ballistic. 'Didn't he know safety switches only saved about 90% of electrocutions? Why was he so foolhardy? He could have been killed ...' On and on she went and Joseph had just quietly listened, seemingly unaffected by both the tirade and the danger he had put himself in.

There was no doubt in Dana's mind that he knew all about safety. He just seemed to have a few blind spots when it came to himself. Dana wondered if he had always possessed this strange ability and that it was just waiting for the right circumstance to become apparent. Could it have been that on some deep subconscious level he knew this and therefore did not worry overly much about the risks, knowing that electricity was deadly to others but posed no threat to him? What would have happened if they had not had a safety switch? Would he have sucked in the electricity and then just spat it out as he had done today or would he have been killed like their mother's ravings had suggested? Were these falling barriers letting strange powers through? And what exactly was the story with herself being able to control the eels? Dana had been able to hear their speech, not the thoughts they threw into everyone else mind's, but the hissing whispers they murmured to each other. She had heard them and understood them when nobody else could.

No wonder the faeries were having trouble coping. They dealt with magic as part of their natural existence and still things were not working as they were supposed to. The rules were changing rapidly and as if to confirm her thoughts another astonished gasp rose from the faerie folk.

Dana looked up to find Azuradien's arm cleansed of blood and healed. The twisted scar remained but not the open wound that Michael had inflicted upon him to release the eels.

'Dana you should have seen it,' Ashley spoke in a hushed whisper. 'My dad just started to pick things up off the table. He looked like he was in a daze, operating on autopilot. I didn't see everything he grabbed but I saw him mix some ashes from the burnt down candle with the nectar. He even crushed some of the flowers we drank from and threw them in. I wasn't really paying much attention but he mixed all of the things together and then poured the liquid over Azuradien arm. To give the old guy credit, he didn't flinch; he just grabbed the cup from my dad's hand and drank the rest down. You could see the pain wash away from his face almost instantly. His arm is completely healed.'

The faeries had been hovering around the edge of the room, erratically flying up to the ceiling to then descent and flutter as close to their king as they dared fly. The soft hum of their wings would rise to an intense buzz then drop back down to a steady hum. Their movement created a constant flickering of light, the low glow the faeries normally produced was sparking in abrupt flashes, creating an erratic kaleidoscope of light. When Azuradien stood, his face was bathed in a warm steady glow of appreciation as his people crowded close to ensure he was unharmed. He accepted their warmth and waved them away to go about their business.

Michael remained at Ashul's side, not yet certain that the faeries would understand, knowing that he didn't fully understand why he acted the way he did himself. Ashul seemed to mirror his uncertainty.

'They haven't bound me yet! And it looks like Uncle Brent has managed to clean up my mess so here's hoping. No harm, No foul.' As Michael said the words he knew they sounded childish but he did not know how to deal with the anguish radiating from his friend.

'Ashul, I will apologise. I wasn't in control. I didn't mean to just slice into his arm. I can't actually even remember cutting them out …'

'It's not that. They will not only understand, they will honour you. Their greatest healers could not remove the darkness, could not breach Azuradien's defences to relieve his suffering. What I abhor is my own failure. I should have taken that charge of electricity, not your father. I am the one who is sworn to protect you and I just stood by and did nothing.'

'But Dana knew Dad was the one that could help. Are you telling me that you have that same power?'

'No, I'm not able to wield electricity as your father has demonstrated. I have my sword, my knowledge and my strength. I was born of magic so I have its power but I know not whether I could have withstood *that* charge!'

'So what would have happened if you had stepped in, if Dana had called on you?' Michael was finding it difficult to follow Ashul's reasoning.

'I would have been honoured to serve her.'

'And died trying, am I right?' Dana said, stepping into the conversation.

'My survival is inconsequential. I would have saved you and spared your father the risk.'

Dana was fed up by this stage. Everyone else was celebrating and now she had another chivalrous idiot to deal with. She was just about to let fly when her mother stepped in.

'Ashul, if you had intervened we would have lost you. That makes no sense. We're in this together. You have to learn to let us take risks also. Who knows a situation may arise when we will have to risk ourselves to save you!'

Ashul froze and his eyes turned to ice.

'This cannot happen. I am your protector, nothing more than a tool. You may never risk yourselves to save me. You are the ones of the blood. You are the one who must be guarded, above all else. Do you understand me? Above *all* else, that is my sworn duty. That is my only purpose. We bonded warriors would all perish to save those of the blood. To do anything less would be a violation of our oaths. It would blacken our souls.' Ashul had taken her hands and was actually pleading his case, desperate for her understanding.

'Have you forgotten so quickly that my son is now a bonded warrior? Are you saying we should stand by and let him perish also?' The steel was back in her voice and there was no arguing with her now. She would drive her point home and take no prisoners. Michael felt sorry for the hardened warrior. He may have fought many foes over the centuries but how many pissed-off mothers had he had to deal with?

Nicola stood hard as granite, watching the realisation of what she had said sink in. She saw his shoulders slump. She didn't want to break him, she just needed him to understand. As with her own children, she had to harden herself when delivering harsh lessons. Only when she understood, did she relent.

'Don't you realise, you are more than a protector to us. Are you not made of the very blood we are descended from? You are family. I couldn't stand by and do nothing whilst you were in danger.' Her eyes softened and she looked at them all with that maternal expression that always embarrassed Michael so much. Right now he quietly admitted to himself, it made him feel like part of something bigger.

'To do anything less would blacken my soul.'

This was too much for Ashul. He just turned and walked away. He didn't storm off nor did he slink away chastised. He just moved away like someone who could physically take no more.

Nicola started to follow but Azuradien stopped her with a gentle hand and bid her to stay.

'Give him time. You have offered him the greatest of all gifts – one that he has longed for, for an eternity. He has ever watched the bond that exists between family, knowing he would never have one of his own, trying to accept that he would never be able to experience this unique gift. You must understand he was not born, he was created. He, more than the others, have always recognised the difference, wishing it could be other than it is.'

'But his brothers, the others of the bonded, they're his family aren't they?' Michael was one of the bonded now too and was the one to ask the question. But he already knew the answer. That there was a bond was undeniable. But did he feel close to the bonded like he did to Dana? Michael knew he did not.

'Michael, they're comrades, sworn to the same purpose, held together by magic, not choice. There is very great difference.'

'But he will either learn to accept this gift or he will not. I suspect, dear lady that once someone finds a place in your heart that is exactly where they remain. Now not wanting to be rude but there is much we need to talk about. But before we sit in conference, Michael I must thank you. My flesh has been contaminated with those foul creatures since I was a young fool. You have released me from their curse, for the first time in an eternity my head is clear of their voices. I owe you a debt of gratitude no words could ever convey. Know only that if you ever have need and that need is within my powers to give, so shall it be given.'

And here Michael was wondering how to apologise. He had an idea of the depth of gratitude Azuradien was trying to express. He had felt the eel's foul presence in his body. The thought of having to endure their existence slithering under your skin for years ... Michael suppressed a shiver. He nodded his acceptance of the debt.

Michael was glad Azuradien held no ill feeling towards him. A gash from wrist to elbow was more than an acceptable price to pay for the removal of the eels.

Ashley jumped in and asked the question that Michael had been trying to find a polite way to broach. 'Azuradien,

I'm sorry but the curiosity is too much. Can you tell us how you came to have those awful things under your skin?' Ashley she wasn't rude, as such – she was more straightforward. And if she needed to know, she asked the question.

'Well, that is a tale that needs telling over a cup of tea. Please let us remove ourselves from this room. It's quite overly gore covered, don't you think? My old body needs to rest, please join me in my private suites.'

So after looking around at the table that was littered with blood splattered sheets, and the floor with its oily black smudges they all decided that another room sounded like a good idea.

Empathy, Electricity & Something Else

They followed Azuradien to his quarters. Malcarielle joined them fussing around her father as much as he allowed. When Michael entered Azuradien's room it was nothing like he had expected, which Michael had to admit was more towering walls, strange furniture and sweeping domes. This was a small comfortable room, furnished as you would expect a well-off eccentric to decorate. An eccentric who was human.

Chairs with plump velvet covered cushioning. Thick rugs on both the walls and the floor. Side tables in beautiful polished woods. The woodwork did not look like anything Michael had ever seen before. It looked to have been grown rather than carved. He doubted if any tools had been used in the creation of the furniture. Tables boasted anything from one to five legs, all of varying thicknesses with a structure that suggested they had grown straight out of the ground. The room had a more organic feel compared to home but it was a far cry from the cloud furniture they experienced in the great hall. A large fireplace dominated the room and with another of those casual flicks of Azuradien's wrist, the coals and wood burst into flame. Not a stick had been lying in the grate when they entered and the fire that danced before them was blue and purple in colour.

'Do make yourselves comfortable.' Azuradien gestured around at the couches and chairs.

When no-one moved to comply, and he realised that they were all staring at the fire, Azuradien laughed and explained, 'Oh the fire, I spent quite a time in the mortal realm and grew fond of a lot of your ways, comfortable furniture, plush rugs and roaring fires. Many a night I spent with one king or another discussing matters of great importance with my feet stretched out, sharing his footstool, enjoying the simple pleasure of nice warm feet. We do not have the same use for fire that you do and do not use nature's abundance in quite the same fashion but I managed to convince a couple of fire sprites that if I helped them out sometime, they could help me out here.' And he finished by indicating the fire as if that explained everything.

Luckily Malcarielle noticed the puzzled glances travelling between them and requested that the sprites present themselves to the mortal guests.

The fire stopped its random dance and separated and reformed into five little blue and purple sprites. They looked very similar to the faeries. Small delicate creatures with hair that was a blaze of flame, their eyes too seemed to be made of fire, and when they opened their mouths to speak a thin crackling sound emerged, the exact same sound a fire makes as the wood pops and sizzles. Their colours shifted and merged between the blue and purple they'd already seen, right through the full spectrum of the rainbow.

Dana and Ashley crept forward and they both turned to Nicola in wonder. 'Just like your stories, Aunty Nic. They're just the same as you always described them.'

A slow blush creep up Nicola's cheeks 'I never ... I dreamed and just made that into stories.' Azuradien and Malcarielle shared a puzzled glance at this. Michael was getting ready to ask them exactly what that look meant when a fire sprite bouncing past him. It landed on Joseph's head and then burst into a shower of exploding sparks. Embers glowed on his dad's shoulders for a couple of seconds then faded away to nothing.

As the last ember died away the explosive sprite appeared back amongst his friends in the grate. With five distinct pops they dissolved back into the fire from which they had only moments before materialised.

* * *

Dana and Ashley sat on the rug in front of the fire mesmerised. Occasionally, a small face would wink at them from amongst the flames and both girls would jump back enchanted.

Michael had moved to stand beside Ashul being more interested in the tale the faerie king had to tell.

Azuradien sat back for a moment enjoying the warmth from the fire, collecting his thoughts. When he began to speak all eyes were upon him. 'I was young and foolish once. It may be hard to imagine under all this silver hair and wrinkled skin but it is true.' Malcarielle had moved to stand behind his chair and had placed her hand upon his shoulder, encouraging him to continue.

'I was a fool! At the peak of my power, I was forced to watch as many mortals, people I counted as friends, died in their attempts to destroy the black foulness of the eels. I, who had been named the greatest power our people had seen in generations, awash in their praise sought to breach the covenant. I attacked the evil directly, sure in my own power.' Azuradien chuckled at his own arrogance.

'I acted. I let forth a bolt of energy, its purpose, to annihilate the creatures. I succeeded in doing nothing more than stripping myself of all my magical protections, something that I would not be able to do consciously.'

'Our magical barriers, you must understand are to us like your skin is to you. Any magical folk, be them faeries, sprites or even Ashul here, could not willingly remove this protection, any more than you could shed your skin. But this is exactly what my attack had done. Sensing my unprecedented weakness, the black tendrils struck. My body was covered in a matter of seconds. Then their search for a way inside began.' The already weakened faerie paled during his recollection.

Michael was finally starting to realise the scope of what he had done. He had broken through the magical field of one of the most powerful faeries of his time. Ashul nodded to Michael when their eyes met and urged him silently to listen.

'I don't suppose there is any of that amazing tonic left is there? No? Well, we may impose on you to make us up another batch during your visit.' Azuradien suggested raising his eyebrows towards Brent. 'It does give one an amazing buzz.'

Malcarielle began to fuss at this point, plumping already overstuffed cushions and straightening the sleeves on his gown. When she tried to throw a rug over his legs, Azuradien's patience finally snapped and he kicked the rug towards the fire, where the sprites greedily materialised and reduced the cloth to glowing threads and a puff of smoke in a matter of seconds.

'I will not bore you with the struggle that resulted. But if not for Ashul ripping the majority of those things from me, I would have perished.' Azuradien nodded towards his friend. Ashul, still locked in thoughts of his own, barely acknowledge the gesture and seemed annoyed that the lesson should be interrupted by such an insignificant fact.

Resigned to this quirk in his friend's nature, Azuradien continued, 'It took only minutes for my strength to return, my barriers automatically reactivated. Unfortunately, the eels you encountered today were trapped within this barrier, trapped inside my very skin. Not even the most skilled of our healers are able to breach another's barrier and therefore the eels could not be removed. Destined by my own pride and stupidity to be their unwitting prison. Tormented in mind and tortured in body as they fought to escape. When escape proved impossible, their evil turned to manipulation of my mind.'

Michael had been completely transported by Azuradien's words.

'This is why what you have done today Michael is doubly a miracle. You not only sensed the evil hiding under my skin, you managed to penetrate my magical protection. So before we go any further, have you any more surprises for us? I don't think my old heart could take any more excitement today.'

Azuradien's story was a lot to take it in and Michael felt that he should clarify some points. He had not acted to save anybody. He barely remembered reacting at all. The eels had whispered in his head, echoing through his mind. Something deep inside him had had enough and his next clear memory was holding the handful of writhing darkness and his desperate need to be rid of them. There had been no heroism on his part. Dana's undeniably, but not his. But before he had a chance to speak, the conversation had moved on and there was a deep discussion in progress about where each of their powers lay.

Azuradien listed their 'talents' in the same fashion his mother would tick items off a shopping list.

'We have a wielder of the wild magic.' Azuradien indicated to Nicola. 'Unfocused, but powerful.' One of his long delicate fingers went up.

'A bonded mortal, something never been seen before.' Another finger was raised.

'A… what did you call him, Michael? A human lightning rod, which to our minds means power over the elements of water and air. It may be that Joseph can be trained to work with more. Do you have an affinity with any other element that you can think of?'

Without hesitation or consultation everyone yelled out, 'Fire!'

They all had a story that could be told about Joseph and fire. Fireworks, bought by the case load, set off for any occasion. Barbeques, where a full truck load of charcoal had been used to fry a couple of sausages. Open fires at home where they could almost have roasted a pig if they wanted to.

The stories almost always ended in disaster, almost. But Joseph somehow managed to get control of things just in the nick of time. He had never lived down the time he had got rid of an ants' nest with petrol rather than traditional pesticides. Once he'd properly dowsed the ant hole with petrol, Joseph had stepped back and thrown a match. With a resounding *whump* fire spewed up out the ground in five or six different places around the garden.

Joseph hadn't considered the fact that an ant hole would have more than one entrance. Michael and Dana had found half the back garden ablaze, a plastic slide melting and their father standing nonchalantly in the middle of it all, an amused half smile on his face.

In Dana's mind things were starting to make sense. The electricity, the fire – her dad definitely had some level of control of these things all along, albeit unconscious. The fire sprite, dancing above his head raining embers on his shoulders, had obviously recognised his talent.

And as if to confirm her analysis had been correct, the playful blue sprite popped out of the fire, screeching as it danced first on one of her father' shoulders then the other. Each time it dissolved into flame and burned its way over his head, reforming with a pop and sizzle, where it would settle for a few moments dancing happily before it melted back into flame. The sprite emitted an extraordinary amount of heat that Dana instinctively shrank away from. She had a healthy respect for fire that made the whole encounter somewhat uncomfortable. The sprite was enchanting but the fire itself made her heart beat erratically.

Joseph on the other hand was thrilled by the whole thing. He held out his hand in invitation and it was surrounded in flame instantly. The fire in the grate suddenly extinguished as the family of sprites exploded into life dancing over his knuckles and up his arm. The cracking sound was almost deafening as their enthusiasm grew.

Azuradien threw the fire sprites a stern look, the flames dancing over Joseph's hand disappeared and a second later the fire exploded back into life, Azuradien wiggled his feet in appreciation of the returned warmth. Joseph, however, looked mournfully at his hand before lowering it back down to his side.

'Good. That theory seems to be confirmed. Fire will be a very powerful weapon.' Azuradien looked pleased.

'A potion master.' Another finger raised as he nodded towards Brent.

'An empath who can project,' Azuradien continued.

Michael had started to kick haphazardly at the edge of the carpet. He had no idea what a projecting empath was, he just hoped they would not project all over him.

Concentrate: there is no time for your humour now. The voice of Smoke broke instantly into his thoughts. She sounded a lot like his mother, and he had to smile at the comparison. *'She sounds like a wise woman. Focus!'* Smoke retorted and then broke the link. Michael tried to apologise. This was all going a bit over his head. But a faint snort of derision was all that he received.

Michael turned to see Ashul suppress an awkward smile, Smoke had obviously broadcast her opinion to all of the bonded.

Finally Michael realised it was Ashley that Azuradien was talking about. Apparently an empath was someone who could pick up on another's feelings and someone who was sensitive to those around them. Being able to project meant she could make those around her feel that same emotion and amplify it if needed. Apparently it was Ashley who had broadcasted the sense of calm they had all experienced. It was Dana who had been in control. Ashley had been able to pick this up and broadcast the message out to calm the group.

This surprised Michael not one bit. Ashley's moods were always catching, be it good or bad. Michael had just classified her as having an infectious personality but nothing was as simple as it seemed.

Then Azuradien turned towards Sarah, his bushy grey eyebrows raised.

Almost apologetically Sarah answered, 'I can sew.' She quickly looked around the group embarrassed.

'Be not ashamed. Binding magic is very powerful and has a wide range of applications. Although it is harder to learn, if we had access to the ancients' writing with our protection you would be able to read the text and unlock more of the power. Alas I think the book was lost long ago.'

Without thinking Michael jumped in: 'Mum has a special book. She read it to find out about the evil little bastard Anarcus.'

Azuradien's foot stool flew towards the fire as he jumped up from his chair. The stool was consumed by the sprites in a burst of intense fire, the heat less scorching than the gaze he threw towards Ashul.

'You allowed them to access the archives alone and unprotected.' Azuradien no longer looked the old, kindly faerie but an untamed force to be reckoned with.

'I did not! They have not attempted such foolishness on my watch.' Ashul stood forward, a warrior that would no longer stand with head bowed.

They faced off against each other, neither gaze wavering. The air in the room thickened with the power they unconsciously generated. Malcarielle tried with a gentle hand to direct her father back to his chair but to no avail.

The awkward silence was finally broken when Nicola stood up, adding her own anger to the charged atmosphere. 'What was I supposed to do? Watch my son being tortured, in his dreams no less, by that sadistic freak and its pet family? Wait while a force I didn't know existed came in to save the day? Or should I have just sat back and waited, just as the faeries were doing, to see how things played out. No, I chose to take the risk and protect my son. I choose knowledge over denial.' The last five words echoed through the room, as if many voices had spoken. The power behind the words was immense and undeniable. Generations of anger added their own force and the intensity was far too much for a human mind to channel let alone contain, and so, drained, Nicola crumbled to the floor.

Battle Training

Spluttering back to consciousness, Nicola felt the sweet taste of Brent's elixir firsthand. It was powerful stuff: her limbs tingled with an almost uncomfortable buzz, like having a straight shot of caffeine, times one hundred. But her heartbeat was slow and her mind felt clear for the first time in ages.

She opened her eyes to find a group of faces looking down at her anxiously. On some level she realised her words had been harsh but she also knew they had been fair. She would not take back what she had said. Her children's lives had been in danger and she would risk more than her own sanity to save them and if anyone had a problem with that then it was their failing not hers.

Her eyes were steely as she raised herself to her feet accepting only Joseph's firm hand in assistance.

'Do you know the danger you placed yourself in?' Ashul asked gently.

'Yes, I think I do.'

'Think? You need to know. The book is dangerous. A tool that should only be used when the appropriate wards are in place. It is a tome for more than just knowledge. With every use the book gains more power because this is part of the transactional nature of magic. For the information received you will have given something of yourself.

Joseph spoke up now, concerned, 'Do we have any idea what this book has taken? Azuradien, can you tell us?'

'Not without access to the book. I will make it my first course of action to uncover this very detail once you have been trained. But you still have not grasped the importance of my words. The book contains fragments of every mind that has already accessed the book. A bartered moment of memory taken by the book to enhance its own store of information. Every fragment has only the knowledge of the pain that drove them to the book in the first place. In the days of the book's creation, it stood open for all hands to access its knowledge, so the book was balanced by the intent of the queries posed. But as the power grew the book was only used in extremis, thereby changing the nature of that held within the pages. These poor slivers of consciousness know only their moments of need. Their emotions are not tempered by a lifetime of experiences to enable some form of balance.' Azuradien had taken Nicola's hand and looked at her with open concern.

'The powers in that book could have possessed you. I have read into your consciousness and found that some may have already taken root in your mind.' Nicola snatched her hand from Azuradien and jumped up with a ferocity that belied her recent condition.

'Read me again without my consent old man and you will have a battle on your hands.' Nicola heard the echo of a multitude of voices giving her words power and threat. She could feel the minds contained behind a barrier trying to break through but the elixir or something stronger gave her the ability to endure without being overwhelmed.

'I have placed a block in your mind where the others are bound. I did this because you were unconscious. There was one mind so wracked by torment that he would never have allowed me to block him. Your mind is in great peril from one named Trevlor. He will seek control.' Azuradien defended his actions but in a subdued understanding almost apologetic voice.

'I honour your bravery,' Ashul said. 'But you must understand, the risk was too great.

'No. The book and Trevlor gave me the knowledge to call you, to protect my family.'

'When choices are few, we all do what we must. The faerie have done you a great wrong when we sat in observance, underestimating the danger.' Azuradien lowered his head with the weight of the words spoken, but he was a king and he soon raised his eyes. 'In the interim, if the lady does allow it, I will continue to strengthen the barriers, to protect your mind. I know the burden of having another's presence fighting for dominance.'

Nicola nodded, but still gave no apology for her outburst.

Michael sensed Ashul's approval.

They were both alike, blinded by single-minded opinions, convinced they were always right. Michael wished he felt the same kind of certainty.

When Ashul's eyes turned toward Michael they held nothing of the king's empathy. He approached towards Michael, placed his hand on his shoulder and asked,

'Ready to train?' Without waiting for a response Ashul had strode past and Michael followed behind wondering if this was really the time for soccer.

* * *

When Michael thought of training he thought physical activity, movement, speed. This wasn't training; it was more like school. And it had been in session for days. He had come to the realisation that adults could make anything boring if they tried hard enough. Azuradien had already spent one day going through the principles of magic. He sensed Smoke linked closely to him, attentive on the discussion. Today was about maintaining balances, sensing the flow, drawing slowly, focusing intent, blah, blah, blah …

'So, young Michael, you find this boring? Well maybe now you can show us what you're capable of?' Malcarielle had not been present for the majority of their sessions, claiming she had important work she needed to complete. Although each time they had a break, she would join them, supervising the distribution of food and drinks, ensuring everyone was being well looked after. Her face looked strained and her skin had an almost translucent sheen, but she was always unerring polite. Michael found that each time he looked up, usually just as he stuffed a honey cake into his month, he would find her green eyes boring into him as if she were looking for some further flaws in his personality.

She had only just walked back into the room when she pointed out to the group how bored Michael appeared. Her ability to read him was fast beginning to annoy him, but her tone was encouraging this time, not challenging.

'Come, I have made this for you.' She unwrapped a bundle of green silk to reveal a sword with an elaborately decorated scabbard. With some effort she drew the sword and handed it to Michael. Holding the sword in an awkward grip initially, Michael admired the blade. He realised that it very much resembled Ashul's. It was silver down the length of the blade but it looked to have traces of black woven through it, as if a wisp of smoke had been folded into the metal itself. The handle was wrapped in black leather and she had engraved the same strange symbols that appeared throughout the faerie realm, around the hilt.

Before he could think of anything to say, Malcarielle stepped behind Michael, reaching around his chest and carefully buckled on the scabbard so that it now hung across his back. She rested one hand on his shoulder and another on his waist. After a brief pause her magic flared and the scabbard disappeared. Michael could still feel it resting across his back but most of the weight had lifted. He found Malcarielle's delicate touch much more noticeable.

As he sought the correct words to thank her for the awesome gift, his hands found their correct position on the hilt.

Azuradien nodded approvingly at his daughter. 'The queens of our realm have always gifted the bonded with their arms. My daughter has wrought well, the balance seems perfect.'

'The balance is sweet.' Michael had not really been listening to Azuradien. He was instead captivated with the sensation of spinning the sword in his hands. He was able to roll the sword around, from hand to hand without any loss in balance. It felt part of him, designed for him. When he finally turned to thank Malcarielle, she had already taken one step closer.

'I have watched you, studied the way you move. I have also added all the strength I could. Please show my rambling father what you can do.' And she whispered to Michael, 'Do not think, just do. Imagine power flowing through you, enjoy it.' Malcarielle smiled up at Michael. 'My father often forgets that part.'

Ashul halved the distance between them as he drew his own sword. Joseph sat on the edge of his chair. The disinterested look had left his face. Joseph's eyes were wide, darting from Michael to Ashul eager to have something to watch.

'Alright brother, let us spar. Don't hold back. I will have my protections raised so you need not worry.' Then he added with a mocking pause,' about *me.*'

Michael wished not for the first time in his life that he had kept his thoughts to himself. The intensity of the light increased as a score of faeries flew in, hovering around until they each found an unobstructed view of Michael and Ashul. He had become the main event of the evening.

Dana and Ashley were sitting side by side and Dana looked ready to pounce forward and intervene if needed. His mother had a slight frown on her face.

Ashul drew his sword and with not so much as an *en garde* he raised it above his head and swung ready to strike.

Both instinct and Smoke's guidance helped Michael raise his own sword in time to parry the blow. Their swords met with a clash of steel on steel. Michael's hands took the majority of the impact with his palms stinging and wrists temporarily numb.

He was holding his sword much too tightly, echoed through his mind. His bonded brothers were offering advice. It seemed this contest was being watched by many interested viewers.

The bonded laughingly wanted to see their leader get bested so long as it was by one of their own. Rather than finding these thoughts confusing, they somehow harmonised and focused Michael's own.

Michael knew that even if Ashul didn't hit him – he hoped such things were frowned upon in training sessions – Michael wouldn't be able to match his strength, speed or endurance. And Ashul wasn't holding back. With blinding speed Ashul turned and swung his sword low trying to sweep across Michael's midsection. He had been warned. Smoke knew Ashul's style. Michael managed to jump back and catch the sword on his cross-guard. Malcarielle's runes flared brightly, slowing Ashul's movements for a few seconds. She winked at Michael from the sidelines.

All of this seemed a little unfair. Ashul had been doing this all of his life, his very long life. He was a warrior after all. Michael was just a … well to be honest he wasn't sure what he was anymore. But being distracted at this particular moment by a pretty winking faerie was not his most clever move.

Ashul wasted no time. To add a little sting to the lesson he had the nerve to somehow spin Michael around and then slap Michael across the backside with the flat of his blade.

Michael heard the bonded's sympathetic cries in his mind. Ashul could be a harsh teacher.

Smoke remained a rock as her strength gave Michael speed and focus. It was like having another mind, another set of eyes watching out for him, warning him, guiding him.

Slapping someone across the bum didn't seem knightly; it seemed kind of childish to Michael and he was supposed to be the king of childish. The giggling from the watching faeries didn't help matters either.

Enough was enough. From that moment on Michael took Malcarielle's advice: he forgot to think, he just did. He was able to synergise all of the messages and guidance coming from external sources and channel the result. Michael was doing something for the first time but his body responded as if he had practised a million times before.

Michael fell into the rhythm of parry and thrust. Spinning away from an attack only to sweep his sword double handed above his head and come through the move on the offensive. He could almost anticipate Ashul's next strike. It was a dance and Michael knew the steps. He had Ashul on the back foot, but Michael knew the knight was stronger and that eventually he would win. He needed to draw power and then he might stand a chance.

He focused his intent, drew slowly as instructed. He could feel the power building and was about to let Ashul have it with a spinning sweep that was supposed to take his legs out from under him and at the same time deliver a nice jolt, but … nothing happened. No blazing light flowed down the blade, not even a dull glow. Absolutely nothing.

Ashul sensed his complete failure and chuckled to himself and made his own sword flare. And with an uncharacteristic smirk he advanced. Michael backed away barely managing to keep Ashul's sword from his skin.

Ashul had started to take things just a little too seriously and with an ease that showed he had just been playing with Michael all along he broke through Michael's defences and drew a line of fire down his left arm. It stung like a bastard not just as a result of the slice on his arm but because Ashul had added a nice kick of magic to the blow, as if to make a point of what Michael had attempted but had been unable to do.

Michael had been pushed too far, pushed to a point where he really didn't care anymore and all he could focus on was the smirk. Not the power or the training. Michael had no intention of being fancy, that wasn't his style. He wasn't going to try and swat anyone across the backside. Michael was hoping to knock Ashul's sword aside just for a moment so he could smack Ashul hard in the mouth. But Ashul flicked the sword around as if weighed nothing. It was an extension of his own body, and every small opening Michael made was soon defended.

Sweat trickled down Michael's back and his arm shook with the effort required to keep his sword raised. His pulse throbbed steadily in his temples indicating just how exhausted he was becoming. Michael knew he was starting to lose his grasp on the sequence of the fight, and a fight was exactly what this had turned into. Not a battle to the death, nor until someone fell. This was a fight for something more elusive, harder to describe. It wasn't quite pride but Michael would be lying to say that was not a factor but it was something more, self-worth maybe. Not having the words to describe it didn't make the wanting any less. It was something he needed to do, and it allowed Michael to completely focus on attaining that goal. Seconds, or maybe hours later – he could hardly tell anymore – Michael saw an opening and with all the skill that Dana had tried to teach him, Michael punched Ashul clean in the mouth.

Before Michael could feel true satisfaction, Ashul swung backhanded. Michael's sword rang with the impact and was thrown into the air, landing quivering point down inches in front of the watching crowd.

Michael noticed the small trickle of blood at the corner of Ashul's mouth just as he twisted and threw all of his weight against Michael.

He might not have been a seasoned warrior but Michael had been pushed off the ball many a time in his soccer career. It took a little more than a forceful shove to make him lose his balance. His body moved of its own accord rolling away and landed back on his feet facing Ashul.

His anger finally broke and a ball of energy appeared above his head. With reflexes acquired over years of training he jumped, and with a flying scissors kick he shot the ball directly towards his goal. Ashul!

As always, Michael knew when the kick was true. He didn't need to watch to know the ball would hit Ashul in the middle of his chest. His magical protection saved him from the blast, but not from the force of the kick. The bonded in Michael's mind cheered loudly. He hoped Ashul would hear them too.

The smirk was gone and had been replaced with a smile, a very genuine, very warm, although somewhat pained, smile.

'Unorthodox, but effective! It seems the apple does not fall very far from the tree, Lady Nicola. You were right. He needed to be angry with me to release his power. Perhaps you may also have taken the time to warn me that that game he plays can also be used as a weapon. That, I was not expecting.' Ashul rubbed at his chest as he walked towards Michael.

'I think you deserved that. I certainly didn't suggest cutting him to get him mad either. That was all your idea.' Nicola walked over to check Michael's arm.

'You two planned this? You tried to get me mad?' Michael snatched his arm away from his mother's grasp. 'Well sorry to disappoint everyone. If not for Dad's help with the ball, it all would have been very anticlimactic.' Michael walked away, a bit disappointed with himself, but mostly with the others. They had played him and he didn't enjoy being played.

'Michael, have you not wondered how you managed to get through a bonded warrior's defences.' Malcarielle asked and pointed to the ceiling where a black streak ran from a point just above everyone's heads all the way down a nearby wall.

'And sorry, buddy but I didn't create any ball of energy either; I would have if I had thought of it. But I think you took care of that all by yourself.'

Michael looked around at them all in turn.

Ashul walked over and slung his arm around Michael's shoulder. 'You almost took my head off, magical protection or no.'

Apparently when Michael had decided to belt Ashul in the mouth, his sword had flared with a white streak of light, deflecting Ashul's sword and carving a line down through the wall and floor. Smoke confirmed Michael had also been the one to create the ball of energy, using her strength of course.

Michael wasn't so impressed. So he could do magic as long as he was mad, bleeding and not actually trying to do it at the time.

Real handy.

He must remember to let the bad guys know the ground rules before any battles began.

* * *

It finally knew where they had gone. One of Its many minions had reported seeing them enter the land of faeries. So they were going to try and enhance their powers. Learn what had been lost. Such a shame that the faerie folk only knew half of the powers that were available. Without the burden of scruples, power could be generated and acquired in many amusing ways. And with the only ones who knew how to stop It away at faerie camp, It had been out collecting. Not many had given willingly, but power was power regardless.

And with Its power slowly increasing, It found many approaching, offering their allegiance. And those who were not willing to pay the required joining fee, well they were simply acquired.

It had also had time to plan. It had everything set up. When the despised family returned to this plane they would be in for a big surprise. And all that It needed to do now was find a way to appropriate Ashul's power for that was all that was required to finally have dominion. It sensed that his bond to the humans was the key, but It had yet to happen upon the exact nature of his undoing.

Boot Camp

They had been training for nearly a week. Sometimes in groups, sometimes with individual faeries who specialised in varying forms of magic. Michael mainly trained with Ashul, day in, day out, and as time ticked by Michael's apprehension grew. Each second that passed seemed to wind him tighter. He could physically feel the passage of time as the tension built in his body. His neck and shoulders were knotted and twisting nausea plagued his stomach. There was an almost painful buzz of adrenaline stressing already overworked muscles.

He felt they had been away from home too long.

Even though everyone assured him that time ran differently in the faerie realm and that only one night had passed in real time, Michael's instincts told him that they needed to get back home, and soon.

When he felt a soft tap on his shoulder, he had his sword magically in hand and was halfway through a one handed swing designed to decapitate his adversary when he realised his opponent was Dana. With a curse, Michael called his sword back into himself. The result was his silver blade exploding out into a million fractured particles that could barely be seen but could be felt as a cold, tingling sensation that intensified then just as quickly disappeared as the sword was absorbed back into the scabbard that hung across his shoulders. The outward concussion blurred the vision and only became visible as the metallic shimmer condensed like smoke around Michael's shoulders to disappear entirely.

'Far out, Dana, you can't just walk up behind me like that. I could have seriously hurt you!'

'Can you chill with the boy turned warrior routine it is getting old already. I just wanted to come over and talk to you for a while not play at being 'wonder twins'!' This was said in a droll monotone, her usual enthusiasm for sarcasm gone.

It was in that moment that Michael realised the impact the forced isolation was having on Dana. Michael was struggling himself, living in the 'cave' – no matter how ornately decorated it may be, he still found it draining. He needed light, he needed open spaces, he wanted to run and now that he could, he wanted to ride. But Dana was being smothered.

Her skin was pallid, her hair was lank and lacked its usual shine and the spark had gone from her eyes.

'Dee Dee, are you okay?' Dana had already eased herself down to the floor and Michael bent down concerned.

'Micky, I can't take this much longer, I know we have to learn but these guys have nothing to teach *me*.'

Dana had at first loved Azuradien's tales of magic, engrossed in all the ideas he was trying to teach. But the forced isolation was physically and mentally suffocating her. Azuradien had been able to identify that Dana's skill lay in her empathy for animals, her ability to understand and maybe even control animals. But the faeries had little actual training to offer her. They seemed to know all the species of animals that existed, and even creatures recounted in fable that had at one time existed, or still did, live, albeit in other worlds. Goblins, elves, giants, unicorns, gryphons, dragons all had a place in Azuradien's lessons. But the faeries' isolation had made them a purely elemental race. They could teach about the channelling of power and the manipulation of the basic elements; air, fire, water and earth. They could hear the voice of the land, the stones, even the rivers, all which had a story to tell. Though when it came to animals the faeries were like zoologists who had learnt everything from a book. They had no practical exposure.

'I have been assured that other faerie clans can still feel the animal's presence, even communicate to some degree. But not this clan. Elsewhere, I may find a faerie to teach me. Not here though. According to Azuradien, my innate skill has already surpassed any in this clan.' Dana did not say this with pride or superiority but with remorse for how little she had been able to learn.

Dana could now channel power. It was a little too easy, really, and she soon realised that her family had all been subconsciously touching the source for years. It was in their blood and with the weakening of the breach, the power available had simply increased.

Not being able to practise any technique specific to her gift, Dana was left with time to think. Ashul had already told them they had all been drawing on this power – cloaking was just one of the easiest examples to pinpoint. The more she thought about how subtly magic worked the more she questioned the extent of its use in everyday life. When she stopped and thought about how many occurrences were put down simply to luck, coincidence, even intuition, she reasoned that some of them had to be the result of the use of power, be it intentional or not. The thought didn't comfort her.

'Michael, we need to get back. We're not the only ones able to use the power. I think everybody can, to some degree. But one thing we know for sure is that Marcus and his family are using it. And who knows what they're planning while we're sitting here with a bunch of well-intentioned, but let's be honest, slow moving, self-important faeries.' Dana stood up and began pacing back and forth.

Normally when troubled she would walk outside and sit with Sheba. Her presence calmed Dana, allowed her a moment of mindfulness that she was not able to find amongst the highly strung faerie-folk. With this simple comfort denied to her, Dana found herself rooming the hallways like a caged animal.

'There is nothing natural down here. This place is barren. There is no sunrise, no sunset, nothing to gauge the passage of time. It is driving me crazy.' She tried to add energy to her voice to make Michael understand but the lack of emotion proved her point more despairingly than any inspiring speech.

The sheer lack of life in her voice convinced Michael.

'We'll speak to Mum tonight. I will talk to Ashul. I don't think Azuradien will get it – but you can't stay down here any longer.' Dana dropped into her little brother's arms, glad that somebody understood.

* * *

They just had to get through one last lesson. Azuradien liked to conduct his theoretical teaching in what resembled all too closely a lecture hall. On entering the room there would only be empty space, with not one piece of furniture, at least not to begin with. As Azuradien walked in, chairs and lectern would appear out of the seemingly thin air. Michael hadn't had a chance to speak to anybody but it soon became obvious that the impatience to leave, the need to do something was becoming endemic. Everyone was either fidgeting of slumped in their chairs with impatient or glazed expressions on their faces.

While Azuradien detailed the type of enemies they could face and the best way to focus energy, Michael simply zoned out. He had already worked out that if he changed his philosophy to believe everything he had ever read, been told or dreamed then he would be pretty close. Michael didn't care about specifics. There was scary stuff out there. He got it.

He was brought back to the moment when Joseph whispered to Michael, 'Don't they realise I *do not* need to know how a fully worked 5.0 litre fuel injected V8 engine generates torque to know that if I put my foot down on the accelerator the car will go really, really fast.' The exasperated tone to his voice showed they were all struggling with this forced inactivity. Joseph had mastered the practical lessons very quickly. Throwing fireballs as well as calling down lightning. Whether through boredom or frustration Joseph convinced a fire sprite to sit on Azuradien's head during their last session. Joseph could control the heat the sprite generated so Azuradien continued the whole time seemingly unaware, until Azuradien flicked his wrist. Banishing the sprite and then sending a bolt of light towards Joseph.

Michael dodged out of the way but needn't have bothered. Joseph caught the bolt, juggled it between his hands a couple of times and then clapped his hands together releasing a small shower of light. He then nodded smugly towards Azuradien with a 'is that the best you've got' kind of air.

Even Dana smiled.

The slow clapping from the front of the class showed that the prank had not been appreciated.

Azuradien rose above the ground. His aura glowed and his eyebrow met in the middle with the angry frown that covered his face. 'Enough of this, you mock our knowledge. If the student would become the teacher then one of you must step forward and prove your worth.

'Nicola, if your knowledge surpasses mine, then meet me!' Azuradien commanded.

'I can't,' Nicola replied, resigned. 'I cannot control the power, you know that.'

'No you cannot. Magic is all about balance. Wild magic is about extremes. You will need to learn how to handle both.' Azuradien instructing tone rang throughout the training room.

They had learned, as the name suggested, wild magic was the dangerous and the most powerful force of all. The faeries had likened magic to a simple chemical reaction, where the power generated by wild magic was closer to splitting an atom.

'I realise that but I will not just let emotions rule me!'

'Cannot or will not?' Azuradien demanded.

'Will not!' Nicola replied, her voice edged in ice. Her face looked impassive but Michael had seen it before. They all had. Behind her eyes she had the potential to go nuclear. 'Do you think I could have survived my years of illness if I allowed every moment of hopelessness to overcome me? I will not be controlled in that way.'

Nicola's emotions were her trigger and if that was truly the case the old man was in a bit of trouble if he didn't button his lip on this one. The whole idea of losing control did not sit well with Nicola. She did not like to allow her emotions to take control. The disease in her ear made responsibility and control a key part of her existence. She needed focus to block out pain, to control the dizziness. It was part of her nature. If she allowed emotion to rule her, she would be overwhelmed by all of the symptoms of her disease. Logical process, control, ownership were her strengths. To find that she needed to give this control away to tap into this so called 'wild magic'. She was just not certain she could allow herself to do that.

So she banked the fire and asked the only question that mattered to her. 'Azuradien, how do we stop Anarcus? Enough theory and discussion. How do we stop that creature from harming children?'

'The answer is not so simple. We need to understand how the breakdown of the magical barriers has occurred. Can the process be reversed? Was it Anarcus' doing or was it just time for the magic to return?' Azuradien lowered himself to the ground.

'In case you hadn't noticed my son is strung so tightly he might snap at any moment. My vibrant daughter is having the very life sapped out of her by this existence.' She raised her hand to indicate their bland undefined surroundings, seemingly unaware that she now hovered above Azuradien. 'And my niece is suffering the emotional impact of these conflicting energies. While you theorise, we're suffocating!'

Hovering in front of Azuradien, theory was forgotten.

A power akin to electricity crackled out from around her, surrounding her in a halo that was painful to look out.

Michael's sword, which hung almost permanently across his back, flared in what he hoped was sympathetic harmony, but may have been in response to a perceived threat. Ashul, likewise, now glowed with a faint aura.

'We cannot wait for your analysis, we must act. Evil grows with each passing second!' Her voice resonated with the power of too many voices. But this time she did not crumple to the ground. She forced them to her will.

'I will protect my family!' As she lowered herself to the ground the cracking, simmering energy remained.

Michael felt the pull of the same wild energy flowing through his veins. He had already stepped to her side when his mind was rocked with a call from the bonded. They had sensed a massive drawing of the power and it had nothing to do with what was happening here.

'Anarcus moves,' Ashul announced. 'We have delayed here too long!'

Nicola's eyes burned intensely, pinning Azuradien, forcing him to claim some responsibility for their delay. Her aura intensified until it was almost impossible to look at her. The air surrounding her sparked with what could only be likened to static electricity but was somehow more erratic. Everyone in her immediate radius felt the uncomfortable prickling tracing across their exposed skin. With a dull 'whump' a snaking burst of energy shot out towards Azuradien. The very room changed composition: the walls and floor shook and took on the same strange aspect of Nicola's aura, the chairs and lectern simply dissolved as the energy spike travelled through them.

Just as the energy was about to reach Azuradien, Nicola turned her head aside and the stream split and separated so that it encircled every member of their group.

With a gesture that resembled an embrace, Nicola pulled her family towards her, then ripped them out of the faerie realm.

* * *

Azuradien and Malcarielle were left alone. The white cloudlike walls were gone, replaced with a surface that was painful to look at, remaining in a constant state of flux. The multi-coloured array pulled their eyes in opposite direction and created in them a nauseous reaction as if the room were spinning.

Azuradien dropped his head in despair.

Had he just allowed the wild magic free reign?

Return Home

A painful moment of disorientation followed. Time, space and all the dimensions altered. Michael felt his heartbeat slow so dramatically that he thought that it had stopped only to have it race in a series of fast almost consecutive beats, blurring with the tempo of his breathing. He couldn't define up, down or even depth. The constant of gravity was gone – there was no weight from his muscles, nor even the gentle tension gravity created between hair and scalp. Yet somehow it felt like other dimensions had been added rather than removed. Experiencing a string of altered realities concurrently, his mind spun in the centre of a maelstrom of conflicting sensation.

His mind burned with a fire that he realised on a cellular level had the ability to not only consume but to create. It was apocalypse and genesis combined. Michael felt a fearful moment of separation not just from his family but from himself as his consciousness became disconnected from his being. In the eternity that existed between heartbeats, Michael's body dissolved and was reformed by nothing more that the sheer force of what he instinctively knew to be his mother's will, by her unwavering control.

* * *

After Michael was rudely reconfigured by Nicola's wild magic, it took him a moment to be able to grasp the familiarity of his surroundings. Mild nausea and the chaotic afterimage of wildfire made coherent thought difficult. He clenched his hands in an effort to stop the world spinning and with the unmistakable feel of grass between his fingers he began to suspect his mother had wrenched them out of the faerie realm.

The sudden return of gravity kept him on his hands and knees and he stayed in that position for a moment, forcing some stability to return. The green itching smell of the grass beneath him, the manicured hedges at the edge of his vision, the mild chemical smell of chlorine all confirmed that he was in his own backyard.

Michael rose to his feet, mentally counting heads as he did so. Dana already had her arms wrapped around Sheba, gaining something more than stability from the contact. His mother seemed to be the only one unaffected by the disorientation. Everyone else seemed to be kneeling, as he now was, or seated on the rocks that surrounded the lawn, fighting the nausea that pinched every face.

Ashul harboured no such disorientation and strode purposefully towards Michael. The warrior made mental contact with the bonded as he moved, and Michael, privy to the communication, was not surprised when the air soon shimmered and Lightning appeared.

'Be wary, we know not the nature of the threat. I will search the second realm and return.' Ashul clasped Michael's arm as he spoke, nodded as if satisfied and then threw himself onto Lightning's back. The horse kicked off into the air and then in a mere three strides vanished into the second realm.

Michael itched to call Smoke to him and ride beside his comrades but his place was not as clear. He belonged with the bonded, but also with his family. Ashul's voice spoke clearly in Michael's mind. 'You are with us, hear our thoughts. You are with them, relay what we find. Proximity matters not. Focus. The threat is real!'

'No shit, Sherlock,' Michael muttered to himself. He could sense that something was wrong. The sun, high in the sky, suggested that it was a little after midday yet a cold wind blew against his neck sending shivers down his spine. Where there should have been the background noise of suburbia, there was only the slow penetrating wail of a siren somewhere in the distance.

While the rest of her family went inside the house, Dana, attuned to a whole other world, paused trying to understand what she was hearing. The sounds of animals in distress surrounded her. Dogs howled mournfully, cats yowled in the obsessive way they so very rarely do in daylight hours and the delicate background song of birds and insects was silenced. Sheba's usual playful doggy demeanour was gone. Her tail and ears were down, and everything about her looked like a dog waiting to be kicked. As Dana moved from the sunlight of the lawn to the shade of the trees that lined the fence line of their property, she repressed a shiver. It had felt like a cold finger had traced its way down her spine. She turned towards the trees and the shadows pulled away from her gaze. Sheba snapped at the darkness and Dana got the brief impression of thin black fabric before the image blended back into the shadows surrounding her.

'Guys, I think we have company.' Turning she became aware that only Michael had remained outside.

* * *

The tension had never left Michael's body and he felt the weight of it through his shoulders. Another breeze caressed his neck and he rolled his shoulder in an effort to dislodge the chill. Cold hands gripped his upper arms as Dana shouted her warning. He spun, sword instantly in his hand. A frigid breath sighed against his neck and the weight lifted from his arms. Michael continued to circle he moved towards Dana and saw a billowing shroud hovering above her. A pale faced woman with elongated features. Her maw opened, and she lowered her gaping mouth towards Dana's neck. Sheba jumped and ripped at the being with a ferocious snarl, her teeth caught flesh and for a second the form became less insubstantial, and more solid. Long lightly muscled arms, and skeletal hands tipped with wickedly hooked nails reached towards Dana. The form was surrounded by constantly shifting shadows, worn like a cloak. Shrieking, the wraith dissolved and faded back into the ether.

'What the hell was that?' Michael cursed as he pulled Dana towards the house.

Before they had time to move, Michael felt the weight drop back upon on his shoulders and long fingers curled once again around his arms. He spun, grabbing at the form on his back but he was unable to find purchase. His hands passed through nothing more than a pocket of ice cold air yet nails still tore at the skin on the back of his neck. Sheba ripped at the nebulous fabric and the form once again gained weight and substance. The wraith released another piercing scream and this time Michael was able to grab at the creature's neck and throw her over his shoulder. The body slammed into the ground. But she nimbly flipped herself and scuttled towards Michael.

Through ropes of matted black hair, bleached white eyes pouring milky tears stared at him with naked hunger. The creature shook her head like a rabid dog and the ribbons of thick drool that hung from her cracked lips flew in all directions, burning wherever it touched. With another shake the form become less solid but before she disappeared completely, Ashul strode through the trees, lifted his sword over his head and pinned the creature to the ground. The wraith writhed against the blade, feet drumming the ground. Long pale hands clutched the steel piercing her chest.

As Ashul pulled his sword from the ground the body dissolved and inky black rivulets of ichor pooled and were absorbed too quickly into the soil.

'Where there is one of the weeping women, there will be many,' Ashul warned them. Before Michael has time to react the shadows around him coalesced into a dozen shrouded forms.

'Michael, go! Smoke has discovered trouble in the street. I will handle this.' Michael hesitated but Dana pulled him resolutely towards the house. They needed to regroup.

As Michael turned to look back over his shoulder Ashul was joined by a handful of bonded warriors. The wraiths shrank from the horses thrashing hooves and screamed their defiance as the warriors drew their steel.

The screech of the wraith diminished as he made his way through the house, pushing Dana ahead of him. Within moments Michael was behind his parents and as just as quickly they passed through the front door where the shrill wail of sirens blared. He had received clear images from Smoke and if she was correct, and he had no reason to doubt her, the fire engine would be stopping only a few houses up the block. He experienced a kind of mental double vision, being able to perceive what was in front of him as well as the battle that was being fought with the weeping women behind him. But due to his training in the faerie realm he was able to focus on his own circumstance while still tracking the bonded.

Smoke had been not been mistaken: the fire engine came to a stop outside of the Sanderson's house. The blue Ford Falcon was quickly becoming a charred ruin. Billowing black smoke rolled out of the broken windows and the fire that had licked up its side was already moving. Firemen jumped out, hoses quickly connected, and they ran towards the fire that was greedily making its way up the struts of the carport towards the Sanderson's house. If the carport caught both their house and the one next door would be in danger.

But in surprisingly little time the firefighters had the fire under control and at that point Joseph and Brent walked over to offer assistance.

'Stay vigilant, Michael, this is no ordinary fire,' Smoke called into his mind. 'Get your father and uncle away.' Before he could act a dry whispered chuckle replaced Smoke's voice; his eyes locked with those of his father as a cold wave of hatred washed past them both, heading directly towards Mrs Sanderson's smouldering wreck. And Michael knew the doll had just joined the battle.

Joseph, having already sensed that the fire was no longer natural, grabbed Brent's arm and turned back towards Michael.

The air rushing towards the car turned backwards and the fuel tank on the car exploded, sending a wave of burning heat searing towards where they stood. In horrifying slow motion the super-heated air around him caused branches and leaves on plants fifty metres away to singe and ignite. To Michael, the explosion seemed totally out of proportion to its relatively small source.

Michael's eyes were stinging as the greasy clouds of smoke blew towards him and he soon lost sight of his father.

Blindly running towards the blaze his vision returned in time to see his father's hand raised as a second greater blast ripped outwards from the crater that used to contain an almost new blue Falcon.

* * *

For every weeping woman that writhed on the ground another emerged from the shadows. They dropped on the necks of the bonded, eager for the life force that flowed through their bodies. But every cut of a blade gave them substance and the bonded closed ranks and purposefully sliced through the nebulous forms that surrounded them.

The horses themselves became powerful weapons against their enemy and the wraiths shrunk from their hooves as they reared up, crushing bodies beneath their feet that dissolved with each blow. The air was filled with piercing wails as the darkness solidified and even more pale faces emerged.

* * *

Amongst the chaos, the firefighters took shelter behind the engine. The area surrounding them was badly scorched; the engine offered the only protection available. For them, a simple car fire in the suburbs had inexplicably turned into a major conflagration, and the fire was behaving in a way that made no sense.

A secondary concussion sent flame blazing out into a relative circle that left the Sanderson carport nothing more than a pile of rubble. The colour bond steel roofing that remained had started to warp and melt under the extreme heat. Debris showered outward and molten pieces of metal cut through fences and embedded in bricks twenty metres away. The firefighters had some cover but the couple of spectators that stood by in a zombie-like trance should have been toast.

As the fire grew more intense a shimmering wall appeared before the firefighters. The fire flared and met with resistance, finding it could not penetrate deeper.

Michael followed the shimmering energy to its origins, and found the source was the centre of Joseph's outstretched hand.

The air was displaced as a string on energy vortices flew past Michael. Another wave of cold malice washed towards the circle of fire, sensed more than seen. The flames flared maliciously just before another concussion blew towards Joseph. Driven to his knees, blue flame advanced to within inches of his hand. Joseph's clenched fist shook with the force it took to maintain his circle of protection.

Three things happened simultaneously: first, the fire engine was rocked by another impossible blast and thrown onto two wheels. Second, the fire, fed by the unholy energy from next door, emitted black oily smoke that flowed forcefully against the wind directly towards Joseph and Brent. Thirdly, Nicola, having never lost her hold on the wild energy that crackled around her, threw her sister towards Joseph and Brent and then turned and ran flat out toward the fire engine.

Michael was completely unprepared for a foe that he could not fight and found himself standing mutely with Dana and Ashley. The fire had momentarily blocked everything from view.

Michael felt his energy being drawn and instantly knew his dad was struggling and in need of help. With a quick communion with the bonded, he funnelled not only his energy but that of the full twenty-eight bonded directly towards his father.

Through this link he sensed more than saw the effects of this energy boost. Joseph's defensive circle strengthened. His ring of influence rippled and then expanded outwards, forcing the fire back onto itself.

Dana could feel the terror radiating from the animals around her. A group of birds, curious things that they were, had flown too close and were now suffering the smoke's poisonous effects. Dana felt their pain as they dropped to the ground, felt their tiny bones break. She broadcast the warning that the smoke did not move with the wind. It had power and malicious purpose behind it. The minds that were not overcome with panic listened and flew away, while others terror-stricken flew mindlessly towards their death.

Sarah, having been thrown into the thick of things, had realised that the smoke posed an equally real danger. She had closed her eyes and was mumbling to herself; all the while her fingers twisted and turned in intricate patterns.

When her eyes opened her arms shot upwards and a net of incandescent energy hung suspended in the air above her head effectively blocking the smoke's all too calculated approach.

Sarah managed to trap the bulk of the smoke but the insidious vapours that remained outside of her net searched for life. Travelling with or against the wind, whatever drove it closer to its goal, seeking out life wherever it could be found.

Things seemed to be slowing down and Michael turned to watch the final drama play out. His eyes followed the course of the smoke which seemed to have lost interest in smaller prey. It now condensed and changed direction back towards the fire engine.

* * *

Everybody had been so intent on fighting their own battles that no-one seemed to notice that the fire engine was sheltering half a dozen people. The firefighters had carolled the unresponsive onlookers into what should have been relative safety behind the engine not realising the fire was operating outside of nature laws. The engine was rocked by one concussion after another. Each time it took a little longer to settle back onto four wheels.

* * *

A blood-piercing wail rang from behind them as the last wraith fell. Ashul spoke in Michael's mind, 'Hold we come!'

Another explosion, greater than those before, rocked the ground beneath Michael's feet. The engine stayed poised for what seemed like an eternity, finally the front tyre was unable to stand the heat and pressure, blew, sending the engine toppling towards the group sheltered beneath it. It took Michael's overtaxed mind a couple of seconds to realise the group included his mother.

He had already called out to Smoke when the final concussion hit.

Fourteen horses materialised at full gallop in mid-air.

Instinctively, Michael reached up and pulled himself onto Smoke's back, joining his brothers.

Michael might not have had a direct enemy in the battle but now he had purpose. The bonded surged forward, now galvanised with Michael's directions, and with energy in differing forms blasted out from them. The engine's descent slowed as surge upon surge of force bombarded it.

Grappling hooks flew through the air. Tearing against his eardrums was the screeching wail as metal dragged against metal fighting for purchase.

The horses lowered their heads, readied themselves for the agonising jolt as the ropes pulled taut and they took on the weight of the fifteen tonnes of toppling metal.

Their forward momentum halted and their muscles bunched as they strained against the weight. They lost ground and the gap between bitumen and scorching metal closed. Even if those sheltered were not crushed under the engine's weight the searing heat would burn flesh in seconds. But these were no ordinary horses and this was no ordinary situation. For long moments their hooves dug at thin air and strove to shift what appeared to be immovable, but with the next timed bunching of the horse's flanks the engine lifted.

The horses flew upwards sharply with a fifteen tonne engine following behind. They flew over the houses until they were clear of bystanders. In concert, the riders cut their ropes and the engine crashed to the ground twenty metres away from where it had previously been located. Two horses broke away from the group, one grey and one black, while the others disappeared into the sky, fading as if they had never been.

When Michael dropped to the ground beside Ashul, Lightning and Smoke joined the other bonded on another plane, unseen to those around them.

Michael looked down at the circular indentation where the fire engine had been certain to fall. He knew his mother's power had made this hole. He had felt the surge when the engine's weight shifted. Her power had cut not only through grass and dirt. The fire engine had been parked in the street when it was thrown over by the blast. She had been forced to blow a hole through bitumen and the underlying network of steel and concrete that travelled under most suburban streets to shield the people about to be crushed by the toppling engine.

A number of perplexed soot covered faces looked up at Michael from the shallower edges of the hole. The bravest, or just the less dazed, were already using the concrete protrusions in an effort to get back onto surer footing. Michael reached down and helped those he could. The couple of people who had stopped to watch the blaze now wandered back to their homes oblivious to what had transpired around them.

One of the firefighters had his head bent over the broken form of Nicola.

Michael felt a pulse of mocking hatred that radiated from behind him, which made him pause and turn.

He heard his father's shocked intake of breath when he saw Nicola lying unmoving in the crater below.

Laughter rang in his Michael's head as Marcus and his family sauntered out into their front garden. Marcus lifted one hand in a kind of cocky salute, while his other carried a suitcase. They piled into their BMW and started to reverse out of their driveway.

Another forceful wave of hatred hit Michael. So close and intimate, it took Michael a few seconds to realise it came from the back of the car. Marcus must have carried the doll out of the house in the suitcase.

As yet more tangible loathing from the doll poured over him and the image of the crumpled body of his mother was forced into his mind.

Michael felt hate of his own. Maybe this was the role in the battle that he must play. Finally he had a target. The enemy had shown itself and he had no intention of letting it escape. He ran forwards, drawing all the power he could. He felt his family drop to the ground as the energy he drew weakened them further.

His strides ate away at the distance separating him from the car.

Ashul was at his side but Michael was going to make sure he was the one to rip open the door. He was the one who was going to wrench the suitcase out of Marcus' grasping hands.

He knew his mother was conscious. He could feel her drawing on the wild magic. A blast of wild energy flew through Michael as Nicola used him as a conduit for her attack.

The back door of the BMW blew from its hinges. The tyres of the car screeched across the driveway as the car was forced sideways. Still reversing at speed, the rear of the car hit the letterbox with a crash of broken brickwork.

In the hole, a firefighter was still bent over Nicola, trying to breathe life into the seemingly broken body. Her eyes opened, their dark blue burning with anger and determination.

Michael felt the sudden surge as he was overwhelmed with power. His bones burned with the wild energy that was forced through him in levels he never thought possible.

Ashul cried out a warning.

Michael barely registered the frightened eyes of Marcus in the backseat. He saw only the case – singed and blown open with this latest expulsion of power.

The doll lay barely moving at the bottom of the case but still managed to exude an ungodly energy. It hurt Michael's eyes to look at it but he refused to turn away.

Marcus' father was desperately trying to reverse, but the car was wedged up on the destroyed letterbox. Wheels spun, metal screeched but the car didn't move.

The doll, although inert, was not defenceless. Cold hatred pulsed outwards. Michael saw the lips on the doll stretch back in a corpse's smile.

Michael required strength to shield himself from the attack and so he drew this from all quarters as he had been trained. Ashul fell beside him, one knee buckling under the strain.

'Michael, no!' Ashul cried. 'You will destroy us all. Your family first of all!'

Michael could feel all of the links to the network of energy supporting him. He was like a spider sitting in the centre of an elaborate web. As he traced each strand he could feel the tension each individual was under, some near breaking.

Dana dropped to the ground.

Sheba stood beside her and Michael was all too aware

of the link between them. Sheba's strand of energy pulsed. But Dana had blocked the flow, deliberately shielding Sheba from potential harm. Sensing the danger she was protecting those she loved where she could.

Michael, feeling all too like a spider, tried to stop the flow of energy as Dana had done but it had its own momentum now and would not be so easily stemmed. A pulse of incandescent energy flew through the spiritual strand linked to his mother.

'Finish it!' he heard a hoarse voice shout.

'*No!*' shouted the bonded in his mind.

Michael was faced with an impossible choice. Destroy the evil that he now knew would kill others but save lives, sacrificing those he loved, or protect his family and let the evil get away.

The laughter of the doll echoed through his mind. It won either way.

Michael used the faeries' training and forced barriers in his mind to close. As he did so he felt the pulse of wild magic he associated with Nicola flicker and then drop to a level that was barely detectable.

The BMW suddenly gained some traction and rocketed out of the driveway, the force of the reversing vehicle slamming the suitcase lid shut.

Michael walked back towards where Nicola lay and stood amongst the circle of family that now surrounded her. Her eyes were open – the blue startling against the pallor of her face.

'You let *It* get away.' Her lips barely moved.

'I had no choice, it would have killed you.'

'*You let It get away!*' The startling blue eyes blazed with a fire that contained no warmth. 'After all the energy we fed you, you let it *get away*.'

Michael stumbled back from the hole unable to bear her disgust.

Ashul grabbed Michael's arm, trying to steady his friend.

Michael looked around, his eyes pleading for understanding but the face that rose above him knew no mercy.

'You let *It* get away. You had your chance. Time has made you weak, so I have taken this form. This way, I will ensure you will not fail again.' His mother's face looked down on him, but her warmth was no longer present.

Nicola was there no longer. The faerie king's barriers had been broken.

Trevlor had taken control.

Epilogue

They sat in a kind of mini war council. Huddled around the kitchen bench as if fearing detection. Both families were present. Except for the one they now thought of as Trevlor.

Azuradien and Malcarielle had come at Ashul's call. They appeared almost human in the first realm. Something not remarked on by the shell-shocked families.

Azuradien understood what had happened. He had sensed the combined memories in Nicola's mind fighting for control when she ripped them out of the faerie realm.

'But her will was so strong. She had kept them subdued, forced them to her purpose.'

'Then how …?' This was all Joseph could manage.

'Her energy was depleted. She had a choice. Protect herself or protect you!' Azuradien's slender arm swept around to include all of Michael's family.

'She chose well!' Malcarielle murmured looking towards Michael, trying to give him back some hope.

'Hush,' Azuradien whispered, 'not without a shielding, say no more.' Malcarielle sat back, chastised.

Malcarielle and Azuradien bowed their heads.

Azuradien spoke in a manner to soothe them, 'All is not lost. Anarcus' energy is vastly depleted. It will have to return here soon, where the breach is at its greatest and the source flows freely. Michael inflicted great damage. It will need to recover quickly or it may not recover at all.'

Joseph rose. 'Do you really think we care? I've lost my wife.' Dana sobbed quietly beside her father.

'Only lost,' Azuradien said, 'but not *lost to us*. For what is lost can also be found. We have only to look in the right place.'

A Sneak Peak from Book 2

Battle for
the Second Realm

Prologue
Thirst for Knowledge

Nicola looked down on the circular hole that the wild magic had created in the quiet suburban street. The blast area resembled some kind of war zone, with shattered concrete, rubble and dust-laden smoke spreading over more than a ten metre radius. Soot-covered faces emerged through the haze. The hiss of broken pipes and the steady tick of cooling metal were the only sounds breaking the uncomfortable silence.

Firefighters moved aside chunks of broken concrete; working together they were able to climb the network of pipes and steel that lined the inside of the crater. Two men remained, kneeling in the mud that had formed at the base of the hole, slowly getting soaked by the water leaking from the ruptured pipes. A pale arm, remarkably untouched by the chaos, was lifted as the firemen searched for a pulse. Urgency seemed to enter the scene as the men who had scrabbled to the surface ran back to the edge of the crater, handing down portable resuscitation equipment.

Who had she missed? She had tried to protect everyone.

She ran through the faces surrounding the hole, ticked off Michael, Ashley, Dana. All were safe. She couldn't be sure but the firefighters all seemed to be accounted for and the person who lay struggling for life was not wearing protective clothing.

As the fireman in charge reached up to grab the resuscitation gear, she was able to glimpse the owner of the pale unmarked arm. Her own unblinking blue eyes stared back at her. She had been the one unprotected, exposed as the wild magic tore through her. She couldn't remember the moment when her consciousness had left her body, but she had been in this position before and she knew what she needed to do.

Her heart had stopped once before, during a gruelling ten hours of surgery, and she had awoken to the disorienting experience of looking down on her own body. The surgeon, controlled and purposeful, had gone about the task of resuscitation.

Nicola knew at that time, as she did now, that moments mattered in this one instant more than at any other time in life. Instinctively knowing that panic, if allowed a foothold, would literally kill her. She forced her mind to focus, to be as controlled as the surgeons had been and forced herself to become more.

More what? More solid, more real, more tangible. The words mattered little, the concept was everything. She needed to refocus her being. She could not allow herself to dissipate.

With only thoughts to ground herself, she found the gentle pull of her body. Once found, the connection grew a kind of weight and she allowed herself to descend. Resisting the uncomplicated comfort that surrounded her, she embraced the complication of self, knowing that now was not her time. Her mind flinched as it re-entered her body – the restriction felt claustrophobic, but she had known what to expect, and stretched her senses to regain contact with fingers and toes.

As her consciousness poured through the vessel that was her body, she encountered an unexpected resistance. Pathways were blocked, areas that should have been empty were already filled. Nicola felt a moment of panic.

Was she too late? Had she been out of her body too long? Was the damage too great?

Struggling for composure, she felt the resistance flex, her hold on her own body was forcibly pushed outwards and her grip lessened. Trying to regain focus, she searched for any mental or physical handholds that could help her anchor herself.

Because she was desperate to find a way to pour around the blockages, Nicola sensed the other's presence too late. As the pathways and avenues that led into her own body were being barred against her, Nicola recognised the mind behind this unexpected expulsion.

Trevlor had somehow taken control.

Nicola was losing cohesion. Knowing the fight for her own body had been lost, her mind raced for a solution. The wild magic, linked so intrinsically to the physical, was not available to her and she quickly felt her clarity of thought diluting, distracted by the images of her family before her, so bright, so complex, so engaging, she almost became lost in their light. There were so many points of brilliance surrounding her, each begging her attention, her mind split in a myriad of directions.

How different everything looked now that the connection to her body had been severed.

As she felt her consciousness drifting down the many paths before her, she heard whispered voices accompanying her journey.

Need to see.

Need to know what happens.

Never went this far last time.

Need to know.

NEED the answer.

The voices were one from many and a prickling of annoyance disrupted her gentle journey into dissolution. Her focus became drawn to the whispering that surrounded her and she tried to understand the many voices, tried to understand what they were talking about.

Need the answer.

Will never get another chance.

Need to know.

NEED.

THE.

ANSWER.

What answer?

What opportunity?

The greedy hunger in the words was almost obscene in its blatant need. A prickling of recognition, she had encountered this single minded thirst for knowledge once before.

She had been on the receiving end of this unwavering, unforgiving transfer of information and she now paid the ultimate price for the answers she had received.

As Nicola focused on the whispers, the tone changed to include the rustling of pages. The hungry voices faltered as Nicola recognised her opportunity. She remembered the dry dusty feel of the paper, and traced the now familiar symbol with her mind's eye.

With each layered detail of remembering, her scattered thoughts gained weight and descended, not towards her own body but towards the greedy pages of the gypsy book. She had no idea whether the book could support life, but when needed the devil drives. She flooded into the pages of the book, felt a moment of resistance, and then the cover slammed shut and she was encased in pages of memory.

About the Author

Petra has lived in a world where plans mean little and dreams are the only constant. Diagnosed with ear disease at the age of eight, she turned to books to escape the constant medical procedures that would be a part of her life for two decades. She always had an open view of the world around her, having grown up on stories of her gypsy ancestors, but a near death experience during surgery confirmed what she had long known: the world has many layers and the people that reside within it have even more.

Petra runs her own Finance IT Consulting business and writes about her strange 'what if' view of the world in any spare moment she has. She is married with two children, and the characters in her books have a tiny bit more than a passing resemblance to her family. All of their strengths are their own and all of their weaknesses are pure fiction.

9 781925 585971